When she stopped, he stopped with her.

She turned to face him, and his pulse sped up. Moonlight hugged her face, showing Rafe all the details he had been hoping to see. He held his breath.

She had high cheekbones and a wide brow. Though she was lean, her full lips lent her a softness that was lacking in her attitude. Her neck was long and graceful, her skin a smooth, unblemished ivory. Her large eyes, framed by dark lashes, dominated her other features. They were a bright Lycan green.

She took a step, bringing her close enough for Rafe to feel her breath on his face. She said suddenly, in a hoarse, velvety whisper, "It's you, isn't it?"

Then she waited in silence as if daring Rafe to find meaning in those words.

THE BLACK WOLF
&
ENTICING
THE DRAGON

LINDA THOMAS-SUNDSTROM
AND
JANE GODMAN

Recycling programs
for this product may
not exist in your area.

ISBN-13: 978-1-335-45149-1

The Black Wolf & Enticing the Dragon

Copyright © 2019 by Harlequin Books S.A.

The publisher acknowledges the copyright holders
of the individual works as follows:

The Black Wolf
Copyright © 2018 by Linda Thomas-Sundstrom

Enticing the Dragon
Copyright © 2018 by Amanda Anders

This edition published by arrangement with Harlequin Books S.A.

For questions and comments about the quality of this book, please contact us at CustomerService@Harlequin.com.

Printed in U.S.A.

CONTENTS

Linda Thomas-Sundstrom writes contemporary and paranormal romance novels for Harlequin. A teacher by day and a writer by night, Linda lives in the West, juggling teaching, writing, family and caring for a big stretch of land. She swears she has a resident muse who sings so loudly, she often wears earplugs in order to get anything else done. But she has big plans to eventually get to all those ideas. Visit Linda at lindathomas-sundstrom.com or on Facebook.

Books by Linda Thomas-Sundstrom

Harlequin Nocturne

Red Wolf
Wolf Trap
Golden Vampire
Guardian of the Night
Immortal Obsession
Wolf Born
Wolf Hunter
Seduced by the Moon
Immortal Redeemed
Half Wolf
Angel Unleashed
Desert Wolf
Wolf Slayer
The Black Wolf
Code Wolf

Harlequin Desire

The Boss's Mistletoe Maneuvers

Visit the Author Profile page
at Harlequin.com for more titles.

THE BLACK WOLF

Linda Thomas-Sundstrom

To my family, those here and those gone,
who always believed I had a story to tell.

Chapter 1

Hot Miami nights in September were the bane of tourists and locals alike…but they suited Rafe Landau just fine.

Werewolves seldom reacted to heat the same way humans did. With body temperatures so elevated most of the time, a few degrees one way or the other didn't matter. And humidity was Rafe's friend. Sultry nights like this one were perfect for keeping criminals inside in front of their air conditioners. Or so he hoped. A detective's job didn't involve much downtime in a city this big. Having a night off from the usual chaos was a blessing.

Rafe sipped his soft drink on the narrow balcony of his semi-affordable oceanfront apartment, where the crash of waves almost completely masked the more invasive city sounds. Behind him, the blonde he planned to share a couple of hours on a mattress with shuffled toward him on bare feet.

"Got anything to drink in your bachelor pad besides sodas?"

Her voice was grittier than her looks. Rafe liked his temporary bed partners natural, without medically enhanced curves, dyed hair or overdone makeup. His preferences could have been a throwback to the times when wolves ran naked in the wild and nature ruled, but the fact was that he liked to see, taste and feel the women he dated with nothing artificial in his way.

Tonight's date had already discarded most of her clothes; she was down to flimsy green lingerie that looked good on her. Her shoulder-length hair was tousled, her lips pouty. And her current state of undress made her invitation perfectly clear.

"Cupboard by the sink," Rafe said, directing her to the stash of wine people had given him on various occasions, which he never drank. Other than a few swigs of beer on social occasions, the acuteness of his Were sense of taste and smell made alcohol off-limits.

"Wine?" she called out from the small kitchen, and followed that up with, "Warm wine?"

"I wasn't expecting company" was Rafe's standard reply in situations like this. He liked his women to feel special. This one was extraordinarily beautiful and probably damn good in bed, but she wasn't the first he had invited home this month.

He supposed that he had been compensating for the painful memories, finding comfort in random companionship.

He had started feeling sorry for every woman who had caught his eye lately, believing him to be trustworthy because of his detective status and hoping that he might be available. The main thing he needed from a human female partner, however, was something none of them had been able to provide. Not that any of them could help being human. Although he could pass among them most of the time, he wasn't really like them, and he had a secret to guard.

The fact that he was one of more than two dozen werewolves in a tightly knit Miami pack wasn't exactly something he could be open about, and it kept him from any real connection.

He glanced over his shoulder. Hell, he was fairly sure he remembered this woman's name. Brenda? Brandi? Something starting with a B.

Maybe he was wrong about the B. *Randi? Candy?*

He might call her again sometime when he was lonely, even though they had nothing in common, really. It was dangerous for Weres to fraternize for too long or become regularly intimate with a species outside their own.

But available she-wolves were a rarity in Miami and tricky to be around due to that little phenomenon known as imprinting. A lingering meeting of the eyes, Were-to-Were, or one outstanding sexual climax between them, and a werewolf was as good as engaged.

"Do you want some?" his date asked, clinking glasses on the counter.

"No," Rafe said. "You go ahead."

A breeze had come off the ocean to ruffle his hair—hair that was too long for a cop and too short for Rafe's taste. It was a good wind. Felt nice.

He closed his eyes.

The scent of lilac perfume preceded his date onto the balcony. "Nice view," she observed.

"Yes," he agreed. "I'm damn lucky to have it."

He took in the long lines of towering hotels perched along the beach. Lights glistened on the water. Colorful umbrellas dotted the scene during the day. His place was the only remaining small, privately owned building among those multistoried stucco behemoths. A holdout. His refuge. The manager liked having a cop around.

"How much is the rent?" his companion asked, making conversation, interrupting Rafe's communion with the darkness and the breeze. At this point in the evening he should have been paying more attention to the green lingerie, but he frowned.

Some little thing nagged at his consciousness, served to him on that wind. A new scent arrived that was hard to define with Brandi so close. It wasn't salty ocean waves or the usual array of smells wafting in from the restaurants down the street. This was something else. *What?*

Rafe's pulse accelerated slightly as he caught and held a breath, searching for a way to reconcile the new scent with the sudden burning sensation at the back of his throat. He set down his drink and peered at the ocean, hoping to attach a name to what he couldn't quite capture, though his unusual talent for identifying and categorizing problems was what had made him the youngest decorated detective in the Miami PD.

Not perfume, he decided. The incoming scent wasn't floral. It couldn't be the warning signal of a wolfed-up Were, since the moon wasn't full tonight, and anyway, he was intimately familiar with the scents of his kind.

The way his body had automatically tensed suggested he would have to find a polite way to send the woman beside him on her way and find the source of the mysterious smell that had taken precedence over her lilac perfume. There was the slightest suggestion of danger in the other scent, and his innate sense of justice demanded he focus on tracking it down.

Mysterious scents were almost never good. More often than not, they were attached to trouble. Still, he actually would be sorry to see Brandi go when the night had been so promising. What male, human or Were, wanted to pass up such an opportunity?

He just had a bad feeling about what might be out there...and he couldn't let it go.

Cara Kirk-Killion stared out the window of the black SUV, feeling anxious and trapped. She didn't often leave her family's secluded estate. She liked the freedom of open spaces, wind, trees and being alone to commune with those things...and all of that was about to end for a while. The SUV had already entered the city, which meant that she had less than ten minutes of freedom left.

She hated the promise she had made to her father to behave. It was time, he had said, for her to see more of the world...in moderation, and in carefully controlled circumstances. It wouldn't do to turn her loose in Miami without strict supervision, she had heard the Elders say, and she understood the need for such precautions. So she was to see more of the world under the protection of one of the largest and strongest werewolf packs in Miami. Her father's people...though they weren't really people. They howled each time a full moon came around.

Every instinct at the moment, however, told Cara to run in the opposite direction. Seeing more of the world wasn't necessary when deep down inside her so many worlds already existed. She hadn't actually begun to believe she might be a freak until a week ago, when some Were Elders showed up and the plan to take her away became a reality.

That's when the dreams began. And the lectures.

Cities were dangerous places, her father had warned, which was likely the reason her parents had hidden her and themselves in the country. Cara also got the impression that the Kirk-Killions wouldn't have fit in anywhere else. Her family was different, and Cara hadn't needed anyone to point that out.

Colton Killion's body was covered with scars that no one ever spoke about, probably because his Were blood should have healed them. Her father's hair was as white as his skin. He liked to roam in his wolfed-up shape and seldom came into the house. A pure white wolf. Lean. Strong. Fierce. Ghostly.

Her mother was neither human nor entirely wolf. Though she had been born a pure-blooded Lycan, it turned out that Rosalind Kirk also shared her blood and DNA with other types of beings. Her mother's hair was sometimes as black as the night and at other times white. Her features had a tendency to rearrange on occasion, and her deceptively delicate body reeked of old power.

Her mother liked to disappear for hours and shapeshift when the moon was full so that she could run with the white wolf she had lived with for years. The eerie sounds Cara's mother often made—not howls or growls, but something much more powerful—had echoed through Cara's mind from the time she was born.

It hadn't taken Cara long to realize that she also possessed some of her mother's special traits, and that the Kirk-Killions might seem scary to the humans beyond their gates. Because of all that, her parents weren't accompanying her to Miami. There were two strangers in the front seat of the SUV, and they refused to meet her inquisitive gaze.

Werewolves. Both of them. Half-breeds, in that unlike her, they had been human once. Cara smelled the old bites that had sealed their fates and inducted them into the moon's cult a long time ago. They'd probably been warned about her being a freak of nature, and it crossed her mind that maybe she should give them a demonstration. Show her fangs. Bring out her wolf. Give them a thrill and make them turn back so that she could again plead her case for staying home.

She wasn't actually going to do any of that. At eighteen years old, she was no longer a child. She could remain calm and follow the plan that had been made for her. She would try to behave, if only because her dreams had also pointed her this way…to Miami and what she might find there. *Whom* she might find there. The male who had been haunting her dreams lately and had contributed to her current state of restlessness. The guy who had destroyed whatever kind of peace she had been able to find with her unusual little family for the past few weeks.

If she happened to find the guy, she would make him pay for bothering her and piquing her interest. Then she'd go home dream-free.

The city's glittering lights surrounded the car, but Cara stared at the back of the seat in front of her. Through the open window she caught a whiff of a salty scent that could only have been the ocean she had heard so much about. It was a lovely scent, unique, and served to scramble her sense of duty.

Suddenly, behaving herself and allowing these guards to take her someplace she didn't really want to go just didn't suit her at all.

So when the car slowed for the next red traffic light, Cara opened the door.

Chapter 2

Standing on the sidewalk, Rafe stared at the darkest stretch of beach with his senses wide-open. The wind had changed, taking the mysterious scent with it. He listened to the waves and muted music from one of the hotels. There were no police sirens tonight, and for the moment, no noisy tourists. It was just him and the beach.

Nevertheless, his pulse continued to race as if he was about to discover something. He hoped whatever that was justified his reluctantly giving Brandi the heave-ho. She hadn't gone without a pouty fuss.

Rafe buttoned his shirt and tucked it into his jeans. He scanned the beach, looking pretty much like anyone else who might be out for a nighttime stroll, except for the badge pinned to his belt. He hadn't taken the time to put on his shoes.

A half-moon overhead made the wave foam look silver and the sand appear as soft as velvet. Yet all was not so calm beneath the surface. The farther he had walked from those glittering hotel lights, the more his senses nagged about something being different tonight, something he had to pay attention to. If the strange scent had reached him on his balcony, its source couldn't be far off.

When his cell phone buzzed with a text message, Rafe cursed the interruption. Still, the number that came up on his screen was an important one. This would have taken precedence over a call from his department anytime. It was his father asking him to come home. Judge Landau seldom made such a request.

"Okay," Rafe muttered without immediately texting back. His attention was fixed on the water, where a solitary figure had emerged from the waves.

A woman.

She stood near the sand with the water swirling at her feet. He was pretty sure she was naked. Although the idea that occurred to him was insane, Rafe ran a hand over his eyes, imagining that he could be looking at a mermaid.

Of course, there was nothing strange about someone taking a nighttime swim, so he should just turn around and head home. But the feeling of stumbling onto the mystery that had called him here had gotten stronger, along with that unidentified scent.

Using the special abilities that allowed all Weres to see in the dark with more precision than their human counterparts, Rafe stared hard at the woman near the shore, even though his mind issued a warning about infringing upon her privacy.

The moonlight shone on the water behind her, presenting him with her slim silhouette. Her legs were slender. Long wet hair cascaded over bare shoulders.

Though Rafe couldn't see the woman's face in the dark, even with his considerable Were talents, he knew she was looking straight at him with the same kind of scrutiny. The intensity of her attention was electric.

"You all right?" he called out. "Are you alone? The tides can be quite treacherous for anyone swimming solo."

The mermaid offered no response.

"Well, I'll leave you to it, then," Rafe said. "Sorry if I interrupted whatever you were doing."

Maybe she thought he was some kind of pervert for staring at her. Could he blame her? On the other hand, if she did turn out to be a mermaid...

He shook his head sharply, clearing away that ridiculous notion. Again, though, he got the funny feeling this woman was connected to what brought him out here tonight in the first place. Since there was no one else around, he had to consider that she could very well be ground zero for the sensations running through him.

He didn't see a towel or a pile of clothes that might belong to her on the sand. She made no move to turn away or cover her bareness with her arms. Being naked all alone was one thing. Being naked on a public beach was another.

"Do you need something to wear? Maybe someone took your clothes while you enjoyed your swim?" he asked.

The woman didn't speak. Her earthy, not quite identifiable exotic scent floated around her like a cloud.

"You can have this." Rafe removed his shirt and held it out to her, then shook it as an enticement for her to take his offering.

"Fine." He lowered his arm when she made no move

toward him. "But you really can't walk around like that. Not here."

"Why?"

Her question rendered him speechless for a few beats. She had a deep, throaty voice unlike any he had heard lately. Sort of a whisper. Almost a purr. It moved the wolf buried deep inside him with the kind of physical response usually reserved for a full moon.

Rafe shook that off, too. "You might scare the tourists," he managed to say. "Or receive a proposition or two that you find offensive."

When the woman shook her head, her waist-length wet hair swirled. Though he wanted to see more of her, Rafe figured she already thought he was a perv.

"There are no strings attached. The shirt is a gift."

"I don't know you," she said.

The sexiness of her tone produced a strange fluttering sensation in his chest, which Rafe also found absurd given the circumstances. Hell, he wasn't going to arrest her for indecent exposure, because he was the only one out here at the moment, and honestly, what he could see of her was quite decent. What he had to do was to go away and leave her alone.

And yet her rapt attention kicked his pulse upward another notch, and the air between them seemed to be charged with ions like those preceding an oncoming storm system.

There was danger here, his instincts warned. He had to tread lightly if he hoped to understand what that danger was.

"I'm with the police," he said to explain his continued presence.

"And you're a werewolf," she returned with way too much insight and confidence.

Rafe was stunned. "Werewolf, is it?"

She spoke again. "I've heard that Weres around here have to try to fit in. You look human."

"Why would you think I'm anything other than human?" he asked.

"Practice."

After waiting a few more heartbeats, Rafe said warily, "If I'm a werewolf, what does that make you for recognizing me as such?"

"I guess I'm harder to define."

"Maybe you can try."

"I've been cautioned not to do that," she said.

"Who cautioned you?"

"One of you."

"A werewolf, you mean, or a cop?" Rafe pressed.

Although a cloud passed over the moon, bringing a brief, temporary dullness to the night, Rafe saw her nod her head.

She said, "The ghost warned me."

Another spike of surprise struck Rafe. Though he didn't have the specific details about this woman, her reply made who this had to be extremely clear to him. The scent that had drawn him here and the prickly premonitions about the possibility of danger finally came to a head. Mystery solved. One part of it, anyway.

"You are Killion's daughter," he said.

This was the female his pack was expecting. She was supposed to be an extremely rare kind of shape-shifter hybrid. Hell, maybe she *could* have been a mermaid.

"Yes," she said.

"What are you doing here, and without your companions?"

Rafe connected this shapely vision in front of him with the text message he'd received from his father moments before. Cara Kirk-Killion must have escaped from her transport and her guards. His pack would be looking for her.

"Those guys were responsible for your safe passage to the estate," he continued.

"I don't need guards. Maybe you've heard why?"

She didn't give him time to reply. With a quick turn on her long legs, the female that everyone in their pack had been warned to avoid at all costs until proper introductions had been made…just walked back into the sea.

Leaving Rafe to stare after her.

Cara didn't stop to consider the possibility that the Were on the beach would follow her until she felt the pressure of a hand on her arm.

The touch came as a shock. No one had dared to touch her in the past for fear of what kind of shape she would end up in and how far into their souls she could see. One touch was all it took for her to adapt her form to the shape of whatever kind of being had reached out. Sometimes all it took for her to shift her shape was closeness, eye contact or a connecting thought.

Once she had melded to their shape, she could read them easily and see into their souls. She could at times predict their futures and understand their needs.

This Were had broken with tradition. Possibly he didn't know better than to get too close to a member of the Kirk-Killion clan. Yet if he knew about her guards and the estate, he had to belong to the Landau pack and be privy to their secrets.

"It isn't safe out here," he warned, letting his hand drop.

"It's never safe," Cara replied, longing to get back to the silence and buoyancy of deep water, dreading having to go to the Landau place, where more Weres like this one awaited her arrival and she would be fenced in.

"I mean that if you're as special as everyone seems to believe you are, you'd be a hot commodity around here and possibly hunted for your many talents," the Were said. "It's not safe to be on your own in a strange city."

Cara still felt the burning sensation of his hand as if his fingerprints had been stamped on her skin. Did he also feel the heat? Had the call already gone out about the necessity of finding her?

More time was what she needed. Time to herself. Time with the water, which had been lacking at her family's inland estate. Time to experience a few more precious moments without the shackles of Were society.

"I'll take you there," the Were beside her said, skipping over all of the things they hadn't yet mentioned about why she was in Miami and how she had gotten away from the guards. "To the house," he added.

She had escaped one net only to be ensnared by another. The big Were next to her, with his moon-streaked brown hair, lean, muscular build, chiseled features and light eyes, looked capable enough of handling any surprises that were in store.

Because he was in human shape tonight, Cara maintained her human countenance. She also kept her voice. However, she sensed the wolf curled up inside this guy as if it were her own and knew that it was strong, like hers. Being near him messed with her delicate equilibrium. She was drawn to him without knowing why.

He looked at his hand suddenly, as if he also felt the burn caused by one brief, simple touch. Then he glanced back up at her.

"I don't like being caged," Cara said, watching him closely, observing how he fisted his hand and the way the wind played with strands of his hair. He was as good-looking as her father, with prominent cheekbones and wide-set eyes. He was tall, with broad shoulders and moonlight-dappled golden skin. All of those things reinforced the Were's wolfish nature, and yet he wasn't a full-blooded member of the species. Human blood also ran in his veins; she perceived the slightest hint of an altered fragrance. One of his parents had, at one time or another, been human.

"That's what you believe will happen when you accept our hospitality?" he asked. "You'd be caged?"

His voice disturbed her with its low, cautious, controlled quality. The Were's earthy, masculine vibe caused another new ruffle in her widening awareness of the world outside her family's gates. This was her first time meeting a male Were who looked as if he might not be too much older than herself.

"Why else would my parents shun this place and everyone in it, if not that for the fact that they no longer fit in?" Cara replied.

"From the stories I've heard, your parents withdrew from the rest of the pack because it was in their own best interest."

Yes. She knew that. But it was only a small part of why the Kirk-Killions had withdrawn. And she didn't owe this Were any explanations.

"I need time to get myself together," she said. "It's not easy for me to come out of the seclusion I'm used to."

To her surprise, her companion seemed to get that. After a brief silence, he nodded and said, "I'll wait for you on the beach."

Cara didn't know what to make of that. He was going to leave her alone for a while?

"What if I swim away?" she asked.

"Then you will be someone else's problem."

He didn't mean that the way it sounded. Cara heard how his pulse pounded with the effort it took for him to let her have her way. She had no doubt that he would come after her if she tried to leave the area, and that shaking off this guy might be a difficult task. The strength of his inner wolf and all those rippling muscles made him a worthy opponent.

"Who are you?" she asked, more intrigued about him than she wanted to be.

"Name's Landau. Rafe Landau. And I can assure you that though my family's estate has walls, those walls are there only to keep trespassers out."

Landau...

The Miami pack was both run and protected by his family.

She didn't really believe in coincidences, and yet what were the odds she would run into a Were of this caliber so soon after ditching the guards his family had sent to bring her there?

"Can you promise me that's the truth? I won't be a prisoner behind those walls?" she asked.

"I can."

The handsome Were allowed one little thought to slip past his mental defenses, and Cara caught hold of it easily. Neither fear nor anger ruled Rafe Landau's thoughts. He wasn't afraid of her at all. When she saw the image he held in his mind, she smiled.

"I could be one, you know," she said. "If there were such creatures."

He was staring at her openly. His heart continued to pound.

"Who knows?" she added. "Since you're granting

my wish by letting me explore the sea, maybe your wish will come true."

"What wish?" he asked, frowning.

Cara's answer was meant as a subtle warning of her power. This Were might be strong, but he wasn't truly in control now that a werewolf-vampire-banshee hybrid like Cara Kirk-Killion was in Miami.

"About mermaids," she said as she dived beneath the next incoming wave.

Chapter 3

"Well, this is going to be a challenge," Rafe muttered as Cara Kirk-Killion disappeared from sight. He feared that the word *challenge* didn't begin to cover things.

She was swimming away, and he wanted to go after her. What if she decided not to return? Would he let her go? Let her become somebody else's business, as he'd said?

Not likely.

He found himself much too interested and curious about her. And besides, his family was responsible for her safety.

Rafe ignored the tug of the outgoing tide on his legs. He needed more time to think. If Cara was anything like her parents, he could sympathize with her reluctance to meet the pack that had helped her family out of a jam so long ago.

Rosalind and Colton had departed from Miami soon

after a battle with a particularly nasty nest of vampires that had almost killed Cara's father. Colton Killion had been so severely injured that he had ended up a rare ghost wolf—the name Weres had for survivors of such heinous, life-threatening attacks.

Given Colton Killion's state of health and his appearance after the attack, the wolf's desire to go into seclusion was understandable. But in addition, from the stories Rafe had heard, Colton's mate had turned out to be something even rarer than he was, making it even more necessary to retreat from the city. Now, Killion's sole offspring was here, and heaven only knew what traits she possessed.

Rafe walked farther up the beach and turned without taking his eyes off the ocean. Cara hadn't seemed dangerous, but what did he know? Wasn't it a fact that looks could be deceiving?

He clutched his phone. The next step was to call and check in with his father, who would probably send a car to fetch her. But he didn't do so. Not yet. Rafe empathized with her plight. Cara had to know how different she was and that his pack would be wary.

Still, whatever other forms she could take, Cara was a wolf. Both of her parents had been full-blooded Lycans before the events that had changed them, and Lycans carried the purest blood in the Were world. His hand felt hot. His insides were feverish. It was likely that his wolf was reacting to that part of Cara. Was his desire to see her again due to obligation and the threat of danger in his own backyard, or did it have to do with meeting a new kind of being that he wanted to understand?

Maybe she'd ditch him and appear somewhere else. If she did, where would she go?

"I won't call them," he said as if she still stood beside

him. Then he sent that same message silently through the telepathic channels all Weres used to communicate.

"But I won't go away," he warned out loud.

The return of the fluttery sensation in his chest made Rafe stand up straighter. It was as though Cara Kirk-Killion had heard his little speech and had placed her own silent comment inside his chest instead of his mind. She knew he was there, all right, and that he would be here when she decided to be reasonable. She was also letting him in on some of the special things she could do.

The only question now was how long she might make him wait for another chance to see her, and if she already knew that was what he wanted most.

The Were wasn't going away. Cara sensed his determination to corral the guest who was MIA and fulfill his obligation to the pack. She also sensed that he was genuinely interested in her for reasons of his own. This Were male had a different agenda. He seemed to be as curious about her as she was about him.

She rode the crest of another wave, feeling extraordinarily light, but guilt over the promise to behave that she'd made to her father left her nauseous. Her family never broke their promises. Would she be the first to do so? If the Landaus' walls didn't keep her in line, her family's reputation for integrity would.

As the wave that brought her back to shore receded, Cara stood up. Taking a few steps forward to avoid the drag of the tide, she said to the Were on the beach, "You are persistent."

"Persistence is my middle name," he returned. "I've been told it's a virtue."

Cara didn't wipe the water from her face, liking the

coolness it provided. "You'll take me to your pack yourself? You aren't afraid of being alone with a member of my clan?"

"Should I be afraid?"

"Not tonight."

"Then yes, I'll drive you to the compound, if that's all right with you," he said.

"Do I have a choice in the matter?"

"I suppose you can do whatever the hell you want, though the invitation to be our guest stands," he replied.

She watched the tall Were brush sand from the hem of his jeans. In the moonlight, his bare shoulders appeared to be perfectly sculpted. She allowed her gaze to linger there.

"One thing, though," he said, glancing up. He held out his hand, offering her the damp shirt he had removed before wading into the water after her. "Nakedness won't do if we meet anyone else on the way to the car. This is the best I can come up with unless you remember where you left your own clothes."

Cara glanced up the beach. "I came from that way."

He nodded. "Maybe you can wear the shirt until we find your stuff."

If she followed his suggestion, she would have to take the shirt from his hand…the same hand that had touched her and given her the first real thrill she could remember. She wasn't sure she wanted another one. She was fiercely aware of his body, and the fire in his eyes held her strangely captive.

She took another step, then paused. The Were's scent saturated the shirt he held out to her, overwhelming her senses.

Seeming to understand her reticence, he closed the distance and stopped an arm's length away from her with the shirt dangling from his fingers. It was a dare. A challenge. She took the shirt and held her breath as she slipped it on. The musky fragrance embedded in the fabric surrounded her body like a cloud until she could barely smell anything else.

"Better," the Were said. "Now let's get the rest of you covered up, shall we?"

Cara only then dared to take a deep breath.

"You have to understand that my family is personally responsible for your safety while you're in Miami," he said. "That was the pact we made, and pacts must be honored. I'm guessing there would be hell to pay if we don't keep you in our sights."

The shirt was soft, well-worn, and the same color blue as Rafe Landau's eyes. Cara liked those details, and she liked looking at Rafe. He was a fine male of the Were species, she supposed. But the way she felt around him was disturbing.

"What if I asked you to postpone the inevitable for a while longer?" she asked.

He said, "I thought you already did."

"Your pack thinks I'm a freak."

"Then you can prove them wrong."

"How do you know I'd be able to do that?"

"Call it a hunch," he replied.

Cara blinked slowly. Like her, Rafe was quick to make judgments. But that didn't mean he was right.

"It's just a feeling I have," he explained.

"You don't know me."

He shrugged those fascinating bare shoulders. "We can walk along the shore to get your clothes. I like the sand. Moonlight makes it sparkle."

Cara expected him to say more. He had to have questions.

"Maybe we can come back here sometime after you settle in," he said. "Would you like that, Cara?"

Hearing a stranger say her name gave her a jolt of pleasure that she tried to ignore. She wasn't experienced in the nuances of male-female relationships, though she wanted to learn. And she could do worse than having this handsome, understanding Were as a teacher.

Rafe Landau didn't know her, though. Not really. Not at all.

So what would he think when he found out her secrets?

The time it took for them to reach the spot where Cara had left her clothes was too short for Rafe's liking.

With Cara dressed only in his shirt, which hung a little below her hips, the whole situation felt too intimate. They weren't lovers out here to enjoy the moonlight. He had become her guard—and her jailer, to hear her tell it. Still, having this rare and beautiful creature beside him made Rafe feel oddly content.

He had to wonder about the hidden dangers Cara represented. Her father had achieved legendary status among those of Rafe's pack. Her mother was only mentioned now and then in whispers. What kind of life could Cara possibly have had with a family like that?

"Are you much like your mother?" he asked, undeterred by the probable insensitivity of the question.

"Yes," she replied.

"Are you afraid of being like her?"

She glanced at him as they walked. "Sometimes."

"Would your family have sent you here if they had suspected trouble for you among us?"

She shook her head. "Only at home can I truly be free."

Rafe said, "I believe... I hope...you'll find that doesn't have to be the case, and that you'll make friends here."

The desire to see her face up close and in better light had become an urgent necessity. Rafe wanted to get to know every line and curve of her body. Cara might be dangerous, but she looked so fragile and delicious in his shirt.

Maybe *fragile* wasn't the right word.

If Cara was anything like her mother, formidable was more like it. Rumor had it that Rosalind Kirk could shape-shift into many different forms any time she wanted to and that few enemies could stand against her. Nevertheless, if Cara was like her mother, and not entirely wolf, why did his wolf recognize hers? And why didn't he sense any animosity in her?

"I won't be here long. Surely you know that I can't live among you," she said, acknowledging his thoughts as if he had shared them with her.

"How do you know you can't be happy here?" he asked. "At least you can give us a try."

She gave the ocean a long look and said, "I have promised to try."

Cara's feet seemed to skim the sand. She was incredibly beautiful. Stunningly so. Yet there was no mistaking the powerful aura that surrounded Cara like her own personal fog. Rafe could only imagine how she might use that power if she wanted to.

Despite that, it took all of his willpower to keep his hands to himself. He wanted badly to console Cara, to reassure her that her visit would go well. He knew he was lying to himself about the possibility that she wouldn't want to leave when the time came. For the moment, he tried to stick to the story that they could be friends, though that too was revealed as a falsehood each time Cara leaned into the wind and his shirt clung to the outlines of her sleek, wet body.

When she stopped, he stopped with her. She turned to face him, and his pulse sped up. Moonlight hugged her face, showing Rafe all the details he had been hoping to see. He held his breath.

She had high cheekbones and a wide brow. Though she was lean, her full lips lent her a softness that was lacking in her attitude. Her neck was long and graceful, her skin a smooth, unblemished ivory. Large eyes, framed by dark lashes, dominated her other features. Those eyes were a bright Lycan green.

She took a step, bringing her close enough for Rafe to feel her breath on his face. She said suddenly, in a hoarse, velvety whisper, "It's you, isn't it?"

Then she waited in silence as if daring Rafe to find meaning in those words.

Chapter 4

She knew she had surprised Rafe. There was no way he could even begin to comprehend her remark. But this had to be the Were who had haunted her dreams. Why else had they met like this—him, out of all of the other wolves the Landaus could have sent to find her?

Was there such a thing as coincidence, after all, or had there been some other hand at work here?

Cara had anticipated this meeting with her dream man and had vowed to pay him back for the sleepless nights. Now she wanted this moment to go on, and for time to stop with the two of them right here, near the water.

Eventually, she broke the silence. "Six days. I'll stay here for six days and then I'll go home."

He said, "Are you worried about the moon being full right after that?"

Cara didn't have to look up at the sky to know the exact position of the moon, and that it was half-full tonight. The pull of the moon on her system was a constant reminder of what it could do, and what she could become. She also felt the movement of the tides and the rhythm of the blood in her arteries.

She felt Rafe's attention on her as if it was another touch.

"It wouldn't be wise to stay any longer," she said.

"What would happen if you did?"

He wore a serious expression that made his eyes gleam as he waited for her to explain herself.

"Unwanted guests might arrive," she replied.

"We've had quite a few unwelcome visitors in the past and know what to do with them," he told her. "Have no doubts about that."

"These uninvited guests wouldn't be any of your concern and are merely another part of my existence."

"Are you talking about vampires and what happened to your parents here?"

"Among other things."

He leaned toward her. "What would other creatures want if they did come?"

"The same thing you want," she replied soberly.

"And that is?"

"Me."

Her answer didn't seem to surprise him. He didn't feign ignorance or pretend to misunderstand her meaning. But he took in a breath and held it before speaking again.

"It's natural, I suppose, that I'm interested in you. Wolf-to-wolf attraction has a heady allure, and being at the beach doesn't help any, because moonlight on the water is romantic. Then there's the fact that you're exceptionally beautiful and half-naked. All of that can mess with a guy's head. I'll admit that it's messing with mine."

Ribbons of pleasure wound through Cara with an exotic flutter. No one had ever told her she was beautiful. She hadn't really been sure how others perceived her looks. She'd never understood why other creatures wanted a piece of her, except for the vampires. Her mother had warned her about that. Having a Banshee's spirit nestled inside her would allow her to lead bloodsuckers to their next meal by pointing out human weaknesses. If caught by them, she'd become a vampire's dinner bell.

The heat caused by Rafe's remarks left Cara uncertain about what might happen next, and what she should do. Her legs felt weak, and that was a first. Her stomach twisted as if the thing she housed had come alive. Rafe had an almost mystical allure for someone who had gone without companionship for most of her life.

They had reached the place where she had discarded her clothes, but he hadn't noticed. Hadn't he said he liked her half-naked?

"You haven't seen a naked woman before?" she asked, noting how he stared at her as she started to take off his shirt.

"I've seen a few," he replied. "But none quite like you."

A shiver moved through her as she brought her head up and whirled around. A new feeling had invaded her senses, and it didn't register as anything remotely like pleasure. It was an announcement that they had company. The kind she had warned Rafe about. Trouble was coming, and the wolf beside her was about to find out what her world could be like.

Rafe spun around, his senses on high alert. Cara was already on the move.

He caught up with her in four long strides as his cop

reflexes kicked in and he stepped in front of Cara to block her way while he searched the beach and the sidewalk. She placed both of her hands on the center of his back and applied pressure to move him out of the way.

"Wait," he said to her. "Just wait."

He didn't have his gun. Hell, he wasn't wearing shoes. The shove Cara gave him sent him forward a few inches, but he rallied. Determined to do his job and protect her, Rafe hit a number on his cell phone to call his father and said to Cara, "What's out here that I can't see?"

"Fangs," she replied.

"Fangs, as in vampires?" Could that be right? Had vampires found Cara already? How was that possible?

"One of them," she said.

"Close by?"

"Very close."

"How can I find it?" Rafe asked.

"Smell."

He was supposed to smell a damn vampire when his lungs were filled with Cara's rich scent?

"Describe the smell, Cara."

"Dark earth, dirt and other things more difficult to define unless you've met with vampires before. They're masters at masking those smells, which makes them hard to find if you were to go looking."

"Can we get to the street, or another block down the beach?" Rafe asked.

When she didn't answer him, he took her silence for a bad sign. Keeping his eyes trained for any movement in the distance, Rafe automatically reached for Cara's hand. The surge of electricity that hit him when their skin met was a shock. But he couldn't let it distract him from getting Cara out of there. Even if she had faced these creatures before, he had to guard her with his life. Or try to.

"Follow me," he instructed, lacing her fingers with his and absorbing charge after charge of electricity that felt like nothing he had ever experienced.

Adrenaline took over. Cara didn't protest when he pulled her forward. "Warn me if I'm heading for trouble," he said.

She tugged at him hard enough to stop him after a few steps. Frustrated by this, Rafe turned to face her.

"It's you," she repeated, but with a different emphasis this time.

Her face came close to his. As she met his eyes, her wet hair brushed against his bare arms, causing alternating heat and chills. Cara, the hybrid shifter he was trying to protect, could adopt a vampire's form if one were to appear on the beach, but the need to get her to safety was strong enough for him to override his fear of that happening.

"What is it, Cara?" he asked.

Her next words shook him up more than touching her had.

"You smell like them," she said.

"What are you talking about?"

Cara didn't honor him with a reply. She turned toward the dark remains of a hotel under renovation, taking him with her. That's when Rafe saw what had attracted her attention. Someone was standing on the sidewalk in front of the hotel. Someone Rafe thought he knew.

"No way," he muttered in surprise. But in the time between that remark and his next breath, the figure materialized beside them…and Rafe hadn't seen anyone move.

Perfume. He smelled perfume, and it was familiar. Also familiar was the tangle of blond hair and the green shirt that did little to hide an exquisite body.

Holy hell...it was Brandi. She was a goddamn vampire?

Shock kept him from moving as fast as he should have. His date from earlier that night was there beside him, hissing through a pair of lethal-looking fangs as she went for his throat.

In a flash of speed that rivaled the creature in front of him, Cara had Brandi's hair in her fists. God, it really was Brandi...or whatever the hell Brandi really was.

"My problem. Not yours," Cara said to him over her shoulder.

"The hell you say," Rafe snapped.

Cara was already liquefying. That was the only way to describe what happened. Her body just seemed to melt into a kind of being that was Cara, and yet different, as the fight began in earnest without him.

Cara snapped at the vampire with a fresh set of fangs that made the creature in her grip hesitate for a few seconds too long. Uncertainty flashed in its red-rimmed eyes as Cara's hold on its hair tightened.

She felt the vampire's hunger and the incessant throb of its need to feed. Hunger was everything. Starvation meant oblivion. Vampires killed in order to feel alive— otherwise they were merely animated corpses without any real direction. This one was old, and masterful in its ability to disguise itself, at least on the surface. Once the fangs came out, its human semblance began to decay.

Cara's fangs, on the other hand, brought on a hunger of another kind—a defensive desire to rid the world of the monsters she was cursed to emulate.

The Landau wolf joined in the fight. Using his weight to press Cara aside, he struggled to get one of the vampire's arms behind its back. The harsh sound of a bone breaking was alarmingly loud as the vampire's arm shattered near the shoulder. Louder still was Rafe Landau's startled intake of breath.

Fangs brushed her arm, ripping her sleeve, leaving a long trail of flapping fabric. Cara maneuvered her way between Rafe and the snarling bloodsucker with her own fangs exposed and her hands moving almost subliminally fast.

Rafe, who was incredibly strong and used to fighting, by the looks of things, wasn't to be left out of this fray. He also wasn't going to allow a female to help him do his job, no matter who or what that female was. With great force, he leaned his shoulder into the vampire, and it teetered. The bloodsucker hissed again through its treacherous fangs and spit out his name.

Hearing that made Rafe Landau hesitate. Cara pushed past him. Even a few seconds of hesitation when facing the walking undead meant certain death, and this abomination whose distant relatives had helped to make Cara like them in so many ways wasn't going to win tonight. She hated vampires. She hated when they came to find her, sensing kinship. She hated every time her fangs dropped and she became like them.

Foul black blood spurted from the vampire's shoulder when Cara's fangs found purchase. The blood was evidence of the creature's recent meal. There would have been none otherwise, only a spill of dark gray ash, the same ash vampires dissolved into after being dealt a death blow by a worthy opponent.

"Let me have her...have *it*," Rafe directed. But this was Cara's own personal war.

Cara dug into the bloodsucker's flesh with her fangs. At the same time, Rafe landed a right-handed punch to the vamp's shoulder, and the fanged parasite shrieked, probably not from pain, but from anger. It lost hold of its feminine disguise as it rallied, and the undead creature whose looks previously could have fooled most humans became the bony, skeletal, red-eyed abomination it really was.

Cara felt no kinship with this vampire and refused to acknowledge being like it. This was one of the many monsters that ruled her nightmares. Vampires were the enemy, though this one had likely believed at first that Cara Kirk-Killion, with her pale skin and fangs, might help take Rafe down. But vampires like this one had nearly killed her father. To most of the world, her father had died.

Colton Killion's DNA had been compromised by too much vampire saliva and too damn many bites, and he'd become a legendary white ghost wolf one fateful night here in this city, an albino whose skin and hair would have stood out anywhere as being freakish.

The same thing was not going to happen to Rafe. *Not tonight.*

Though this bloodsucker was fast, Cara moved faster. She possessed a secret weapon that hadn't yet been revealed. Her heritage. All of it.

She snapped her fangs in the creature's face and made it look at her…made it look into her eyes. A far older spirit than this vampire was beginning to show itself. This was death calling. True and final death. The Banshee inside her had awakened.

The shriek that came from the vampire's open mouth when it realized its fate dictated what would happen. One second passed, then two more, and Cara, with her dark spirit's extra push of power, punched through the vampire's bony concave chest with both hands. Gripping hard, she squeezed the blackened heart that had not beat in centuries until the useless thing crumbled.

"Don't breathe," Cara shouted to Rafe, who was beside her and struggling to get his hands on the foul creature. Seconds later, the bloodsucker exploded like a bomb had gone off, and its lifeless body disintegrated into a flurry of foul-smelling ash.

Chapter 5

A dark, sticky rain was falling. But it wasn't rain, really, and nothing that resembled water.

Rafe let out the breath he had been holding and stared at the spot where the vampire had been standing. He was afraid to look at Cara in vampire mode. Shock over witnessing what had happened here made his stomach turn. This was something he would never forget, though the whole event had happened so fast, he hardly believed it had happened at all.

Finally, he did look at Cara. He had to see her to try to make sense of it all. She hadn't just exposed a gleaming set of fangs—she'd exposed one of her secrets. And even with her fangs, pale skin and flat black gaze, she had the ability to mesmerize.

Many features remained of the Cara he had met earlier tonight, only slightly rearranged. She had sharper cheekbones with gaunt hollows beneath. Dark crescents underscored her eyes, contrasting with the whiteness of her skin. The only color she possessed was in the tiny drops of blood speckling her lips, which were half-closed over a daunting pair of unnatural teeth.

The rumors were true. Cara had transformed into this new version in less time than it had taken for him to catch his breath. Rafe found himself equally fascinated and repelled by her new look and by what he had seen Cara do to the vampire. No stranger to violence himself, he sympathized with Cara, and how her life probably consisted of one fight after another. He wondered if she would ever be able to find the kind of peace she might crave.

Hell, he was speechless, and therefore couldn't ask her how a shape-shift like hers was possible, or what it felt like. Plus, it wasn't his place to ask her tough questions or make her feel any more ill at ease than she already did.

Cara Kirk-Killion, in whatever incarnation, had just possibly saved his sorry ass from a date with a vampire. He couldn't believe it Using fangs had likely been Brandi's intention all along. The skimpy lingerie had been camouflage. Lilac perfume had masked the unfamiliar scent. They probably never would have made it as far as the bed.

Cara had freed him from having to deal with his first vampire—a bloodsucking parasite so like a human, he had fallen for its charade. What about the curvaceous body Brandi had sported, and the silky tousled hair? Would he have discovered the truth if he'd gotten close enough to the creature to discover that her chest contained no heartbeat?

And what about Cara? Did her vampire form come with a vampire's thirst? If she had those kinds of urges, she was controlling them well. She stood three feet from him with her hands at her sides, radiating no perceptible aura of danger, though for a few seconds back there, he'd had doubts. His ears still rang with the sound of her fangs gnashing.

"Can you change back?" he asked, slightly out of breath from the recent adrenaline surge. "Will the vamp characteristics fade away on their own?"

Maybe those weren't the questions Cara had been anticipating, but they were the only ones she was going to get from him at the moment. Her eyes were trained on him. She said nothing in reply as he led her down the sidewalk.

In the glare of his building's exterior security lights, Rafe glanced away from her lingering gaze long enough to note the rips in the shirt he had loaned her and the blood soaking it in several spots. She didn't seem to notice any of that.

"We'll need to see to those scratches," he continued, stepping aside so that Cara could precede him to his apartment. "We can make a quick stop at my place if you're up for that," he added. "I have a first-aid kit."

When she shook her head, Rafe paused, then rallied enough of his wits to say, "Thank you, Cara."

Her red-rimmed eyes, still dilated by an interior darkness, met his. The tips of her extremely white fangs seem to glow against the color of her blood-flecked lips.

"That's what you meant when you said 'it's you,' right? You smelled that vampire on me?" With the adrenaline still flowing, he kept up the nervous chatter. "Now that I think about it, I invited that thing inside. What kind of a fool does that make me?"

Cara finally spoke. "I told you they are deceptive in their disguises. Like we are."

Like we are...

She meant werewolves masquerading as humans.

As Rafe watched, Cara's face began to shift back, resuming the beautiful human features Rafe had first seen on the beach. The hollows in her cheeks disappeared, and some color returned.

He couldn't have explained what the process actually was or how it worked. When the redness around her eyes faded, Rafe wondered whether the face she now showed him was what Cara actually looked like, or if its beauty was another kind of stunt for suckers like him to fall for.

In the light from the building, Cara was even more beautiful than she had been in the moonlight. Could he trust his eyes?

Werewolves didn't shape-shift easily. Transformations were always painful. Some Weres shifted faster than others, with full-blooded Lycans being masters of the pain game. Cara's switch to vampire mode and back had been different. It was silent, fluid, as if she had merely coaxed another shape into existence.

She continued to observe him with a keenness that made his inner wolf anxious. *Just another shape-shift in my repertoire of them*, her expression suggested. *Nothing special.*

Hell, did she even know what special was?

"Can you control when you become like them?" he asked, unabashedly curious. "Do you make it happen?"

"It just is," she replied.

Though the fangs were gone, flecks of blood still dappled her mouth. Rafe tried not to look.

"There's no control button or on-off switch?" he pressed.

She shook her head.

"Can you do that with any supernatural creature, Cara? Look like anything that comes your way?"

"For the most part."

"Christ," Rafe muttered. "I see why you'd rather not be in an unfamiliar place when the moon is full. What could your werewolf side possibly be like when coupled with so many other talents?"

"My wolf side isn't much like yours," she said and left it at that.

The weird thing was how much Rafe desired to get closer to Cara in spite of the warning flags his mind was waving. He should have felt sorry for her and her burden, yet she seemed to be up to the task handed to her, if tonight was any indication. Though her family and background were intimidating, part of him needed to see past all that and find the real Cara. He tried to guess whether anyone had ever seen the real thing.

Telling her he'd like to help in any way he could seemed ludicrous, given the fact that she had just killed a vampire with relative ease. Still, when he gestured again for Cara to precede him to the stairs, she obliged docilely, as if she trusted him and they were fast friends.

As they began to move, the soft growl of a well-tuned engine broke the silence. Rafe had almost forgotten about the emergency call he'd made to his father before the vampire attack and had mixed feelings now about how quickly the call had been answered. He would lose one-on-one face time with Cara. There would be less of a chance to get to understand her.

Cara was listening to the same sound. When she turned to him, her eyes were again the color of polished emeralds, flashing with curiosity as she wiped the flecks of blood from her lips with the back of one hand.

"I'm sorry," Rafe said as the musky scent of approaching Weres became more pronounced. "We've got company, but it's all right this time."

Almost immediately, he caught sight of his silver-haired father and Cameron Mitchell, another large Were Rafe knew very well, who was a senior detective on the Miami force. They were heading their way.

"I'll go up and get more clothes for you," Rafe said to Cara. "We never found yours, and the picture you present in my shirt is…"

Cara tilted her head to one side, waiting for him to finish. He didn't. Couldn't. This hybrid Were was sexy, lithe, strong and more than a little bit scary.

Yep, he was a fool, all right, for sliding into sympathy with her so effortlessly. Telling Cara he was attracted to her, scary bits and all, wasn't going to help their situation and would confuse them both. But that was exactly what Rafe was thinking when he'd only known her for, what? About an hour? As she had said, he didn't really know her at all.

"Rafe?"

His father's deep voice was only a sampling of the kind of power Dylan Landau possessed. Cara looked at the alpha coming their way with a flicker of interest. Before stopping to think, Rafe reached out to offer her his support with a light touch on her arm.

Fire erupted inside him as her eyes met his. More flames licked at his throat, bringing on a whole new level of heat. There was no way to acknowledge the suddenness of these feelings, their origin and what they might mean.

"Cara. Are you all right?" his father asked, slowing as he reached them.

When she remained silent, Rafe didn't answer for her. He was struggling to control his own feelings. Cara had told him she needed time to adapt and get her bearings, and time was exactly what he needed, too, because his heart seemed to stop each time their eyes met. The reaction was not only absurd, it was irresponsible.

"Come with us," his father said, gesturing with a wave of his hand toward the car parked a short distance away. "And welcome to Miami."

Rafe's father hadn't gotten to be a respected judge without having serious social skills. The alpha's tone was calm and free of any hint of chastisement over her earlier escape. There was no anxiousness in his bearing. There usually wasn't.

Between his father and Cameron Mitchell, Cara was in good hands. Rafe should have been relieved to let her go.

Yet he didn't feel relieved. Far from it. He felt as if he wasn't going to allow them to take her.

Cara slowly turned toward the two men without visibly revealing the concern Rafe knew she felt. On the inside, Cara was on fire, just like he was. They shared the flames that had been kindled between them tonight. He should have feared that, or at least been wary of the speed with which this had happened.

Ignoring the others, Cara said to him, "That vampire wasn't after me. It wasn't waiting for me out here tonight."

Rafe gave her a questioning glance.

"It was here for you," she said.

Cara was probably right, Rafe realized. Having missed her earlier opportunity, Brandi had been waiting for another shot at draining him dry, whether or not he had company.

But there was a slight problem with that, if the stories were true about werewolf blood being a turn-off to vampires. He chose not to point that out for the time being. Brandi had been trying hard to seduce him. If it wasn't dinner that wily creature had wanted, what had she been after in her attempt to take him down?

Cara wasn't in a position to protest the presence of the two new Weres, so she tucked those arguments away. She didn't like this interruption of her time alone with Rafe Landau. In less than an hour, she had become comfortable with him. Now, with the other Weres present, she again felt tense.

The stab of regret she felt when Rafe dropped his hand and spoke to the others was a new kind of pain. She didn't like pain. A fresh round of defiance rose inside her over the idea of being separated from him.

"What vampire are we talking about?" the silver-haired Were asked nonchalantly.

His scent was similar to Rafe's. The older wolf was notably alpha, and had to be Rafe's relative. Father? He was tall and handsome. His long hair was tied behind his neck, and he had a younger Were's build that made him appear half the age he'd have to be if Rafe was his son.

Rafe answered the Elder Were's question. "We had an argument with a vampire a few minutes ago."

Cara observed how the alpha moved with the same kind of grace Rafe possessed. However, she could tell the older Were was a pure-blooded Lycan and wore his power like an emblem of high birth and rank.

"Cara, this is my father, Dylan Landau, host for the duration of your stay," Rafe said, interrupting his father's line of questioning. "And this is Cameron Mitchell, a good friend of ours."

"Please forgive the lack of introductions," the alpha said with a polite dip of his head. "We were very worried, and happy to find you in good hands."

The alpha took in the scene through pale eyes, missing nothing, assessing the situation without comment. When his gaze landed on the tears in her sleeve, Dylan Landau said, "Not a heated argument, I hope, with that vampire?"

"Nothing too bad," Rafe lied.

The alpha nodded. "I knew your father and your mother, and I'm glad they agreed to let you visit. I'm sorry you didn't have such a warm welcome, Cara, and would like to make that up to you. Would you come with us to see where you'll be staying?"

Cara didn't look at Rafe. She could have been wrong about the tension that seemed to be building up in him. She knew he wanted her to comply, to reach a safer place than this one. He had worried about her from the start.

Even more interesting was the fact that Rafe's father didn't appear to be too concerned about their encounter with a bloodsucker. Every Were here should have known this was worthy of further investigation.

Unfamiliar sensations continued to flood Cara's system when she stole a closer look at Rafe. The flares of heat were new and something she didn't fully understand.

As if he had the ability to read minds, Dylan Landau addressed her last thought. "Rafe, why don't you ride along with us? Maybe you can loan our guest some clothes until we get her home."

Rafe's father didn't ask how she had lost her clothes in the first place, and Cara felt herself warming to his social skills.

It looked like there was going to be a benign ending to this eventful evening, although she'd now witnessed for herself the vampire presence in Miami and how far this city's bloodsuckers had evolved. The appearance of the one she'd met tonight, along with the fact that it had purposefully lain in wait for Rafe, was highly unusual. Vampires tended to act on instinct when finding their next meal, and didn't usually set traps to ensnare their victims. Yet it seemed to her that this one had.

"Male or female vamp?" Rafe's father casually asked.

"Female," Rafe said.

The alpha asked Cara the question directly. "New or old?"

"Not too ancient," Cara replied. "But talented."

Dylan Landau nodded. "Well, it will be a relatively short ride to our home. It won't take long. We aren't going far."

Unlike with his father, Cara could read Rafe's emotions as easily as she had read the tides. Rafe wanted her to go along with the plan his father had laid out, and at the same time, he was sorry she had to.

Cameron waved a hand toward what Cara supposed had to be the waiting car. She looked to Rafe, whose nod indicated it was all right for her to follow.

She was trapped. There was nowhere for her to run, and she couldn't rely on the ocean to take her away.

"I'll be right behind you," Rafe said. "I'll just get those pants. I hope you like jeans."

Cara followed the two Weres from the beach without argument, already counting the minutes until Rafe would again be at her side. She continued to watch Dylan Landau closely, gauging his strengths, needing to ask the alpha what he knew about her parents, while knowing she'd have to behave and honor his wishes if she were to piece together the puzzle of what had happened to them here nineteen years ago.

Had her mother and father been cast out of this pack

for being different, or for being dangerous? What had made them outcasts? Who had been alpha of the Landau pack back then?

Her parents had never spoken to her about these things. Questions about the past were taboo. Getting answers was part of the reason she had gone along with the plan for her to visit Miami. It was the reason she was going with these Weres to the car. Still, there was another path to explore here in Miami as well. The path revealed by her dreams…and the wolf that had haunted them.

Right here, tonight, whether it had been coincidence or the fates had played a hand, that wolf dream was no longer just in her imagination. The wolf had come to life, and his name was Rafe Landau.

They were in some way connected. Even in the reality of the moment, Rafe Landau was haunting her. His looks, his presence and strength, all pointed to something she had yet to grasp. If events were lining up and falling into place, did that mean she was on the path to get everything she wanted?

The questions she needed to have answered were the reason she had helped Rafe fight off the undead attacker, and was wearing his clothes. Her curiosity had prevented her from making Rafe pay for appearing in her dreams and disturbing her sleep. It suddenly seemed to Cara that Rafe, for good or ill, was going to be the key to what lay ahead. He was the central clue in the mystery of her existence that she had to unravel.

Do you know this, Rafe?

She didn't send that question to him over Were channels because the answer would have been about what lay ahead. If she stayed.

Chapter 6

The Mercedes sedan seemed crowded to Rafe as Cameron pulled away from the apartment building. Cara didn't look at him from her side of the back seat. She had withdrawn. He couldn't read her.

They traveled in silence. The car's interior temperature felt cool, and the leather seat was luxuriously soft. For once, Rafe was relieved to leave the beach. Thoughts of his close call with the vampire nagged at him. He hoped this wasn't a prediction of what the future might bring.

Several things continued to bother him, but the image of Cara with fangs was foremost in his mind. He would have preferred that others in his pack not be exposed to the kinds of things Cara could do. *Freak* was the word she had used to describe herself, and actually, was that so far off?

Then there was the attack itself. Why had the vampire gone after a werewolf when a human tourist would have been much tastier fare?

Rafe kept those thoughts locked away as buildings and lights shot past the window. At this hour, people crowded the streets in search of food and entertainment. Six police cruisers crept by, keeping up a show of law-enforcement presence.

By comparison, the estates on the far side of the city were quiet, secluded and seemingly a world away from the neon and the noise. His family's property was one of the largest in the area. Its three landscaped acres were entirely surrounded by an eight-foot stone wall that was monitored by the pack, and there was a small manned guardhouse at the front gate. A well-respected federal judge lived there. Wolves lived there. The Landau house was a place of secrets.

Rafe stole a glance at Cara as they neared the front gate, thinking she had to feel the heat of his attention even though she didn't turn her head. Or was he just making that up?

He sighed and rubbed his temples, not sure what to expect when they arrived. Who would be among the welcoming committee? He assumed that most of the pack would have been kept from meeting Cara, at least for tonight.

"Here we are," his father announced as the surroundings grew darker and the long stretch of gray stone came into view. Cara had told Rafe she feared being trapped behind those walls. He'd have given a lot to know what she was thinking now.

The car stopped in front of the ornate iron gate and was quickly waved through by a familiar guard when it opened. As the Mercedes cruised down the driveway, his father turned in his seat.

"It's past dinnertime, but you can have whatever you like as soon as you're settled in. You must be famished," he said.

Rafe could almost hear Cara silently say, *What I'd like is to go home*. To her credit, she didn't voice that response.

"Not many of us will be here tonight," Rafe's father continued. "We thought you might prefer some time to get to know the place before we introduce you. Is that all right with you, Cara?"

Cara was looking at his father. She barely nodded her head. He knew this was the moment she had been dreading, probably since the plan for her to come to Miami had first been hatched. On the surface she looked calm enough, but small quakes rocked the seat he shared with her, and every one of them was like a stab to his heart.

"Cara," he said, needing to speak, hoping to ease her trepidation. "Look. See up there?" He pointed at the brick house that rose two and a half stories above a meandering lawn. "Top floor? Can you see it?"

Her eyes glided that way.

"Your mother stayed in a room there. Your father, too. Maybe you'd like to have that same room while you're here?"

He had snagged her interest. The air in the car became charged.

"I'm sure that can be arranged," he said.

"It can," his father agreed.

She was tuning in now and sending Rafe messages over silent Were channels. *"Will I be a prisoner?"* And *"Will you be here?"*

"No. Not a prisoner. I've told you that. And yes, I'll stay if that's what you want," he messaged back over

airwaves his father would also be privy to, as well as every other Were within a short distance if they weren't careful with their transmissions. He'd have to warn Cara to erect her own inner walls.

Here, in this pack, where so many secrets had to be kept, unspoken messages were the normal mode of communication. That didn't necessarily ensure privacy but there were ways to get around being overheard at times.

"After what happened tonight with that vampire, it might be best if you stayed away from the walls for a day or two, Cara. Just to be safe," his father suggested.

The next shudder that rolled through Cara felt to Rafe as if it had been his own. The word *trapped* echoed in his mind like a shout. When the car stopped in front of the columned southern portico and Cameron opened the door for her, Cara got out. As Rafe's mother emerged from the house, Cara paused. But she didn't have to be worried.

Dana Delmonico Landau had turned *casual* into an art form. That showed now in her outfit, a faded pair of jeans and white T-shirt. His mother had never been a fan of anything fancy. She had been a good detective for years and had risen through the ranks to become a captain in the Miami PD. She had only recently retired and therefore had too much energy in need of release.

His mother had been born human. She had also been here when Rosalind Kirk and Colton Killion had briefly been in residence. From the stories of that time, he knew his mother, along with his father, had helped Cara's parents in the final showdown with the vampires, after which both of Cara's parents had disappeared.

Did Cara know anything about that, or about the part his pack had played in those last days? If she housed spirits similar to her mother's, would being in this house seem like déjà vu?

"Cara." His mother had stopped on the bottom porch step. "I'm Dana, and I'm glad you made it here. Would you like to come in, or would you prefer to take a look at the grounds first? Please understand that we're not as grand as this place would make us seem, and we're happy to have you join us here."

Cara didn't speak, but Rafe noticed that her eyes gravitated toward his mother's.

"Rafe," his mother said, turning to him, "why don't you show Cara around while we find her something to eat? Let her catch her breath before joining us inside."

Rafe looked to his father, who nodded in spite of his earlier warning to remain clear of the walls for the time being. Both of them knew the importance of that warning, and also that Rafe would take it seriously.

"Cara, what do you say to a little more fresh air?" Rafe asked. "Just to get the feel of the place."

She nodded. And as though she was merely any invited guest instead of the daughter of two Were legends and potentially as dangerous as both of them, everyone else went into the house, leaving Cara and him in the driveway, alone.

She had never seen a house as large as the one in front of her. Actually, Cara had never seen any house besides the small one she had grown up in. Nevertheless, she sensed a certain familiarity with the Landau mansion that didn't make it seem as foreign as she had expected. There were plenty of ghosts here, something she was intimately familiar with.

"How long?" she finally said to Rafe, looking up at the house. "How long were they here?"

The fact that he was keeping up fairly well with her line of thinking was reflected in his reply. "Your father was treated here after being gravely injured. My grandmother took care of him and helped him to heal. Your mother was also a guest at the time and helped keep watch over him. This was before your parents had bonded."

"My mother was a guest?"

"She was here with her father. Your grandfather. It was also Rosalind's first time away from her home, and she skipped the warnings about remaining inside, and breached the wall. She must have found your father in the park, in a fight with the fanged hordes. It was her call that brought other Weres to your father's aid before it was too late."

Cara eyed the wall in the distance and the trees topping it. "That park?"

"The same one," Rafe said.

"So close?"

"The vampires had infiltrated a section of the park that's still some distance away." Rafe was eyeing her intently. "Does being near to it disturb you?"

Cara shook her head.

"No one mentioned those things to you?" he asked.

"My parents don't speak about the past," she replied.

"Not even to explain why things are the way they are?"

She turned to look at Rafe. Getting to the heart of her parents' past had been a burning desire for as long as she could remember, and Rafe was telling her things she had long waited to hear, but how much of what he knew was the truth, and how much of it was either hearsay or exaggeration?

Rafe probably hadn't been born when her father and

mother had been here, and neither had she. To Rafe, the past was just tales. To her, the real story of what had happened and who she was had become the main puzzle of her life.

"Vampires," she said. "Vampires made my father a ghost."

"It took a hell of a lot of them to do so, I've heard," Rafe agreed. "Colton was one of the strongest Lycans around in those days, and also a damn good cop."

"Cop?" Cara echoed.

He nodded. "Your father was a cop, like my mother. They protected Miami's population from bad things that dwelled both in and out of the shadows."

"Until those shadows gained strength," Cara noted.

When Rafe smiled, she was taken aback. There was no humor in anything that had been said, yet his smile was spontaneous and sat as easily with Rafe as his wolf-ishness.

He said, "We've both sprung from some pretty good genes. My mother was a badass, too, I hear. She's actually pretty formidable even now."

His smile dissolved into a more serious expression. "How did you know that vampire would be after me? I'm asking you because I'm wondering if maybe you purposefully gave me a trail to follow that took me away from her tonight. Could that be right, Cara? You lured me out of my apartment in time to prevent those fangs from reaching my neck?"

When she broke eye contact, Rafe seemed to read into it. "Well, then I doubly owe you, don't I." he said. "And I'm not going to ask how you managed it, because whatever you did worked."

She let that go. Had to. Rafe was looking at her differently now—more warily. Her earlier show of tricks might have scared him. Either that, or he was perplexed by what seemed to be an overly complex plan.

She could read in his expression that he had more to say on the subject. Instead, he changed tack. "We can walk in the grass. In the evening, and this far inland, it's the coolest place around."

"Where are the others? Your packmates?" she asked, wanting more of her parents' story but not ready to ask. What Rafe had already told her was food for thought, and better than any dinner the Landaus could have served up. Her parents had both stayed here, in this house, and some of these Weres had fought beside them.

"The others will be waiting to be called," he said.

"Will they come tonight?"

"A few of them, especially because of the vamp sighting. They'll keep a close watch on the park. You won't have to meet more of them until tomorrow."

So, she had been wrong about being a freak show for this pack. There was no crowd. She wasn't going to be the main event for tonight. Rafe's immediate family members and the Were who had accompanied the alpha were the only wolves present at the moment. She could breathe easier, and almost relax.

Maybe not too much relaxation, though. Because there was a new scent in the air, and a sense that someone on the other side of the wall was silently calling her name.

Chapter 7

A chill reached Rafe as he watched Cara turn toward
the section of stone wall not far from where they stood
in a way that made it obvious she sensed something
he didn't.

After years of having to protect herself, Cara was
probably a master of the art of self-preservation. He'd
hate for it to be another bloodsucker out there, though.
His grandfather's pack had culled vampire-nest numbers
years ago. As far as he knew, there hadn't been a vamp
sighting near here since he was a kid.

Rafe maintained his neutral expression while keeping
a cautious eye on Cara. The electrical current she radiated eased after he took a few deep breaths, testing the
air the way most Weres did when their inner fur was ruffled by a disturbance. Her frozen stance had produced
waves of anxiety in Rafe that made his muscles twitch.

Reluctantly, he tore his focus from her to check out

the wall. Cara took a step toward it. Though it was only one small step, Rafe sensed that she wasn't going to be chained by any rules governing her confinement, even if they were for her protection. Actually, he couldn't imagine who might stop her. The memory of Cara Kirk-Killion in action tonight wasn't going to fade any time soon.

Ebony lashes fluttered over her eyes. Strands of midnight-hued hair, still damp from her swim, looked like streaks of ink against her ivory neck and the shoulders of the borrowed shirt, which was too large and made her look waifish. In his jeans, Cara seemed even more like a kid playing dress-up.

"What is it?" His voice was low and steady.

"No one is watching us now?" she asked, her gaze intent on the wall.

"I wouldn't say that—" He didn't get to finish. Cara was already heading for the barrier at a sprint. She was more like a streak of lightning than anyone moving on two legs.

Rafe swore out loud. Then he gave chase, hoping to God that he could catch up with Cara before anything else did.

He didn't see her top the wall and didn't stop to analyze his actions in following her. There were eyes on them from the windows in the house and also from somewhere else nearby. He and Cara hadn't truly been on their own, and she must have known this.

He breathed a sigh of relief with the knowledge that backup would be right behind him if it was needed. Uttering oaths beneath his breath and pushing the limits his patience, he followed her into the park.

She was fast. Cara ran like she was on all fours, much like their ancient wolf ancestors. He had never seen anyone go from zero to thirty in just a few seconds on foot. But he was also no slouch when it came to running. Pack training readied all Weres for speed a few nights each month after the sun went down. Plus, he spent a lot of time sprinting after bad guys in the day job.

In his favor there was the fact that he knew every corner of the park that lay beyond his family's property. Most of the officers in law enforcement did, because the western section had a notorious reputation as a gathering place for gangs and criminals. There would be a cop or two on duty out here tonight, keeping watch for illegal activity. There would also be a party of Weres scouting around. It was unfortunate that a place so haunted by an unsavory past was connected to the estates beyond its borders, but that was part of city life.

He ran without breathing hard or breaking a sweat. Cara, just ahead of him, had slowed to a jog. She darted from tree to tree like a bloodhound on the scent, and he still had no idea what she was after.

Damn it…why didn't he know what she was doing? He was supposed to be a good detective.

After nearly tripping over something on the ground, Rafe slowed. Cara had removed the jeans, possibly in order to get around more freely…which meant that she was again half-naked. He was an idiot for allowing her the freedom to get away like this.

He was also an idiot for harboring thoughts of what he'd like to do with all that ivory bareness of hers if the situation were different. And, well…even if it wasn't.

The disturbing scent Cara had noticed was strongest near the trees. The humid air had filled with whispers.

Night had a strange feel to it here, too. The darkness was thicker, denser, as if unseen things took up space in the shadows. The pressure in her ears was a warning. Strange odors left a tang on her tongue. Her pulse thundered, though she saw nothing.

She slammed to a stop beneath an old tree, where her search turned up no one. Ready to shout a warning to some unseen foe, Cara waited a few more seconds to gather what information she could find.

The bark of the tree she stood beside shimmered like gold in the moonlight. Leaves shuddered and fell at her feet, as if the season were changing. There was movement. Rustling.

Cara glanced up.

Her equilibrium wavered. She gave a soft roar of protest. Clinging to the tree's branches was a kind of darkness she hadn't seen before. The treetop had become like a black hole in the atmosphere that was filled with chatter.

She swayed, unsteady on her feet, finally realizing what this was. What it had to be. Vampires were here. Lots of them. The damn bloodsuckers had called to her in a way only they could.

That realization caused the night to blur. Bloodsuckers unlike any she had seen before began to drop to the ground, one after the other. Five. Ten. More kept coming. Too many to count. The sheer number of them took the air from Cara's lungs. For the first time in her life, she felt afraid.

They moved like a monstrous incoming tide of malevolence—a wave of dark disjointed bodies with shockingly gaunt white features and skeletal frames. Things out of nightmares. Throwbacks to ancient times when vampires were nothing more than the walking dead. Their black eyes sank into dark sockets. Mouths were open and hissing, exposing lethally sharp yellow fangs.

An odd sensation of déjà vu hit Cara and rooted her to the spot. Sickness roiled in her stomach as nasty odors churned up unpleasant things inside her. She was going to be surrounded and vastly outnumbered. She'd be dead if she didn't act fast.

Fear of what she was seeing caused her wolf's energy to blaze. She didn't want to become like these monsters and had to do something to stave off a transformation she refused to accept. But could she manage to trick the traits built into her system by avoiding the rules?

Yes...

Like a caged animal finally freed, Cara let a rush of energy take her over. That energy flowed through her like a river of fire, burning everything in its wake. A new, crazed kind of power fueled her fury. Fangs filled her mouth before disappearing again.

"Not like you..." she whispered.

As she raised her hands to fight, Cara felt the sharp pop of claws springing through her fingertips. She called her wolf to the surface and made it obey. The wolf barreled upward and through her with the force of a runaway train.

Her spine cracked. Muscles seized and began to lengthen as she took her first swipe at the darkness gathered around her with preternaturally curved claws that would be a match for any oncoming pair of fangs. The shift was painful because it went against her nature—she had chosen her wolf, instead of becoming like the fanged parasites breathing down her neck. Cara had never attempted this before, and she had to bravely hold on.

Breathing became difficult. Her discomfort turned white-hot. Cara rode out the pain until her body finally accepted the shape that ruled most of her genetics. Werewolf. She-wolf. Not just any Were, either, but one with the ancient European designation of *wulf* that denoted the early masters of the breed who were powerful shamans.

This is who I am. What I am.

The urge to fight roared through her. The need to kill the creatures that had nearly killed her father here a long time ago became too difficult to ignore. She was strong, fast and fierce. Her wolf shared its soul with the spirit of a Banshee, just like her mother, and that spirit told her she was not going to die tonight.

All she had to do was kill every last bloodsucking fiend surrounding her.

Her blood sang with that goal until her head felt light. But her plan encountered a hitch. The vampires dropping from the trees didn't come after her. Every one of them suddenly moved en masse in the opposite direction, as though they had been drawn elsewhere by something more appetizing. As though they hadn't seen her at all.

There was someone in the distance. Cara turned her head, and the sickness inside her tripled. *Rafe?*

A ripple of horror accompanied the idea that Rafe had followed her, though she should have known he would. Rafe was a protector. He watched over her. As strong as he was, however, Rafe would be vulnerable without a full moon overhead to shift him. Against so many abominations, he'd have little chance of surviving an attack.

She ran, plowing through the haze of vamps, wielding her claws like the weapons they were originally intended to be, slashing at everything in her way and swallowing growls of anger and the sudden fear of losing what she had only recently found. Rafe Landau.

Her claws went through vamp bodies as if they were composed of air instead of strings of decaying flesh and bone. Although the vampires shrieked with terrible, unnatural voices, none of them noticed her. Not one of them fell.

The shock of her inability to stop them tripped her up. Cara stared at the dark moving tide with wide wolfish eyes, seeing clearly, shocked by the sight in front of her and how she wasn't able to do anything about it.

Then her system was jolted with a new awareness. The gaunt creatures were attacking a fully wolfed-up werewolf, brown-furred and massive in size. *Not Rafe. Someone else.*

The werewolf fought the oncoming horde like a pro, swinging his arms, using his legs, snapping his jaws. He fought hard, though he had to realize all that energy was useless against so many sharp teeth.

Cara couldn't stand to watch. She started again toward the rapidly tiring werewolf in the center of the fray and heard a voice in the distance say, "I'm here."

Or…had she uttered those words?

She flew to the middle of the fight, whirled, lashed out and made no headway. The big brown Were, now tiring, didn't once look her way. He looked past her at something she would have had to turn around to see.

Another sound broke through the grunts and growls she and the brown werewolf were making. At first, Cara thought it was a howl of distress or a warning call going up about the fight taking place. But that wasn't it. She recognized what it was. She had heard this sound before.

The shrieking noise seemed to split the darkness into multiple shadows. The power in it sucked the fight out of Cara. She stilled, frozen in place as the scene continued to unfold in front of her.

Helpless to do anything but observe, Cara witnessed the downfall of the beautiful brown wolf as it forfeited its life. Fighting on wouldn't have helped the Were, she realized, because this scene wasn't actually taking place in her current reality.

The brown wolf wasn't here. There were no vampires. What she was seeing was an image projected on the spot where this battle had happened in the past.

Cold gripped her. Energy that had been white-hot now turned icy. She panted with the effort to understand what was being shown to her as her limbs trembled and spasms threatened to drive her to her knees.

The Banshee spirit inside her hadn't predicted death here. The shriek had been a Banshee's cry, yes, but her Banshee hadn't made that sound. Someone else had used the Banshee's voice, but in a different way— maybe not to predict this brown werewolf's death, but to save his life.

And that just wasn't the way things worked.

Banshee spirits predicted death, and this one hadn't. There were no other dark, death-bringing spirits in the area, except the one sharing space in Cara's soul. And yet she had heard that wail.

She stared hard at the scene that she now knew to be unfolding in a different time. Her claws had been useless against the monsters because they were ghosts, like the rest of the images she had been shown. She was experiencing a memory, a projection, an imprint of what had happened in the past, in this spot. And that meant the sound she had heard had to have been made by her mother…long ago.

Others were coming, rushing toward the fight in

this alternate reality. She watched with fascination as several Weres flooded the area. They had come to the brown wolf's rescue nearly too late, drawn by the Banshee's wail.

Once the Were pack took up the fight, it became even more fierce and bloody. But Cara couldn't be a participant, since this was a dream. She had seen this battle, had lived it, had experienced the horror of an event that took place long ago…all through her mother's eyes. Rosalind Kirk had been here then and had made the call that had ultimately saved Colton Killion from death.

The park had shown her another piece of the puzzle. What had happened here all those years ago had been so awful that it still resonated in this space.

Witnessing the attack that had made her father what he was today made Cara's knees buckle. Colton Killion. Ghost wolf. Outcast. Survivor.

But how could he possibly have survived this?

She closed her eyes to shut out the rest of the fight her parents had endured. It was a gruesome thing that made that sickness inside her grow.

Releasing the breath she had been holding, unable to fight the wobble in her limbs, Cara slipped toward the ground without hitting the grass…saved from falling by the strong grip of two powerful hands that had come out of nowhere.

Chapter 8

What the hell just happened?

The question echoed inside Rafe's head as he reached Cara in time to catch her. She was breathless and wolfed up. He had no idea why her heart was racing so fast. There was nothing out here to see. He and Cara were the only two Weres in the area. And yet she, who was supposedly the strongest of them all, had folded up as if life had suddenly become too much for her to bear.

He held a werewolf in his arms. Cara had shifted without the moon to guide her, and without other external stimulus. There were no furred-up werewolves present to initiate such a change. She had taken werewolf form as quickly as she had adopted the vamp semblance earlier. He'd have believed this was also impossible if he hadn't seen it with his own eyes.

She was also incredibly beautiful, and he shouldn't have noticed. In a shape that was more familiar to him than that of a vampire, Cara looked both feminine and feral. Yet she didn't exactly look like any werewolf he had known. She retained more of her human features than was normal for Weres. Same light eyes. Same dark, silky hair. There was no hugely elongated face or altered body shape. Upon closer inspection, it was easy for him to see the female he had met on the beach.

She was taller, thinner, stringier. She had more angles. Sharp bones jutted under her skin, and there were shadows beneath her eyes. Ten curved claws edged her fingertips. Her spine, through the shirt she still wore, felt to him like a string of pearls.

Maybe she had gotten stuck in a partial shape-shift. It was possible her shift hadn't been completed before he'd found her, and because he looked human, her changes had hit a pause button. Whatever the cause of the way she looked at the moment, Cara's uniqueness fell way beyond the scope of his experience.

Rafe sank to his knees, holding her. Cara's eyes were closed. Her face was chalky and pale. He wiped away the tears that glistened on her cheeks and listened to the growls rumbling in her throat. She'd had a shock of some kind that he hadn't been able to share. His eyes had been on her and not their surroundings. Whatever had shocked Cara into her current behavior had been the impetus for this latest version of herself. So, what the hell was it?

"What did this to you, Cara?"

His only concern now was to make sure she was all right. While he wanted to point out the consequences of breaking rules put in place to prevent incidents like this, Rafe didn't speak of those things. He didn't take the time to search the area again in case he had missed something. All he could do was comfort Cara and encourage her to shift back to the shape that best resembled his in case anyone from the pack came looking for them—which would be any minute now.

"Change back," he whispered, his face close to hers as he pressed dark, silky tresses away from her cheeks. "Do it now, Cara. Do it for me."

She shuddered once before he heard the soft sucking sounds of her body realigning that meant her wolf was in retreat. Jutting angles melted back into curves as her tautness eased. Her face blurred back into full human mode, though it remained as white as a sheet. The last to go were her claws.

With them together like this, the moment felt exotic. He was holding a she-wolf in his arms, one he was attracted to in spite of all the warnings and inexplicable phenomena he'd witnessed tonight.

His inner wolf gave a roar that shook Rafe up. He swallowed back an inappropriate human-voiced growl. Were to Were, wolf to wolf was how attraction among his kind worked.

Cara was again only half-dressed in the torn shirt he had loaned her. Her lean legs were bare. Broken buttons on the shirt exposed far too much neck and the graceful sweep of her collarbone for him not to notice.

The scene was as rich as it was surreal. His wolf, tucked deep inside him where it belonged, continued to respond. Pressure built up in his chest, and these feelings weren't supposed to happen. Shouldn't happen. He and Cara were sampling a forbidden closeness that would get them into trouble with their respective families if they found out. Killion's daughter was off-limits. Her presence in Miami was merely temporary.

So why was it happening?

Why was Cara here, uncomfortably out of her element? Who in their right mind had forced Cara to visit a world she knew so little of?

When her eyes fluttered open, Rafe felt immense relief. "You're okay, I think," he said. "Am I right?"

Chances were that she couldn't talk yet. Maybe she didn't want to. The air around them vibrated with questions he needed to ask her.

"We have to get back to the house, Cara. This is far too dangerous. I'm not sure what just happened, but I'm guessing it wasn't normal, even for you. There are tears in your eyes. You're shaking. Please tell me you're all right."

She reached up to encircle his shoulders with her arms, in what amounted to the first show of vulnerability he had seen in the short time he'd known her. The slide of her palms across the back of his T-shirt felt extremely sensual and gratifying, though he knew better than to classify it that way.

Her face was so close to his, he had to look into her eyes. The hardest part of this whole ordeal was the effort it took him to keep from kissing her...because that would have been a really stupid thing to do under these circumstances.

As he fought that internal tug-of-war, Cara drew back suddenly, possibly only then realizing the position she was in. She pushed him away and scrambled to her feet. Looking down at him, she said in a quavering tone, "Don't tell them about this."

Rafe got to his feet. "Tell them what?"

"Swear," she said.

Didn't she know it was too late to hide her show of rebelliousness? As of a few seconds ago, they already had company. Of course she would have noted that, so what, exactly, was she asking of him?

"They know you're out here. It wouldn't be wise to forget that you are a special guest," he said. "I have already mentioned our responsibilities regarding your safety. You do understand that going against what's asked of you doesn't win you any points?"

"It was something I had to do," Cara said.

"And it was terribly dangerous."

"Dangerous for my father. Not for me."

Her remark dropped a big black net over the conversation, stifling anything Rafe could think of to say. He didn't know what to make of her words as he ventured a glance over his shoulder at the park.

"This is where it happened," she explained. Her shaking hadn't eased, and not much of her color had returned. "This is where my father nearly lost his life."

Rafe's gaze drifted back to her. "How do you know?"

"My mother told me."

"When?"

"Minutes ago."

Rafe rubbed his forehead, trying hard to follow what she was saying. "You didn't have a cell phone. No place to hide one. How could she tell you that?"

"She called me to this place in another way."

Could he believe her? Rafe wasn't sure. There were so many odd and questionable things about Cara Kirk-Killion, he didn't know where to begin to catch a glimpse of the full picture.

She was a complex creature and way out of his league, but did that lessen his desire to kiss her?

No.

He was hot, energized and on edge. He also knew exactly how far he had to move to again enfold her in his arms. His attention kept returning to her face and the sensual mouth that had trembled with vulnerability a moment ago. Though no trace was left of the tears he had wiped from her cheek, those tears had been there for a reason. When she had first opened her eyes, they'd contained a silent plea for support.

So…no. The desire to hold Cara and kiss away whatever had shaken her was strong, even though part of her allure could be a trick. She could have been using her wiles to attract him.

Yet what she had gone through had seemed real to her. He had seen that in her eyes.

Confusion over this dilemma drove him to silence. Cara moved first. She pointed a slender finger at the darkness they both had the ability to see into.

"This is the place," she repeated. "I now know why my father became what he is. I saw how it happened. I experienced that fight with the vampires as if I also took part in it. But I wasn't there when he was. I didn't run to help the brown Were fight off so many fangs. It was my mother who did that. She moved in to help. I saw all of this through her eyes."

"Because she called you here," Rafe said with a skepticism he couldn't hide.

Cara shook her head. "This place called to me with her voice. Violent acts leave residue on a place. This was a memory for me to access because I have that brown Were's blood in my veins. My father's blood. After the attack, my mother's spirit became tied to those vampires, not out of any choice she made, but because she was born special in ways that left her open to roaming demons."

Weird as it might have been, Rafe was starting to believe her. As a cop he sometimes experienced sensations tied to past events at certain locations. At least, he imagined he could. To see those past events firsthand

was an entirely different matter, and a level of awareness well beyond his capabilities. However, who was
to say that Cara didn't have those kinds of talents, and
that she spoke the truth?

Meanwhile, they were taking too much time outside
the wall. He wasn't exactly sure how many minutes had
actually gone by, but it had been long enough for the
pack to find them. Others were close now, and closing
in. The night had become pressurized due to his packmates' imminent arrival.

"How will we explain your quick exit if we don't
mention what you saw?" Rafe asked.

"Will we have to?" Cara asked.

"Yes. They're coming now, as you well know, and
are merely giving us some time to work this out. They
will be watching us to see what we do next."

What she did then beat every single explanation Rafe
could have thought up. She closed the few inches of
distance separating them, stood on her toes, lifted her
face…and pressed her lips to his.

Chapter 9

She had meant to distract the pack that was observing from a short distance away, pretending she and Rafe had retreated from view for a few private moments alone. But something unexpected happened.

The second her lips met his, Cara felt another kind of shift taking place. Not a physical alteration. Something different, new and exciting.

Rafe's mouth was hot and unmoving. He had been as surprised by her forwardness as she was. The heat he radiated through this meeting of their lips flushed her face and throat. The charge created by touching him so intimately quickly spread to her chest, where her heart raced.

She had done this without thinking, and sensed that this latest move had been dictated by the spirits she harbored. What did she know of kisses, feelings, planned distractions and relationships? She'd had a vision that had shaken her and in the aftermath had wanted to share her wayward energy with someone. Rafe Landau just happened to be the easiest to reach.

Or so she told herself.

Beyond that, she had no idea what might come next. She had expected that this closeness would make her feel better, but she actually felt worse. Rafe Landau was pure electricity, and he was sending her bottled-up energy into overdrive. Scrambled images flashed in her mind like small bombs going off, all of them connected to the emotions she held in check. Vampires were cold. Werewolves were warm. Rafe Landau was volcanic.

The world around her dimmed as the sensations she was experiencing took over. Air shivered. The ground moved. This one little meeting of their mouths sent Cara's stomach into free fall and numbed every warning message her nervous system kicked up.

She had dared to get close to a being that was most like her in terms of species, and they were connecting. Here, so far from her home, she had seen her father mauled by bloodsuckers, and she had found comfort after that vision where it was least expected…in the arms of one of the Landaus, who were gatekeepers to a past she desperately needed to find.

For another second or two—mere blips in the scale of time—when Rafe's lips parted and his emotion caught up with the surprise, the kiss became a real one. As his breath became her breath and his hands slid around her waist, Cara imagined that she also might have become nothing more than an image projected onto this place— someone both experiencing this closeness firsthand and observing it from afar.

His heat was her heat. Rafe's breath was sweet and his mouth was sublime. His body felt extremely masculine and toned, and that new awareness seemed to cue something in her body that had been dormant.

More changes were growing inside her, rising to engulf her, and all of them were centered in her chest. Her heart beat furiously and in time with Rafe's. His strength became hers as if transferred by the meeting of their lips. Their bodies were trysting on a physical level, and she didn't know how to deal.

In the periphery of Cara's awareness, sounds rang out that she couldn't concentrate on or identify. Rafe's mouth was everything and her sole focus. He was the epicenter for needs she had never before accessed.

His thoughts whirled like cyclones in her mind as their connection continued to deepen. When their tongues tentatively touched, more inner fires sprang up to engulf her. He silently repeated her name, moving his lips over hers. It was like a song that got progressively louder. Like a tune she had heard somewhere in the past.

She was listening to the call of the wild. The sound of one wolf attending to another in a time of need. Male to female. Were to Were…except that her world had spun her beyond all that and into a category all of its own.

"Cara, I'm here."

She couldn't take any more input. Circuits were frying and their mouths were sealed together in a way that neither of them had the power to disconnect. Half-hearted phrases she had once used for her dream man, such as *Make him pay* were something she no longer wanted. Not now. Not yet. Maybe never.

The outside world finally intervened, interrupting these moments of sensual chaos. Voices other than her and Rafe's inner messages to each other became too prominent to ignore, and her companion's lips left hers.

Rafe's blue eyes bored into hers as if he had also been drowning in emotion and regretted coming up for air.

"Rafe," someone called out. "This is folly. Come home now."

Her wits returned too slowly to have aided her if this were an enemy. Cara shook her head hard and broke eye contact with Rafe. She turned her head to refocus, feeling as if she were tipping off balance until her attention landed on the silver-haired alpha of the pack, and recent events quickly filled her mind.

This kiss had been a distraction meant to cover up a rebellious act and had turned into something more.

Beside her, Rafe called out, "She's okay. We're okay. We just took a little detour."

There was a sharpness to his voice that made Cara's nerves buzz. Surely Rafe's father had heard that edge? Still, Rafe hadn't lied about the detour. So would there be repercussions for ignoring his father's suggestions and for kissing the freak he was supposed to have been protecting?

Back in action and mentally armed, Cara sensed a new disturbance that might have explained the seriousness of Dylan Landau's tone. There were other Weres here, and they were easy to locate by scent, but there was an alternate presence not quite so easy to assess. A presence that wasn't willing to be detected.

Not a vampire.

Not a werewolf like Rafe or his father.

Cara now regretted being the cause of this latest round of troubles for Rafe and his family. But she knew for a fact that more trouble was on its way.

His father had sent up a silent warning that Rafe barely heard over the words of Cara's messaged apology.

"I didn't mean to bring this down on you, but it was an inevitable consequence of my coming here."

Bring what down on them? Danger? Lust?

Rafe took a sideways step, holding up a hand to signal Cara to wait while two members of his pack glided in behind his father. Danger was a signal that made all werewolves twitchy. These Weres were on high alert, their muscles corded.

Rafe looked to Cara for guidance. Who else might be out there in the dark, able to avoid his extraordinary gift of sight? He had become aware of this other presence by reading her mind, though her face showed no hint of anything out of the ordinary.

His father strode forward like a silver bullet—fast, purposeful, geared up for the task at hand, whatever that might be. "Foreign," his dad said to the small group that surrounded Cara. With a few sharp gestures, he encouraged everyone to move in the direction of the wall.

There was no reason to disobey that directive. His father rarely issued commands, so when he did, everyone listened. Nevertheless, Rafe got no real sense of what Cara believed could be out here spying on them. In all the time he had worn a badge, his radar for anomalies had been trained on human criminals and rogue Weres. Tonight, he had added vampires to that list, but he didn't catch their odor on the sultry incoming breeze.

They swiftly hustled forward in their small circle, with Cara quiet in the center of this man-wolf show of testosterone. His father had brought the gate guards, two big guys used to tackling problems head-on. Against an invisible foe, however, muscle would be useless. Even so, though Rafe didn't often regret leaving his gun locked in a safe in his apartment, he regretted it now.

If nothing else, he could have waved the weapon around as an added incentive for unseen interlopers to back off.

They reached the wall in tight formation. Rafe's father held out his hand to help Cara over, but she shook her head. Finding grooves in the stone with her fingertips, she simply hoisted herself up and over the wall with ease.

Rafe went next. He was used to climbing this wall, having mastered the skill as a kid. The others followed. Although he'd been afraid that Cara would be long gone when they landed, she was there on the lawn. Quiet and oddly calm, she nodded her thanks to each Were in turn, and then paused to search Rafe's face.

"They're not coming here," she said. Her voice was steady. "Not tonight."

Then she walked toward the house as if nothing had happened. All eyes turned to Rafe for the explanation. Regretfully, he had only one.

Privacy was the word that came to his mind, and also the worst possible thing he could have said.

"Sheer lunacy," Dylan Landau countered, with a hard look at his son.

Had they seen the kiss? The intimacy he and Cara had shared?

Cara had asked him not to mention her vision. If he was trustworthy, he'd honor that request and dig deep for another way to smooth over this breach of etiquette with his father. For werewolves, lies were tough to maintain. Weres read Weres. There was no option here but to speak as much of the truth as he could, in spite of what his father and the others might think.

"I'm attracted to her." Rafe shrugged his shoulders.

"So I see," his father said. "Does that make you mindless and blind to your responsibilities?"

"Neither, actually. If I couldn't handle what might have been out there, Cara certainly could have."

His father dismissed the other Weres with a barked thank-you, which meant that Rafe was going to have a one-on-one with the alpha.

"Seriously?" his father said, turning back. "You'd put Cara at risk after she ignored the rules a second time in a single night?"

"I had no real choice but to follow her. Should I have let her go out there alone or taken the time to call for help?"

"Is that what you call protecting her, Rafe? Holding her like that?"

So, his father had seen the kiss...

Instead of following up with further objections, though, his father added, "I get it. It was that way for me when I met Dana. I was instantly attracted to her. But your mother, who was forbidden as a mate for me at the time, was human until she had a lesson from the bad wolf that changed her. While Cara is...more."

Rafe smiled warily, able to feel the lingering softness of Cara's mouth. He recalled that Cara had been segregated from others for all of her young life, and that what had happened in the park tonight might have been her first dip into the realm of adult pastimes.

The thought gave him a few seconds of pleasure before he responded to his father.

"We haven't imprinted, so you can skip the birds and the bees lecture. She's safe. We're here. End of story," he said.

"I hope that's true, Rafe. I haven't set eyes on Colton Killion for more years than I can count on both hands. He was a tough bastard before fate rose up to bite him, and I can only imagine what he's like now. Entrusting his daughter to us was a miracle in itself. How she fares here is up to us."

"Maybe," Rafe countered. "However, it's not that straightforward. Cara has a mind of her own. She is unlike us, yes, and I'm not convinced that she wants to be like us, or if she even could be if that was the purpose for this visit. Cara is merely tolerating us and is used to having more freedom. Who among us would like to be displaced or caged?"

"No one is caged. Cara can go home any time she decides to. This is an invitation, not a life sentence. It's our home, not a prison."

"I hope she sees it that way," Rafe said.

"Cara will see it like that if she has no reason to believe otherwise."

"And if she jumps the wall on occasion in order to assure herself that she's free?" Rafe asked.

His father had no answer for that and didn't try to make one up. Dylan Landau had built his reputation as a lawyer and, eventually, a federal judge on honesty and fairness. He had always played fair with his son, as well as the other Weres in the pack he had inherited from Rafe's grandfather. No one could say this alpha didn't try to understand all sides of an argument. And Dylan Landau was still, after all these years, deeply in love with his wife.

"Kissing her was the only way to stop Cara from whatever she was going to do out there," Rafe said.

His father nodded thoughtfully. "Be careful. That's all I ask."

Their little chat had gotten them nowhere, really, and both of them knew it.

"Dad. Why would a vampire come after one of us if the stories about their appetites are true?" Rafe asked.

"Like the one you met tonight?"

Rafe nodded. "What did it have to gain if our blood disgusts them?"

His father eyed him thoughtfully. "I suppose that it might have been to take you out of the picture."

"I wonder what picture that would be?"

They both looked at the house as if they could still see Cara walking up the steps.

Rafe spoke first. "Believing that would mean that the vampires somehow knew about my affiliation with this pack, and perhaps even that Cara was coming here."

"Yes. And I don't like the sound of that," his father said in a sober tone. "Or that fact that vampires have returned and dare to show themselves. It will bear looking into."

A heavy silence fell as they contemplated the ramifications of what had been said. Finally, his father smiled and clapped Rafe on the back. "Hungry?" Without waiting for an answer, he led the way to the house. The house that felt different to Rafe now that Cara Kirk-Killion was here, stirring to life so many of its secrets.

Chapter 10

Cara stood by a window, fighting the need to go back out there, beyond the wall, to find more of her mother's memories and the elusive presence that had disturbed her.

At the moment, there were only three wolves in the house with her. No army. No bolted doors. Rafe and his father were on the lawn by the steps, deep in conversation. Here in a house where privileged werewolves lived and so many others came and went, sensing anything beyond the werewolf presence was impossible. Cara had to shelve her curiosity about that wall and what lay beyond it for the time being and try to get along when small aches plagued her from the way she was clenching her teeth.

The house was grand in spite of what Rafe's mother had said, and too large for Cara's simpler taste. There were rooms and doorways everywhere. The expansive salon she stood in had high ceilings and a polished wood fireplace. Pictures lined the walls. Each piece of furniture looked as though it had been placed with care. This was in direct contrast to her home, which was a sprawling cabin filled with rough-hewn furniture, surrounded by trees and reached by way of a seldom-used dirt road.

But her mother and father had both been guests here in the past, so Cara didn't feel completely isolated from them. It was possible that their spirits and memories remained in these hallways, as they had in the park. If that were the case, she would find them.

"Would you like to see your room before having something to eat?" Rafe's mother asked from an open doorway.

"Yes. Thank you," Cara replied, not used to being civil with strangers, no matter who they were.

"Hang tight, then. I'll just be a minute," Dana Delmonico Landau said before disappearing into the room beyond.

The offer to stay in the room her mother had used was another example of how these Weres seemed to know a lot about her parents, while she was at a disadvantage, knowing nothing about this pack. *Well, almost nothing*, Cara silently amended as she ran a fingertip over her lips. Some things about Rafe Landau were clear, and most of that information was as disturbing as everything else.

Though strong and capable, Rafe had not pressured her to behave. He had gone along with her without complaint when he could have turned things around. Would he honor her request to keep what she had seen in the park to himself, as well as the fact that she could wolf up without the help of a full moon?

Her treacherous body hadn't lost the sparks their intimacy had ignited and wanted her to return to Rafe now.

Cara crossed her arms over her chest to hide the ongoing thud of each heartbeat as her thoughts stayed on Rafe.

When he turned and followed his father toward the house, she backed away from the window.

"Okay," Dana said from somewhere behind her. "If you'll follow me, I'll take you up. Your things are already in the room, having arrived before you did."

This could have been a small dig about Cara's earlier MIA status, though the tone didn't seem accusatory.

"If you'd prefer to have a tray in your room, that can be managed," Rafe's mother offered. "Just tell me what you want to do, and what would make you the most comfortable for your first night away from home."

"Tray, I think," Cara said gratefully, and Dana waved her toward the stairs.

"You knew her?" Cara asked as they climbed higher into the house, thinking more of her family than of food. "You knew Rosalind?"

"Not really. I loaned her some clothes once when she needed them," Dana said.

Cara wondered if this was another allusion to the fact that she was in a similar circumstance, dressed only in Rafe's torn shirt.

"I left my clothes near the ocean," she said.

"That's where you met the vampire?" Dana asked without looking back from the step above.

"Yes. There."

"Sensing vampires is a talent that comes in handy. Things could have been easier around here in the past if more of us had that capability," her hostess remarked.

"You've fought them before?"

"Oh, yes. And I'm lucky to be here to say so."

They reached a landing on the second floor and kept going to another set of stairs that led to a compact space high above the yard. Cara saw only one door here, which led to a small room. After so many years had passed, the small space somehow still carried a diluted version of Rosalind Kirk's floral scent.

Behind Dana's back, Cara finally smiled.

"The room hasn't been used in a while," Rafe's mother said. "We haven't had guests in years."

"It's fine for me."

Compact and spare, the room contained only a bed, a dresser and a chair. The ceiling slanted toward a window that someone had already opened to let the night air in. Her bag was on the floor.

Leaning against the doorjamb, Dana said, "Your mother jumped from that window once. No one knows how she accomplished that without breaking a bone."

Cara moved to the window to look out, noting the distance to the yard below.

"I hope you'll use the door while you're here, Cara," Dana said. She was smiling. "The bathroom is behind the curtain beside the closet."

Cara nodded.

"Now, about dinner," Dana said. "I'll get that tray and be back in no time."

"Thank you," Cara replied, though she was tuned in to the view of the yard and picturing her mother leaping three stories to freedom. Why Rosalind had taken such an action was the question that plagued her.

Rafe couldn't wait to see Cara and didn't appreciate how that thought kept taking precedence over others. He hesitated on the porch as his father went inside before he backtracked to the yard.

Taking his time, trying to remain calm, Rafe walked to the side of the house. It had only been occupied by his mother and father for the last ten years, though they had visited his grandparents here often before then. He knew which room was Cara's and that she would be there. That room, high under the eaves, was another part of the Kirk-Killion legend. Out of all rooms in the house, Cara would be the most comfortable there, when everyone else avoided the space.

He found the window he sought—Cara was framed in it. She hadn't changed her clothes. The fact that she still wore his shirt gave him unexpected pangs of pleasure. This was a category of female he had never expected to find. Cara was seductive, secretive, part animal and extraordinarily beautiful. He wanted not only to protect her, but to possess her.

And it was a good thing he hadn't imparted that piece of information to his father.

Can't have her, his mind argued. *I know better.*

Nice try, his mind kicked back. But the reminders weren't working. Rafe had a hard time convincing himself that he didn't really need to see her again so soon.

They hadn't had time to get to know each other. Their conversations had been sparse and their meetings filled with strange activity. Despite all that, Rafe felt as if he knew Cara on a level way beyond normal and that the extremes of their emotional connection bypassed any need for further details.

This thing between them, whether wrong or right, remained inexplicable. Maybe it was a case of animal magnetism at its best. Surely it was a hell of a lot more than lust at first sight.

"Are you all right?" he called out to her.

"She jumped from here," Cara said.

"Rosalind? Yes. So the story goes."

"Does the story say why she did that?"

"I don't suppose anyone would know the reason, except for your mother," Rafe said.

"We didn't sit around telling stories. My parents aren't legends to me."

"How did you pass the time out there?" Rafe knew he was pressing his luck, and he didn't actually expect Cara to reply. Plus, they were speaking loudly enough for anyone around to hear.

"We hunted," she said.

"For food?"

"For monsters."

Rafe blinked slowly to hide the fact that he should have seen that one coming. "Were there a lot of monsters?"

"An endless supply," she replied.

"Did anyone help?"

"Now and then, but it was a task for us in the end."

When Cara shook her head, her jet-black hair, dry now and sleek, ruffled in the breeze that also moved the curtains beside her. The desire to catch hold of those shiny tendrils drilled at Rafe's insides and caused him to take a few backward steps.

He heard another familiar voice through the open window and watched Cara turn her head. She then turned back.

"Dinner?" he asked.

After nodding, Cara left the window. Moments later, she was beside him on the lawn.

Rafe flinched with surprise.

She maintained a distance of several feet between them this time and seemed to be waiting for him to say something. Rafe rallied with a casual remark. "Maybe you can show me how to do that teleporting trick while you're here. Other officers on the force would be envious."

"It's a family secret," she said.

Rafe thought her tone was light, as if she might be teasing him. The fact that she could dig up some lightness, with everything going on, seemed like a good sign and provided him with more insight into the Cara he wanted to know.

He willed himself not to look at the bare legs she didn't seem at all self-conscious about. And that was hard. He was a male, after all, and it was a toss-up where to actually keep his focus, since all parts of the female standing in front of him were worthy of attention. He had to constantly remind himself that she was off-limits and that she would leave soon, in spite of those wicked inner flames and the desire to take her in his arms.

"Are we alone?" she asked, training her gaze on him. Her big green eyes were alight with excitement.

"No," he replied. "I think you know that without me having to tell you."

"Can we walk? Will they stop us this time?"

"That depends on the direction we go."

"Near to the wall."

"It wouldn't be a good idea," Rafe said.

"Just near to it. Not over it."

He waited for Cara to say more.

"Not over it," she repeated.

He nodded. "We can do that."

"Go ahead and say what you're thinking," she suggested.

"I might be arrested if I did."

The remark appeared to throw her. Dark hair curtained the sides of Cara's face when she tilted her head questioningly, so that she appeared to have been swathed in reams of black silk.

"Never mind," Rafe said. "Let's walk."

"I expected you to ask me to promise to behave myself," she said. "Why haven't you?"

"I don't recall how many times I broke that kind of promise," he said. "I'll just trust you and leave it at that. Okay?"

She nodded.

Rafe balled both hands to keep from reaching for her, wishing she had put on a damn pair of pants and that she didn't look so immensely appealing. Both man and wolf were twitching with appreciation for the opportunity to be with Cara again. After her little excursion to the beach not more than a couple of hours ago, and a little wall-hopping after that, watchful eyes truly would be on them at all times.

He didn't like being observed. However, his father's trust might have slipped somewhat where Rafe's dealings with Cara were concerned, and with good reason… because as soon as they were out of direct light, and with others watching them or not, he planned on kissing Cara again. Anyone who protested that could go to hell.

Eyes like green fire met his, as though Cara had read that last thought, as well as the thoughts preceding it. Feeling as though he had been caught in a tractor beam, Rafe had a sudden sensation of falling through space.

Chapter 11

Within the chaos taking Cara over, two things stood out. The first was the idea of making it beyond the Landaus' wall as soon as the chance presented itself. The second was an almost dire need for more intimacy with Rafe. Right then, both desires carried equal weight.

In the open, with the grass under her feet and Rafe beside her, the hope of running away began to wither. So far, no one had mistreated her or allowed the rumors about her family to dictate the terms of her confinement. All in all, the Landaus had gone out of their way to make her feel welcome and as though she was just another potential packmate.

Once they got wind of Rafe's budding feelings for her, however, all that might change. If given a choice, Rafe would have to stand with his pack. It was useless to imagine otherwise, or that she and Rafe could develop a true friendship within these massive stone barriers. She had never had a friend. Had never needed one until now, though already Rafe felt like so much more than that to her.

With his scent in her lungs and his eyes following each move she made, Cara wished things could have been different. That she hadn't been born a creature whose segregation was necessary in order to protect outsiders from feeling the wrath of the monsters that regularly appeared at her family's gates.

Did friendship involve subjecting each other to danger? What if this thing with Rafe went well past the definition of that term?

Dealing with isolation was a lesson she had been taught early on, and it made good sense in the long run. If Miami's population knew nothing about the existence of werewolves and vampires, what would they think about demons? What would they think about a creature like her, who was a conglomeration of all those things?

She was the main attraction for monsters, just as her mother had been. Dark recognized dark, and inheriting the spirit of a Banshee meant she carried death's breath inside her in spite of the fact that housing this Banshee had been the result of a good deed done by that ancient spirit in her mother's family's past.

Tonight's vision in the park had shown Cara that her mother had used the dark spirit to save her future mate, in a daring replay of the incident in the dark spirit's ancient past that had tied the Banshee to Cara's ancestors. What this also insinuated was that the Banshee's purpose could somehow be manipulated, and that the spirit could possibly be persuaded to help with a cause that was contrary to a Banshee's reason for existing. Or else maybe the Banshee now owed Cara's family for giving it a place to exist.

The problem was that the black breath, however it

had gotten inside her, attracted anomalies of all kinds. Her mother had lived with that same problem for many years before unknowingly passing it to her daughter. Darkness was part of Cara's birthright. In contrast, everything in Miami was colorful and blindingly bright.

The only saving grace for her predicament, as far as Cara saw, was having her father's pure Lycan blood as a stabilizing factor. With the added infusion of his worldly, humanized Lycan DNA, she was able to tolerate having a dark spirit trapped inside her. So far. But she had vowed never to have children of her own for fear of passing that spirit on and gifting a life like hers to anyone else.

"Do you want to talk?" Rafe asked, walking beside her.

"I'm not sure what there is to say," Cara replied.

"Is talking about yourself prohibited in the grand scheme of things?"

"My life might read like a nightmare to you."

"Sometimes sharing nightmares can dilute them," he suggested.

Cara wondered what he'd think if she told him about the dreams she'd had of him before she had met him, and what she had planned to do if she were to meet the male who had given her so many puzzles and helped to lure her from her home. What she hadn't considered back then was the reason for fate bringing them together, when surely there had to be one.

"I guess that's the reason behind me coming here," she said. "Diluting the nightmares and securing my future."

"I've thought about that, Cara. What if coming here is some kind of a test?"

Cara paused to encourage Rafe to explain that remark.

"You aren't your mother," he began. "Maybe the test is to see if all those monsters can track you here or whether you've given them the slip."

He hesitated thoughtfully before continuing. "It's also possible that those monsters you've met are tied to the energy surrounding your home, and not to you. Could your family be giving you the chance to find out if you can live in the world with the rest of us, instead of being banished from it?"

Those theories resonated for Cara. They were perfectly viable explanations for the decision her parents had made, though she just couldn't see how it would all end.

"Brandi—that's what the vampire on the beach called herself—wasn't after you. That's what you told me," Rafe went on. "If you're such a monster magnet, why was I her target? Once she saw you, wouldn't she have changed her plan?"

Cara shook her head. "She had your scent already, which means that you were marked. It can be difficult for a bloodsucker to veer off a mark. Next to impossible sometimes."

"Even after you appeared and were a much tastier treat?" he asked.

"That's the way they operate. If they come for my mother, they have no interest in me until they find out too late that she has given the dark spirit to her daughter. Some remnant of that spirit must still remain either inside or around my mother. Enough of it to temporarily deter the monsters."

"Dark spirit?" Rafe asked.

"Banshee. You do know what that is?"

He nodded. "But maybe dealing with the vampire on the beach was the first test, according to my theory, and you passed it. The vamp went after me, ignoring you entirely until you made yourself known."

He stopped there before saying in a lighter tone, "Hell, Cara. Maybe you're not so tasty after all. And maybe," he added slowly and with careful precision, "the true test of your presence here is to see if I'd be the one to bite."

Rafe's hand was on her shoulder. With a gentle tug, he turned her to face him. She didn't meet his eyes, needing a few seconds to think about what he had said and how to understand his latest remark. She and Rafe were alike in many ways, but not nearly enough alike to keep him from being hurt if his theories were wrong and the bad guys came after her here.

What she didn't mention was the idea that the vampire had been after Rafe to get him out of the way, having been alerted to her arrival and the Landaus' plans to host her as a guest. One Landau down would have meant fewer werewolves to deal with when the bloodsuckers came after her.

"Well," Rafe continued, "I guess I could be mistaken about you not being like a magnet, because you've been like catnip to me since I first laid eyes on you at the beach. How's that for a confession? So, I have to wonder if you're seducing me on purpose, and if so, what that purpose might be."

With a nice show of Were speed, he brought her within the circle of his arms. They were hip to hip. Their chests were touching, and their thighs. The intensity of Rafe's attention was like facing a whole nest of vampires at once and demanded that she look up. Feeling the sensual energy he radiated as her gaze traveled from his neck to the blue gleam of his eyes, Cara realized that Rafe Landau had misjudged things.

He was the magnet...and she had unknowingly been caught in his force field.

Unprepared for the cascade of emotions hitting her, Cara let Rafe's mouth hover inches from hers. She could no longer look at him. She couldn't breathe when he smelled so fine. She was used to monsters, not strong wolves who teased new emotions from her instead of the usual shape-shifts.

"You're being hasty in your conclusions," she pointed out.

"I know that. I just thought I'd better get all that out in the open."

"Are you always so honest?" she asked.

"No. Not always."

Candor was something Cara understood, though she didn't know what to do with his. Rafe Landau was a daredevil, and proving that here. He was also a rebel, dodging the limitations that had been imposed on him by his family and his pack. But he didn't know the full extent of what carrying around a Banshee's spirit meant, and that through her brief connection to him, she already perceived that death was coming...not for Rafe, but for someone close to this pack that she saw clearly in her mind and had not yet met.

"I have only an inkling of what you're capable of," he said softly in a voice that made Cara's insides ache with longing for a hazy kind of fulfillment that was still unknown to her. "But this is nice, at least for now, isn't it?" he asked. "I'm glad you're here. I hope you'll stay awhile. More than six days."

"I'm trouble, Rafe. More trouble than the politics of this visit are worth."

"I'm sorry you think so. Saddened, actually."

Cara's body knew what was coming when her mind

hadn't fully grasped it. Everything he had said was a lead-in to his next move, and as Rafe's lips brushed hers, she closed her eyes.

Just this once I'll allow another round of closeness. And then I'll put a stop to whatever you're thinking.

That plan faded away as the fleeting touch of Rafe's lips added another layer to the tumultuous emotions already bringing her dangerously close to a precipice. That precipice was the only obstacle standing between her and all hell breaking loose in Miami. It was the dividing line between good and evil, as well as the one thing she had dreaded to encounter all along—a mate.

She could not think of fitting in when so many Weres could be hurt if she remained. She could not with good conscience do anything that would involve passing this dark spirit on. Therefore, she couldn't continue to pursue this relationship with Rafe, for whom she had quickly developed her own soft spot.

This Landau wolf might cause a hitch in her getaway plan and interfere with her ability to focus if things got more serious between them. There would be more danger. More hurt.

Stop the madness, her mind cautioned.

Do it now, or all will be lost.

She had never wished so hard or fervently that she had been born normal as she did right then.

Rafe felt prickling sensations in his muscles as he feathered his lips over Cara's. The back of his neck chilled in direct contrast to the white-hot currents he encountered each time he got near to her. So, what was this sudden chill all about?

He was an ass for daring to ignore the warnings his family had issued. In his defense, Cara's physical

strength and the softness of her lips were a tough counter to those inner arguments. The others didn't know
her the way he already liked to imagine he did. He and
Cara shared a bond that, though hard to define, very
much controlled his actions.

He couldn't have stopped what was coming if he
had tried.

Her lips were warm and supple as he increased the
pressure of the kiss. Her breath was hot. Cara's mouth
was an inferno. This was no ice queen from the bayou.
He was almost completely sure that no frigging Banshee
looked at him through those half-closed green eyes.

And yet the chills persisted.

He backed off. With a careful finger, he tilted Cara's
chin upward again so that he could see all of her beautiful face in the light from an outdoor lamp. The face
he searched was perfectly molded into feminine perfection, and a little too pale. He couldn't imagine what
it must be like to house any spirits other than a wolf.

She avoided his gaze by lowering her lashes. Nothing
in her expression suggested coyness or that she might
be ill prepared for the attentions of a male. Cara could
easily have pushed him away, and didn't. She could
have used some of her incredible speed to outdistance
him, but she stayed.

"I wonder if you believe any part of what I've said,"
Rafe began, uncertain about trusting himself for the
next few minutes after having come this far. "Or if it
makes sense."

Warning signals were flashing madly in his mind.
His head was filled with whispers. *Do not get closer
to her. Back away, you fool.*

Spikes of flame hit him when he noticed how Cara's
face whitened more, and the way her lashes kept her

eyes hidden. She hadn't moved, and yet something behind all that pale, beautiful skin did, as if there was something coming alive beneath the surface.

"Cara?" His voice was hushed.

Only silence answered him. When Cara finally opened her eyes, the deep green color he had hoped to see was gone.

The eyes looking back at him were now a dull, flat black.

Chapter 12

Death was calling.

The intensity of that call punched through Cara with the force of a battering ram. The spirit had risen unannounced, and it was necessary to distance herself from Rafe to hear what that spirit had to say.

Brittle thoughts took shape in her mind—hard, unrelenting, violent thoughts. She had to leave Rafe, get away before the spirit overtook her completely. The message was that someone was coming. Something was near. And there was going to be a loss of life.

Night crowded in. Internal wailing sounds echoed in Cara's mind, and she struggled to contain them. Clamping her teeth together proved useless. Her hands were shaking. Her head hurt and her jaw ached.

She shook her head at Rafe's expression over the suddenness of her rejection and bit her tongue to keep from showing him again that all the fuss and rumors about this Kirk-Killion freak of nature were true. The need to free the Banshee's cry was a terrible burden.

Swaying slightly before widening her stance, Cara opened her mouth to try to speak, and no words came out. As her throat began to loosen, the sound that emerged traveled upward through her body from the depths of her soul. But it wasn't a dark spirit's cry that came out. It was a haunting wolf's howl that rolled on and on as if it had no end…because she had avoided the Banshee's appearance by calling upon her wolf for help.

In seconds, her howl was answered. One response came from the direction of the house. Another came from someplace beyond the wall and was followed by a third and a fourth. Weres had emerged from their hidey-holes, lured by the sound she had made. Not the kind of Weres that would be in human form tonight. These responses were the vocalizations of a few full-blooded Lycans able to shape-shift without the lure of the moon—creatures almost as rare as she was, since very few werewolves on Earth could perform that trick.

It seemed the Landaus had a few secrets of their own, besides the obvious ones. Lycans were rallying to her cry as they would have in the wild, and she hadn't meant for that to happen. She had just needed to outwit the dark spirit she carried within her, at least temporarily, so that Rafe wouldn't see it and change his mind.

Recruiting every wolf molecule in her body was what it took to overpower the Banshee, and Cara succeeded. But that spirit coated her insides like an internal mist. The ancient thing that predated the wolf species swirled near the base of her throat, soaking up the last of her wolf's cry.

The spirit had to announce a death. That was its sole purpose. It had veered from this purpose twice in the entirety of its long existence, and each of those mistakes had cost it dearly. This Banshee could no longer live on its own and was doomed by its past transgressions to exist inside a host tied to the family it had helped instead of hindered centuries ago.

Death was coming, though. No mistake.

It was coming here.

With a roar of protest, Cara tore off her shirt and dropped to her hands and knees, feeling the escalation of Rafe's tension without being able to do anything about it.

He had seen her as a vampire and was about to find out more of what she could do. More secrets were going to be exposed, and Cara saw no other way to manage the next few minutes than to become a creature that could outrace Rafe and his pack.

"Do not follow," she warned him over Were channels as her body began its downsize into a new shape. *"It's already too late."*

Rafe stumbled back as if he'd been struck by an invisible hand. *Holy hell...* The partial shape-shift he had witnessed earlier had been a convincing disguise, but Cara was now a wolf. A real one, on all fours in a full transformation, with a rippling coat of black fur that shone by lamplight like liquid onyx.

When Cara's head came up, her eyes again shone with green fire, but nothing else about her was familiar. She growled menacingly. Her whole body shook. When her eyes met his one last time, Rafe understood what she was telling him. Cara was inside that shape. She was in control of this shape-shift and had changed for a reason that made this shift important.

In the distance, resounding howls that would have

scared the pants off anyone in the park rolled through the night. The sounds shook Rafe up. Cara's latest trick seemed like a dream. Like the stories about her mother, Cara could become a rare black wolf.

Christ. What could he say, except…

"Do what you have to, Cara. We'll deal later."

She wheeled around so quickly, Rafe barely saw her move. Like a streak of supernatural lightning, she took a run at the wall and hurdled it before his next full breath.

Rafe heard the pounding of each thundering heart-beat in his chest. He replayed all the warnings he'd had with regard to Cara, knowing he had ignored them all, believing that she could handle being here and eventually learn to assimilate with the pack. He saw now that the idea had been a mistake, and that Cara was beyond anything his pack could have tamed.

He just couldn't get a take on the real Cara, or how this had happened to her, which left him more determined than ever to find out. So he lit out after her for the second time tonight, not sure who he'd find behind the rest of those answering howls, but envying those Lycan bastards for the ability they had to get to Cara faster than he could.

He took aim at the wall and scrambled over it, glad he had put on his boots. Dropping down on the opposite side, he traced movement to the west by the trees where he had promised himself to have that second kiss with Cara.

It turned out to be a werewolf, suited up in jeans, missing a shirt and running on two legs that Rafe saw. He knew this guy and blew out a sigh of relief. At least one Lycan was accounted for. It was Jonas Dale, one of the strongest Lycans in Miami, who was also in law enforcement. Jonas had been trolling the park tonight with the intention of keeping people safe.

Behind Rafe came the soft thud of someone else landing. A quick turn brought him face-to-face with Cameron Mitchell. The fiftysomething detective wasn't Lycan and therefore not in an altered shape, though his muscles visibly quivered across his wiry frame.

"You heard it?" Rafe asked.

"You'd have to be deaf not to," Cameron replied. "Where is the she-wolf?"

"Chasing something. I have no idea what."

"The others who responded?"

"Jonas is the only one I saw."

The more time spent at a standstill, the greater the possibility of losing Cara, so Rafe spun around and raced off. Since he knew this park well, as most of his pack did, he had a good idea where to start his search. No self-respecting criminal would go near the public streets on the opposite edge of the park. Off to the east were darker patches of ground that provided better camouflage.

The only wolf who didn't know any of this was the one he needed to find. Rafe had to understand what Cara's latest shape-shift was about and whether he could reach her in time to help.

He ran like the wind with his packmate beside him, scanning the dark, avoiding the lighter places near the boulevards in the far distance. Nothing could throw him off the scent. With Cara's fragrance embedded in his lungs, he was soon able to pick up her trail.

Cameron swore between breaths. "I saw her from the porch. I did see that correctly? She can make herself into a…"

"Wolf," Rafe replied over one shoulder as he pulled

slightly ahead of Cameron. "We've all heard the tales, so this shouldn't really have been a surprise."

He failed to mention that it had been a complete surprise to him.

"Yeah. Well, good luck with that attitude," Cameron said, rocketing into a higher pace that made Rafe dig in. Cameron continued to mutter to himself. Between the obscenities and a few human growls, Rafe heard him say, "This is something I've got to see up close."

As they covered more ground, Cara's scent grew stronger. Just as Rafe had suspected, she was making for the next notoriously troubled spot in this damn park as if she had a nose for these things. He wondered if there actually was someone out here or if she had again been taken in by a vision of some kind.

The night had gone quiet. Each breath he took seemed labored when he wasn't the least bit winded. *"Have to reach you,"* he messaged to Cara. *"Please wait."*

Cameron said, "You expect her to listen?"

"No."

Cameron grunted a nonverbal response as they rounded a line of trees that threw long shadows from the partial moon overhead. The scent became more convoluted here with a breeze from the north. And there was something else—a new scent that again chilled the back of Rafe's neck. It was an odor that he didn't recognize, and it tangled with Cara's fragrance. Cameron had no such problem pegging it.

"Hunter." Cameron spit out the word with a vehemence that could only have come from firsthand knowledge.

Rafe's stomach turned over. His mind rebelled. There hadn't been hunters in this part of Miami for years, and the idiots who had trespassed in the area in the past had been lethal. Not only that, they had been led by Cameron's mate's father. Having gone through tough times like that, Cameron had to be furious about the possibility of a replay.

"Cara is wily," Rafe sent to his packmate. *"She will watch for this."*

"And if she is in wolf form, her pelt would be worth a few million bucks on the black market," Cameron sent back. *"That kind of money would make a hunter real hungry."*

"It would also mean that someone else would have to know about her and her whereabouts."

Rafe's protective instincts spurred him on with new determination. He couldn't wrap his mind around the idea that hunters were what Cara had perceived. Surely she would understand that his pack could deal with any black-market lackey that came along hoping to make his fortune? Even then, however, there would have to have been a leak of information about her visit and what Cara was capable of. But how, when her many talents had been a complete mystery to the pack? Until now.

For a hunter, Cara would be the rarest of the rare, the catch of a lifetime if trapped while in wolf form. But she was used to fighting for her life and for freedom, and was no fool. Since she and her family battled vampires and demons on a regular basis, what chance did a human with a weapon have against power and knowledge like hers?

The familiar report of gunfire split the night, adding another surprise to an evening full of them. Guns were a bad sign of the times and something he had to deal with on a daily basis at his job. Here, with Cara out of reach and a Lycan or two taking up the chase, the dreaded idea of silver bullets fueled Rafe's anger... and the thought that though a pair of fangs might not do damage to the daughter of two legendary Weres, that damn metal could.

He had the scars to show for it, as did a couple of his packmates. Worse still was the glimmer of a memory of the well-aimed silver round that had taken down the only other female he might have dared to love, once upon a time, in his youth.

So it was a damn good thing he wasn't stupid enough to have immediately fallen for the she-wolf they were chasing, in case she turned out to be the kind of adrenaline junkie whose life would end long before he could solidify a relationship with her...if, in fact, that's what he wanted. And if, in fact, he had a choice in the matter.

Too late, his mind argued. *It's already too late.*

The look Cameron threw him after Rafe finished that thought had sympathy written all over it.

Chapter 13

Sifting through so many odors kept Cara occupied as she sped from shadow to shadow hunting for the one scent she sought.

"Wait," Rafe had urged from somewhere behind her, but she was onto something he couldn't be involved with. Vampires were bad enough. This new presence was outrageous.

She locked her thoughts behind an iron wall in her mind that was much more secure than the Landaus' protective pile of stones. Without the ability to read her, she'd be invisible to most Weres. In full wolf form, she could outrun all of them put together.

The park wasn't as large as she had been led to believe. Skirting the trees, Cara located the shadows she searched for and the abomination hidden in them. Using her exceptional vision to separate other forms of darkness from the night, Cara saw the demon that was cloaked as a human.

No disguise could mask the stink of a demon, and their cunningness was legendary. This one had been waiting, having lured her here with insightful fore-knowledge of what her reaction to its presence would be.

She didn't give the abomination time to appreciate how well its lure had worked, or to pounce. A single leap took her to the monster with her teeth bared and her claws swiping.

The thing hissed like a vampire as her first blow landed and fought back with maniacal energy derived from an innate connection to the others of its kind. The energy of one of these demons was siphoned from the energy of many, no matter how separated they all were from each other.

Being in human form didn't slow its reflexes much, though Cara didn't allow the freak leeway to discard the layers of its temporary disguise. She snapped at the hell spawn's moving limbs, caught skin in her teeth and tore away a large chunk of its muscle while trying not to breathe in the fetid smells emanating from wounds that should have bled and didn't.

This creep was old, treacherous and used to fight-ing. It managed to catch hold of her muzzle with both of its bony hands as she wheeled, temporarily delaying the damage she dished out.

Cara shook it off with a fluid show of wolf flexibil-ity that brought her snapping canines dangerously close to the demon's face. It got to her again by yanking on the fur covering her left shoulder. Using a viselike grip, the demon lifted her front end off the ground, causing a round of pain Cara didn't have time to process as she heard the snap of her right paw breaking.

Had it broken every bone in her body, she would have continued to fight.

You don't belong here and can't be allowed to stay.

No one who knew about demons could have afforded to let this one go so near to a densely populated pocket of civilization like Miami. If granted free rein, others would follow. They might already be here somewhere.

Cara closed the remaining inch of distance to the creature's face and snapped again. Demons had two vulnerable spots, whatever form they took. Since one of those spots was their face, Cara dug deeply into this demon's cheek with her wolf-sharp teeth.

The monster screeched in anger and flailed wildly in an effort to dislodge her. Cara hung on, her strength centered in her jaws, until she was able to free herself from its grip.

As the demon leaned back to begin its own shape-shift, Cara heard another sound that drowned out its screech—a sharp crack followed by a puff of air that sailed past her right ear.

A gunshot.

The demon flew backward as if it had been knocked off its feet. Cara lunged toward it to regain her advantage as the demon's human semblance further dissolved. What remained in its place was an ugly six-foot-tall mass of jellified flesh with a pair of dark red eyes and matching horns.

There was no mouth with which to bite because half of its face was gone, but she hadn't done all of that damage. The bullet had torn a hole in the demon's face a few millimeters from where her teeth had clung. Even then, the demon should have recovered. Their composition wasn't like a human's. Usually it took a lot more than one big hole to bring a demon down. Yet the monster dissipated in a puff of black smoke as if it had been composed of air rather than a thick coat of recently adopted flesh and bone.

The surprise of such an easy victory stole Cara's breath. She backpedaled, already whirling to search for the second intruder. What she found instead was a huge, half-furred-up werewolf skidding to a stop in front of her.

The Were's growl shook the ground. She had to look up to see this guy, who was the biggest werewolf she had ever seen. Male. Lycan. Fierce. Dangerous and furred up. His chest was broad. His legs were thick. Though he had a werewolf's enhanced musculature, his face retained many recognizable human characteristics, which meant that he also had been bred from an ancient wolf lineage from a time before wolf blood had taken a hold on human anatomy.

Her new companion stared briefly at the spot where the demon had stood. With an incredible display of pure-blooded Lycan speed, he then caught hold of her. But Cara wasn't afraid. This was not an enemy. One of the answering howls in the distance had been his, and he had come to her aid.

He wrapped his claws in her fur and dragged her closer to him. Her injured paw pulsed with pain. Her heart boomed as the Lycan's gaze swept over first her face and then her paws. He pounded his chest to show his good intentions and then lifted her up as though she weighed nothing. After settling her into his arms, he walked briskly toward the sound of more running.

"Cara!" Rafe's shout was weighted with anger and concern as he and another Were closed in.

She couldn't blame him for being angry but was glad nothing of that demon remained for the Landau pack to feast their eyes upon. This one time, she had gotten away with leaving most of the Landau Weres behind as she performed her mission. She had tried to save them from the onslaught of problems caused by her nature. Nevertheless, she hadn't killed that demon, and whoever had done the honors remained at large, a mystery.

"We heard shots. Were you hit? Are you okay?" Rafe demanded, eyeing the Lycan holding her.

His blatant concern brought Cara a degree of warmth that she couldn't have explained even if she'd had vocal cords. Through Were channels, she sent him a thought. *"I'm all right."*

She began her reverse shift, shaking off the wolf, making the Lycan holding her tilt back and forth in order to keep her in his arms. Once she'd discarded the wolf semblance, she sank against the unknown Lycan's massive chest, slightly out of breath.

"Jonas," Rafe said to the Lycan holding her, "hand her over. And thanks."

The big werewolf did as Rafe requested, then took off again, possibly to search for the party responsible for the gunfire that had downed the demon with a single, specialized, well-targeted bullet.

"I'll help him search," Rafe's packmate said. "If it's a werewolf hunter, the idiot is a piss-poor shot."

Rafe waited until both Weres had gone before looking directly at her. "If you keep this up, your invitation might be revoked. It's too dangerous letting you do whatever the hell you please. You do get that? Hell, Cara, I'll take you back myself."

Cara said breathlessly, "You have no idea what's out there clinging to the shadows."

"More memories?"

"Not his time."

"You're injured, and on my watch," he said in a tone

that again said he had truly been worried about her, not for the sake of the trouble he might be in with both of their families, but because he honestly cared about what happened to her.

Another flush of heat crept into her face as Cara acknowledged his words.

"The hand will heal," she said, adding to herself, *and that demon won't come calling again.*

Rafe didn't look at her hand. His focus remained on her face. Cara felt the intensity of desire he was withholding. Rafe wanted to let his attention slip to her naked body. His pulse moved beneath the skin under his left ear.

Now that she was in his arms, her injured hand seemed like nothing compared to the ache she felt in other places. Deep inside her, a distant thrumming vibration was producing longings she was now beginning to comprehend. In spite of what had just transpired, and with the acknowledgment of demon presence in Miami, she wanted Rafe to look at her. She wanted to remain in his arms for a while longer.

As strong and independent as she had always been, Cara was caving on the idea of remaining close to Rafe Landau. There was no look of horror on his face about her latest shift. None of the feeling she had for Rafe had struck her while she lay in the other Lycan's arms. Only Rafe made her feel this way. She sensed a strong, rapidly forming bond. Their bodies were in sync on this, although their wishes went unspoken.

"We have to get you home," he finally said. "Some damn fool has a gun. Is that what you were after?"

Cara shook her head. "He found me."

"How did you break your bones?"

Cara supposed Rafe might understand about the

demon if she answered him truthfully, but she didn't yet dare to do so.

"Let's get you home," he said, continuing to stand there, holding her, as if he didn't want the moment to end despite the possibility of more gunshots.

"Does it hurt badly?" he asked, shifting his focus to her hand.

"I've had worse."

Cara studied Rafe's handsome face, expecting to find clues as to what he might be expecting from her at this point. She had to accept the fact that she truly was inept at deciphering some of the expressions that crossed his face.

"My mother will help with your hand, though she's not as gentle as my grandmother was when it comes to healing injured limbs," he said. "I suppose I'll have to loan you another shirt."

Cara wasn't sure how to respond, so she didn't try. She was thankful that the demon hadn't found any of Rafe's friends tonight.

Finally, he moved.

"I can walk, Rafe. There's nothing wrong with my legs."

"Yes. I suppose you can. But you're naked. In my arms you're not so exposed."

He was lying about his motives. Rafe wanted to hold her.

"Being without clothes will bother the others?" she asked.

"Probably not half as much as it bothers me," he returned.

The thrumming inside her was growing stronger. Cara slid her gaze downward, past Rafe's lips, his chin, to the broad muscular chest covered by a T-shirt that stretched tight. She fought the urge to tear that T-shirt to pieces with her teeth and get at what lay beneath. She would have liked Rafe better with no barriers between them and his bronze skin exposed.

Maybe she had been too long in animal form tonight and these urges belonged to the wolf—to the more primal parts of herself that had never been explored. As if she had just awakened to the world of a mature female's physical needs, Cara smiled at Rafe...and then found herself pressed to the bark of a tree with his hard body tight up against hers.

"Damn it." His curse was a whisper of molten air on her forehead. "They won't like this. Won't appreciate it."

He swore again, then added, "But what the hell?"

Chapter 14

Rafe was ravenous, and he let his instincts take over as he leaned against Cara in a way that indicated how the idea of friendship had evolved into a new kind of madness.

It didn't take a specialist to tell him that the state he found himself in had to mean he and Cara had imprinted. He was acting contrary to every rule he had in place to govern his behavior in the world so far. Somehow, and after such a short acquaintance, their souls were making these decisions for them.

Cara was a seamless, flawless turn-on, and having her naked or half-naked most of the time didn't help his willpower. Unlike his human partners, she had torn through his defenses as if none of them existed.

Her lips were there for him to taste. Her breath was sweet when he did. Musky wolf scent perfumed the dark tangles of hair that Rafe ran his fingers through. He had a very real need to explore every inch of this magnificent she-wolf hybrid whom everyone else secretly feared.

With her thighs against his and her high, firm breasts against his chest, self-control was quickly becoming nonexistent.

Cara appeared to be as stunned as he was by this latest act, though she didn't resist. He tasted the blistering-hot tang of passion coating the inside her mouth. She had closed her eyes.

He kissed her as if there wouldn't be another opportunity, as if they were the only two Weres in the world… devouring, taking, possessing Cara's mouth the way he wanted to possess her body, and as though he too had become possessed.

He wasn't gentle. Didn't take his time. Her tongue was malleable and an instant addiction. For now, Cara's mouth was everything. It was the connecting link between two souls that hadn't expected such a pairing.

Although tearing his clothes off was not an option, Rafe felt feverish and confined. He maintained the hope that he could handle this and that things actually wouldn't get out of hand. Danger remained each moment they stayed in the park. They would be expected back behind the walls. But as Cara's palm slipped up his back, the caress burned through his shirt with the heat of a falling star. When she tugged at the hem of his shirt in order to reach his skin, his body rippled with anticipation.

He broke the connection with her lips just far enough to speak. "You're new to this, and I'm taking advantage."

In response, Cara raked her nails across his lower back. The sting told Rafe that though Cara might not be as experienced as he was in dealing with sexual desires, she was also part animal when it came right down to it, and all animals instinctively knew what to do in a situation like this.

Her touch turned him on. Spurred him on. The pain was real, which meant that Cara also was real. She was neither wholly pleasure nor wholly pain, but both things rolled into one. To love her, to make love to her, would be at her partner's peril, but that was just the kind of challenge a werewolf lived for.

He kissed Cara again with a vengeance, and she met him halfway as her fingers moved over him as if seeking a deeper connection. How could he tell her that she had already gotten under his skin?

The brash devouring that seemed to go on forever left him unsatisfied. Rafe vowed not to take this seduction farther tonight and to give Cara a chance to learn and adapt to the ways of the pack—and in particular a male Were's physical urgings. Yet even that promise was fading.

Animals.

Yes, we are animals inside, Cara.

You and me.

His hand moved without conscious direction, running over the length of Cara's smooth right thigh. She gasped and growled again, and the sound made Rafe want her all the more. The possibility of imprinting with Cara made adhering to former promises seem impossible.

He slid his hand down her leg, cursing the action, knowing what he would find and also that reaching that place would lead him to a state of mindless, blissful oblivion.

He was almost there when the word *don't* lit up in his mind with the brilliance of a neon sign, followed closely by *can't.* Because, hell…he might be an animal in human guise, but he was also an animal who cared about the female in his arms and about what would happen to her if the imprinting sequence had truly begun. Mating with Cara would seal the deal for good. No out. No exit. After imprinting, no other partner would do for either of them. Ever.

Did they truly want that when they knew so little about each other, and when so much was already at stake with Cara's visit here?

Do you realize what's happening, Cara? Are you seeing the larger picture?

He had to stop now, before it was too late. Before more of Cara's delicious heat corroded his sense of what was right.

Damn, that was hard.

Nearly impossible.

When he pulled back, she opened her eyes. He had no words to offer her that might explain the rashness of his decision to stop what he had started.

Rafe had no idea whether or not Cara got this, got that he had only halted due to his concern for her. Before he had taken his next breath, she had slipped from his grasp, melted back into full wolf form and was limping away on three legs without looking back.

Cara had sensed Rafe's reluctance to indulge in this intimate moment before he had stopped kissing her. She hadn't wanted to face him after that.

She couldn't afford to let him see how being close to him affected her, and how breathless she was. So she walked away from the beauty of their moment of passion, unclear about what would happen from here but not willing to change back to her human shape in order to speak of those things.

Rafe followed her, keeping a distance of a few steps between them. He said only one thing. "Let me carry you back. I can get you in without anyone seeing you. I've spent a lot of time there and know the place well. I can at least try to ward off the questions they will have."

Ignoring his suggestion made her feel better in spite of the fact that her paw hurt like hell. She was being stubborn, when shifting to human form would have taken her weight off the broken bone. Still, the discomfort of a fracture didn't last long for any werewolf, and was a minor thing for a Kirk-Killion. The same combination of wolf and vampire blood that made her so strong also allowed her to heal more rapidly than most Weres. She would never have survived this long if that hadn't been the case.

She stopped near the wall to look at it, expecting to see more Weres looking down at her from the top. No one was there.

"They trust me," Rafe said, coming up alongside. "They trust me to do the right thing."

Growling at him did no good. Rafe added, "Follow me, then, if I can't help you any other way."

He turned and began to walk along the base of the wall, pausing once to make sure she was trailing him.

"Being naked in your human form might be less intimidating to others than your current incarnation," he continued, speaking to her calmly, as if nothing had happened between them that should have caused her silence. "It's up to you, though."

She thought about biting him and decided against it. Uncertainty had muddled her thinking where Rafe Landau was concerned, and the only way to stave off these new sensations was to keep her wolf shape and her distance. The discomfort of her broken paw was preferable to the strange longing she had to mate tooth and nail with Rafe.

"There's a break in the wall near the guardhouse," he said. "It's a small one, but sufficient to get through if you know about it. When we reach the other side, we can skirt the house and use a rear door. Hopefully Cameron hasn't returned with news about the shooter. If he had, there would be plenty of activity, and I don't see evidence of that. And just so you know, Cameron won't tell them about you unless you want him to."

They found the break in the wall and Rafe ushered her through it, touching her only once as she slid past him by running a quick helping hand over her black coat. The heat in his hand, so like static, raised the fur on the back of her neck.

If Rafe thought it would be easier on the rest of the Weres to see her in human form, she owed her hosts that much. She would change back for them as soon as she reached the grass.

She didn't have that chance. Just five steps across the Landaus' yard, the game of hide-and-seek came to an end. Lights came on. An alarm set for Were ears went up. And her Landau hosts appeared like apparitions near the driveway wearing grim, worried expressions.

Rafe moved forward without hesitation. "Possible hunter out there," he said. "Cameron's searching."

Their eyes were on her.

"Cara injured a hand," Rafe said. "It should be looked after."

"Yes," Dana Delmonico Landau agreed, observing Cara. "Did that hunter hurt you?"

"No," Rafe replied for her.

"Another moment of privacy needed?" Rafe's father asked with a hint of warning in his tone.

"Someone or something has been luring Cara out there. I'm not sure what. She will have to tell us if she wants to," Rafe explained.

Dylan Landau searched the rim of the wall before returning his attention to her. "Maybe you'd like to tell us about that now, Cara, so that we can be better prepared if there's trouble. I don't like the sound of this or the news of a shooter, whether or not it's a hunter stalking the park. And I don't like the fact that someone else might know you're here when that's private pack business."

As Rafe's mother removed her jacket, she said to both of the men, "Why don't you head to the house? Cara and I will be along shortly. I'll just have a quick word with her."

When Rafe's gaze returned to Cara, his expression was as intense as his kisses had been. The rising heat was a continuous indicator of what he could do to her body. She could not have been hotter. Concentration was next to impossible with Rafe beside her, and her injured paw ached from the pressure she was putting on it in order to stand on all fours.

Rafe didn't argue with his mother, probably because he realized that she'd removed her jacket to cover Cara's nakedness after her next shape-shift. The Landaus seemed to be good at reading others and sharing.

Her wolf shape hadn't seemed to bother or surprise them. But the mention of hunters had unsettled everyone here. Surely they would send more of the pack after the hunter, but they had no idea they'd been so close to a real threat in the form of a demon, or just how much trouble having a Kirk-Killion here could bring.

She watched Rafe go.

"I haven't been taught the ins and outs of social graces, Rafe. I'm merely stumbling along, trying to find out how to deal." She sent the message to him on Were channels, hoping he'd understand.

Obviously she was taking too long to deal with her own issues, because when Dana Delmonico Landau turned back to her, the older woman's tone had changed.

"Now," Dana said. "Why don't you get on with that shift and tell me what is really going on."

Chapter 15

Rafe's mother was going to interrogate Cara. You couldn't truly take the detective out of a person, even after they had left the force in order to be the mate of an important alpha. His mother was no exception. She was also kind and intuitive, though, especially gifted in reading thoughts and unspoken intentions.

Having been on the receiving end of these interrogations while he was growing up, Rafe didn't envy Cara. But he figured she could handle it, even without him there.

"Did you know about her abilities?" he asked his father as they climbed the steps leading to the front porch. "About how special her wolf is?"

"I assumed Cara might have inherited that talent," his father replied. "We had never seen anything like her mother. I was sure I'd never see anything like Rosalind again, and for a minute there, I thought I was back in the past."

"Rosalind was a black wolf? A real wolf? That wasn't just a rumor?"

"Oh, yes. She was terribly strong and unfailingly rebellious."

Rafe nodded. "That rings a bell."

His father rested a hand on the white-painted pillar. "You would have had to meet or see Rosalind to fully understand what all those combinations of spirits could do. What they were, and how they reacted. Nevertheless, Rosalind's rebelliousness and her strength ended up saving many Were lives in the end."

"Colton Killion's life among them. I believe Cara might have come here to find out about the past," Rafe said.

The remark earned him a thoughtful sideways glance.

Rafe went on. "I don't think Cara knows much about her family history or the part her parents played in Cara's current situation. It's normal for her to want to learn about her origins, isn't it, and why she is the way she is?"

"Do you believe it's our place to enlighten her?" his father countered.

"I do if she needs that information enough to have agreed to come here to find it despite her reluctance to do so."

His father paused near the front door. "What was calling to her out there?"

"I don't think it was a hunter she was after, but there were shots fired. After shifting, she got away too quickly for Cameron and me to keep up. Whatever it was that Cara found out there broke bones in her hand, and yet we didn't see any intruders near where we found her and she wasn't willing to speak of it."

His father searched the wall in the distance. "We heard that howl."

Rafe was sure he'd never forget the haunting sound Cara had made. "You sent Jonas?"

"Without you here, he is the fastest."

"And the only shifter around tonight who is able to manipulate the moon for his own purposes," Rafe added.

"There is that," his father agreed.

"You do know that Cara won't be a willing prisoner here or mindful of the rules?"

"I never would have expected anything else from the daughter of an exceptionally talented Lycan like Colton Killion, even if Rosalind hadn't been tossed into the mix."

Rafe followed his father's gaze. The wall seemed darker by moonlight and even taller from where he stood. Cara had gone over it as if it was no obstacle at all. He had now seen three of her transformations and wondered how many more of them might be in store.

He said, "Maybe you should tell Cara about her father, and what you know."

"That would be good," his father agreed, "if I knew where to start. Colton wasn't part of this pack. His family kept to themselves. His was a very old family line that was more powerful than most, and the Killions had no interest in being part of a pack. Their sole purpose was to fit into the world around them. They tried hard to do that."

Rafe turned, wanting to go to Cara but willing to give her the time to settle down after whatever encounter she'd had out there. Unanswered questions kept arising, chief among them: *If not another vampire, what made you run?*

He didn't ask that question of Cara over Were channels, though. The need to hop over the wall and have another look at the park was making him anxious. He wasn't used to leaving hard tasks to others and hoped Cameron would return soon with news. Barring that, he'd have to find out what the holdup was without letting Cara see him leave. She would try to follow.

"You'll have plenty of time to find out what she was after if tonight is any indication of what we can expect," his father said, noting Rafe's fisted hands with a nod of his head.

Rafe said, "You knew this going in, and the kind of trouble she could bring."

"Yes. I just didn't expect things to happen so soon."

"Neither did I," Rafe muttered beneath his breath.

His meaning was different from his father's, though. He hadn't expected to bond with anyone, let alone their guest, which was what was already happening. The desire to go to Cara was like another fist curled up inside his stomach. He could hardly stay away from her. He couldn't keep his gaze off her.

Chastising himself wasn't working, so he headed to the side of the house to find an out-of-sight spot to get over the damn wall. As confusing as the night had been, doing what he did best would put him back on track. Chasing the bad guys. Sweeping the park. Getting it done. He could forget Cara for a while.

"Rafe?"

He turned back.

"I've been through this before, son. Nothing is different about this, and we can handle it," his father said.

Anxious to get going, Rafe shifted his weight nervously from boot to boot. "I'll be back when there's something to tell you, and not before then."

"Cara will be all right here," his father promised.

Rafe nodded. "I'd have no doubts about that if in fact you could keep her here."

Cara was in good hands with this pack on guard. The doubts he didn't mention were about himself and what he might do next if he didn't get the hell out of there.

Cara wasn't with him now, and yet it felt as if she were. Her taste was in his mouth. Her fragrance stuck to his skin. Each time he thought her name, the image accompanying it melted from one shape to another, just as Cara had done several times now.

Maybe the pack could handle a shifter like Cara on a temporary basis. The question was whether they could handle her for much longer than that.

I'm acting like a besotted fool...

"Later," he called out to his dad as he launched himself at the wall.

He dropped down on the other side, relieved to be free to pursue other things than the compulsion to mate with the only female on the planet who was off-limits to him.

"That's better," Dana remarked as Cara completed her shape-shift. "Now, if you'll put this jacket on, we can have a conversation. Are you good with that?"

Cara took the offered clothing that smelled nothing like the shirt Rafe had loaned her earlier that night. She was sorry she'd had to ditch the shirt in the park.

Dana was tall and wiry, with a more petite bone structure than her height suggested. Her hair, so like Rafe's, was brown, but curly. Her skin, also like Rafe's, was a smooth golden bronze. She had an ageless face and large eyes that took in everything around her. And all of her attention was on Cara.

"I'd like to know what made you go out there, against the suggestions we made for your protection," Dana said.

Blunt and to the point. Cara was used to this. Telling Dana part of the reason for her escape couldn't hurt. She didn't have to lie to her hostess.

"I heard a call," she said. "Something called my name."

She watched Dana process this. "Does anyone else know you're here in Miami?"

Cara shook her head. "No one any of us would like to meet or acknowledge. That doesn't mean certain beings can't find me if they're in tune with what's going on around them."

"Like the vampire at the beach?"

"The vampire was an accident. It hadn't gotten wind of me before I sensed its presence."

"And Rafe just happened to be there when you all met up?"

Withholding information that Rafe might find personal and sensitive wasn't lying, so Cara said, "Unlike the vampire, Rafe sensed my presence on the beach and found me first."

Rafe's mother took some time before speaking again. "I've fought vampires on several occasions. They pass along information on channels similar to ours. Could it have been one of them calling to you in the park?"

"No. Not a vampire."

Cara could tell Dana wasn't saying what she was thinking, though she had to know Cara could guess what that was. If not a vampire, then what kind of creature had detected Cara so soon? That's the question Rafe's mother would likely want to ask. And since Cara didn't want to lie outright, she had to evade the question before it was voiced.

"If you press me, I'd have to tell you things you might not want to hear," Cara warned.

"And if you withhold important information that could potentially harm this pack, you'd be responsible for whatever might happen," Dana countered.

"Not wanting anyone to be harmed on my behalf is one of the reasons I didn't want to come to Miami."

"Yet you ultimately agreed to come," Dana pointed out.

"I'm trying to make peace with my decision, which isn't so easy for someone like me now that I'm here and trouble has already begun."

Dana's scrutiny was like having a bright light turned Cara's way. "But you like Rafe," Dana said.

Cara needed a moment to process the remark. Was it a change of direction intended to trip her up?

"Yes. I like him," she replied. "Just as my family must have liked their hosts and the Weres here who fought beside them in the ghost war."

The term *ghost war* caused the she-wolf across from Cara to flinch. Dana said, "You're alluding to the fight near Fairview Hospital?"

Cara mentally filed away what Dana had said about a hospital. There had been a battle near a place called Fairview, and that was information she needed in order to piece together more of her family's history.

"I was alluding to the attack in the park that left my father a white wolf and introduced him to my mother."

"Ah, yes." Dana's tone was solemn. "If we listed each and every time we came up against creatures unlike us looking for a fight, that list would extend from here to the ocean and back several times."

"I'm only interested in one of those incidents," Cara said. "For now."

"Of course." Dana nodded. "I can tell you what I know, having been in the fight near Fairview, if that's what you want, but how about if we postpone that conversation for a while and get you inside? I don't like the way the wind has changed in the last few minutes."

Cara inhaled the night air. "Humans," she said.

"Well, that's a relief." Dana sighed and took a quick look down the driveway. "After all, we're just like them, as far as they are concerned. I used to be one of them, you know."

Cara did know that. The she-wolf across from her was the reason Rafe had a human scent mixed with Were. Dylan Landau had mated with a human who had been either accidentally scratched or bitten by the wrong kind of wolf, because no human would willingly defect from the known world to a much darker and more secretive one in the shadows.

Everyone had a story, it suddenly seemed to Cara. Though her story had to come first.

In spite of what Dana had said, Rafe's mother was showing outward signs of being concerned about the human scent that now permeated the air. She fixed her attention on the gate in the distance long enough for Cara to follow her line of sight, then looked at the wall.

"A hunter wouldn't come here, surely," Cara said.

"No hunter in his right mind would. But then, hunters are by their very definition morally off track."

"I didn't get a sense of humans in the park where we were," Cara noted.

"But you heard the shots?"

"Yes." One of those shots had sent that demon back to the hell it had sprung from, saving her the task.

Dana was looking at her when Cara turned back. She said in a tone reserved for sharing secrets, "How did you hurt your hand, Cara?"

Cara focused her senses outward in search of something to use as a diversionary tactic to avoid Dana's question. She found it.

"They have found your hunter," she said.

Dana stepped forward to see who might be approaching by way of the manned front gate, but it was too far away to get a good look, even for Weres. She again glanced at the wall, sensing what Cara had. The human presence was strongest there.

"Human male," Cara explained. "Smells like metal and hatred."

What she didn't say was that it also smelled like death, and that the Banshee's stifled cry in the park had been reserved for whoever this was.

Dana turned to her. "Hatred has a scent?"

Cara pulled the borrowed jacket tighter around her and nodded. "It's like nothing else."

"Please go to the house and wait there, Cara. Will you do this one thing I'm asking?"

Deciding to honor the request, Cara headed for the house. Yes, she could do this one thing, because who the hell cared about hunters? Humans were no match for werewolves. Weres had three times their strength and five times human speed. If a handful of humans knew about the existence of werewolves without understanding those facts, then hunting werewolves had to be a doomed sport.

The real reason for going to the house, however, was

Rafe. Avoiding him right now was a necessity for everyone concerned.

This had been a night full of surprises...

And it wasn't over yet.

By the time she reached the porch, her arms were tingling in a reaction reserved only for her. Rafe was still close. Though she couldn't see him, she had picked up on the beat of his heart as though hers had been jump-started. Her hands began to shake with anxious excitement over how she was able to differentiate Rafe's presence from the others' and perceive his approach so easily.

There was shouting near the wall, but Rafe's wasn't among the raised voices. His scent had accompanied the smell of the human she had detected while standing with Dana on the lawn, though.

And now he was here again, moments later, on this side of the wall, Cara's senses screamed. Rafe was closing in as the attention of others was drawn elsewhere.

He was in front of her. Beside her. Pressing her against the brick with a replay of what had happened in the park, and with a body that was strong enough to steal her breath away.

He was looking at her, and she could not look away.

Rafe's blue eyes were bright. He wasn't smiling or willing to explain his actions. His lips brushed hers, creating sparks that lit up her insides. When his mouth covered hers with a hungry, almost angry devouring, it seemed to Cara as if no one else existed.

His kiss was very wicked in the way it tortured her. His body was unrelenting in the pressure it applied. Rafe's needs formed their own kind of power that wrestled with her former desire for independence. She was afraid that this time, she wouldn't so easily get away.

She was slipping, becoming someone she didn't recognize, and was aware of the moment her carefully guarded restraint started to go.

For someone like her, losing control was never a good thing.

Chapter 16

Seconds.

They had mere seconds to break the rules this pack had set in place and be together.

Rafe hadn't planned to behave like a madman, but he wasn't completely surprised by the impulsive forwardness of his actions. He had reached Cara here without the usual argument with himself. Nor had she offered any.

It was now pretty damn clear they were going to be together for long periods of time no matter what anyone could have expected. Detective Rafe Landau had been cuffed to this incredibly beautiful hybrid without a key to extricate himself. Did that make him weak, or merely smitten?

Too late to decide...

Already, he was caught in an inexplicable undertow of feeling, though in the periphery Rafe heard the voices that were getting closer. He was needed at the wall and wasn't there. If he and Cara were discovered in a wayward embrace, it would prove to be worse for her. The pack might send her home if they were to comprehend the rapid evolution of the bond forming between two unsuspecting souls.

Cara's breathing came in rasps when their lips parted, and he fared no better. She was waiting for his eyes to find hers, and she shook her head when they did. It was possible that Cara, who hadn't seemed frightened of anything since he had met her, might be afraid of him.

"There can be no shape-shifting your way out of this one," he whispered to her. "We just have to be sure about what this is."

"Is insanity the conclusion you've come to?" she asked.

"Yes, possibly. Probably, in fact. But does that realization change things?"

"It means I can't stay."

"Doesn't it also mean that you can't get away?"

"Watch me," she said.

Rafe took a step back to allow Cara to test the truth of her reply. She didn't accept the challenge.

"You should tell me now if you've made this happen," Rafe continued. "Is this a trick that you wield?"

She was all eyes and lips and velvet-smooth skin. He wanted to drink in that beauty. Now that he had gotten that kiss out of his system, a replay was first on his agenda. However, the voices at the wall were now almost right on top of them.

There was to be no next kiss or further closeness. The stolen seconds had been used up, and the world was again encroaching.

After the voices, a sudden hush made the absence of sound seem sinister. Rafe's duty to his family and his pack made him turn. Behind him, Cara said, "Death has come," in a soft, knowing tone that instantly cooled him.

Hell. How did she know? How could she?

Troubled by a long list of seemingly impossible theories about Cara and tonight's events in the park, not to mention her latest announcement, Rafe left her. He hustled back to the wall, feeling her heated gaze follow.

Death had come. Yes. And it had struck while Cara was in the park. Since Cara was also part Banshee, he wondered if her howl had been for this poor human being they had found, and if she had covered up her knowledge of that death with a timely, wolfish shape-shift.

Hurling himself over the wall, Rafe found that his father, Cameron and his mother had gathered there. They were all quietly staring at the lifeless body lying at their feet.

This was not a Were they looked at, and no one Rafe recognized. Still, the shock of Cara's prediction about the body he and Cameron had found left Rafe uneasy.

"This could be our hunter," he said to the others.

"I believe so as well," Cameron agreed. "There's a smell of metal on him, though we found no weapon."

"Did you…?" his father started to ask.

"We found him this way," Rafe said.

"Cause of death?" Rafe's father asked.

Cameron said, "Looks like his spine has been severed. The poor bastard didn't have a chance of surviving that."

Rafe didn't have to glance over his shoulder to know that Cara would be watching. She might have had fore-knowledge of this death, but she could not have had a hand in it. The time lapse between hearing the gunshot tonight and finding Cara with Jonas had been no longer than a minute at most. He had accompanied her here himself. So who else had been out there?

Going into full cop mode, Rafe reasoned that only two things he knew of could have severed this man's spine.

"Has to be either a strong werewolf's claws or a chain saw," he said. "What about Jonas?"

"Never," his father replied. "Jonas would not harm a human like this, and we all know it."

"I meant, has there been word from him yet about this?" Rafe clarified.

His father shook his head.

"So, who did it?" Rafe's mother asked. "Jonas isn't the only Lycan in the world with a gift enabling him to change tonight and do this kind of damage to an intruder wishing us harm."

"After handing your houseguest over to us, Jonas was long gone," Cameron said. "While Rafe went east, I followed Jonas to the west. It was on our return that I met up again with Rafe and we found this guy."

"There might have been two hunters, and Jonas went after the other guy, leaving this one to us," Rafe added.

"You found him here, where he lies?" his mother asked.

"Yes, but my guess would be he was dumped here," Rafe said.

"I agree," Cameron chimed in.

"Well, if this guy was a wolf hunter, it would seem that someone did us a favor, though it was a particularly grisly one," Rafe's mother remarked.

"And it would also suggest that he didn't know anything about Weres," Rafe said. "Unless, of course, this guy and his friend had gotten wind of Jonas prowling the park all wolfed up. But how would any human know about that when very few Weres do?"

"Jonas often prowls that park," Cameron reminded them. "Maybe one of these guys saw him and hatched a plan."

"Or else someone besides a nasty vampire or two knew about Cara's arrival," Rafe's father suggested.

All eyes turned to the alpha.

"No one else could know about Cara," Rafe countered. "Hell, only a select few know about us."

"So why would a wolf hunter be in this park tonight or be dumped at the foot of our wall?" Rafe's mother asked. "Maybe we're wrong about this guy being a hunter. Perhaps he was just an idiot with bad intentions, shooting at the wrong person out there who then retaliated."

"A person with the ability to sever his spine?" Rafe said.

"It seems that we have more investigating to do," Rafe's father concluded. "And we just happen to be good at that."

Cameron nodded. "I'll call it in and let the PD try to reason this one out. Determining the cause of his injuries will keep everyone busy. But finding him so close to the wall means we will be involved."

Rafe's father nodded. "We'll have to be doubly on guard with so many others snooping around."

His comment had mainly been meant for Cara. Had she heard it?

Rafe still felt her attention on him and didn't mention anything about the possibility that Cara's howl had covered up a Banshee's warning to the others. Especially after seeing her in full wolf form, everyone knew what Cara was capable of. He didn't need to fill in the details. His take was still that she had shape-shifted in the park

so as not to scare either him or Cameron by presenting
a part of herself she preferred to keep hidden.

Death has come, she had said.

"You wouldn't have liked it," she messaged to him
now after gaining access to thoughts he hadn't protected from her. *"You wouldn't have understood what
the spirit inside me does."*

Rafe didn't want to ask the next question, but he
did anyway.

"Did you have anything to do with this guy's death?"

Her reply was immediate. *"It's a hellish injury inflicted by a monster. But I also smell wolf around it.
The Banshee can't kill. She merely predicts death and
calls death to its mark."*

"Merely?" he messaged back.

The lips he had kissed would have uttered those
words of explanation aloud if Cara had been there beside him. Cara's hidden entity was a death caller, so
Cara also had a kind of forced relationship with death.
It was no surprise how well this would go down with a
species like vampires.

What it also could imply, however, was that through
the spirit she carried around, Cara might be able to predict the time and place of the death of everyone standing here. This realization should have turned him away.
The barest hint of the idea should have made him re-
think his connection to her.

As if that was actually possible.

"Rafe."

His mother brought him out of thought.

"Is it too late to say I'm sorry?" she asked.

Cara didn't require the help of Weres in law enforcement to find the answers about the body at foot of their

wall. She could get those details if she was allowed more time in the park. But in order to get that time, she needed Rafe's understanding. She'd have to explain more to him about herself, and that would be more discomforting than a few broken bones.

The injury had become little more than a nagging ache that any wolf could have handled. By tomorrow, she'd regain some use of her hand. Dana would see to bandaging the injury soon. Rafe's mother would also come looking for Cara about her missed meal, avoiding any inquiry about the body at the wall in favor of treating a guest with kindness and respect.

The party near the wall began to disperse. Cara supposed all of them realized she was there, observing them from her perch on a shadowed section of that wall, though they let that slide.

Only the strongest and smartest Weres had successful and long-lived wolf packs. The silver-haired alpha of this pack took the wall as if it was a minor hurdle. Dana followed him. Cameron headed off across the park, speaking on a cell phone. When the other three were gone, Rafe said, "You can come out now."

Cara walked toward him along the top of the wall with the agility of a cat rather than a wolf.

"Do you know who did this?" he asked, looking up at her.

"No."

"But you knew it would happen?"

"Yes."

She gave Rafe time to absorb her answer. He then said, "Are there going to be any more surprises before the next sunrise?"

An expression of wary relief crossed Rafe's handsome features when she didn't answer.

"I'm going to be called in to investigate this body," he said. "Other cops will arrive in force any minute now. Can you hear the sirens? If any part of this was the work of a Were, the humans on the force can't be allowed to figure that out. If this guy was a human on a bender with a gun, they'll have to hunt for the missing weapon, as well as the blood an injury like this should normally have left behind."

He hesitated before continuing. "Did vampires have anything to do with the lack of blood at the scene, Cara? Did they get to this guy after he was injured? If he was dumped here, who brought him? All those questions need to be answered to start the ball rolling."

"Vampires got to him," she said. "I can smell their presence as well."

Rafe didn't like that news. "Damn it. Monsters and wolves and vampires, all at once, would muddy things up. This was an act of brutality against a human, and we don't condone such things."

"What do you do when the hunters come?"

"In the past, we turned them in."

"And when they talked about the existence of werewolves?"

"They were declared certifiably insane."

Cara supposed that might be true. "We can find the weapon this human used if we look."

Rafe shook his head. "What you need to do is get out of sight before everyone arrives."

The wail of the sirens he had mentioned became louder, and was in some ways similar to the Banshee's cry. Cara decided to share that thought.

"Sirens also mean that someone has died, or could be about to die, right? In that case, death is only a possibility. I don't have the option of offering a way out for the victims my spirit attaches to. When the Banshee cries, death answers."

She took a breath and continued. "Only one dark spirit has ever dared to try to change that outcome, and that spirit was doomed to reside within the living body of my relatives. After my mother's turn at playing host, she passed that spirit along to me."

"I'd like to know more about that, and about what you feel," Rafe said earnestly. "I can't begin to imagine what it's like." He swore under his breath and waved a hand at the park. "There are deaths all over a city like Miami. Can you see all of them, or only a few?"

Because he honestly wanted to know the answer to that question, Cara obliged. "Through the spirit, I can see the deaths of those closest to me."

Rafe looked at the body on the ground. "Then this guy got close? He could have been the shooter?"

"Yes. But…"

Rafe's gaze came back to her. "But?"

"He wasn't the one who got closest to me out there."

He stared at her as if not knowing what to make of that. He didn't know about the demon or the other presence she had sensed on the sidelines. Perhaps that mysterious second person had been the killer Rafe's pack would seek. She could help Rafe in one small way if she broke the rules that had been imposed on her, and on her family before that. She could give him a heads-up and face the consequences if there were to be any.

"You won't find the next body for a while," she said. "But there will be one."

The fact that there was to be another death and he now knew about it made Rafe's head swim. His next question was a no-brainer. "Who, Cara? Who is going to die?"

"I don't know," she replied. "It's not information meant for me. Telling is cheating, don't you see?"

He didn't actually see that at all, but there was no time to delve deeper into spirits and curses. The sirens had ceased. Officers parked along the boulevard would now have entered the park. The ground shook slightly with the effort the officers were making to get to the scene.

"Go, Cara," Rafe directed. "Go now."

He was happy to see that she heeded his request so he could face the oncoming investigators. These were guys he knew. Guys he worked with. Besides himself and Cameron, there were three more Weres disguised as human cops and detectives in this area, and Rafe hoped at least one of them would be on duty and know whose wall this was.

Still, he also figured that Cara wouldn't go far. Not only that, but she was withholding information that was pertinent to this case. Any cop worth his salt could have picked up on that.

"I'll see you later," he said aloud with a glance at the house. "Count on it."

Chapter 17

It wasn't Dana waiting for her this time. The silver-haired alpha stood on the porch.

"Tell me about what happened," Dylan Landau said calmly. "Dana said someone called to you from out there tonight. Who was it? What was it about?"

Did she owe this alpha the truth in payment for the help the Landaus had given her family in the past?

"Demon," she said.

Creases appeared on Dylan Landau's forehead. He hadn't really been expecting that kind of a reply. His tone changed to one of concern. "Can you explain?"

Dana interrupted, emerging from the open doorway. "About that injured hand?"

No one here had been fooled by her sudden appearance. Dana wasn't going to be left out of these discussions.

"There hasn't been a demon sighting near here, as far as I know," Dylan said.

"Demons are everywhere and rarely show themselves unless they want something," Cara explained. "This one looked like a human and smelled like cooked flesh."

Her description was graphic enough to cause a temporary silence on the porch before Dana said, "Actually, we have seen them."

The alpha looked to his wife.

"In those older times, when Rosalind called them out of hiding," Dana said.

"Why would it call you, Cara? How did it know you're here?" Dylan asked.

"It's possible that rumors spread after tonight's vampire event at the beach," Cara replied. "This demon could have sensed my vibration the way Weres sense disturbances in the areas they frequent. It was waiting for me out there."

"It knew your name?" That question was from Dana.

Cara shook her head. "It called to a dark spirit, and I showed up. That spirit is chained to my soul. Where it goes, I go."

She doubted whether either of these Weres could comprehend the complexity of spirits and vibrations. For them, even vampires were a nuisance of the past. Banshees and demons would be on another level.

"So this demon knows about what's hidden inside you?" Dana asked.

"Everything composed of darkness knows that about me," Cara replied.

Dana said, "Could the demon have killed the human in the park?"

"The demon that called to me was killed by a bullet that might have been meant for me. Maybe I was your hunter's target, and he missed."

"In which case the demon couldn't have killed the man we found," Dylan surmised.

"Unless there were two hunters out there tonight, as Cameron and Jonas thought, and only one of them got away," Dana said.

Dylan looked at Cara. "Perhaps the best thing to do, for your safety, would be to take you home. Then again, if there are demons around, it's possible that only you could recognize their presence from far enough away that we could do something about it. If you stay here, you can help."

Dylan Landau had given her an out by suggesting she could go home. All she had to do was say the word and that big black car would pull up, ready to whisk her away. Hadn't that been her wish from the start? However, there were now reasons to stay. The past had to be put in order.

And then there was Rafe.

"Do you want to go home, Cara?" Dana asked.

"No. But it has been long day. I'd like to rest."

"One more thing," Dylan said before she reached the door.

Cara easily anticipated what he would say next.

"It would be wise not to let Rafe be the deciding factor in what direction your next few days take," Dylan said. "I think you know why."

She repeated the word she had thought to herself earlier. "I've never had a friend. Rafe is the first."

That wasn't actually a lie. But already, Rafe was so much more than that.

Tired, hungry, Cara followed Dana upstairs to her room. Dana had a tray that contained an assortment of food and a mug of aromatic, rapidly cooling liquid for her to drink.

For all of that, Cara felt grateful.

Real fatigue didn't set in until she had been left alone in the room her mother had used so long ago. Though Dana also had brought up a bag of medical supplies and quickly bandaged her hand before leaving, intuition told Cara she wasn't going to be alone for long.

She could almost imagine what Rafe's upbringing must have been like in a mostly normal Were family that was so different from hers. Was she wrong to envy Rafe for that?

It was after midnight and the room was warm in spite of the open window. A soft breeze did nothing to alleviate the stifling weight of Miami's humidity. Cara sat on the sill with the mug of tepid tea. At home, she and her father would have been hunting until dawn if a demon had dared to set foot on Kirk-Killion land. They'd be scouting for more of them until the sun came up.

Here, Rafe and other city law-enforcement officers would take care of the surface mess associated with the body they had found. Even after sunup, however, they'd be in the dark in the search for an intruder able to sever a human spine.

As part of both investigating teams, Rafe would have a long night ahead. Like Rafe, she wasn't used to resting until a task was done. But she had to leave this to others for now. In a city as large as Miami, there could be hundreds of demons. Each shadowy street might hide a nest of hungry vampires.

Cara studied the area from her perch at the window. There were lights on the other side of the wall, and more raised voices. Those disturbances alone would keep lurking demons and human hunters away. Light had always been the bane of monsters while being a relief to everyone else. Instead of having her father watch over things, the Landau pack would take on that task.

With new memories of her own, she turned to stare at the room where ghosts of the past still lingered, hoping for once that thoughts of Rafe Landau might chase those ghosts away.

All of the big boys in law enforcement were there eyeing each other as forensics techs surveyed the scene. There was plenty of muttering among them. Four Weres, two in uniform and the others in jeans, studied the scene with blank cop faces, though their thoughts came to Rafe like shouts.

"Looks like we have a new problem."

"We'll need to gather the packs and get to the source of this mess."

"Has to have been a wolf. Who else could manage something like this?"

"These forensics bastards will have a field day and get nowhere."

"We'll have to make sure they get nowhere."

"We have to beat them to the place where this guy was killed and see for ourselves what turns up."

No one had seen anything like this before, and anxiety made them tense. Too many secrets were at stake if a Were had a hand in this gruesome deed. Packs thrived on the stories about the past, so the Weres here were thinking of the time when their Elders fought off whole armies of nasty things that went bump in the night.

It was important that they found the spot where this guy had been murdered, and Rafe knew how. He knew who could easily lead them there, though he was loath to suggest such a thing. Two of these cops were pack and two weren't. No one outside the extended Landau family had been privy to Cara's visit for reasons that now had been made abundantly clear to Rafe.

Someone was after Cara. Someone, possibly with a gun, planned to hurt her, and the best way to do that was to lure her into the open without backup.

Who would die next, as the damn Banshee had predicted? And when? Death's next victim could be anyone here, but he couldn't announce that fact to those standing around him.

Without the others knowing of Cara's visit and her many talents, predicting another dead body might turn up would incriminate whoever mentioned it when that turned out to be the truth.

Rafe was suddenly very tired of secrets.

News trucks were already circling on the street in the distance. TV personalities would be salivating for gory details worthy of morning headlines. Every cop on the force was familiar with the sound of those engines and what they meant. Tonight, due to the body's close proximity to Judge Landau's estate, the news vultures would be held back, at least for a while.

When his father appeared, each of the officers present nodded to the judge. He spoke to them calmly. "Those of us behind this wall will go on record as volunteers to help with this investigation in any way we can. The sooner justice is served, the better we can all rest."

There would be no rest, of course, not until this crime was solved, one way or another. With sunrise several hours off, members of the Landau pack would race through this park in search of details before anyone else got around to it. If a wolf was involved in this heinous act of violence, Weres would deal with it. Self-policing was the only way to handle problems pertaining to the existence of werewolves.

And if vampires had messed with the scene, as Cara had confirmed, Were secrets in the area were going to be sorely threatened. Smack in the middle of this dilemma was an unpredictable hybrid she-wolf who had not learned how to play well with others. Still, her help might be the key to solving the case.

Rafe's father wore a worried expression that ran counter to his usual calm outward demeanor. Things had gotten messy since Cara's arrival, and his father was showing the strain. Tonight had offered a concentrated sample of what they could probably expect as long as she remained in Miami.

Rafe had to be especially careful about messaging his father on Were channels, but he had more to say. *"If you were Cara, and not yet grounded in a new city or a new pack, would you choose to go or stay?"*

Cara might have heard that, of course. Though he had been cautious, her ability to tap into thought systems came to her as easily as hurdling eight-foot stone walls. Cara was indeed special. So he had to wonder if the reason she had been kept in seclusion was due to the danger that followed in her wake—or because she was the danger.

She had proved to him in one night that she had more secrets than the rest of them put together...

But just when he thought things were hard enough to figure out, he picked a word from his father's mind that set his hair on end.

That word was *demon*.

Chapter 18

She'd paced for so long, Cara was afraid she had worn down the carpet. But the lights beyond the wall had dimmed at last, and some of the people had finally dispersed.

It was time to find out if that demon she had encountered had friends, and if one of those hell spawns had murdered a human.

By the looks of things around here and the Landaus' reaction to tonight's events, this pack must have avoided real trouble for some time. She couldn't imagine a long stretch without the kind of problems that followed her around.

Her parents must have realized that by sending her to the Landaus' she might crave the kind of lives others led. So why send her here? Why put these Weres through a night like tonight when more of the same was a given?

Cara stood at the window her mother had long ago jumped from. She had no clue as to what might have precipitated that leap. Rosalind could have either been running away from something, or to something. That piece of the puzzle was unsolved.

"I'm ready to see this part of the picture," Cara muttered with a hand on the sill. The sensation of sharing the room with ghosts of the past had grown stronger. The sharp sting in her mouth was also a part of that.

Needle-sharp incisors pricked her lower lip. Cara wiped her fingers across her mouth, and they came away with tiny droplets of blood. Dark blood. With no vampires present. This was the second time tonight she had altered her appearance without the proper motivation. She spun toward the bed with her senses sparking. On the bed was a filmy, reclining figure.

"Rosalind," it whispered to her.

Dazed, Cara hit the wall next to the window with her shoulder as something blew past her with a speed that was little more than a time slip of barely disturbed air. A second ghostly apparition appeared beside her and gracefully leaped onto the sill, where it paused in a knee-bending crouch.

As Cara stared, more details about this apparition filled in. It was a young female dressed in a glossy black shirt that swirled to stillness as she settled on the sill. The ghostly spirit remained there for a moment more, outlined by the night beyond, long black hair billowing in a nonexistent breeze.

The female glanced at the bed, wiped a hand across her mouth and held up two bloodstained fingers as if to show them to whoever was in the room with her. She uttered a sob of fear and disgust. And then the appari-

tion turned back to the window, pushed off both feet…
and jumped.

Cara stood there, frozen beside the window, feeling
like she was the one who had jumped. But she hadn't
moved, and there was no one on the bed. She had fangs,
like the female apparition, and blood on her fingers…
didn't she? Or had the blood been someone else's burden?

Her mother's burden?

A knock at the door shook her, but she ignored it.
She'd just received another vision of an event from the
past, as if it had answered her request for enlightenment.
The ghost at the window had been Rosalind. The figure
on the bed must have been her father.

Cara leaned out the window with a sense that time
had been suspended. The knocking sounds at the door
grew louder and were a distraction she didn't need.
Whatever had happened in this room to her parents remained a mystery that she would have to decipher later
when the distractions ceased.

The door opened without her invitation. A deep voice
said, "Can we talk?"

Rafe's powerful presence chased away all remnants
of the room's former occupants and replaced her chills
with familiar warmth. But she couldn't go to him or
try to explain what had happened here with a mouthful of fangs.

Avoiding the directness of his gaze, Cara covered
her mouth and reined in a shudder, not sure how she
was going to get out of this.

Rafe didn't cross the threshold into Cara's room. Her
appearance was a warning to stay where he was.

Her face had again lost color. Her dark glinting stare

was trained on the window, as if something had happened there.

Clearly, she wasn't all right.

Why?

He scanned the room to make sure she was alone, rechecking each corner twice. After that, all he could manage to say was her name.

"Cara?"

Her silence wasn't necessarily anything to worry about. The way she covered her mouth might have been, though. She was hiding something from him.

"Hey," he finally said. "I came to tell you that I will take you home in the morning if you still want to go."

She continued to stare at the window, and that made him curious. She hadn't dropped her hand from her mouth. He had to get her to talk so that he could see what he was dealing with.

"Are you Cara?" he asked, hoping nothing of her dark side would start wailing. "Is Cara here?"

He was afraid to crowd her by advancing. Putting her in this room might not have been such a good idea after all. She'd probably find no real comfort sharing a space that had long ago been occupied by other spirits in various states of distress.

Why hadn't anyone here considered that?

Why hadn't he?

Cara was haunted and in need of help she wouldn't ask for. At the moment, she was wan and lifeless. Maybe remaining in Miami was going to harm her in ways none of his family could detect.

Worried, Rafe said, "I'll take you home right now. You can gather your things and I'll get a car."

She took one small step toward him as if drawn by the firmness of his tone. Rafe kept his eyes on her.

When she again glanced toward the window, anxiousness over what she was thinking made him consider blocking her path to it.

"Tell me," he said. "Tell me what happened here."

Cara blinked slowly, as if shaking off the spell she had been under. She dropped the hand that had covered her mouth and looked at him.

"You might go through this all the time and be used to surprises, but it looks to me like you might have had a different kind of shock here. Am I right about that?" he asked.

There were shadows beneath Cara's eyes that he hadn't noticed previously. Her green eyes had a dark cast. To be honest, Rafe had had enough uncomfortable silence to last him a lifetime, so he walked toward her with his hands in his pockets to make reaching for her impossible. Cara, however she looked and no matter how haunted she was, remained an ongoing temptation for him. He had to accept that.

"Taking you home won't solve the problems that are haunting you, but it might be a healthier option," he said.

Cara shook her head.

Rafe persisted. "If you're going to stay, I need to understand what's going on so I can help. Please let me in."

She spoke at last, repeating what she'd said earlier. "I came here to find the past."

That's when Rafe saw the fangs.

He hid the anxiety this caused him. "You're finding part of that past in this room?" he asked, wanting very badly to hold Cara. "What did you see?"

Speaking slowly, as if she hadn't yet shaken off her recent shock, Cara said, "I don't think my mother knew she could be like the vampires before coming here. I think she found that out in this room, and the revelation frightened her."

Rafe waited for her to go on, sensing she would. Cara was wild-eyed. Her body was rigid. She had to get this out.

"My father almost died by fang, and my mother had developed a pair. Think how that might have gone down with my father, Rafe, if his lover started to look like a vampire."

He tried to comprehend the meaning of what she had just told him, and spoke carefully. "You've connected with another moment in your mother's past?"

She nodded. "Those fangs might have been the reason she jumped from this window. She needed to hide them from him."

He was catching on to the importance of that. "Rosalind fled because she developed a new talent for growing fangs? Was there a vampire in this room to instigate such a change?"

Cara's voice lowered. "No. That's the significance of this memory. She had changed on her own. She had grown a pair of fangs for the first time, possibly because my father had so much vampire venom in his system and she was near to him here."

Rafe waited, not sure what to say. What Cara said made sense in a Kirk-Killion kind of way that he wasn't up on.

"My father was here also," Cara continued. "He was looking at her, and there was blood on her lips from dealing with those fangs."

"Your father was here?" Rafe asked.

She nodded. "He was on that bed."

"Do you think she bit him?"

"I think she was afraid to be around him when the

fangs appeared. She was shocked and afraid of what my father would think after he had been so brutally attacked by the kind of being she was starting to become."

Rafe's insides twisted with the reminder that this visit to Miami hadn't been good for Cara. She couldn't have been paler. He felt her tension from two feet away.

As far as he could see, finding out about her parents' past wasn't making Cara feel better. It was only making things worse. If she wanted family history so damn badly, why hadn't she asked her parents to shed some light on the past? She was so brave in facing monsters, it seemed absurd that she couldn't face her parents for some answers.

"So Rosalind had discovered a new shape-shift and was terrified," he said.

"Yes," Cara replied breathlessly.

"What does that have to do with you? Why was discovering that such a shock?"

"She didn't understand how it could have happened, I think. Maybe she believed she could no longer control the shape-shifts in the way she had always believed she could."

"And that might lead to hurting your father? Hurting others?"

Cara's eyes grew wider. "Something sinister had taken place. In becoming like them, it would mean that vampires had some degree of kinship with her, and that she had become something else again, other than the previous merging of wolf and Banshee."

Cara took a step toward Rafe. "I think maybe she didn't actually know about the Banshee until then."

A light in Rafe's mind clicked on. He suddenly understood why Rosalind's jump from the window had been so important to Cara's understanding of the past.

Rosalind had been a rare black wolf before the attack on Colton, but afterward, as a result of the part she had played in rescuing him, Cara's mother had learned that she housed another entity, along with more abilities that she could have dreamed of.

Speaking was a chore for him after that surprising streak of enlightenment. Cara had just located the moment that her mother's life, and hers, had been forever changed.

"Do you want to leave?" he asked, cautiously gauging Cara's emotional state. "Do you need to? You don't have to be a tortured guest here where so many ghosts roam. Get your things or leave them, and come with me."

"I'm not going home. Not yet," she argued. "I have to see this through."

"See what through, Cara?"

"There is more to come. I wasn't just sent here to try to assimilate. I'm here for another reason. I'm sure of it."

"I won't take you home if you're not ready for that, but this room is no longer an option. We can go to my place. We can find out how many vampires will catch on to our bait-and-switch routine."

The darkness faded from Cara's eyes as though it had simply drained away. Was that because he cared about her and had offered some comfort?

The premonition and shared memory stuff should have scared him off, but a detective who was also a werewolf couldn't admit to being so easily intimidated. For better or worse, they were now a couple and he had to see this through. He had to help her, protect her, in whatever kind of situation arose next.

"What happens to you also happens to me by proxy,

Cara. Together, we're stronger. You just have to tell me what we're facing, and why, so that I can prepare."

She nodded again. "I don't know what's next, but I'm going to find out."

Rafe closed his eyes briefly to assimilate all of this. Imprinting could be a bitch or a boon, but it had rules.

No exit.

No detours.

Nowhere to run.

And damn it, he had no intention of trying to get out of this relationship, even if that were possible. As difficult as tonight had been—dilated eyes, wolf shapes, vampires, dead bodies and Banshees—he was in for the count. He was all hers, whoever and whatever Cara really was beneath all that black-haired beauty. This just wasn't the time or the place to tell her so.

She was moving toward the door. The idea of leaving the estate where she should have been safe from the rest of the outside world had been tempting to Cara. He took her bag from her. When they exited the room, he closed the door to seal off those damn ghosts.

They headed down the staircase. The house was quieter than it should have been, given the chaos surrounding the discovery of that body by the wall. Abducting their guest wasn't going to sit well with his folks, but Rafe had an argument ready in case he and Cara were caught making a quick exit.

He had gone over most of the possible consequences of taking Cara away. Rafe understood that he'd be breaking trust between the Landaus and the Kirk-Killions, and that he might be leaving the way open for more danger. Removing Cara, shielding her from so many watchful eyes, just seemed the right thing to do, if not for Cara's sanity, then for his.

She might find a few moments' peace in a smaller space that her parents had never seen or occupied. If they had to stake every damn vampire that found her, so be it.

They made it down all flights of stairs and halfway across the entrance hall before someone got in the way of their reaching the front door.

"Going somewhere?" his mother asked.

Chapter 19

The strange thing, Cara discovered as she studied her hostess, was that Dana Delmonico Landau wasn't half as put out as she appeared to be. Beneath the stern exterior lay a palpable aura of understanding that led Cara to believe a getaway might have been expected, at least by one member of this pack.

"Too many unwelcome newcomers know she's here," Rafe said. "It's too damn dangerous for Cara to stay right now."

Dana studied her son for a long moment before turning an inquisitive gaze on Cara. "Nothing can get past those walls out there, Cara. That, I can promise."

Though Rafe nodded in agreement, he said, "What about what's in this house?"

Dana didn't quite get what Rafe was saying. "No one here would hurt Cara."

"That's where you're wrong," Rafe countered. "Who's

to say that ghosts can't cause their own kind of damage to someone who is open to them?"

"Ghosts?" Dana echoed.

Rafe nodded. "Who is to say what can and can't hurt someone so unlike the rest of us?"

It was the first time Rafe had actually addressed the differences between them. With him, her inner wolf wanted dominance. The she-wolf wanted to reach out to Rafe, but the darker aspects of her soul were getting in the way.

"So you'll sign on as Cara's sole guardian?" Dana asked Rafe.

"For a night or two. Then we'll return," he answered.

Dana again looked to her. "You're okay with this, Cara?"

Cara nodded.

Dana gave them both a last once-over before stepping away from the door. "He won't like this," she said.

"I'm sure you can help with that," Rafe replied. "And you know where we'll be."

"So will those bloodsuckers, most likely."

"I hope not," Rafe said, and Cara saw that some of the strength of his will had been inherited from his mother.

The standoff was over. Rafe had chosen to be her champion, although he had no real notion yet of what he had signed on for. Did that make him a hero, or merely misguided in his affections?

A delicious warmth overcame Cara when Rafe took her hand. He liked to touch her and wasn't afraid. Slinging her bag over his shoulder, Rafe nodded to his mother and tossed Cara a quick look that said *Here we go.*

Leaving his father's house might have seemed like a stupid move to some, but it was based on solid reasoning. If vampires were like bloodhounds on a scent, Cara's lingering fragrance in and around the estate would occupy those bloodsuckers' cravings for some time. By taking her away, Rafe hoped Cara might have a brief respite from all that before they tracked her again. The bonus in all this was having Cara to himself.

He didn't dare lead her through the park or anywhere else on foot. With monster deflection in mind and a plan to try to leave no trail for others to follow, Rafe headed for the garage.

There were six cars parked there for him to choose from. He picked a small silver sedan that would blend in well with other cars on the road.

After opening the passenger door for Cara, he climbed behind the wheel to find the keys conveniently dangling from the ignition. The engine turned over with a soft roar, and they headed out. At the front gate, the guards waved him through, and then he and Cara were on their own.

"I wonder if you realize how powerful this thing is between us," he said.

Cara's gaze slid to him. She said, "Yes."

"If this location change doesn't work, we'll try something else to avoid the monsters," Rafe explained.

"You live near the water, and water can divert them," Cara said.

"Water?"

"It's what kept that vampire from seeing me on the beach. Salt water is a purifier," she said. "The smell distracts vampires by hampering their sensitivity to things around them. They hate it. Avoid it."

He said, "You're serious?"

Green eyes gleamed when they turned his way. Cara

had just given him another lesson in a course titled Vampires 101.

Those green eyes of hers did more than that, though. The seductive quality of her gaze produced enough heat to ease his tenseness. He began to relax as his mind retrieved images of him and Cara in the park, backed up against a tree, and how badly he had wanted to kiss her.

He wanted that same thing now.

"I have never been alone with a wolf like you," she confessed.

"I consider that a point in my favor," Rafe returned lightly. "It will be okay. You can rest and I'll stand guard."

"Do you understand why I wasn't allowed to be with others, Rafe?"

Several reasons came to mind, most of them having to do with her parents and the many forms she could take, but Rafe didn't say so.

"I've never been safe for anyone to be around. And I've certainly never been with someone willing to break down the barriers that have been erected for their own good," she said.

"Is that what I'm doing? Breaking barriers?"

"Yes."

"I'm willing to take my chances and see where this leads," Rafe said.

"Maybe that wasn't your choice, and our attraction is being guided by invisible hands," she suggested.

"Whose hands would those be?"

"Your parents'. My parents'. The imprinting phenomenon you keep thinking about could be derived from chance, or fate."

"Maybe all of those things combined," Rafe said.

"You believe that?"

Rafe nodded.

"I can read your thoughts, you know," Cara confessed.

"So, what am I thinking now?"

"You want to kiss me," she said.

Of course he did. Having Cara next to him drastically threatened his vow to not take advantage of her while she was in his care.

"It really is too late to fight the truth, and too late to question how we got this close so quickly," Rafe said. "It doesn't actually matter how, does it? Only that it happened. You do get that, Cara?"

He pulled the car to a curb near enough to his building for them to get to it quickly. Cara's only response to his remarks was a slow blink of those mesmerizing emerald eyes.

He turned off the engine and faced her. "From what I've witnessed, you fight for the right side, just as your parents did. You want to stamp out the evil that comes your way, and that objective makes you dangerous only to the bad guys."

Cara shook her head. "The spirit inside me is harder to control than anything you could imagine. She twists me into shapes I see only in my mind, and her hold on my soul doesn't diminish over time. That's where she resides, Rafe. In my soul."

She took a breath before continuing. "There's no option for releasing that spirit and no way to predict what she might do if I let down my guard. Vampires and demons want that spirit released. Death is their accomplice. If they can't have that spirit, then they will make do with the body sheltering it. Guess who that is."

"I thought the Banshee's deal was to predict oncoming death, and only that. Are you saying my understanding is wrong?"

"Wrong, yes, because of what happened all those years ago."

"How wrong?"

"The dark spirit can never be freed," Cara said.

Rafe thought that over. "You said freed. Does that mean you could release it if you wanted to, or if you found a way?"

"We made a pact to protect her, and that pact can't be broken."

"Who agreed to such a thing?" he asked. "Did they understand the consequences of such a vow?"

"My ancestors knew very well what they had agreed to. Those were the ancestors this spirit helped. If it wasn't for her help, I wouldn't be here. My mother wouldn't be here. My family's bloodline wouldn't exist."

"It's a her?" he said.

"The Banshee is a female spirit, or the closest thing to it. She can only exist within a female host."

Cara's explanation shed more light on things. She was bound to this dark spirit because of a blood vow by a family member in her past. This might mean that she could conceivably get rid of that spirit if she had a mind to, and instead she chose to honor that ancient pact.

Rafe nodded in understanding. "You said that instead of calling death to someone in your family, this spirit saved a life, and in doing so, went against its purpose for existing."

Cara nodded. "And we agreed to save the spirit, in turn."

"By passing it along in your family from soul to soul, which in essence hides it," Rafe said.

"That was the deal, yes."

"Yet other creatures seem to be able to find you and the Banshee with relative ease."

"And so some of us have become her protectors. We keep her safe."

He hadn't considered that line of reasoning, and it came as a surprise. Cara wasn't just unlucky to be inhabited by the dark spirit she spoke of. She was its guardian.

Or was she its jailer?

He didn't have a clear picture of what would happen if Cara were to release the spirit. The whole thing sounded ominous and inconceivable. It was no wonder that Cara had tried to keep the Banshee from appearing by shape-shifting away from it. Like his task of protecting the people of Miami, Cara was looking out for the spirit and had no choice in the matter.

"What would happen if you didn't adhere to that old vow?" he asked.

"Dark forces would come to deal with us all for that past transgression, and for harboring her."

Hell, that sounded bad. It also sounded like supernatural payback.

They were parked and couldn't afford to linger in the open, though Rafe wanted to remain close to Cara. He was beginning to comprehend the direness of Cara's position and the little effect he could have on something so serious.

She had said dark forces would come after them.

Damn it. All this made his job as a cop seem like a cakewalk. Because would anyone have liked the sound of that?

Chapter 20

No shock registered on the handsome face of the Were facing her. Cara found the whole idea of sharing confidences strangely intimate. Like their kiss in the park, talking things over with Rafe was also a new experience for her. By accepting Rafe as a confidant, she was allowing him a fair amount of power in their relationship. How he might direct that power was the question.

She was tired. Sleep had always been difficult, and it would be a luxury tonight if she managed to close her eyes. Things at home had been straightforward. All that mattered was living day by day to fight creatures that sought to limit her freedom. That wasn't so simple when others became involved with her story, and when Rafe had so quickly found a way to earn her trust.

He opened her car door for her but didn't offer a hand. His reluctance to touch her wasn't born of fear. It was a compassionate attempt to give her time to process what they meant to each other.

He gestured for her to precede him toward his apartment building. Their arms brushed when she did, and that slightest of sensations again set her senses ablaze.

"Cara?" The tender quality of Rafe's voice amplified her body's sudden buildup of heat. She couldn't let down her guard, but she was better prepared for ghosts and demons than the delicious distraction Rafe Landau posed.

The adrenaline surge that hit her now was similar to fight-or-flight syndrome. Yet Rafe wasn't the enemy. She couldn't take her eyes from him, and her body tingled all over. He had caused her to question the future and had made it clear he would have preferred to have her all to himself, with no dark spirit standing in the way of their union. Rafe was ingrained in her thoughts now and was therefore haunting her, still.

"The beach isn't safe tonight," he warned. "Too many people might be out, enjoying a late-night rendezvous, which could potentially bring more trouble if there do happen to be any vampires around. We should stay inside until dawn. I'd be willing to bet that sunrise can't be too far off."

He was avoiding the next question he probably wanted to ask her by circling the conversation back to the vampires. Still, she knew what Rafe might be thinking after telling him more details about the Banshee.

"I can't release the dark spirit, Rafe. I can't ever do that, and it would be useless to suggest such a thing."

He said, "I do understand about promises and vows, Cara."

As they reached the stairs that led to his apartment, she said, "This means I can never be free in the way you might wish me to be."

"Maybe you're wrong about what I wish," he returned, pausing on the stairs to look at the beach. Thankfully, he changed the subject. "Is anyone out there?"

"No one that should concern us at the moment."

Rafe sighed with relief and used a key to unlock his front door. Then he waited for her to precede him inside. A light switch near the door illuminated the room with a wash of soft ambient light. It was easy for Cara to like what she saw.

The space was relatively small and not crowded with furniture. The flooring was a cool gray tile. Closed shutters on two front windows blocked out the night and the view. Rafe's furniture consisted of a leather couch with a small table beside it and a pair of fabric-covered chairs. Three interior doors led to other rooms. One of those would be his bedroom.

She turned her attention to the wall of glass that led to the balcony where she had first seen Rafe and the trouble he was in. Only a faint trace of the vampire he'd brought here remained. Most of Rafe's surroundings smelled like him.

The apartment was the exact opposite of the luxurious Landau estate, and it suited Rafe's personality. Free of pack rules and onlookers, Rafe could be his own man here.

Ocean sounds pervaded the room. Though the glass doors were closed, the rhythmical lull of waves washing onto the shore created a backdrop of comforting sounds that Cara welcomed.

"Home sweet home, small and simple," he said, watching her.

"This is more like my home," she told him. "Minus the trimmings."

"Hell. I have trimmings?"

Cara resisted the smile she felt tugging at the corners of her mouth.

"I'd like to hear more about where you live," he said, dropping her bag and crossing to the windows to make sure the shutters were closed tight. He pointed to one of the interior doors. "The bedroom is over there. Bathroom is to the right, and the kitchen is opposite. I don't suppose you ate whatever my mother fixed for you tonight, which was probably a good thing. She was a great cop. As a cook, she's not quite so special."

He waited a few beats before adding with a lazy smile, "You do eat normal food?"

The teasing was supposed to put her at ease, and worked. Rafe wanted her to like his home enough to feel comfortable. Everything he had done tonight had been for her, and she was learning a lot about Rafe Landau in bits and pieces.

"Do you have tea?" she asked, because he was waiting for her to speak.

"Sure. How about something terribly fast food—like to go with it?"

"Anything would be nice, as long as there's a lot of it," Cara replied.

When he offered her a dazzling, contagious smile, Cara couldn't quite recall the last time she had let herself enjoy a moment like this, however brief it might turn out to be.

This sense of having encountered unexpected happiness wasn't going to last, of course, because that would have been asking too much. She and Rafe weren't people with typical needs and wants. And they had too many secrets left that hadn't, out of necessity, been shared.

Dressed in her own clothes, Rafe's houseguest was no less seductive than she had been in his shirt and not much else. Cara seemed to prefer black—a black shirt and loose black pants. She had dared to kick off her boots, which might have meant that she would stay put for a while.

She had sleepy eyes. Now and then, her dark lashes lowered over them. She sat on the sofa with both hands folded in her lap as if she were a prim and proper schoolgirl instead of one of the world's most dangerous creatures. She had already removed the bandage on her hand.

Rafe noticed how frequently her gaze returned to the glass doors. She probably yearned for the water he had first found her near, but they both knew it would be a bad idea to let her go. Impossible, really. The goal was to evade vampires, not to send them an invitation.

It was 5:00 a.m. when he finally looked at the clock. Only a couple hours of seclusion were left, and then Cara could swim to her heart's delight while he found a way to finagle another day off from work—an especially difficult request with the investigation of that body underway. Harboring a sexy hybrid werewolf in need of a guardian wouldn't cut it as an excuse with his human boss.

He was curious about that body, though, and how deeply it might be wrapped up in Cara's business. Had it been deposited near the wall as a warning for the pack harboring Cara? Could the damage to that human have been caused by the same creature that had gotten close enough to Cara to break a few bones in her hands? The thought of that made him sick.

He hadn't kissed Cara again. True to his own personal promise, he hadn't gone near her, though waning willpower kept him riveted to the chair by the front door.

She had eaten a sandwich and drunk four cups of tea.

Neither of them had slept, because who could have on a night filled with so many dark deeds?

Cara didn't talk or offer any more confidences. She didn't request a shower or look around the other rooms. Her gaze connected with his every few minutes, inviting him to get out of the chair, but he refrained from acting on his instincts. The result of ignoring all those feelings and physical desires for closeness was a thickening of the atmosphere that made the room seem even smaller than it was.

Though the coffee in his mug had gone cold, Rafe drank it.

Guilt was also part of his new dilemma. The pack would have discovered more details about that murder in the hours before dawn, and he should have been there with them. He would have been there if he had left Cara in his family's care, but again, that hadn't been a choice.

His wish to keep her in his sight was strong enough to override other necessities. That's the way the imprinting process worked. Though still in the early stage, the compulsion to mate with Cara took precedence over most other things. Until they fully mated—on a bed or elsewhere, with him settled between Cara's thighs— every waking thought revolved around personal needs that both of them were pretending to ignore. Cara also felt these needs. He saw it in her big green eyes.

Since tone of voice and sharing confidences were other components of seduction, they didn't speak. Prolonged eye contact had to be avoided.

When golden streaks of sunlight finally filtered into the room, Rafe got up to stretch his legs. After removing his shirt and his boots, he took Cara by the hand and led her to the door. He preceded her down the steps and across the sidewalk that bordered the sand. There, he pulled her around so that she had to look at him.

"Freedom at last," he said. "But that also means no getting naked in the daylight, so we'll have to make do in our pants."

He wanted nothing more than to get Cara naked, and cautiously guarded that thought. The call for him to get to work would come any time now. Sun worshipers from the hotel and surrounding buildings would soon hit the beach, and his moment alone with Cara would be lost. Until then, they could relax their vigilance. Monsters didn't roam when the sun came out.

Cara was all his.

The sand felt warm on his feet and already reflected the sunlight. Cara dug in with her bare toes as she turned toward the water. She removed her shirt and tossed it aside, but kept her pants on as she broke into a run.

Rafe followed her, leaving a few feet of distance between them. When Cara reached the water, she didn't hesitate to wade in. He caught the item she tossed to him as he followed her into the surf. It was her pants.

Everything after that happened in slow motion.

Cara turned around in waist-deep water. Across the lapping silvery foam, she gave him a wide-eyed stare.

"Oh, no, you don't," Rafe said, his warning muted by the crash of the next wave. Damn it, he had misjudged the freedom he had just offered to her, and what Cara would do with it. He had believed she was on the same page.

The back of his neck prickled as he waded in after her. But it was too late. In a repeat of the night before, and in spite of events that had taken place between then and now, Cara was suddenly gone. She just vanished.

Knowing that it was futile to go after her, he nevertheless had to try. Rafe moved into deeper water and swam in a direction parallel to the shore. Strong strokes took him halfway up the beach, where there was no sign of the female he had promised to protect.

He had let her go, and there would be consequences, though the worst of it was the way he felt. "Cara…" he messaged to her. "Don't do this."

The only response he got was the steady drumming of the waves and the irregular beat of his heart.

He couldn't wait all day for the runaway to show up. An hour had passed since he had lost Cara, and he needed to retrieve his cell phone and get down to other business. He'd have to also confess to his family about having lost her in broad daylight. And really, where would a naked woman go? How far would she get?

Rafe walked back to his apartment, dropped Cara's clothes beside his on the floor in the bathroom and stepped into the shower, not sure what was worse… thinking about Cara out there, or in here—as a runaway, or as his lover. He tried not to imagine her sleek body turning to him, and the way he might have pressed her to the cool, wet tiles as he readied for the move he hadn't been able to get out of his mind since meeting her.

He could almost see the water dripping down her face, and the look in her eyes that told him she wanted the same thing. He could feel his hands on her, his mouth on her, his hardness entering her softness. It all felt so real, and so right, he wondered if this was a premonition of things to come or merely more wishful thinking, and if those two things had become inexplicably intertwined. The images and sensations were so vivid, so potent and realistic, he cut the damn shower short so he could again breathe properly and regain perspective.

Hell, this imprinting business was a bitch.

Soon he was fully dressed, armed with his gun and his badge and ready to roll. He left his front door unlocked in case Cara returned and headed for the street, wishing that his only problem in the next half hour was the ribbing he'd get from other cops if they saw him driving his father's luxury car.

It turned out he didn't have to worry about that. Cameron had beaten him there and was leaning casually against the silver sedan at the curb.

"Thought you might need some help," the Were said, adding with a wry grin, "with the car."

Chapter 21

The Were who had captured a piece of her heart in so short a time didn't return to his apartment before the sun went down. Cara's boundless need for freedom, even from her new feelings for Rafe, continued to resonate in every cell in her body.

At sunset, most of the humans on the beach had dispersed. Despite the few people still around, Cara finally left the water, figuring the others who saw her were so skimpily clad themselves, they might simply let it go. And there was no evidence of vampires flooding the area. The salt water would have covered her tracks if there had been a fanged scout or two.

Rafe had left the door unlocked. Her open bag was on the table where she had left it that morning. Damp clothes, Rafe's and hers, had been hung up on a rack to dry.

She had trouble in the shower that not only smelled like Rafe, but reflected happier things related to his life.

His thoughts seemed to linger there. Those thoughts made her blush.

Dressed in dry clothes, Cara walked from room to room studying the details. Rafe was neat. Several framed photos of his family lined one hallway. There was a television set and a radio in the bedroom. She ran a hand over the mattress, feeling for hints of Rafe, though no one had slept in that bed last night.

She didn't have any family photos at home, or a refrigerator filled with things to eat. Although comfortable and snug, the Kirk-Killion cottage served up more basic fare. She hadn't felt any lack of comfort while growing up, or the necessity for company other than her mother's and father's until the dreams had started. Dreams that turned out to be of Rafe, and a life like his.

When a knock broke the silence, Cara whirled to face the door. Rafe had returned. He had known she would be here. Would he be angry? Upset about that morning?

"Are you decent?" he called out. And Cara let go of the breath she had been holding.

Rafe's familiar scent preceded him into the room like a separate being. Contrary to her misgivings about seeing him after her disappearance, Cara felt relief. She was sorry she had given him the slip. Rafe had become her mooring, her stabilizing rock in a new world, and he had been confident about her return.

Their gazes connected. Through that meeting of their eyes, their thoughts and hopes melded together. Rafe's expression showed his hunger and his need for more than just speaking to her, but he said, "Are you ready?" without acting on those needs or chastising her for the earlier defection.

"Yes," she replied, gleaning a picture of where Rafe

wanted to take her—the place that took precedence over their desires and what they both would rather have done.

Their wants were to be put on hold.

They were going back to the park.

She was to help him find a killer.

There were working streetlights surrounding the park on three sides, but not to the east, where gangs occasionally used the globes for target practice. The east side was where he took Cara.

Rafe parked his older SUV next to two unmanned police cruisers and Cameron's showy beige sports car. "Cops are in the west and Weres are everywhere else," he said to her. "The body we found near the wall has been taken to the morgue and the investigation is well underway."

Cara's eyes were clear and focused, he thought. A good sign. Still, he would have preferred to have been with her anywhere but here.

"There haven't been any other deaths today, such as the one that dark spirit predicted. Not yet, anyway. So now," he said, leaning back in the seat, "tell me about that gunshot. The one that came too close to you for comfort."

Cara replied quickly. "One shot."

"You're sure?"

She nodded. "Only one."

"Pistol or rifle?"

"He wasn't close."

"Rifle then, maybe. It came from which direction?"

After scanning the park through the windshield, Cara said, "Where it was the darkest."

"Figures. Can you show me where you were? Do you think you can find that place again?"

"Didn't the big Were named Jonas tell you?"

"Jonas has been inconsiderately MIA today, so it's up to you, if you have anything to show me that can help with this investigation."

"You believe that whoever fired a shot at me could have had something to do with the death of the human?"

"I don't believe that. We have to start somewhere, however, and you encountered trouble near the same time that body was being mutilated. I wanted to take another look around without the rest of my police team here, since I'd have a hard time explaining about you or keeping you from getting mixed up in the investigation."

"Won't we be interfering?"

"That depends on how it turns out. If a Were had anything to do with that human's murder, it's our job to find him. If it was something else, well, we wouldn't want to cause a panic about that, would we?"

Cara and Rafe got out of the car and he rested a hand on the warm metal hood. In any other situation, he would have hurdled the car to get at her.

She looked at him soberly. "I didn't tell you everything."

"Yeah, I figured as much," Rafe said. "Better late than never is how the saying goes, so any light you can shed would help. Would you like to tell me what it is that you didn't mention?"

Rafe rounded the car slowly, careful to give Cara time to respond to his question.

"I'm sorry about today," she said.

All he could think to say was "Okay."

Her eyes narrowed on the park. "I don't think that bullet was meant for me, as you all supposed. I don't think it was a wolf hunter out there."

"Why do you think that?" Rafe asked.

"The bullet carried a strange scent."

Rafe drew in a breath, anticipating that Cara would mention silver. He carried silver rounds in a hidden pocket on his belt because a bad werewolf was a danger to everyone, not just to humans.

"Can you describe the smell?" he asked.

"The bullet smelled like fire."

All right. He had not expected that.

"A wolf hunter would have used silver," he pointed out.

She nodded. "No hunter."

Rafe had to process what she had said. If Cara was right about the shooter not hunting Weres, what could the imbecile have been after, and with a bullet that Cara said smelled like fire? Cara, who was a kind of monster hunter herself, would be able to tell what kind of bullet had come anywhere near her.

Needing more thinking room, Rafe absently tugged at the collar of his shirt. It was important for them to find that bullet. Imperative, actually.

With a little luck, maybe they'd locate a casing on the ground or the damn bullet embedded in the trunk of a tree. It might not help to explain how the murder victim got a severed spine, but there was a chance that bullet could provide some kind of a clue that could give this investigation a kick in the right direction.

"Can you show me where it happened?" he asked Cara.

Cara gestured for him to follow her.

After the events of last night, walking in the dark, with Cara a few steps in front of him, kept Rafe on edge. Cara could drop to all fours at any moment and race away in the opposite direction if she had a mind to. He now knew that her MO was to run away from her feelings for him.

He could still hear the howl she'd made last night. The shock had stayed with him.

The park wasn't quiet tonight, either. Though the perimeter was blocked off by cops on foot and in squad cars, there was still plenty of noise. Muted music came from the boulevard. Sirens wailed in the distance and car horns honked. Those sounds dimmed as he and Cara strode deeper into the darkness with their inner radar humming.

His companion walked with an outward show of confidence he didn't feel. Cara exhibited no sign of having concerns about who or what might jump out of the shadows. After his close call with bloodsucking Brandi, he preferred to place his trust in Cara's expertise in the realm of the supernatural.

"Not far now," she said, as if she could have arrived at the spot they were looking for with her eyes shut.

They had to find something soon or turn back. They were nearing the southeastern portion of the grounds where crimes occurred on a weekly basis. The pack had taken to patrolling the area in nightly sweeps and would likely have been here soon after sundown, along with the cops. It wasn't much past that time now, but Rafe recognized the smell of trouble.

They were going to have company.

Any packmate out for a prolonged stroll would at least know about Cara's visit, so bumping into one would merely be an inconvenience. It was everyone else Rafe had to worry about. Humans pretty much all smelled alike, which made telling the difference between good guys and bad guys a toss-up until their behavior came to light. Bad guys tended to carry guns and knives, but the kind of trouble Rafe sensed smelled like…death.

They moved in silence over dry, trampled grass and beneath trees that didn't yet cast shadows. Overhead, the moon was partially covered by clouds. In five days Weres would come out from behind walls and shadows to howl at that moon. A park full of Miami's werewolves was probably the safest place around if anyone dared to come here to cause problems.

His attention had slipped. Ahead of him, Cara stopped suddenly and stood very still, driving Rafe's nerves to a state of red alert. His right hand went to his weapon and hovered there. He heard Cara whisper, "Company," as he got a whiff of what that company might be.

Cara placed a hand on his to keep him from drawing his gun and shook her head adamantly. She said the words no one wanted to hear in such a precariously dangerous situation.

"Won't do any good against this guy."

This wasn't a memory. What was happening was real because Rafe, beside her, had also picked up on the smell. He also noticed the way she had to speak around the sharp tips of her fangs, and warily glanced away.

"Damn it. Another one?" he asked.

The only questions she had now were how soon that bloodsucker would take to get to here and which one of them would tangle with it first.

Rafe was keyed up in a way that made her nerves dance. He was probably angry the search for the bullet had been interrupted and plagued by the reminder of how he'd been fooled by the ancient parasite he'd invited into his apartment yesterday.

He took a step and Cara matched it.

"Which one of us do you suppose looks like dinner?" he asked cynically.

"This is highly unusual," Cara explained. "Normally, vamps don't come after wolves unless there is no one else around."

"Either their tastes have evolved, or we're just lucky." Rafe glanced at her again. "If they don't usually like wolves, why would they bother to come around here, where there are so many of us? And why did they attack your father here, in this same park?"

"I think they attacked my father to rid the city of one of the oldest werewolf lines. They knew about the Lycans who could do them some major damage. Every wolf they took down would mean more freedom to prey upon Miami's population."

"Well, that plan didn't turn out so well, did it? Maybe this sucker won't overstep its bounds."

Cara wanted to tell Rafe that vampires had no bounds, but just then a tall skeletal form cloaked in black slid into the shadows between two trees...and her fangs began to throb.

Chapter 22

Rafe tried not to show the disgust he felt as he faced this animated corpse. The creature was painful to look at and hadn't bothered to hide its true semblance. Or so Rafe surmised, because nothing could have been worse than this guy.

Unlike the high-gloss version of the undead that Brandi had presented him with, this bloodsucker looked and smelled like it had recently crawled up from a grave. It had a white face and gray hair. Red-rimmed eyes glowered at him from a sunken face that was not much more than a conglomeration of exposed bone. There was barely enough flesh on its lips to hide the bloodsucker's long, pointed fangs. The way it stared was unnerving.

Cara, on the other hand, didn't seem surprised by the awful appearance of this gaunt apparition. Her vibe was calm as she waited for their visitor to make a move. For her, this was a regular occurrence.

Rafe broke the silence by muttering, "Where's a carved wooden stake when we need one?"

The vampire—a male, Rafe thought, but couldn't be sure—emitted a hissing noise through its fangs that was reminiscent of steam escaping from a vent. Rafe got the feeling the vamp was angry, and yet its face didn't reflect that. The creature didn't move. This guy was probably sizing them up and wondering if it could manage a twofer. Or maybe this ugly bastard hadn't expected to find two Weres in the park tonight and was therefore reassessing its options...as if it had any.

"Wait," Cara softly cautioned Rafe.

"Which of us is the target?" Rafe asked, ready to tear this creature apart with his bare hands if it showed any intention of going after Cara. Those bones looked brittle enough to snap without much force.

The vampire finally took a step, which was actually more like a glide, as if it wore skates beneath the rags covering its body.

That was creepy.

"You don't belong here," Cara said.

Rafe heard the warning in her tone. Her voice was like steel.

"What do you want?" she asked the creature.

Rafe clenched his fists when it replied in a hollow voice that sounded like it had originated in an echo chamber.

"Information."

"We are not friends or allies," Cara said.

"Yet we are sometimes like cousins, are we not?" the vampire returned, showing more wit than Rafe would have imagined possible given the bastard's tattered state.

"Not even close," Cara said.

The vampire pointed a bony finger at her. Rafe leaned forward ready to act. "The dark is strong in you, wolf girl," the vampire remarked.

Rafe wondered if Cara wore her darkness like a special perfume only other hybrids could smell. Vampires, it seemed to him, were another kind of hybrid. They weren't completely one thing or another—not completely dead, or they couldn't be walking around, and not fully alive, either—which made them creatures able to somehow bridge the gap between life and death.

Did they like being in limbo and feasting on the life force of others? This wasn't the time or place to ask that question. Rafe avoided looking at Cara to see how she had reacted to the vampire's remark. It would have been suicidal to shift his attention from the creature in front of them after seeing how fast his fanged date had moved.

"What do you want?" Cara asked again.

"Life," the vamp replied.

"Then you've come to the wrong place," she said.

The creature dropped its hand. "And yet you have so much of it. So much life. Surely you can spare some of it for a cousin in need."

"You can't bite me," Cara said. "I think you already know that."

Rafe resisted the urge to glance sideways at her. This was news to him. If vampires couldn't bite Cara, how in hell did they assume they'd be able to get at what her body kept hidden inside?

"She is mine to carry," Cara said.

"Perhaps she would like true darkness for a change," the vamp suggested. "Could it be that you have carried this burden long enough? Perhaps the spirit longs for freedom after all this time."

So that was it. The vampire wanted to become the Banshee's new host. But according to Cara, that kind of transference couldn't happen, and she'd never allow it even if it was possible.

"I do not own the spirit," Cara said. "She is not mine to give away. Nor would I try. My family owes her a debt of honor. The Banshee must remain with us, and it is my place to guard her."

The vampire's eyes darkened considerably. "I am sorry to hear that."

"Why?" Rafe broke in. "Why are you sorry to hear that?"

He didn't like the way the red-rimmed eyes turned to him.

"I am old. Blood no longer sustains me," the dark-eyed sucker replied.

Rafe didn't really want to know what that meant. Chatting with this vampire was disconcerting enough. Finding out that vampires—at least some of them—retained their wits and could speak in proper sentences was worrisome. The questions pummeling him now were crucial ones about what this bloodsucker would do next. Would Cara, who hated the breed that had sent her father into exile and plagued her current existence, let this one go?

There were rustling sounds from the west that brought Rafe a wary moment of relief. A new scent filled the air. Weres were coming. They would see this creature, and if the vampire valued what was left of its pitiful existence, it would have to flee.

He watched the vampire turn to look in the direction of the noise. In the moonlight, Rafe caught the gleam of exposed fangs between Cara's full lips. If the vamp stayed, Cara's fangs would also stay, and the Weres searching the park would see them. But the dilemma of outing Cara seemed trivial against the prospect of his friends in a face-off with an ancient bloodsucker that looked like death itself.

As the sounds got closer, Rafe's tension escalated to a higher pulse-pounding frequency. What would happen? Would this creature do something to save itself?

He didn't have to wait long to find out. The bony parasite nodded to Cara as if acknowledging defeat, then spun around with almost subliminal speed…and vanished.

Rafe kept his focus on the spot where it had stood, not at all sure why the fanged creep had retreated so easily without a fight. Cara seemed to know the answer, but she didn't offer an explanation.

She shook her head hard, as if she could rid herself of the fangs that way. Whereas she hadn't given any hint of concern over meeting the vampire, she now buzzed with nervousness over the possibility of meeting the approaching Weres.

To vampires she was no freak, only an adversary.

Right at that moment, Rafe wasn't so sure about her ability to fit in with the pack, either. The fangs had not retracted, and he hurt for her. With her. The fierceness of his need to protect Cara kicked in so swiftly, he had little time to think about anything else.

The others were almost here, and each passing second made Cara more anxious. She was as white as a sheet.

"It will be okay," Rafe said, moving closer to her. "Touch me, Cara. Let me hold you."

There were other things he didn't say. Couldn't confess.

"Touch me." Not for the sake of the lust I feel, or my

need to possess you, body and soul… "Touching me will bring out your wolf."

She let him slip his right arm around her and met his eyes when he demanded it. And as easily as that, with no more words spoken, and as his eyes bored into hers, her razor-sharp incisors disappeared and a hint of color crept back into her cheeks.

Cara tasted blood, and it was her own. She had bitten down hard on her lower lip when Rafe touched her, mindful of what he was doing, and why. But she had also heard the thoughts that had preceded his willingness to help her—thoughts about lust and possession that again ignited sparks of desire deep inside her.

If they had been alone…

If no one had been coming…

She would have acted on those desires.

They way Rafe made her feel was exciting. She was comforted by the knowledge that though he saw what she was capable of, the son of Miami's alpha wanted her anyway. They were connected by a thread that had stretched tightly between souls. She had no further doubts about this connection or what it might mean, and the remark Rafe had made the night before reappeared in her mind now like a haunting refrain.

Maybe the true test of your presence here is to see if I'd be the one to bite.

Was there a possibility that her parents had sent her to Miami to meet her mate and Rafe had been part of the plan all along?

Who would dare to concoct such a bond when she didn't resemble the rest of the Weres and would never fit in? What kind of parents did Rafe have if they had agreed to such a thing?

She was missing something. They all were. But she couldn't afford to be any more distracted than she already was. The vampire they had faced wasn't alone. Very old bloodsuckers seldom traveled solo, and this vamp had likely walked the earth for centuries. Older even than the term ancient, it had confessed to be nearing a state of nonexistence. Maybe there had been no fight left in it, no real strength, other than a short list of last needs.

"There are more of them," she said to Rafe. "We have to prepare."

Rafe frowned. "More vampires?"

"That one was a master. A leader, and the head of a nest. Others fight for him and do his bidding. The loss of control over his body means nothing when he commands his own fanged army."

"When he snaps his fingers, how many will come?"

"I'm not certain," she confessed.

"Does that bastard believe it can take the spirit from you by force if you refuse to relinquish it?"

Cara shook her head. "It will try to kill everyone and everything around me so that I might change my mind about giving up the Banshee."

"It will go after those it perceives to be the weakest first?" Rafe mused.

She closed her eyes. "Yes. Then they will go after the pack the way they went after my father, hoping to eliminate werewolves one by one."

Rafe ran a hand over his eyes as if that could erase the image of the fanged monster they'd just encountered. "Run away," he said to Cara. "Get behind the wall. We can handle this."

She shook her head stubbornly.

"Why did you let this vampire go if it was so dangerous?"

"I let it go because…" Her reply faded as Cara sensed Were presence that was so strong and vibrant, it undermined what she had been about to say. Along with that vibration came a faint sense of familiarity.

She turned, and Rafe turned with her. The three Weres who appeared didn't reek of the kind of power she had detected in the periphery. They didn't cause the air to change or the night to shiver the way the other more elusive presence had.

Again, she heard her name whispered and looked to Rafe, whose lips didn't move. She tuned in to Rafe's thoughts and found them directed to his packmates and the need to catch the vampire.

There was no time to tell him that she had let the vampire go because she was beginning to see a pattern in the things taking place, and that this vampire might yet have a part to play in her future. As sickening as that thought was, it had taken root.

"Vampire," Rafe said when Cameron and two other Weres Cara hadn't yet met drew up beside them. "And it has friends."

All eyes landed on her before drifting off to check out the surrounding area. Cara had no idea if any of these Weres had ever seen or even believed in the fanged hordes that existed in their city. For them, this was going to be a wake-up call.

"Five," she said, inhaling deeply, sure now about the tally. "There are five of them, moving like a bad wind."

Chapter 23

Rafe watched Cara's eyes glaze over as she stared into the distance. She seemed to have retreated into a space only she could access, where sight and scent and hearing provided her with foreknowledge of what might appear in the next few minutes.

There was no time to waste. Nor was there a need to guess what these creatures wanted, since the pasty-faced master of this little oncoming group had been quite clear about that.

The ancient bloodsucker wanted to get its talons on the dark spirit Cara harbored, believing the spirit could prolong its existence, such as that existence was. If blood no longer bolstered it, surely a Banshee could. And if a vampire played host to such a powerful darkness, there was no way to calculate the kind of damage it could inflict.

It was imperative that the sucker never got close to Cara again.

"Cara, go," he said. "You've done your share of fighting here."

She ignored him, just as Rafe feared she might. This was what Cara did, what she had been bred for. Fighting was the price she paid for being born a Kirk-Killion.

"Rafe," Cameron called from beyond the closest trees. "Are you coming?"

This time, he and Cara would fight together. Beside him, she was gathering herself and her energy. If anyone looked more closely, they might have seen the glow of all her talents coming together for a singular purpose.

God...he wanted her. Badly.

One look passed between them before they both took steps toward the oncoming red tide...and it was the only look that could have counted.

The night stank of death and bad intentions. Cara wasn't the only one who noticed. Rafe and Cameron had been joined by the two other Weres she had seen before while behind the Landau walls. Theirs was a formidable group, but only she could change shape tonight to call up more strength and power.

Against five wolfed-up werewolves, five vampire fledglings wouldn't have stood a chance. But werewolves in human shape, though fast and dexterous, didn't have same kind of speed these bloodsuckers had. Cara wasn't sure what was going to happen. She silently promised these Weres that she would fight for them with every last ounce of her strength.

The first wave of attack brought three fanged creatures. One after the other, the emaciated, white-faced, skeletal apparitions appeared. Silent. Ghastly. Deadly.

Cameron hit the first one head-on. Rafe leaped toward the second. She took the third, backed by the two large Were guards who'd probably also been instructed to keep her safe, when it was actually going to be the other way around.

Sounds of their struggles echoed in the dark. If these vampires assumed darkness was on their side, they had another think coming. Werewolf sight was as legendary as the stories about the moon that ruled their changes, and each Were here carried a weapon—a bone-handled, silver-bladed knife that could stop a vampire if placed correctly, though the best way to seal a vampire's fate for good was to sever its head from its body.

She had something better, something besides the fangs and the claws that had appeared simultaneously to combine two very different parts of herself. She had an intimate knowledge of vampire behavior that was a fast pass into their messy, often jumbled thoughts. Cara used that now.

"Two more are coming," she shouted to the others.

The push was on to make sure these three were out of commission by the time the next two arrived. The Landau Weres were fighting fiercely, bravely, honorably. She pressed past Rafe and turned to stand back to back with him. The fanged invader Rafe was fighting was large but might not have had as much at stake in the fight as these Weres did. She prayed this would give the werewolves an edge.

"Throat," she shouted to Rafe, who swore vehemently as he repeatedly blocked the vampire's almost subliminally quick fang strikes. "Or heart."

"I thought these suckers were heartless," he tossed back with a grunt as his vampire opponent's fangs got a little too close to Rafe's face.

"Their bodies don't know that. You have to make them see it."

Cara slashed at her attacker and caught hold of it with her claws. She felt its hunger and its need to follow a directive. That, too, was necessary information. These beasts were here because their master demanded it. They would never have attacked a group of Weres otherwise.

The other approaching vamps hadn't yet joined in. They were now waiting on the sidelines for the Weres to weaken with fatigue. Through the sounds of fighting, Cara heard their jaws snapping.

Rafe's Weres fought to the best of their abilities and were still standing, but no one had turned the tide or gained the advantage after several long minutes. These vamps had speed and the Weres had strength, but how long would that strength last?

Something had to be done, and she had to do it. The solution might shock Rafe and the others, and yet there was only one way open to her for getting rid of these emaciated parasites.

She called on her wolf, demanding that it listen to her and take shape in spite of the fangs in her mouth. Since she still had claws, part of her wolf was already in evidence. All that was needed was for her to tip the balance.

She had done this before to avoid the wail of the Banshee, and now she demanded the extra burst of power her wolf would provide. There was a chance the dark spirit would feel the extremes of this shift and use the energy for her own benefit, so caution was needed to avoid the death caller.

Shifting was always dangerous for that reason, and she had undergone too many shape-shifts in the past two days. Still, she had to try.

Wolf…

Come.

Now!

The wolf particles in her bloodstream responded to her command with a flare of molten heat that seared her veins. An image of the shape she needed to find flashed in Cara's mind. Not the animal with four legs this time, but another one that shocked her system with a combined jolt of power and pain that was like being pinned by a silver dart.

The sound of her bones cracking made Rafe turn his head. The shudders of her muscles reshaping brought a slow hiss from her throat. Cara swayed and shook off a brief round of dizziness, but stood her ground. She clamped her teeth together as her heart rate accelerated and the werewolf, half human, half wolf, hot-blooded and feral, soared into existence.

One more strike with her powerful claws was all it took for her to dust the vampire beside her. Rafe, still slashing at his nemesis, shoved his vampire away to look at her.

Maybe it was his expression, or the way he blinked back his surprise, that sent her shape-shift spiraling into another direction than the one she had intended. And maybe it was the way his vampire attacker's red-lined black eyes caught hers that caused the rift between her intended shift and what actually took place.

Her wolf sucked back into itself with a reversal that was so swift and unexpected, Cara's lungs were squeezed. More dizziness hit with a whirl of vertigo that nearly sent her to her knees as the wolf she had called upon suddenly devolved, leaving the space it was supposed to have occupied open for another shape.

And there was nothing she could do about it.

Shock had no place on a battlefield, so Rafe had to swallow his. But his skin chilled so fast, his teeth began to chatter as the temperature around him dropped considerably. The speed of these vampires trumped anything he had ever seen.

A chill wind assailed him from behind. His shirt, damp with the sweat of his exertion, turned to ice. He couldn't turn to find the source of this latest phenomenon, didn't dare, although he figured it was related to Cara, and that he wasn't going to like it.

Even the vampires recognized the change in the atmosphere. Their efforts slowed. They stopped moving as the icy wind blew through the area like the touchdown of a tornado.

Shrieks went up from fanged mouths. Something sticky hit Rafe in the face, and he didn't take the time to find out what it was. A shout went up from Cameron, followed by another from one of the guards. Rafe's hands had frozen in a raised position and he left them there, unable to comprehend what was going on and why the vampires had stopped fighting.

For a long, seemingly endless moment, Rafe thought he might have died here in the park and was about to bridge the gap to wherever his next stop might be. Time had slowed further, dragging the movement surrounding him along with it. Turning his head again took real effort. Breathing was tough. He finally managed to glance behind him, looking for Cara in the last place where she had been standing.

He saw nothing at first because, hell…it wasn't winter and this was Miami, and yet snow was falling, tiny foul-smelling gray snowflakes that drifted down to cover his shoulders.

But these weren't snowflakes. The disgusting flurry of ashy particles was all that remained of the vampires.

There wasn't one damn vampire left. And by the expressions on the faces of his packmates, they were as stunned as he was.

Cameron said, "They're gone. All of them."

Panic struck Rafe square in the chest. He spun around on his heels and called out, "Cara?"

The silence that met him seemed unnatural after all the grunting and shrieks. Darkness hovered over the area like a big black cloud. There was no glint of moonlight.

Rafe strained to focus his enhanced sight. "Why don't you answer?"

His chest hurt. His head throbbed. Rafe's packmates, gathered around him, were staring at something above them. He had never been as afraid of anything as he was right then, when his gaze rose to the lowest branch of the tree beside him.

And damn it…that fear was warranted.

Chapter 24

Cara was there, though unrecognizable. Rafe felt her presence in the tree without having to look. What had happened to the vampires was also suddenly clear.

Cara had beaten them at their own game.

The sight of her latest incarnation rendered him speechless. Cara's shape had altered again, and she might have gone too far this time. She had become a dark entity that was difficult to look at. There was hardly a visible outline, because the area around it wavered like a desert mirage. It looked like a mistake or as if some kind of ancient process had taken over. One thing was certain, though: Cara had killed those vampires by allowing the dark spirit inside her its freedom.

The Banshee facing them was terrifying. With each passing second, parts of its countenance flickered and changed, as if none of them could stick permanently. He saw the flash of a face that was beautiful beyond belief. Following that was a skeletal mask that made his insides roil. Then came the face of a wolf. And after that, the features of an unfamiliar female.

Black hair, so like Cara's and almost invisible in the night, flew in the swirls of a nonexistent breeze, each tendril seeming to have a life of its own. The black clothes Cara had worn became a gauzy dark cloud of moving shadows. The only light spot in this vision was the pallor of the face that finally settled into place. Most of Cara's features were there and recognizable, possibly because the spirit couldn't entirely separate itself from its host.

Cara was there, but she wasn't looking back at him. She had done the unthinkable by letting the Banshee out for some air. Was this how she had taken on the vampires? Had she channeled the spirit's power in order to aid his packmates?

Would she be able to tuck that spirit back where it belonged if she wanted to? The Banshee was an entity that ate souls for breakfast. Rafe hoped this one couldn't see into his soul to locate the fears forming there.

"Can you come back, Cara?" he messaged to her.

The Banshee's silver-eyed gaze made him uncomfortable. This spirit was female, Cara had said, though it seemed so much more than any one thing. She could no doubt track the anxiety present in all of the Weres here without having to turn her head. Crouched on that branch, the apparition, a physical melding of Cara and the Banshee, most resembled a vampire queen ready to pounce.

"I know what you are and who you are," Rafe said. "I'd like to speak to Cara."

Rafe's packmates had been stunned to silence. Up to this point, only Cameron had witnessed the kinds of things Cara could do. And hell, a wolf was nothing compared to this.

The dark spirit again flickered in and out of focus

as if it was more of an idea or a dream than anything truly corporeal. Rafe didn't know much about the Banshee other than the few things Cara had told him. Did it understand that he and Cara had forged a connection?

He was seeing for the first time what lived inside Cara, and it was disturbing. One of the most dangerous and feared entities on earth was looking at him through Cara's eyes. This was what Cara had been protecting.

What few details he had learned about the dark spirit hardly prepared him for this moment. Cara's ancestors must have understood the ramifications of agreeing to house this creature. Was their decision worth the sacrifice? And were there more Banshees in the world to take up the task of shouting about death? Could there only have been one of them to begin with?

The spirit's pale eyes fixed on him in a way that told Rafe his thoughts were transparent. He wondered if it shared Cara's feelings, and if the entity had also shared their kiss. It was possible this Banshee knew him as intimately as Cara did, but what would it do with that information?

Rafe said, "If you were the one who vanquished those bloodsuckers, let me be the first to offer thanks."

The eyes truly were silver, a werewolf's bane. The gaze that pinned him was cold.

Christ! What was normal about Cara giving this thing sanctuary, or about what this entity could do to her if it got tired of hiding?

"How long do you propose to stay?" he dared to ask.

His question drew wary glances from his packmates, who were frozen in place.

"According to Cara, you must remain hidden. That was part of the deal you made with her ancestors."

He has letting his packmates hear things they should

not have been privy to, but this wasn't the time to worry about it. He had to find Cara in all that darkness.

"Isn't it dangerous for you to appear to anyone, including us, though we appreciate your help and your trust in appearing now?"

Still no response. Rafe had no idea if the dark spirit could talk or speak through Cara. Anxiousness lowered his voice.

"We'd like to take Cara to safety. She's supposed to be in our care. My care. I take that seriously."

The idea bordered on being ludicrous, Rafe had to admit. Cara had just wiped five vampires off the surface of the planet in seconds and obviously had used a boost from whatever special kind of power this dark entity possessed. She might owe that spirit for help with this skirmish. Conversely, the Banshee might owe Cara for its current home.

None of this made his goal of protecting Cara any less urgent. Banshees might be powerful and utterly inhuman, yet Cara was in there, listening. The body concealed beneath that black cloud belonged to her.

It was an inopportune time for reflection, but Rafe wondered who Cara might have been without all of the tricks and talents and vows. He couldn't picture what her smile would be like, or her laugh. He couldn't see her as a kid, doing things that occupied most youngsters. Maybe Cara missed what she'd never had.

Those thoughts made him want to yank that Banshee out of the tree and demand Cara's return...and to hell with the consequences.

Speaking in Cara's voice, the thing in the tree said, "I wouldn't try it, wolf. Trust me on that."

Cara felt her own spirit rising through the fog that had taken her over. Free again to speak and to breathe, she fought off the icy sensations associated with the Banshee and waited for the dark spirit to retreat, fully aware that it didn't have to. After getting a taste of long-awaited freedom, the spirit she housed was taking her time to withdraw.

Rafe was watching her closely to see when she would surface. His body hummed with anxious energy. He had dared to address death's right hand and so far had gotten away with it.

She had never been almost completely overtaken by this spirit, and that was her fault. By piling energy on top of energy, she had created a gap that the Banshee had used to take form.

She was the only one here to realize that the dark spirit had allowed Rafe to address her only out of curiosity. Maybe the Banshee picked up on Rafe's need to protect Cara, which also meant he would be protecting the spirit she housed, though it was the deadliest entity around and they all knew this.

She felt nothing of the spirit's hold on her now. For the time being, after sharing its power in the fight with the vampires, the Banshee had simply and willingly gone back inside. All that was left of the icy chill that was the spirit's calling card was a harsh dryness in Cara's throat.

Rafe thanked you, and I thank you, Cara silently said as she jumped from the branch to land solidly on both feet.

The Weres were quick to form a circle around her despite what they'd witnessed, though they didn't get too close. Could she blame them? Nor did they pose any of the questions that had to be running through their minds. Cara appreciated the moments of silence that followed the Banshee's big reveal. She didn't hear the word freak resonating in any of their minds.

"Okay," Rafe said without taking her in his arms the way she knew he wanted to. "Time to go. Are you good with that, Cara? Are we in the clear?"

His packmates again looked to him.

"We haven't completed the search," Cara said, sure that none of these Weres would want anything more to do with the park tonight.

"We'll get you back first," Rafe said.

"Then you'll go out again without me?"

"Don't you agree that would be for the best?"

Rafe followed his remark with another more personal question, even though they had company. "Was this unusual?"

She replied, "Yes."

Rafe was tense, but not twitchy like his packmates. He had what it took to be an alpha wolf, with the necessary outward calmness and candor to back up his courage when the time came for him to inherit the job from his father. His stance was easy when his insides were tight. His face wasn't bloodless or rigid with fear after she had shown him her most terrifying aspect.

He was paving the way for his packmates to accept her. Rafe Landau was slated for big things, not just babysitting a hybrid who would never be truly accepted in Were society.

He was perfect in every way. The hardness of his body alone chased away any doubts she had, and kept her rooted in place when in the past she would have run away from any and all emotion.

The level of her desire to be with another Were was new, exciting and nearly as overwhelming as the Banshee's takeover. However, she couldn't rush into Rafe's arms with others looking on. The Weres surrounding him didn't need any more surprises.

"So, okay. The bastards are gone and no one will weep for them," he said, tearing his gaze from her to address everyone in the circle. "We'll go back now and let the others in on what's happening in this damn park."

He didn't touch her when she walked past him, though he raised a hand as if he would. His packmates closed around her, forming a barrier of muscle that prevented her from getting closer to Rafe. They were protecting her from monsters, and keeping Rafe from her.

"It will be all right, Cara. I see what this is, and I'm not afraid to face it" was the only message Rafe sent her.

Deep inside Cara, the dark spirit moved.

The spirit feels what I feel, she should have answered. *As long as she is part of me, she knows all.* But that information was too scary to share.

"You take me, you take it all, Rafe," she messaged to him. *"You do get that?"*

The look he gave her sent her doubts scurrying.

Chapter 25

Cara was taunting him with her closeness. Recovering from the dark spirit's appearance, she would need comfort when they got back to the house. Hell, strong as he was, he also needed comfort after this.

The damn Banshee might have been trying to scare him off, to keep from sharing Cara with anyone else, but his craving for closeness with her was insane. He had to hold on and pretend to be detached when his heart was revving and his body ached for Cara in places too numerous to mention.

If love were to find a place in Cara's heart, would that displace her internal parasitic spirit?

His father had warned him not to indulge in fantasies regarding their guest, yet it was too damn late. His world had narrowed down to Cara, and his view of things had changed. She was the central focus, the epicenter of the emotions he now struggled to keep in check.

He realized that with Cara headlining every thought

that popped into his mind, he'd be no good to anyone in the search for a killer. Cara was causing a rift in his sense of duty. That was a first. Meanwhile, there was an ancient vampire on the loose that had been bold enough to confront them in Were territory. While his mind was filled with anticipation about making love to Cara, who could predict what other kinds of atrocities lurked in the shadows, wanting a piece of her?

He'd take her to his parents and hope they could exert some control over her rebellious ways. He needed to rejoin the search party. Keeping the Were world safe was paramount, and a hell of a lot more important than his love life.

So why didn't he actually believe that?

"I can help." Cara's voice was soft and earnest.

"There's too much at stake to keep you out in the open," he said.

Each time her eyes met his, he seemed to lose his place in reality. Cara was dangerous, all right. Most of all, she was dangerous for him.

"Home," he said in a tone that encouraged everyone to pick up their pace.

Minutes later, the wall and the lights beyond it came into view. Several cops combed the area, sniffing for missed clues. He recognized all of them from afar and had to change direction to avoid their attention and keep Cara out of sight.

His little pack moved in a symbiotic manner without the need for communication. Once they had cleared the wall and were again near pack headquarters, he turned to Cameron.

"Can you make sure Cara goes inside and take her to my mother?"

Cameron nodded. Cara didn't react. Her eyes were

hidden beneath her long lashes, and Rafe felt colder without those eyes on him. He'd be sorry to let Cara go, but he could do this. He would temporarily break the chains binding them, get to the bottom of what the mysterious killer wanted and figure out if the target was Cara.

I can let you go, for now...

That unsent message repeated on a loop inside his head. He couldn't say the words aloud, because he had never been a very good liar.

Cara went with Cameron when she could have refused. Rafe couldn't imagine someone actually making this Kirk-Killion do anything she didn't want to do. Cara was a supernatural force to be reckoned with.

Was he afraid of her abilities? No. If no more creatures were to come after Cara and her life could become more or less normal, could they be happy?

"I'll be back before sunrise," he said.

She didn't stop to acknowledge him, and seemed willing to follow his instructions. She didn't fool him, though. Cara's apparent willingness to listen could be a ruse designed to throw them all off her real objectives. Like her mother, would she leap from that damn window the first chance she got?

Hell, wolf spelled backward was flow...and Cara was nothing if not flexible. In retreat, she gave nothing away about possibly having a secret agenda. He detected no deception in the way she had acquiesced to his request. But Rafe felt the pull she had on his system and wondered if there truly was going to be any way to escape whatever the future with Cara might bring.

"You coming?" he said to the other Weres gathered around him. "Shall we hunt for the killer that threatens to expose us?"

"I'd say that's only one of many new problems," one of the guards remarked.

His father approached, his voice overlapping the guard's. "I just got back from a fruitless search." After taking in the serious expressions of their faces, he added, "What happened out there?"

"More bloodsuckers on a rampage," Rafe said and left it at that.

The guards also remained silent about what had actually taken place. Even though the hierarchy here was nothing like in some other packs, Landau wolves didn't have to worry about retribution from their alpha for speaking their minds or telling the truth as they saw it. Every opinion was taken into consideration by Dylan Landau. But in all likelihood these guys were still questioning themselves about what they had seen tonight.

Rafe's father turned toward the wall.

"The park is still crawling with cops," Rafe reminded him.

"When did that stop us?" his father said over his shoulder.

Rafe didn't look at the house, or for the light in Cara's window. She'd be standing there, watching.

"Dana is there," his father said when Rafe caught up to him.

"Yes." The weight of Rafe's concern was obvious in his brief reply.

"We're not Cara's keepers, merely her hosts, Rafe."

"I understand that."

"One problem at a time is the way to go."

"Cara is at the center of all of them," Rafe said.

His father hadn't seen her all vamped up in that tree, or in Banshee mode, or as a wolf running on all fours. His father wasn't aware of how tightly his son's soul had meshed with hers, and that thoughts of Cara would take precedence until they had fully mated in body as well as in soul.

"We'll skip around to the east," Rafe said. "That's where we left off."

"Then let's get to it," the Landau alpha directed as he leaped onto the wall as agilely as if he was still a Were pup, and Rafe and the guards eagerly followed.

Cara sensed Dana outside her closed door, about to knock, and wasn't in the mood for conversation. She needed a rest and an energy reboot. Her shape-shifts were getting out of hand.

Rafe's theory about her being sent here to see if other creatures would follow or could sense her presence had been proven. Miami was a goddamn creaturefest.

That old vampire hadn't given up easily. The attack he had directed had called the Banshee she housed to the surface and revealed the dark spirit to some of Rafe's pack. It was possible the vampire had meant to do just that and hoped Rafe's packmates would be scared off so she could be singled out. She'd be on her own, without anyone at her back.

That hadn't happened. The old vamp would be furious.

"Do you mind if I take a minute?" she called out to Rafe's mother, stopping the knock before Dana's knuckles connected with the door. "I'll be down shortly."

"Sure," Dana said, with a hint of suspicion in her voice. "I'll wait in the front room with drinks."

Cara leaned against the windowsill. Drinks? They were to sip the hours away while Rafe and the Weres searched through shadows? When vampires and demons had trespassed in the world of men because of her?

She felt the rise of her own inner darkness and held it back. All forms of darkness fed the Banshee.

"It's what the monsters want," she muttered. "What they always have wanted. You."

Her borrowed bedroom was nice, but confining. The breeze coming from the open window stirred Cara's restlessness. Sleep was underrated. Drinks and conversation with her hostess would be torturous. The fact was that trouble had come here because of her, and she had to deal with it before any more deaths occurred.

She needed to see Rafe, and she also needed to stay away from him. She desired to share her secrets and her body with him while danger still posed a threat to everyone in their pack.

This kind of impossible craving was the very definition of the imprinting state. Rafe had warned her of this.

When she again sensed the presence at the door, Cara whirled toward it, thinking that Dana wasn't going to let up after all and might be blocking her exit. Still, she also sensed another presence nearby and turned back to the window.

"Rafe?"

Maybe she had wished too damn hard for this to happen. Maybe Rafe would have come to her now even if she hadn't silently called to him, because he wanted this as much as she did.

He should have been working with the search party. He had no right to be here, but he was.

And her heart was racing.

Sensing the need for stealth and secrecy, Rafe climbed up the side of the house by digging his boots and fingertips into the grooves in the brick. He had not meant to return again. Though he was needed elsewhere, he found himself back at the house and on his way to Cara as though he no longer had a mind of his own.

She was waiting for him, and backed away from the window as he reached the sill. She had expected him. Her heart was beating as furiously as his was.

His need for Cara didn't stop with eye contact. He had a ravenous craving for his mate, and Cara's eyes reflected that same hunger. Their needs were mutual. Cara's desires matched his.

"You must understand why they don't want this," she said with a note of sadness in her tone. "You can be hurt. All of you can be hurt. Those vampires are savages and won't stop coming. The demons you face will only get worse if I stay."

She paused for a breath before continuing. "Keeping the Banshee inside me is at times like swallowing shards of glass. Nothing equals the pain of having all that power and darkness inside me. But in the end, it is separate and belongs to someone else. I have no better explanation with which to warn you about me, Rafe. You have no idea what we've done."

"Too bad it's too late for me to have a choice in the matter, then," Rafe said. "I can't imagine what that must be like for you. What I see in front of me is the most beautiful and courageous she-wolf I've ever laid eyes on. Someone selfless enough to have taken on the burden that was handed to you. Someone who deserves to be loved."

She stared at him with her lips slightly parted. "I have more secrets."

Rafe slid off the sill to stand beside Cara. "Not everyone is afraid of you or those secrets, Cara. I'm not afraid."

He gave her no more time for arguments or protests.

Talking wasn't going to satisfy their cravings for each other. Their wolves were directing how this was to go, and their souls were in accord. They had to imprint, mate, seal the deal, or these cravings would go on and on until they did. He was on fire, and having Cara in his arms was the only way to appease those needs.

Rafe backed her to into the corner and leaned in close. He pressed his lips to hers, hoping she would respond, and drank in her scent as if his sanity depended on it. Because it did.

When she sighed with a heated breath, he came undone. Fire became only the smallest part of the feelings that erupted inside him. Her name was being etched on his soul. Real closeness was what he hoped to find, a permanent connection that would last if they made it to that bed.

Shudders rocked him when she kissed him back. But they had done this before, and this time a kiss or two wouldn't be nearly enough.

Her fingers slipped into his hair. The only way they could have been closer was for him to be inside her... and there was no way to explain how much he wanted that.

She kissed him with fervor now—she was a swift learner with an appetite to rival his. Her skin was hot. Her slender hips ground against his. He was going to claim her as his mate, and his erection was proof of the necessity of their next step. This was what had to happen here with Cara, and no one could stop it. This had been the goal since they had first met.

With a smooth move that required little effort, Rafe had her on her back, on the bed. Looming over her, perched on his arms, he took the time to search Cara's flushed face.

Her eyes were dilated and still green. Her lips were a pale shade of pink that would never bruise beneath the weight of his passion, because Cara was above all a wolf.

Their passion would take them to heights no one had ever seen. He would love her deeply, completely. And after that, he'd come back for more.

Rafe exhaled his next question in a breathless rush as the last few seconds of sanity ticked away. "You did lock the damn door?"

Chapter 26

Cara had no desire to answer Rafe's question, and he wouldn't have let her if she had. Instead he kissed her with a fury that sent her senses haywire. Whether they were safe or not amid the chaos going on outside the Landau estate, this room was going to be their personal haven, just as it had been for her parents.

Still, Cara was instantly aware of a tug on her senses that threatened to interfere in these moments of passion, and the tug was familiar. Her mother and father were crowding the room. Their presence rode on the crest of her emotions. Shutting them out would take more energy than she had and split her loyalties, but she inwardly protested the intrusion. *You did the same thing and survived. Let me have my chance.*

Rafe's hands were on her face. Her body was surrendering to his touch. He lay beside her on the mattress. They had too many clothes on for this mating thing to work. No one had explained about the birds and the bees when she was growing up. She had never seen her father touch her mother, though she had heard their lovemaking on many occasions when they assumed she wasn't around.

It was her turn now to find out what sex and closeness were all about. She was going to find out what being Rafe's mate would be like, and how this act might change the future.

Instincts took over as she curled into Rafe's heat, seeking to be bested by him, and only by him, willing to loosen her hold on her own strength and power. The sheer force of his hunger drove her deeper into the pillows. She tore at his clothes with both hands to get at the smooth skin beneath, and he did the same, reaching her bare stomach in a few mad seconds.

Cara gasped as he slid his hand upward to her breasts and stalled there, possibly expecting an argument she didn't make. He stroked her rib cage and ran his fingertips in small circles without landing in any one place. She strained toward him, offering herself, silently demanding that he comply with her wishes.

It was too much, and not nearly enough. She was determined to take whatever Rafe had to offer. Only in that way would she be able to think straight and get her priorities in order.

His touch, unlike his kisses, became suddenly tender. When his movements slowed to a controlled exploration of what lay under her shirt, Cara began to get a sense of the ecstasy that was to come.

She tugged at him with her hands and nipped at his mouth with her teeth in an unspoken, wolfish command for more. Biting turned Rafe on. He had her shirt over her head before her next breath. His lips left a trail of kisses along the base of her neck, and all Cara could think about was how sanity could be so overrated.

More heat filled her, soaking through every cell. It was the heat of a fever, like sinking into a tub of scalding water. But Rafe didn't focus his attentions on any one place, because time wasn't on their side.

Her pants joined her shirt in a pile on the floor, leaving her naked at last. Though Rafe had seen her this way before, his gaze swept over her longingly, as if he coveted each angle and curve and regretted not being able to linger in all of those places.

His hand moved downward over her hips and her belly, leaving fluttering muscles in its wake. Dipping his fingers between her thighs made her growl. The pressure of his fingers on her sensitive parts made her insides quake. When he found what he wanted there, the place so hidden and low on her body, his kisses stopped long enough for his eyes to again find hers.

"Don't think," he said roughly. "Go with it. Feel. Enjoy our bond. This is what matters, Cara. You have no idea how much. Let me prove that to you."

"And then what?" she asked.

"We go from there."

His fingers tested her willingness, her moistness, her waiting heat, before he stood up to remove his clothes and give her a first full look at the Were she was going to pledge herself to.

Rafe was incredibly well sculpted. He was masculine and beautifully built. His skin was bronze and mostly flawless, except for two small scars near his left shoulder that were evidence of an old fight. And he was magnificently hard.

He was hard for her.

He lowered himself to her slowly, so that she felt his hardness pressing close. His eyes bored into hers as he eased himself into her with a slow, slick slide that robbed her of breath. Muffled cries erupted from her throat, not out of pain, but from her intense need for more of what Rafe had to offer.

She took hold of Rafe's hips and pulled him closer so that he slid farther inside her. Then she growled again, deep in her throat, and tried to hold on to both Rafe and her human shape when the animal inside her threatened to bloom.

Wildness rose in her as her wolf rushed upward to the surface, encouraged by the overwhelming sensations and the new emotions she was experiencing. She had never felt anything like this. Like him…

"Now!" she whispered, feeling the fierceness of her wolf. "Before it's too late."

His next plunge was deeper, and followed by a swift retreat. He then entered her again and again…with a rhythmical buildup of sweet and terrible speed that kept her entranced.

The extremes of the pleasure he gave her caused her body to seize. Waves of heat licked at her insides and that distant drumbeat she had sampled once before spiraled toward Rafe as if it had developed a special relationship with him.

When he stopped, she clawed at him with her fingertips. But he didn't move again, and didn't need to. Buried inside her, Rafe locked her to that beat until sparks flashed behind her eyes and internal fireworks went off…so many fireworks that Cara thought she might die of pleasure. Then he moved one more time…a perfect strike so deep that it seemed to have reached her soul…and Rafe Landau collided with her in the fury of that internal beat that only the two of them could share.

This was the wolf's mating dance, their union, and it sealed the bargain their souls had made without them.

Caught up in the rush, Cara threw her head back and arched off the bed. Rafe's arms were shaking. His eyes were closed. This time when she growled, Cara heard Rafe do the same. When she howled with her newly found satisfaction, Rafe's howl mingled with hers, echoing through the room.

But as the sounds of the culmination of their lovemaking faded and Cara lay breathless beneath Rafe on the bed with her self-defenses on hiatus, something else began to worry her.

The past had again interfered.

Without a word of warning or explanation, Cara slid out from beneath Rafe and reached for her clothes. Uttering just one more growl—of caution this time—she climbed onto the windowsill and crouched there.

Rafe was up quickly and moving toward her, his expression one of shock and surprise. But she didn't take that jump of escape she had been about to make. Instead, she was stopped by the shimmer of air that she had anticipated would gather around her.

Shapes began to form inside that moving shimmer—rippling images that told a story. Her mother and father had been in this room in the past, and they had mated on the bed where she and Rafe had lain together. Cara saw this clearly now, as if that act was taking place on the same rumpled sheets. Two naked bodies were joining. She heard them groaning with pleasure, and she couldn't make the image stop or go away.

Black hair spread across the pillow in the same

way hers had. A muscular backside of pure white skin glowed in the light from the open window as the male drove in and out of the female beneath him with a fierceness that Cara had only moments before experienced with Rafe.

God...they were here. Her parents had taken over the space. Like them, she and Rafe had broken the rules set forth by their respective families by mating. Just like Rafe and her, Rosalind and Colton had thumbed their noses at what was forbidden and sealed their souls together.

The dreamlike images overlapped with Rafe's approach. Cara put a hand to her head to try to halt the whirling that went on and on, with those two commingling bodies centered on the mattress. She had to speak, break the connection to the past. Her voice cracked when she said, "Did we just do this, Rafe, or did I imagine it?"

He was beside her, tall, buff, naked and shining like a bronze star in the moonlight streaming through the open window she huddled in.

"Are you real?" she whispered. "Or are you, like them, a dream?"

Rafe's was the scent embedded in her lungs. His was the body she had shared hers with. Surely she knew this?

"I'm real. This was real. Are you all right. Cara? What are you seeing?"

She didn't stop to listen to him. Pleasure had pushed her over the edge of reason, and only her wolf could cope.

All ten claws sprang from her fingertips at once. The room filled with the sound of bones realigning. There was agony in this transition, possibly stemming from having experienced the heights of a pleasure that went beyond anything she had known mere seconds before. Or maybe the pain arrived like a silver-tipped arrow to her chest because she didn't really want to run from Rafe like this but felt that she had to.

Whatever the cause, the sharpness of her discomfort paused her transition halfway. She looked at Rafe, who was glorious and masculine, strong and caring, and cried out when moonlight hit her face. She roared with her wolf's throat, then turned away from her lover… and jumped.

"Damn it…" Rafe reached for Cara but found the space empty. Pressing himself to the sill, he stared at the drop to the ground below, swore several times more, then hurriedly retrieved his clothes.

Forgoing the door—and whoever would be in the house to question him—Rafe climbed out the window using the foot and handholds in the brick, the same way he had gotten in.

Had Cara not liked feeling vulnerable? Did she regret what they had done? She might not be afraid of vampires and other things that slithered through the night, but it was conceivable that she feared real closeness with another being, and therefore feared him.

That was a hell of a bad thing, given how much he wished for a repeat of what had occurred between them on that bed. Both man and wolf craved that. But her face…the look Cara had given him before she jumped had been…

"There is no escape, Cara," he whispered as his boots touched grass. "It's you and me from here on out, so I need to know what's going on."

He saw no one in the yard. No hint of Cara. Cameron and the other two Weres had been in the park, along with his father. Whether or not they had missed him didn't matter. Only finding Cara did. He had to find out why she had run, and what she had seen in that room that made her question their closeness.

Cara had to be assured that she was not a freak, and that she could be loved. That he loved her.

"It's all right," he messaged to her. *"We both can handle this. Just give me a chance to prove that."*

The three wolves who squatted on top of the wall at the end of the yard nodded to Rafe when he climbed up beside them.

"Did she come this way?" Rafe asked, searching the dark. "Did anyone come this way in the last few minutes?"

The answer was no, so Cara had somehow managed to avoid all these watchful eyes. Rafe landed lightly on the park side of the wall and set off in an easterly direction, not sure which Cara he'd find this time, if he found her at all. Full wolf? Half wolf? Vampire? Human? She was so many things.

Would she let him hold her? Let him take away the fears that made her feel unwelcome and separated from everyone else? He thought he had already done that.

"Cara…" he called out. "Please find me. Let me help you."

He heard sounds that his brain processed as trampling feet, headed his way. Vampires, he now knew, didn't make noise when they moved, so this was someone else. *See, Cara. I am learning.*

Two cops walked forward with their hands on their

weapons, wary of meeting up with anyone in the dark after that body had been found.

"Landau," he called out to them. "Miami Metro."

"Detective Landau?" one of them asked.

"One and the same," Rafe said.

He recognized both of these guys when they got closer, though he didn't know their names. The taller of the two cops spoke first. "We've been over this park twice and found nothing other than a couple of people making out near the boulevard. There are three more officers sweeping the eastern portion. Our guess is that if there is something to be found out here, it will have to be in the daylight. Flashlights just don't cut it on a night like this."

The cop glanced over his shoulder. "You going out there anyway?"

Rafe nodded. "My team is somewhere in the east, running along the edge where the factories are. No doubt they will meet up with your guys, if they haven't already. I got a late start on this and have to join them."

The tall cop pointed to a spot beyond where Rafe stood and said, "That's your wall? Where the body was found?"

"My family's place. I don't live there."

The cops shared a glance that told Rafe they might be wondering what kind of privileges a detective coming from such a prominent family might have had. But that wasn't Rafe's concern. Beat cops and detectives didn't always get along, and the fact that these two might envy his background and his rank was no big surprise.

"Thanks for the sweep," Rafe said, passing them in a few easy strides. "It's my turn. See you boys later."

Though he wanted to sprint, Rafe waited until he

was out of the cops' view. Once in the clear he took off, following the scent of wolf that wafted to him from the north, instead of the east, where it would have been expected.

Breathing in the scent, feeling his body respond with a shiver of pleasure, Rafe smiled. "Got you," he said, and changed direction.

Chapter 27

She didn't usually get winded, but Cara's breath came in gasps and flutters as she headed north. Her body shouldn't have hurt now that she was in the clear, and yet it did. Most of those leftover aches had nothing to do with shape-shifting or leaping from third-story windows, however. They were centered in the place where her and Rafe's bodies had connected. She still felt the flames.

With her claws, she swiped at the trees she passed as if marking her territory and staking a claim. In truth, this was her lover's land. He oversaw everything, and now he also owned her body. What about the portion of her soul that wasn't occupied by spirits? Would Rafe find space there, too?

He was following her, as she figured he would. He'd want to comfort her when she didn't deserve it. Seeing that memory of her father and mother in the room had spooked her. Her father's ghostly, colorless skin and her mother's inky-black hair spread across the sheets were big reminders that the two of them were a species apart from the Were world she was trespassing in at the moment.

Rafe was just a werewolf, and not even Lycan. He possessed no freakish traits other than a dire need to protect what wasn't protectable. While she...well, she was a Kirk-Killion and should have known better than to fall for a good guy.

"Cara. Let me help you."

The messages Rafe sent hurt her and made her want to let him catch up. She would have liked another session on the bed or anywhere else they could have conceived of. But if she kept her distance from Rafe, she might be able to get more insight on who desired her the most... Rafe, or the monsters.

She whirled when she heard Rafe speak to someone else and was again stabbed by jealousy. Cara clung to the bark of the tree beside her, needing to ground herself. Humans also roamed this park tonight, and she was in half-wolf stasis.

"You deserve better, Rafe. I'm sorry it's too late for you to have that chance," she whispered to herself.

The approach of a Were nearby made Cara turn her head. This wasn't Rafe. It was someone else whose vibration was familiar because of the Were's relation to her lover.

"Alpha," she said, dragging her claws from the bark.

Dylan Landau came toward her with a kind of grace only pure-blooded Lycans possessed. The alpha had found her when she hadn't wanted to be found. Possibly he could smell his son's essence, mixed with hers.

"There's no need to take this on by yourself," he said calmly, maintaining a polite distance of several feet.

"Isn't there?" Cara countered.

"We will find the culprit who harmed the human. We always do."

"The pack is strong," she agreed.

The way Dylan Landau was intently eyeing her reminded her of Rafe. It felt to her as if this alpha also had the ability to read things in her that very few others could.

"What's done is done," he said.

So, he knew what had happened in that attic room. She had feared that he might.

"Against your wishes and the wishes of my family," Cara returned.

"We had no preconceived notion about what might or might not have taken place when you two met," he said. "You're both strong individuals with your own minds."

"And yet if there was the slightest chance of an unanticipated connection developing between Rafe and me, why did you invite me here?" she asked.

"We invited you here to fulfill an old promise."

"What promise, exactly, is that?"

"Your father asked that you be allowed to assimilate with other Weres when your time came. I thought we told you this."

"My father left with my mother in order to keep the monsters away from your doorstep," Cara said.

Dylan Landau nodded. "Don't think we didn't realize and appreciate that at the time."

"Monsters are my middle name," Cara said. "I don't belong here any more than my parents did. I believe I have already proven that a few times over."

"Perhaps. But maybe they left for other reasons as well."

"Such as?"

"The desire to protect any offspring they might produce."

Cara stared at the alpha, who spoke again.

"None of the monsters that were left after that last fight at Fairview actually left Miami. They merely went deeper underground, showing themselves now and then by adding to the city's body count. Some of us had to make sure that they remained a secret. We have dealt with the problem as best we could."

Cara tucked her claws inside with a sting and a brief internal whisper. An idea formed in her mind that she wasn't sure she liked, and yet she had to mention it to the Were responsible for so many lives.

She said slowly, "Was I to come here to help with that? Dig up those monsters? Bring them out of hiding so they can be dealt with in a more effective manner?"

Cara breathed out before continuing. "Could that have been part of the reason you would honor an old promise by inviting someone like me here? We were to help each other? Each of us was to benefit by my visit in some way?"

"Yes," Dylan Landau said. "I suppose that was the gist of the plan."

"How do you feel about it now that your son is involved?"

"The only thing your connection with him proves is that your parents were right in the belief that you could assimilate and fit in here, with us."

She almost smiled. "You truly believe that?"

He nodded. "I do, and I am obviously not the only one who does."

The plan had been a good one, Cara agreed, until Rafe had found her on that beach. Who could possibly have expected the result of that one evening spent with him, away from all this?

Rafe was speaking to her now, messaging her along selective channels. But his father had more to say.

"Now that you know about old promises, what can we expect?"

She said, "I don't know." But she did know, of course. Her bond with Rafe was unbreakable—Rafe had told her. Theirs was a deep connection and would last forever.

Her gaze traveled upward to the alpha's handsome face—a face whose chiseled features Rafe shared. Other than Dylan's silver hair, the two of them could have been brothers.

It's too late, she thought again. *I can't live without Rafe, and it might kill us all if I try to live with him.*

"Cara?" Dylan's voice brought her back to the conversation. He was waiting for her decision when there was no decision to be made. None that she could have made, anyway. The only way to avoid the bond she and Rafe had formed was if one of them were to die, and she had no intention of letting that happen. So she had to make the best of things and do her part. She had to honor that old promise, no matter what.

"Rafe has a sadness tucked inside," she said. "I can feel it when I'm with him."

Dylan nodded again. "He once liked a woman who was killed by a monster none of us saw. Maybe you can understand why he wants to protect you."

"She-wolf?" Cara asked, knowing Dylan would follow her question.

"Human," Dylan replied.

"Then they could not have…"

"There was no real bond. There couldn't have been, you know."

Rafe had lost someone he had cared for, and that was the source of his fierce protectiveness for her. Weres didn't as a rule condone human-Were matings, but the alpha across from her couldn't have objected to his son's previous preference, since Dylan had also married a woman who had at one time been human. The difference was that Dana had already become a wolf when she and Dylan had met and bonded.

"Imprinting," Cara said, testing out the word.

"Hell of a thing," Dylan returned. "Wonderful when it happens to the right combination of souls."

Unless one half of that combination is like me. Cara didn't say that out loud. What she said was, "Yes. Hell of a thing."

"Shall we return? Go home?" he suggested. "There are humans in the park tonight, along with the wolves. Keeping you out of sight might prevent anything else from showing up unannounced."

She hadn't considered that, and should have. She didn't have the freedom to do as she pleased in Miami. Dylan was right to be wary.

"There are ghosts at the house," she confessed. "For me, whatever might show up out here is easier to manage."

Dylan raised an eyebrow in question.

"Though there might have been hunters here, as you tend to believe, and although a werewolf could have done the damage that human sustained, it seems like the work of a demon. And where there is one demon, there are always others. Many others."

"Demon." Dylan's tone darkened. A shadow crossed his face.

"That's the monster your shooter took down. A demon came for me and took a timely bullet that missed my head."

Dylan said, "Bullets are never timely, Cara. What you've said changes things dramatically."

"You didn't know about the demons?"

"No," Dylan said. "I did not."

"Do you still want to take me back, behind walls that would never be able to keep a demon out?" she asked.

Dylan Landau didn't immediately answer that question. His attention was torn by the sound of others approaching. Humans, by scent. The alpha gave her a look of warning and moved toward them.

Cara hung back until she heard Dylan's greeting. Then, seeing an opportunity to help with this investigation, which would in turn get this park back to normal for a limited time and perhaps help the pack accept her role as Rafe's mate, Cara melted into the shadows as if she was one of them…and slipped silently away.

Rafe saw his father talking to the cops. He would have closed the whole area off to everyone if he could have and afterward burned the damn park down. This place had been the bane of Weres for years and a death trap for humans who ignored the danger. It made every detective on the job wary, every damn night, and put werewolves in jeopardy each time a full moon came around.

He sensed that Cara had been near his father and wondered what he had missed. When he heard his father shout, Rafe's chills returned. Something was wrong, and he knew what had happened as surely as he knew his own name.

Cara had given his dad the slip. She hadn't just run away from him. She had fled from everyone.

"What the hell are you thinking?" he said aloud. He muscled up to his father when the cops disappeared, and said roughly, "What did you tell her?"

The alpha wasn't intimidated by his tone. "I told her it was okay, and about the old plan."

"What else?"

"Nothing we hadn't told her before."

Rafe rubbed a hand over his face. "We have to find her. I have to find her."

"There are more important things in need of our attention. Cara mentioned demons. Plural. Hell, as if vampires aren't bad enough."

If Cara had brought a demon out of its hole, they really did need to burn this place down.

"You might not realize what you're up against if you go after her," his father said.

"On the contrary, I have a pretty good idea about that," Rafe countered.

"Yes. I suppose you do," his father said.

"I'll help you find her," Cameron said from behind them.

"You're needed here, Cameron. You called in the body. They'll be asking you for more details and may take more statements," Rafe's father said. To Rafe, he added, "I'll come with you to search for Cara."

"No need. I know where she'd go."

"There are several reasons to worry about that," his father warned, deciphering Rafe's thought.

"So there are," Rafe muttered. As he spun around on his heels, Rafe repeated the phrase to himself. "So there damn well are."

Chapter 28

Cara remembered all the cars in the Landau garage and would have taken one if she knew how to drive. Then again, getting out of the Landau compound alone, with a borrowed car, would have been a nightmare. And she'd had one too many nightmares lately.

The body that had been dumped at the base of the Landaus' wall had been meant as a warning—not for the wolves inside those walls, but for her. It was a none-too-subtle reminder that though she had changed locations, there would be plenty of danger wherever she went unless she relinquished the dark spirit she housed.

She was a danger magnet. Coming to Miami and involving others in her trials had been a mistake. The plan that had been set in motion after all this time had been terribly shortsighted and flawed. She would never be like these Weres, even if she tried.

There would be more deaths. She had been warned

about the next one that would soon come. Would it turn out be another mutilated body? This one a Were?

Sooner or later, Rafe and his family would come under careful scrutiny. The Were species couldn't afford that kind of close attention. She owed this pack for adhering to promises their former alpha had made, and she owed them for at least trying to accept her. Everyone would be safer if she left Miami, but leaving was no longer an option. The thought of never seeing Rafe again made her sick.

Her only option was to stay in Miami and go renegade…sneaking away to fight the dirty battles on her own. She could warn the pack each time the Banshee wailed for someone near to them, even when that would be breaking another set of rules. Pack protected pack, and Rafe was now the central core of hers.

That acknowledgment didn't prevent the rumbles of inner protest against the current situation, though. Jumbled thoughts came and went, most of them about Rafe and about how, for a time on that bed, she had experienced what it must be like to feel normal. In Rafe's arms, she had experienced the sublime, and she could look forward to more of that if this pack survived the oncoming tide of monsters.

"Rafe. I'm not sorry we met. I can't be sorry about what we feel."

She sent that message to Rafe without meaning to. She had been thinking about him for too long and too hard. Their bond would ensure that he heard her. He would now know what she was doing and where she would go.

"Don't come after me. This is something I must do."

Would he see this latest defection as an act of selfishness? Or that she hadn't liked what happened in that attic room?

Rafe soon responded, *"I can be with you, help you. Wait for me. Let me do this. Give me a clue."*

Cara erected a mental wall and reinforced it with continued conscious effort. Then she cursed and backed it up with a growl that tickled her human throat.

How would she manage the distance, let alone getting to an unknown location, if she had to traverse the miles on foot? Daylight wasn't too far off. Sunlight would make shape-shifting out of the question. Shifting required darkness and had been born of the secrets darkness hid. She had to hurry, shift now, somehow find her way.

A breeze, warm and steamy, ruffled her hair. The scent of wolf the breeze carried offered no comfort now. She had to find a way out of the Landaus' gates without being seen. The dark spirit was urging her to get going, perhaps for reasons Cara didn't yet know anything about.

Out of a whole host of sounds going on around her, Cara picked out one as being significant. The slamming of a car door.

Footfalls, light but meaningful, became louder as they got closer to where Cara stood. A woman appeared, heading toward her on the driveway. No. Not a woman, really.

"I suppose you'll need a ride," Dana Delmonico Landau said, as if she had either been privy to everything that had happened so far—or possessed a set of talents that she usually kept hidden.

Rafe looked for the black SUV in the garage, feeling guilty about leaving the dirty work regarding the body and finding the killer to the others. But the car was gone. This was curious, since the SUV was seldom used by anyone except the Weres who were out with his father in the park at the moment.

He chose another car and slipped onto the warm leather seat. He had to find Cara. He would bring her back and chain her to the house if necessary until he could get some things done without thinking about her.

It was likely that others had heard what had transpired between them on Were channels. He didn't care. Most of his pack had their own mates and would understand his dilemma with Cara. If she was right about the uprising of monsters in Miami, only she could help to locate and cull their numbers, and yet it was dangerous for her to do so. Having Cara here would benefit everyone, except maybe Cara.

She had closed down communication. He could no longer see her in his mind at present, which would make locating her a problem. Had she gone home? If so, was there a chance he might intercept her before she got there? How would she get away from Miami? Heaven only knew what Colton and Rosalind would think if she returned on her own. Or if he showed up unannounced looking for her.

Rafe waved at the guards at the gate as he drove up and stopped to ask, "Did you see Cara?"

A quick no in reply was all it took for the glimmer of an idea to form in his mind. Cara had not come this way on foot, and she wouldn't have gotten past the guards if she had. She was wily, however, and could have easily skirted the front gate.

Rafe stepped on the gas. Using the GPS, he plotted the secret location of the Kirk-Killions' home that his family had been allowed access to in order to bring Cara to Miami. That place was a couple of hours away. He'd have to find Cara somewhere between here and there.

Barely three miles from the estate, Rafe slowed the car to process another thought that had dropped into his mind. Was it a message? He'd heard a whisper. In that whisper was a name he recognized.

Hell, Cara hadn't gone home. The name he had heard was a place wrapped up in the legends that formed his pack's history.

Fairview.

He made a U-turn and drove at breakneck speed for a few more miles with an eye out for the old sign that had been left standing after the psychiatric hospital had supposedly closed down—*supposedly* being the operative word.

Every Were in Miami knew of this place and that it was where humans freshly inducted into the moon's cult were taken, if they were lucky, to go through their first bone-shattering transition from human to werewolf. Although Fairview's windows now appeared to be dark and the gates were padlocked, there was plenty of activity behind those old brick walls that went undetected by all except for the wounded humans Fairview's conscientious staff served.

It wasn't far to that place. A slight detour only, and one Rafe had to take in case Cara had been the one to guide him there.

Cara sat back on the seat, staring out the half-open window. "This isn't the way home," she said.

"You weren't really thinking of going home tonight, were you?" Dana replied.

Cara gave her a brief glance. "No."

"I thought you might like to see the spot that's been

on your mind," Dana said. "I can always turn around if I was wrong about that."

Cara gave her hostess another sideways glance.

"Do you have any idea where that might be?" Dana asked.

There was only one more place tied to the memories of her parents' past left to see in Miami. Dana had mentioned it earlier. After everything that had happened since then, this trip was to be a fitting finale to her quest for the truth. And Rafe's mother had picked up on that.

"Fairview," Cara said.

"It's only a few miles from us," Dana explained.

Cara studied the landscape intently. Because Dana seemed to understand what was going on, Cara asked what was on her mind. "Was there a reason a fight with the vampires took place there instead of in the park?"

"No one knows that for sure, other than your parents. I tend to think that Rosalind led the vampires here because it was far enough from the city to allow her to do what she wanted to do."

"Which was what?" Cara asked.

"Fight them, once and for all. Prove her dominance over them."

A shiver of apprehension iced Cara's neck when she heard that word. *Dominance.* Out of the corner of her eye, she caught sight of a sign that had long since fallen into disrepair and now hung from its hinges. It would have directed people to the Fairview Hospital Psychiatric Clinic when the hospital was up and running.

She felt an even deeper chill when they turned down a long, dark driveway. Tingling sensations accompanied a new premonition. Something was about to happen here that went beyond her objective of taking a quick look around.

She leaned forward on the seat. Everything outside the car's window had once again become dreamlike, as if she was seeing the landscape through the tight weave of a net. Her sight was limited, but smells came through.

"Wolf," she said.

Dana nodded. "Wolves have always been a part of the history of this place, and still are. One of our pack-mates runs Fairview now, the same as long ago when part of it was open to the public."

"Wolves and humans mixed there?"

"They were kept segregated, of course. No one on the outside ever knew what went on in some of those corridors."

"It's still open?" Cara asked.

"Jenna James runs Fairview now, and she is very good at what she does."

Cara said thoughtfully, "Wolf scent could have been what helped to draw the vampires to the area."

"That certainly could have been a part of why they appeared back then," Dana agreed.

Cara turned to her. "But you don't really believe that was the case?"

"I tend to believe it was Rosalind who purposefully drew them here for a reason of her own, and that she was merely aided by the darker aspects of this place. I think she planned this in order to keep others away."

If that was true, and Dana was right about her mother's motives for coming here, Rosalind had cared about the lives of others and had chosen this place for its remote location. She might have taken into consideration that wolves injured in a fight could have been treated at this hospital.

She was beginning to fill in the blanks of her family's past. She had seen what had happened to her father in the park. She had seen her parents making love in the attic room. Now she was going to find out the rest. The puzzle was about to be solved.

The long driveway to Fairview was partially overgrown with grass and knee-high weeds. There were no lights. As the car wound through a dense stand of trees, the moon ducked behind a cloud.

When the outline of a building came into view in the headlights, Cara put a hand on her chest to try to ease her racing heartbeats. As Dana pulled up to an old chain-link fence and stopped the car, Cara's hand flew to the door handle.

"Wait," Dana cautioned. "Someone else is here."

Cara already knew that, though, and also that the past was about to come alive in a way that could affect them all.

Chapter 29

Rafe drove up to the chain-link fence surrounding the hospital and parked the car. Fairview had a forgotten, forlorn look that was deceiving, and appeared to have been abandoned for years.

Grass had overtaken whole stretches of the circular driveway. The fence drooped in places, and moss crept up the brick near the base of the steps leading to the front door, presenting onlookers with a broody atmosphere that ghost hunters might have liked to explore. Yet Fairview wasn't empty or abandoned, and anyone trespassing here would get a decent shock if they somehow managed to get inside.

He saw no one. Heard nothing. The quiet was so convincing, he almost believed what that boarded-up exterior suggested, when he knew better. Nevertheless, he had to wonder why Cara would want to come here, if in fact she would.

He got out of the car and took several deep breaths.

Then he scanned the area for hints of life beyond the faint scent of wolves that only another wolf would have noticed.

His visits to Fairview were rare and made him uneasy. He seldom set foot here unless called upon to investigate any incident caused by a wolf biting a human. There were several such cases each year, and all of them required the good guys of their species to go after the bad guys afterward to track down those toothy bastards.

Things had been fairly quiet in that arena lately, and now the danger had escalated to include another kind of bite. All of a sudden, the current pack had vampires to worry about. There was no help for humans punctured by fangs, and no private hospitals like this one to take in the undead. Only the cold slabs of city morgues could host a new vampire's temporary stay.

With the back of his neck prickling, Rafe walked toward the padlocked gate. There was something here… but what?

What was he supposed to find?

There was no sign of Cara, but the hum of an engine on the driveway made him turn around. The needling sensations at the base of his neck tripled as he waited to find out if the whisper he heard had been legitimate and if Cara had sent it.

When the SUV rounded a corner, Rafe breathed a sigh of relief. It was the missing vehicle from his family's garage. If his father and others with access to the garage had been scouring the park, who was driving that SUV?

Two headlights coming his way made the night temporarily brighter. Rafe waited by the gate on the opposite side of the building until the car pulled up and the passenger door opened. Cara got out. Following closely behind her was the surprise of the night.

"What are you doing here?" his mother said.

The only sound left after that was the unusual pounding of his heart.

Cara froze when she saw Rafe. She attempted to hide how grateful she was to see him, because there was a downside to meeting him like this, here. Emotions she had tried to leave behind rolled over her. Unable to think of anything to say, she turned to Dana, who stood on her left.

"I suppose he has a right to be here and to share this," Dana said.

"Share what?" Rafe asked, sounding as confused as Cara was.

"Her family's past," Dana said.

Cara realized by observing the way Rafe looked at his mother that he was in the dark about why he was here and might have been following a hunch as to where she would turn up next.

"The bond between you is obvious," Dana went on. "Maybe it's a good thing you're here."

Cara finally spoke up and said to Dana, "You can't possibly find that kind of bond acceptable."

Dana wasn't intimidated by the intensity of Cara's gaze or her frankness. "Why wouldn't we accept it?" Dana said. "Why do you suppose you were sent here, if not to become one of us?"

Rafe stepped closer…close enough for Cara to feel that familiar flush of warmth he gave her and to remember the exquisite seductiveness of his body stretched out on top of hers in that attic room. Her own memories were now of deep, drowning kisses, and how Rafe's scent could chase away thoughts of the bad things in her life.

"This is the place," Cara said.

The set of Rafe's jaw told her he was trying to ignore the compulsion to look around him. For Rafe, what had happed here was part of his pack's dark history.

"What do you want to find here?" he asked her. "More of your mother's memories? Further trauma that might make you feel worse than you already do?"

Rafe was probably wondering if her feelings for him might be nothing more than a chapter in her family's lingering past. If she might have gone to bed with him only because she thought she was dreaming, or reliving something that had happened long ago between her parents.

You're wrong, Cara wanted to tell him, though she wasn't completely sure about that, either.

"My family's memories could be coloring everything," she said in answer to the questions Rafe hadn't voiced. "I have to find out what is here for me, and if I can let the past go once I understand it."

Rafe's blue eyes searched her face in a caressing way that was the equivalent of having his hands feather over her body. He wasn't going to stop her from finding what was here. Maybe he wouldn't offer another protest.

"Trust me," he said. "What we did in that room had nothing to do with Colton and Rosalind. You can forget about that. You were there. I was there. We did what we did because we wanted to, and because we had to. Your discoveries about them and their affection for each other can't cause you to love me any more or less than you do. Neither can someone else's memories or words sway my feelings for you."

She wanted to believe him. She honestly did. The

strange thing was how quickly the imprinting state had taken them over. This was only her second day in Miami, though it felt like she'd been here much longer. Did anyone really know how the mating game could happen so fast, or tie two Weres together so strongly?

Rafe faced his mother. "Did Cara ask you to bring her here?"

"No," Cara said. "Dana merely offered me a ride."

"I thought you ran back toward your home," Rafe said. "I thought you had gone."

Cara shook her head. "It's not over. This is where things in Miami ended for my parents and their life of seclusion began. What happened here was the final battle with the vampires. Something secretive must have been disclosed here that I'm meant to see."

As she had in the park, Cara sensed in the hospital's grounds the remnants of that battle tugging at her. Anger and death lingered in places where lives were lost. She had mentioned that to Rafe earlier, and he could choose to believe it or not.

She didn't look past the fence, already feeling Fairview's chill. The air surrounding the old building was thick and difficult to breathe. No one with an ounce of sensitivity would have been comfortable here.

"Seeing what happened near this place might make me better understand my fears," she said, thinking out loud and avoiding Rafe's gaze.

"What fears?" Rafe asked.

She couldn't hide things from him now, but she didn't want to tell Rafe everything. He hadn't shared the horrors she had seen growing up. Rafe belonged to a pack that supported his species and offered backup in a crisis.

How can you love a monster killer who is also a monster herself?

"No," Rafe objected, having either tuned in to or guessed what she was thinking. "You have to realize by now that you aren't a monster, and neither were Colton or Rosalind. How could you even think such a thing when theirs was the ultimate sacrifice? They gave up our kind of freedom for another one that they believed would suit them better. They offered the same kind of freedom to you before extending the choice of something else."

Cara glanced up, drawn to the tender adamancy of his remarks.

His eyes bored into hers to help drill home a point as he said, "Your parents could have stayed here. No one turned them away. If what they left was so bad, why would they send you here? If they weren't wanted in Miami, why would they expect things to be different for you?"

Rafe's earnestness was as beautiful as his face. What his eyes told her was that he had fallen in love with her. After everything that had happened during their brief acquaintance, their souls had mingled in the way only Were souls could, and he loved her.

The pleasure of that made her sway on her feet. He steadied her with a firm hand that forced her to again meet his eyes.

Could he see that she was desperate to believe him? Was he able to read that in her face?

"This is the final piece of the puzzle," she repeated. "I have to see it in order to understand why my parents made the choices they made."

Rafe nodded reluctantly. His anxiousness surrounded him. But the net of her mother's memory had already dropped in front of her vision, and the process of dipping into the past had begun.

There was no way to stop what was coming, and Cara didn't want to. By finding what she needed here, there was a good chance she could let the past go and love Rafe back. When this was over, she might be able to throw herself into his arms.

At last, she might shed the tears she had held back for so long, and the anger she had harbored for the kind of life she and her family could have lived if things had gone differently and events in Miami had turned out well.

Fears.

There were just too damn many to count. And Rafe had added to them by concentrating, right now, on the word she feared most of all.

Love.

He loved her. It was true.

And she loved him back.

She was Lycan above all, he had said. And as the strongest and fiercest of the breed, Lycans were supposed to be the masters of their own destinies, not pawns to anyone else's.

"Then let's see what there is to see," Rafe said as he took her hand in his.

Blue light shone from his eyes, and that light grounded her. Cara sent the tentacles of her mind into the surrounding landscape and said, "Rosalind. Show me what happened here so that this can be over, once and for all. And so that I can make a choice for the direction my life is to go."

The musty green smell of uncut grass and old trees reached her before it changed to make way for the acrid odor of stale blood.

Cara turned her head…

No, it was someone else who turned to search for the origins of that smell. It was someone else who realized vampires were coming. Cara was experiencing this through someone else's well-tuned senses.

Ten claws and a set of extremely sharp fangs simultaneously altered her appearance. Shuddering with distaste, she set out toward the trees, not half as scared as she should have been when the fate of so many was at stake. Her teeth chattered. Her heartbeats soared.

This isn't me, Cara chanted inwardly, trying hard to remember that.

Focusing on the area beside an old dirt road where the trees were thickest, she put a hand to her chest, barely able to perceive the sting of the grooves her claws were digging. The word *No!* shattered the silence into a million pieces that left a bad taste in her mouth. Enemies were coming, and not just the vampires.

The dark thing inside her stirred, recognized what those odors meant. She felt the cold spiral of that spirit's ascent.

Cara clenched her teeth as if that could keep the sprit trapped inside. Again, though, it was Rosalind who did the teeth clenching. This was Rosalind's picture. Rosalind's answer to Cara's request to view the past. Cara was merely getting a ringside seat at the show.

Cara shook her head to deny what was happening. Rosalind did the same as the dark spirit began to seep through her pores, turning her hands and arms a glossy shade of black. The spirit forced Rosalind to open her mouth. A cry escaped as the Banshee took over with a terrible swiftness, and the wail went on and on, shaking the ground and the leaves in the trees. But this wail wasn't for her.

The first batch of bloodsuckers appeared in the field

to her left. They wore rags, and those rags were bloody. Their gaunt faces were the color of dry bones. Black eyes sank into endlessly deep sockets. Their stink preceded them like a stale wind.

There had to be at least forty hungry, angry, soulless ghouls. And she alone would meet them. She was ready, and she waited for the crush that was to come. These monsters had hurt her lover, and she would make them pay for that.

Beside her, there was a sudden flash of white, as if the storm she had expected had come to ground in the form of a dazzling streak of lightning. That luminous streak sailed by her on two long legs, white hair and skin glowing like moonlight, and issuing growls that were as fierce as anything she had ever heard.

Colton had come. Ghost. Werewolf. Lover.

Her mate would fight by her side.

The white-furred werewolf tore through the vampires like a battering ram. Black blood and ash flew as he hacked his way through them with his claws active and jaws like a steel trap.

Rosalind ran toward him with her claws slashing and her legs moving to the rhythm of her heartbeats. She took one vampire down with a slice to its scrawny neck and another soon after that. A third bloodsucker tried its hardest to avoid her claws and her wrath and didn't succeed. Colton had cleared a path through the fang-snapping horde by circling to her right.

It wasn't until she reached Colton that she heard the sound of oncoming cars and realized what that meant.

The Landau pack had arrived.

More help had come.

The brush of a hand against her throat catapulted Rosalind into yet another shape, and her claws disappeared. With her fangs, she did more damage to the parasites now turning toward the group of Weres who were running toward them. Without a full moon to guide their ancient DNA, none of them could shape-shift into their strongest forms, but that didn't stop them. Ten werewolves joined the fight with silver-bladed knives and carved wooden stakes. Guns would have been easier, of course, but the sound would have carried.

More vampires went down. The scene, gray with a continuous flurry of ash, seemed surreal. Rosalind knew that Banshees didn't wail for the undead, and that vampires had no souls to call to death's door, but none of the Weres had fallen tonight, and still the dark spirit's cry again pushed upward through her to escape through her parted lips.

Blue sparks accompanied the ear-shattering wail. Hearing it, the handful of vampires left standing stopped fighting. In the periphery came the rustling sounds of demons gathering as if they had been invited to a party. Those sounds closed in.

The werewolves cut down the vampires, taking advantage of the suddenness of their frozen state. If they sensed demon presence, they didn't let on. Each dusted vampire was a point in their favor on the road to victory.

The pale faces of another enemy now formed a large circle around the fighting field, shining like small fires in the dark and reflecting the flames from which they had sprung.

When the werewolves stopped to acknowledge the newcomers, the fact that the worst was yet to come was reflected in the expressions of all the Landau pack.

And yet no one moved.

The demons stayed back.

Because the Banshee's wail hadn't been meant for any member of the pack. It had been meant for her.

That realization was the impetus for another shapeshift. As it began, all eyes turned to her. Waves of anxiousness ruffled through the crowd, affecting Weres and demons alike as they tracked her next transformation.

Her skin again became a glossy black before quickly fading to ivory. Her hair, now waist length, hung over half of her face like a shiny black curtain. Something wet trickled down her chin, and black blood stained the fist she raised to catch it.

Banshee.

But the transformation didn't stop there.

Her skin began to dry out. The ivory smoothness became yellowed and cracked as her shoulders hunched forward. From each of the grooves in her chest that she had made with her claws came tiny licks of red-orange flame. As her insides overheated, she blinked through eyes able to see right through the skin of the werewolves around her.

Demon.

Colton was there beside her, seemingly unafraid of this latest incarnation that even Rosalind feared. She was to die. The Banshee had wailed for her...but which incarnation had the Banshee perceived and chosen to call to death's door?

Was it going to be her, as Rosalind Kirk, or the hell spawn that had taken her over? Could the Banshee separate one soul from among so many facets of herself?

The thought that prevailed as she waited to find out was that she might never see Colton again. And in spite of that, she had to make sure he lived.

She lifted an arm and uttered a sound that brought the circle of surrounding demons forward. The reptilian creatures that owed fealty to hell came to her like moths to the flame, hustling forward without realizing they were going to be slaughtered and that she was not really a demon, after all. She just looked like one.

Spurred into action by the gruesome sight, the Weres attacked with force. Mesmerized as they were, the demons didn't know what hit them. And the Banshee, the dark and brutal entity she carried around, wailed again as the last vestiges of the demon in Rosalind died with them.

Within the chaos of bodies dropping and werewolves growling with humanlike throats, Colton was there, again in his human form, and he was speaking to her.

"One more shape-shift" was his request.

Rosalind saw the form of this shift in his mind, and what he wanted from her now. He desired to see her in her own skin. He wanted to look into her eyes. When he reached out to her, she didn't back away.

Her gaze drifted to the werewolves who had fought so bravely. Dylan Landau was there, and beside him his mate, Dana Delmonico. There were others she recognized and couldn't name. All standing. Not looking too bad after their valiant fight.

When Colton took her hand, the next changes began. Glancing down, she saw that her hands and arms were again becoming thin and pale, and that there were no claws. Her lips closed easily because her fangs were gone. No bloodstain remained on her fist. Rosalind Kirk was back to face her lover. But her hair was no longer a deep midnight black. The tendrils covering her shoulders were snowy white—an exact match for Colton's hair.

She had taken on the ghost wolf's whiteness. They were now both ghosts of a sort, and would be feared by the Weres who had come to their aid…though those wolves would never have admitted it. They were Lycans whose systems had been compromised by fate, and by so many other things that lay beyond their control. For them, there was no going back. There was no normal, and never had been.

She and Colton would not find life easy after this night. The Landau pack had seen some of her many variations and would always be afraid of her, or at the very least, wary.

"We will go away," Colton said to appease her fears. "Away from staring eyes and the need to think of ourselves as freaks. We'll go someplace where in the future the monsters won't bother our friends. Do you know of such a place?"

Cara, stunned by all this, nodded along as Rosalind whispered in reply, "Home."

Cara staggered backward as the images she had seen and shared dissolved. She gaped at the spot where Rosalind and Colton had made that pledge.

Some of sickness that had been growing inside her eased, though not all of it was so easily dislodged by what she had just witnessed. Seeing her parents in action drilled deeper into her the fact of how different they had become and how dangerous they were. It was those differences, and the need to feel free, that had taken her parents away from Miami.

And she was like them.

Rafe, her beautiful lover whom she craved with every fiber of her being, would be alpha of the Landau pack someday…while she would always be eyed with distrust if she were to stay.

"You know," a voice said in her ear. Rafe's voice—

deep, masculine and loaded with concern. "The worst trait I can think of is avoidance of a problem that can be solved over time. I don't believe there's a shape-shift for that."

Chapter 30

Cara was shaking. Rafe tightened his grip on her hand, not sure if he should gather her in his arms. There were hints of wildness in her wide-legged stance. Her eyes were glazed. Close enough to whisper to her, he hoped his voice might bring her fully back from wherever she had gone, and that she would believe every word he said.

"You know...the worst trait I can think of is avoidance of a problem that can be solved over time. I don't believe there's a shape-shift for that."

She didn't immediately respond. She didn't seem to see him. Rafe's heart rate sped as he searched for cracks in Cara's demeanor that might provide him with insight on what was happening to her. He had to admit to being shocked by the way she had looked minutes before. There was an added pressure in his chest over the way she looked now. But Cara hadn't gone anywhere. Only her mind had.

Her face had drained of color. Her black hair lay

flat against her slender body, hugging her curves. She seemed frailer, thinner. Inside his hand, her fingers curled into a fist.

"Come back to me," he whispered to her with the re-alization that Cara was not only the epitome of the con-cept of *wild*, but that she always would be. There was no way to tame her inner beasts.

"If you take me, you take it all," she had messaged to him, which now seemed to have been a long time ago.

Born to wildness, and reared on its taste, Cara would always be an enigma who kept her problems, like her Banshee, trapped inside. Who knew what she had seen out here? He hadn't been able to share that, but there was no doubt this had been a very real experience for her. Proof of that was in the rapid loop of expressions her face had undergone and the quakes that continued to rock her. Whatever she had seen had taken a toll.

She must have once again been taken over by Ro-salind for a time. Cara had spoken to him of partaking in her mother's memories, but she hadn't confessed to actually becoming part of those memories. However, he knew that was what was happening. Hell, she had jumped from that window.

Her mother's memories had to be what Cara had found here, and what she had been searching for. Was it done now? Was her search for the past over?

Could they move on?

As for Rosalind…he didn't have to know what had transpired here in order to understand what Cara's mother had done in this place, and which monsters had been present at the time. That too was part of the leg-end and mystique of the Kirk-Killions.

Werewolves had fought vampires and demons in this

field, and had survived. Cara's mother had called them forth and then dealt with the problem they presented.

And now, Cara was so pale and distant.

"I'm here," he said, hoping to get through to her.

Rafe couldn't tear his attention from her for even a quick glance at his mother, who stood by the car. It was highly possibly that his mother had also taken part in that past skirmish. His father as well. This was another example of the tie binding Cara's parents and the Landau pack. They had fought together on more than one occasion, and in Fairview's front yard they had carved out a victory that had chased the monsters off Miami's streets for a very long time.

Like her mother, Cara—his lover, the she-wolf he had sealed himself to—was also an enticement for monsters. But his pack could handle that. He could handle that. If this was his future, then okay. He was all in.

I just want you...

"Think of what kind of a help you can be here," he said. "You can give us a bird's-eye view of anyone or anything intending to ring the doorbell. Housing a Banshee can allow us to see our own futures, if the spirit is willing to show us. Your talents can save lives here, and not just ours."

He had so much more to say. So many things to tell Cara.

"Maybe losing some freedom will be a sacrifice on your part, but I'm willing to help in any way that I can. I will be beside you."

No. Damn it, that wasn't what he wanted to tell her. Was this the time and the place for him to relay the rest? That for better or worse, they were a team forever?

"You are not alone, Cara. I think you know that."

She didn't meet his eyes. Her skin was almost transparent.

"What was once here is over and long gone. It's time to go. It's not safe to remain."

Heaven only knew what could happen if the vampires seeking her found them here in the open with no backup, and with Cara in a semi-catatonic state. He and his mother could put up a good fight if it came to that, but would Cara snap out of her stupor?

Cara leaned forward as if suddenly lulled by his voice. Her long lashes fluttered, creating shadows that contrasted with her skin. She took a big breath, and when her eyes reopened, they were once again a clear, vibrant green.

For now, her inner battle, whatever that had been, had been won.

He reached out to steady her, wanting desperately to kiss her trembling lips. God, how he wanted that. But this wasn't the right moment to indulge his feelings, so he laced their fingers together to reinforce their bond, determined to get through to her and to fix the fallout from a bad situation.

"In finding what you sought, does that make things better or clearer to you? Does it change things here in the present for you or for us?"

She blinked slowly as if finally wakening to the world around her. With another deep breath and in a wavering tone, Cara said, "It changes everything."

She could have meant what she said, though Rafe didn't believe it. Cara was still seeing things through a different lens and was being suffocated by what she had found.

Rafe's soul ached for her and the burden she carried. Hell, what was the life span of a spirit, anyway? Would it have a hold on Cara forever, or until she found a way to pass that spirit along to somebody else?

Was there a way for her to get rid of the Banshee and keep the promises her family had made so long ago?

"Cara, look at me."

Her eyes traveled upward with an agonizing slowness. They were haunted eyes, and thoughtful.

"Nothing changes. Do you hear me? Nothing," Rafe said.

His mother had moved up to stand behind him. Cara turned her gaze that way.

"We all have something that tries to drag us down now and then," his mother said. "The strength of our character is what defines us. You were born with that kind of strength, and that's what will move us forward from here."

"You were here, so you know how this goes," Cara observed.

"Yes," his mother conceded.

"Why did you offer to host someone like me?"

"Because of promises that were made a long time ago, and the necessary fulfillment of them."

"What promises?" Cara asked.

Rafe sensed some discomfort in his mother's reluctance to answer Cara's question, which made it imperative for him that she did. He said, "Yes. What promises?"

His mother finally replied, "That our packs would join forces again when the time arose for such a necessity."

Rafe swore under his breath. "You're talking about the return of those vampires?"

"Yes," his mother said. "Among other things."

Rafe turned that over in his mind. Bringing Cara

here was some kind of payback for the aid the Landau pack had given to Rosalind and Colton a long time ago? Their daughter had been sent to Miami in order to flush the monsters out when and if they resurfaced in this city?

If that was true...

If that was true, Rafe thought with an appraising glance at his mother, then someone here had known about the return of the vampires and had not provided that information to the rest of the pack.

He zeroed in on his mother's practiced cop face, which seldom gave anything away, as the final piece of that idea struck him.

Someone who had known about that old promise had called it in, and Colton and Rosalind had sent their secret weapon in the war with monsters. Their only offspring. Their only daughter.

Cara.

So now you see...
Now you know.

She hadn't just been sent here to assimilate with other Weres, but to help them. Only she wielded the magic necessary for finding anomalies and beasts.

This was a wake-up call. That was the way Rafe was describing his sudden enlightenment in the thoughts he was telegraphing. Yet who among them could have anticipated that their packs would be joined together in other ways, or that she and Rafe would be mates?

He was looking at her. Trying to read her, in turn. Rafe was like a rock in this gathering storm, and so very brave to have gotten this far.

Things were in the open now, so there was no need for any of them to hide what they were thinking.

"So how many demons can we expect, Cara? One of them killed that human who was dumped near our wall, I believe," Dana said.

It was time to do her job. What she had been sent here for. There was no running from this kind of commitment. Still, Cara wondered if this was the reason Dana Delmonico Landau had brought her to Fairview tonight. Dana had used a little added pressure to kick Cara's senses into overdrive.

"Only one demon came for me," Cara said. "A bullet took that one down."

"Not before his friends found out about you?" Dana pressed.

"They share thoughts the way we do. If that one found me, others will follow."

"Christ!" Rafe muttered.

"And the vampires?" Dana asked.

"There's a nest not far from the beach. Vampires don't travel far from their resting places, and that's where the first one appeared. The park shouldn't be part of their area, but that's where I met the second one and his friends."

"That's the vamp presence you detected around the body we found?" Rafe asked.

"Maybe," Cara replied.

Dana cut in. "Wanting what you keep hidden inside can't be the only reason these creatures have come aboveground."

Rafe responded with new insight. "Because whoever brought Cara here might have known of the monsters' return before calling the Kirk-Killions for a favor. Either that, or we have a psychic in our midst who can predict the future. It's possible that Cara isn't the inciting factor for vampires coming out of hiding after all and that her presence here is only coincidental with that."

Rafe tightened his hold on Cara's hand. She would have loved him for that alone when there were so many other reasons for her feelings.

"Our alpha seemed to be as surprised as we were by news of the vampires. If he knew about this, he has become a damn fine actor," he said.

Dana shook her head. "It wasn't your father who sensed vamp presence and started the ball rolling. I would have known about that."

"But the alpha would have initiated my invitation," Cara pointed out.

Dana was eyeing her thoughtfully. "Yes. Dylan sent the invitation, but it wasn't to confront a possible vampire invasion. It was so that…"

"Cara and I could meet and possibly form a friendship?" Rafe finished for his mother.

His grip on Cara's hand could have snapped a human's bones. She relished the minor twinge of leftover discomfort in that injured hand that told her some of her fears about winding up alone in this strange life would disappear if only Rafe continued to hang on.

Had she been promised to Rafe as a mate? Was that one of the promises Dana had mentioned, or had the fates she had blamed after first setting eyes on Rafe Landau been responsible for getting them together, meaning that most of this was pure coincidence?

"Our relationship aside," Rafe said, tensing slightly, "it would seem that there's another mystery to be solved here. Who butchered that body, and why?"

Though the question needed an answer, he quickly circled back to the former subject. "Wasn't it a long shot that Cara and I would imprint?"

Dana didn't shirk the question. "I suppose. However, Colton and Rosalind were willing to take that chance if it eventually led to you being mated." Dana looked to Cara as she went on. "Because if it worked out, Cara would be freed from the burden she carries."

Cara's insides began to twist. Another shudder rocked her. What Dana was telling them would never have crossed her mind. She hadn't thought it could ever happen, or even be a possibility.

Could it be true?

That Rafe was to save her soul?

They would have a child, and if that child was a daughter, the Banshee would have a new soul to share.

When Rafe's gaze came back to her, Cara met it. Though he didn't immediately speak his thoughts out loud, Cara heard them as if he had.

"If we were to have a daughter..."

The thought of that sickened Cara the way it must have sickened her mother when the time came to pass along the dark spirit to its new younger, stronger host...

Because who could have wished such a thing for anyone they truly loved?

Chapter 31

Rafe rallied quickly and herded Cara toward the car. He was silent, though his mind whirled with questions, most of them having to do with sacrifice.

Cara's family had sacrificed their life in Miami in order to save others from harm. Sending Cara here had been about their wish for a hopeful future for their daughter, freeing her of at least one burden—ending her turn with the Banshee. Then there was the fact that Rafe's own family had been willing to tie their son to a Kirk-Killion and all that went with her by honoring promises they once had made.

Sacrifice.

As Rafe saw it, he was the big winner here. Cara was his. What was done was done, and the only direction open to them was forward.

He felt Cara's racing pulse through his grip on her hand and warned himself not to look at her face. If he did, he would likely see her horror over what she had learned about their possible future progeny.

She'd be wondering how she could possibly pass the dark spirit to anyone else after having experienced what that kind of life was like, let alone asking such a thing of a child of her own. She might vow never to have children, which in turn might lead her to contemplate their relationship and possible ways to break the chains binding her to him.

Hell, he wasn't going to lose her. And anyway, that breakup couldn't happen.

Cara stopped when they reached their vehicles, and a new wave of tension ran through her. Rafe turned to search the driveway.

"Even I can smell that," his mother said. And she was right. Foul odors were drifting across the field, emanating from the area beneath the trees that they had just left.

Inner warnings came too fast for Rafe to acknowledge all of them, but one warning stood out and brought him a new round of fear. The only way for Cara to sever their bond was for one of them to die.

If Cara were to sacrifice herself in order to prevent a dismal childless future, perhaps she'd assume the Banshee might die with her. Where would the dark spirit go if that were the case?

"Don't you dare think that way," he said to her adamantly. "Please get in the car. We can outdistance this fight, at least for now, until we know more about it."

His mother didn't waste any time. She dived behind the wheel of the black SUV and started the engine. Rafe opened the door and ushered Cara inside.

"Go," he directed. "Take Cara home." He trusted his mother to take care of her, and she didn't argue.

Anyone who had been a cop, or in any way affiliated with law enforcement, trusted others in the field to do the right thing and make the right choices. His mother took off in a whirlwind of kicked-up dirt and debris, jamming the car into Reverse, then wheeling it around to head down the driveway at breakneck speed. Cara's face in the window became a white blur.

Rafe got behind the wheel of his borrowed sedan but didn't follow the SUV. After starting the engine, he steered toward the trees, determined to see for himself what kind of abomination had come for his lover this time, and if there was anything he could do about it.

"He won't do anything stupid," Dana said as Fairview Hospital slid into the distance. "You don't have to worry about that."

Cara leaned back against the seat, feeling sick and thinking about jumping out of the car. She couldn't see Rafe or the vehicle he had been driving. It was entirely possible that Rafe's mother didn't know her son as well as she liked to think, and his next choice might surprise her.

"It worked," Cara said.

"Yes." Dana didn't pretend not to understand what Cara was talking about. Two families touched by tragedy had been joined at the hip. She and Rafe had become lovers, which had been one of the secret goals for bringing her to Miami that had been exposed at Fairview tonight.

"That must have been some promise your pack made to my family," Cara said. "I wonder what you think about it now."

"I think that had you come here under any circumstances, there would have been the same result. I see the way you look at each other. No one made you do that."

"Rafe knows what I am."

Dana nodded. "We all do."

"Yet you'd accept the consequences of such a pairing for your family? Welcome it?"

"Yes."

"Why?"

"Because everyone benefits, especially you, Cara. And because you've taken your turn with this spirit and deserve some freedom of your own."

"What about Rafe?"

"You'll have to believe me when I tell you that my son can take care of himself and has never once done anything he hasn't chosen to do."

"He chose me."

"Yes, he did."

"And that fell right into the original plan for bringing me here."

"Yes, though none of us could have been sure what might have happened," Dana said.

In Cara's mind, the two objectives for her visit to Miami had been tied together in a nice little knot. She had walked right into this, she realized as she replayed the events of the past few days in search of the details she might have otherwise missed.

En route to Miami, she had jumped from the car that had been sent to transport her and had ended up at the beach…when she now knew that beach was nowhere near the Landau estate. It was in the opposite direction.

This raised the question that nagged at her now. Had someone predicted that she'd try to escape and planned to have her taken in the direction where she had ended up that first night…which just happened to be in Rafe's front yard?

Could anyone actually have seen that far ahead?

Who would have had an idea about the kind of male she'd be attracted to, and vice versa? Her parents?

Had they...could they...have planted those dreams about Rafe in her mind, so that she would recognize him the way she had when they met face-to-face?

Had their union been preordained by the parents who had raised her and who possessed the kind of power and talent to set such a plan in motion?

Cara's fingers closed over the door handle of Dana's car.

"Did you know?" she asked Dana. "Were you in on the details of his plan?"

Dana nodded. "It all came down to freedom."

"That's not the way I see it now. This plan was more like manipulation."

"You weren't forced to make the choices you made, Cara. Neither was Rafe. This could have turned out differently and been a big mistake, but I believe you'd be lying if you told me you'd have changed things."

Silence fell, as dark and weighty as the knot in Cara's stomach. Maybe Dana was right, and she would have fallen for Rafe in any circumstance without interference, but how was she to know that?

Dana broke the silence.

"Rosalind was eighteen and had never been to a city when she came here," Dana said. "You're also eighteen and have led the same kind of secluded life she did."

They were back to an area where streetlights kept the dark at bay. The sun would rise soon, and there would be a short period of relief from finding out what kinds of things the darkness had in store for her.

Closing her eyes was not an option. They had traveled away from Fairview, and yet Cara still strained for a glimpse of Rafe in the side mirror.

"You might have been conceived here," Dana continued. "Eighteen would therefore have been a magic number in all of this."

Cara's sickness doubled as that idea sank in. If what Dana suggested was true, the timing had also been perfectly planned for this visit. She was mating age, and had been hungry enough for companionship to look forward to those dreams of Rafe, in spite of her anger over having them.

Her fingers put pressure on the door handle as thoughts seemed to coagulate...

By mating with Rafe in the bedroom her parents had used, was there a chance she also might have conceived a child—a werewolf child she could then pass the dark spirit along to? A child carrying Rosalind and Colton's superior genes?

She needed to pull over and throw up but couldn't speak.

"I'm sorry," Dana said. "If I had known about all of the logistics of the plan beforehand, I could have approached you about it. I could have spoken to Rafe and armed you both."

"If you didn't know the extent of this plan, who did?" Cara barely got that out. She was millimeters away from opening the door.

"Rafe's grandfather," Dana said. "Landau alpha at the time. And your parents."

She hadn't escaped by the time the gates to the Landau estate appeared, but it was never too late.

Cara pushed down on the handle.

There was dark and then there was *dark*—true darkness that sprang from bad origins. Rafe's car's headlights barely made a dent in it. Like a creeping fog, everything outside the windows was a deep, solid black. So it was a good thing that all Landau vehicles came fully loaded with weapons and a stash of silver bullets in a secret compartment under the floor that only Landau fingerprints could access.

Things like that sometimes came in handy, and Rafe was afraid this was going to be one of those times. The foul odor he had detected had seeped into the car to choke him. Death's detritus was all too familiar to him, except that this time he wasn't in an enclosed room with a week-old dead body. The space around him was wide-open.

"Where are you, you damn bloodsuckers?" he muttered, yanking the wheel to the right to avoid a grove of ancient trees in need of water. Once he had passed the trees, Rafe stopped the car and left it to idle as he pulled up the floor mat and pressed his thumb to the digital lock.

The compartment holding the small cache of weapons and specialized bullets opened with a soft click. He reached inside for the gun, comfortable with it in his hand.

Then he got out of the car.

Cara stopped herself from making her escape, struck by a premonition of her own.

"Turn around," she directed as the gate opened to let them through. "Please. Quickly. Now."

"Cara…" Dana began.

"Rafe didn't follow us. He is out there, searching for them, and shouldn't be alone. He told me he had never seen a vampire before the incident at the beach. What are the chances he's seen a demon?"

Dana didn't balk or argue. She rolled down the window and barked orders to the guard. Wearing a worried expression, she turned to Cara. "Dylan is still in the park, but he will hear me and come. Whoever is with him will follow."

They backed up and headed toward the road to Fairview. Cara didn't press home the point that Dana had been wrong about Rafe and that they shouldn't have left him there on his own.

She shouldn't have left him.

Cara's pulse sped faster than the car. Rafe was going to protect his new mate and had sent her to safety. He was going to face demons for her, in her place, and all Cara could think about was that no matter what the plans had been, if Rafe were to die, her soul would die with him.

The SUV blew through several stop signs and a lot of traffic lights without incident or the police catching on. Dana had gone quiet, tucking her fears inside. Maybe she blamed herself for not seeing what Rafe was capable of. Again, this came down to choices, and whether anyone could accurately predict the behavior of another.

Cara couldn't sit still. How could she when she was sure that Rafe loved her? He had joined up with a monster hunter who was also a monster in most eyes. The thought of a budding love between them, so soon and so very unique, caused another kind of drumbeat deep inside, this time arising from fear.

Was Rafe doing this to give her the choices she hadn't had? Was he willing to sacrifice himself for her?

She felt the tingle of the warmth of the sun that now sat just beneath the horizon like an emerging ball of fire. Its presence was in the air she breathed. The closeness of sunrise was the saving grace in all of this. Vampires and demons couldn't function in daylight. They would burn to a crisp in the light of a new day.

And as far as she knew, another body had not turned up before the stars came out, as the dark spirit had predicted.

Which meant that body hadn't yet been found.

"Hold on," she messaged to Rafe on a channel she was sure he would hear. *"Hold them off until I get there. If you can... If you do...we can..."*

She didn't get to finish that message, and probably couldn't have anyway without the vocabulary necessary to tell Rafe how she felt. Love was new to her.

And it hurt.

Chapter 32

Rafe saw nothing past the beams of the headlights at first. There was no extra weight to the air here and no added foulness now that a breeze had arrived to cut the stink of whatever hid from him. He wasn't alone, though. Were senses told him so.

"She's gone," he called out. "You came here for nothing."

The almost total absence of sound was odd. There were no night birds singing and no crickets or other bugs doing their thing. Rafe's thundering pulse took up the slack.

"Either you crawl back to where you came from, or you come out to face me. What other choices are there?" he said with a firm grip on the gun he held behind his back.

Sudden rustling sounds behind him made Rafe turn. More came from his right, but he stood his ground.

"You know you can't have her. Think of me as the gatekeeper on that score."

Adrenaline turned his skin icy. Sensing these creeps without being able to see them made his stomach clench. Hell, were there vampires out here, or something even worse? What did demons look like, and how fast did they move? He had a nagging suspicion that he was about to find out.

Something slid past him, momentarily blurring the light from the headlights as it headed into the pool of blackness beyond the car. Rafe had no idea what it was. The thing had moved like a streak of misplaced air rather than anything hampered by a solid form.

He turned in a slow circle, watching, searching, waiting, for the next surprise. Each passing second put his practiced cop nerves to the test. "Everyone here has to behave," he muttered to break up the silence and calm his nerves.

Out of the corner of his eye, Rafe caught sight of another blur of movement and brought the gun forward with his finger on the trigger, ready to do some damage if it came to that.

"Show yourself," he said at a reasonable volume, figuring anything that could move so quickly might also have exceptional hearing.

More rustling came from his left. Then behind him. And again to his right. All signs pointed to his being surrounded, and he had how many silver rounds loaded in the damn gun?

Nerves buzzed like loose live wires. Rafe settled his shoulders and widened his stance. He took a deep breath. There was an annoying twitch beneath his left eye. But his hand was steady on the weapon that wasn't aimed at anything…because as of yet there was nothing to see.

He backed up to press himself against the warm metal of the car's side panel. If anything came from behind, it would have to leap over the car and he'd have time to address the threat. His cell phone was in his pocket. He should have made a call before heading in this direction, so his mother could summon backup and return. At least, since he hadn't gone far into the grove on the property, there was a chance that the small staff working underground at Fairview Hospital might have heard the engines and come out for a look.

As if that last thought had kicked up a disturbance in the atmosphere, a solitary form suddenly appeared in front of him. He hadn't even seen anything move, but this sucker was a familiar sight—gaunt, ghostly, white haired, white-faced and all fanged up. Though it might have been human once, it definitely didn't fit into that species anymore.

This was the vamp they had met in the park, the leader of a nest. The decrepit, odorous bloodsucker didn't seem to care about the gun Rafe aimed at its bony chest. After all, it had died once or twice before.

"Glad you decided to show up," Rafe remarked, alarmed by the sight in front of him but still steady enough to deal with this creature. "Too bad there's nothing here for you presently. Surely you've sensed that."

The bloodsucker returned in a mocking tone, "She will come. Surely *you* have sensed that."

The worst part was the ring of truth in the vamp's response. Cara might return when she discovered that he hadn't followed her. She could be on her way now if his mother also realized the potential of the danger he faced.

"She will never give you what you want," Rafe said. "You're wasting your time."

"I have plenty of time to spare. On the other hand, you do not share that luxury," the creature remarked.

"Luxury? Look at you. Time has not treated you well."

"Spoken by a werewolf with a limited life span," the vampire countered.

"At least I don't live off the life force of others. I don't troll the human race for my food supply."

"And yet I would not trade places with an animal that was never human to begin with."

"Yes, well, I don't think anyone would have offered you that choice," Rafe said. "And as a side note, Cara still isn't here."

The old vampire smiled, showing off a pair of chipped, yellowed fangs. Flat black eyes looked beyond Rafe in a way that made Rafe afraid to follow its gaze. He wasn't sure if the sucker had truly seen something or if this was part of an old ruse designed to shift Rafe's attention elsewhere, leaving him vulnerable to those fangs.

He had not heard a car arrive. He didn't sense Cara's return to the area when there was no way he could have missed her. Part of her soul now belonged to him, and he would fight every vampire on the earth if he had to in order to keep it.

Finally, the old creep moved, breaking the standoff with a sideways glide. Rafe adjusted his stance, determined to keep this monster in his sight, and realized shortly afterward that the vampire had detected something else. Not Cara or a car. The rustling noises he had heard earlier were back and seemed to come from everywhere. The strange thing about it was the fact that the vampire across from him appeared to be as wary of the sounds as he was.

This meant he and the vampires weren't alone, and it was possible the two of them weren't going to be the only species represented here.

The car wasn't going fast enough for Cara. But the old Fairview sign finally appeared in the headlight beams and the SUV skidded into a tight right turn.

"Wait," she again messaged to Rafe. *"Almost there."*

When no reply came, Cara sent her senses out to find him. What she located out there turned her skin cold. Chills engulfed her as Dana took another sharp right turn and the outline of the hospital loomed in the distance. Dana had no further questions now. She too was intent on finding Rafe.

Cara was out of the car before it came to a complete stop and sprinted for the trees. Behind her, Dana swore out loud and gave chase. This was a déjà vu moment for Rafe's mother, who had been here back then, when Rosalind was the central focus and monsters flocked to her like lemmings. Dana Delmonico Landau had seen what haunted these woods and was up for round two, bless her.

The distance from Fairview's chain-link fence to the trees was nominal. Cara covered it fast. She didn't stop to listen to the troubling sounds or to pay heed to the creatures that had gathered in such a doomed spot. Rafe was all she cared about. *Now* was the only thing that mattered. That, and the sound of Dana breathing hard behind her.

The vampires that had taken up residence here tonight didn't stop her. Passing the contorted faces of the demons that had come to party with her soul was a breeze. She slowed only after reaching the car Rafe had been driving. The engine was silent, but the headlights were on and the driver's side door had been left open.

The only thing missing from this scene was Rafe.

Cara urged Dana to be silent with a raised hand. *"Rafe?"* she messaged to him and then waited out an adrenaline rush more intense than the one that had gotten her this far.

Had that cagey old vampire found him? The scent of the creature tainted the air and brought bile to her throat. But that wasn't it, Cara suddenly understood.

"Demons," she hissed, as if uttering that word was an act of blasphemy. "We meet again."

Beside her, Dana said, "Shit."

And then the area became quiet again.

The next sound Cara heard was the voice of a vampire she had already met. She had been right in assuming the old bloodsucker would show up.

"I told him you would come," the pale-faced sucker said, appearing in the shadows the car's headlights didn't reach.

Ignoring the vamp, Cara closed her eyes to concentrate harder on Rafe. There were others here, her senses warned. The darkness was filled with a presence that even this ancient vampire would fear.

Vampires walked the earth hoping never to taste the tarnished fruits of the hell they would eventually descend to when their final death came. This was possibly the reason the old vampire desired to claim the dark spirit for himself...so that he could cheat death and continue endlessly on.

Demons were what everyone feared. So, how many of them had come to this place? It was curious how quickly they had located her. And it was a no-brainer that she would have returned to fight beside her lover.

Cara turned in a slow circle to place the positions of the hell spawn in their surroundings before opening her eyes. "Ten demons," she said to enlighten Dana, adding, "Not much of a party at all, really."

To the vampire, Cara said, "Where is he?"

"Right here," Rafe said, causing her heart to lurch as he sprinted from the shadows to draw up beside her.

Cara could have thrown herself into his arms now, the way she had always wanted to, yet she managed to restrain her careening emotions. Rafe was here. He was safe. Whatever happened next would be an anticlimax.

But…why was he safe with so many monsters around? How had he avoided them?

"Bait," he said, reading her thoughts and eyeing her steadily before nodding to his mother. "In order to catch a prize, everyone gets that you have to dangle the bait."

"They used him to get us back here," Dana said, frowning.

"The plan worked," Rafe agreed, brushing up against Cara's shoulder as if he also needed the comfort of a quick touch.

"You have a gun," Dana observed. "And bullets that will count. Why haven't you used it?"

"There's something else out here that I haven't been able to pinpoint. Another presence that has made our enemies as wary as we are."

"But now we have you, dark one," the vampire said without moving toward them. "One of us will be victorious when we shake that spirit from you and eat it alive."

Still, the vampires didn't advance to make good on that threat, and neither did the demons that looked on.

So what was going on? Why were these monsters so anxious about doing what they had come here to do?

Cara spread her arms wide. "All you have to do is come closer, vampire…if you can coax the spirit from me, that is."

"Cara," Rafe warned.

She went on. "If you kill me in the process of taking what you want, you might kill the Banshee as well. Then where would you be? Demon fodder? Demons don't discriminate between the living and the dead. Can't you hear the sound of their jaws chomping?"

The vampire accepted the taunt by stepping forward. Once the signal had been given, the rest of the bloodsucker's fanged friends rushed in from beneath the shelter of the trees.

Chapter 33

All hell broke loose.

Next to Cara, Rafe started shooting, picking off vampires by aiming at their pathetic chests, where their hearts used to beat. Four of them exploded before Dana raised the revolver she had stuffed in her belt and joined in. The sound of gunfire was deafening. The clearing filled with sticky gray ash, which prompted several more vamps to come running.

Given a party like this one, the demons weren't to be left out. Some of the ten Cara had counted flew forward, leaving their human disguises behind. Cara's claws sprang into existence like lethal switchblades as Rafe bumped against her. Wielding them like knives, Cara began her dance of death, swinging, slashing, ducking and lunging at each monster that came her way with a fury and a force they hadn't been expecting.

More vampires exploded. Clouds of ash rained down. Only one demon burst into flames, having gotten too close to Cara, before the fighting shifted into high gear and the demons shrieked with displeasure over losing one of their own.

"Each kill weakens them," Cara shouted. Rafe and Dana were reloading their weapons in turns and fighting with their fists while they did. There was motion everywhere. Falling ash hampered sight.

So far, she, Rafe and Dana were holding their own. The Banshee hadn't wailed for them, so death wasn't imminent, though deep in her gut, Cara had a bad feeling about the outcome of this monstrous barrage. There was another presence out there, Rafe had warned, and she had known this from the start, but besides vampires and demons, what did that leave? Right then, she had no further sense of what sort of visitor could be out there, and there were too many monsters as it was.

Cara had never seen so many bloodsuckers in one place, except in her mother's show-and-tell of shared memory less than an hour ago. These vampires and demons hadn't attacked each other here, which would have been the norm. They seemed to have banded together, with the possible acquisition of a dark spirit as their common goal, though no love was lost between denizens of the darker species.

Cara's fangs appeared soon after the fourth vampire came at her. Black blood covered her cheeks when she used those fangs to tear at the hands reaching for her throat. She moved through the attackers in a whirlwind of fury. Attracted to this kind of power, the dark spirit she held back soared upward with an icy chill.

No. Not now. Not yet, Cara cautioned. She couldn't afford to lose her concentration. If she did, all would be lost.

The clearing crawled with supernatural attackers.

Rafe now mainly used his fists, his fighting fueled by raw, wolf-backed strength. Next to her, Dana, showing no visible sign of fear, had become a fighting machine. And yet even the strongest werewolves didn't come equipped with an endless supply of energy, and their stamina would eventually wane. When it did, the remaining demons would approach, sensing that weakness.

For the first time in her life, Cara began to lose hope. She fought harder, growled with each strike, grunted as she dodged oncoming blows. Her goal was to protect her lover and the spirit that everyone wanted a piece of. She could not have Rafe harmed, especially now that she loved him. She couldn't let her family down.

Those thoughts had barely taken wing when a bolt of white lightning crashed through the crowd, tearing through vampires and demons like a guided missile bent on destruction. It wasn't actually lightning, though, but something made of flesh and bone that moved with the force of a terrible storm.

She had no time to find out what this new interruption was. Slowing down meant defeat. Yet the white streak seemed to be taking out monsters as if it was on her side.

When a high-pitched howl echoed through the clearing, Cara's ears rang with internal warnings. Her stomach turned over. But the howl had a strange effect on everyone in the battle.

Fighting slowed, as if the harrowing sound had contained a command. The vampire Cara held on to paused, shuddered and tried to backpedal. Rafe's demonic attacker lost focus and turned toward the trees. Dana lowered her gun.

Confused, anxious, wary and with their hearts in

their throats, Cara and her companions also turned toward the echo, because every wolf on the earth recognized what such a sound meant. It was the song of triumph and of impending victory when the Weres here were still outnumbered and things didn't look good. And it had mesmerized everyone except Cara, who had heard that same sound once before in a dream sequence of her mother's memories about what had happened to Colton Killion in the park.

The aftermath of the sound was an uncomfortable silence that was dense and disquieting.

Rafe couldn't decide where to focus his attention. The echo of that howl went on and on, even though there were no walls out here for it to bounce off. The sound stirred his insides with hints of a forgotten past that no werewolf now knew. Images of mountains and valleys of trees flashed through his mind, there and gone so quickly he wondered if he had made them up.

All of a sudden, he felt connected to a larger picture that he could only manage to see the smallest part of, and the sensation lifted the fine hairs on the back of his neck. He wasn't the only one affected by the suddenness of new sensations. Every beast in the clearing had frozen in place as if they had been on the receiving end of a stun gun.

Cara looked to be as shocked as he was. His mother was holding her breath. As for whatever had moved through them like a lightning strike in the seconds preceding that howl...intuition warned that this also needed closer scrutiny. However, Rafe didn't turn to glance in that direction, already certain that whatever the flash was, it meant the three of them no harm. The curtain of ash that continued to fall told him so.

He was covered in the foul-smelling stuff. His arms burned with demon fire. The attention of the vastly reduced forces of their attackers had been lured away from Rafe's little threesome by whatever they had deemed to be a greater threat. Fear and excitement ruffled through their ranks. Fangs were again gnashing.

But none of them moved.

The echo of the howl they all had heard was finally broken by another more earthly sound. Cars on the driveway. Engines revved. Doors slammed. Voices called out. Rafe would have said that his pack had arrived in the nick of time if someone hadn't already hit the pause button that had extended to him, Cara and his mother a short respite in which to recoup their strength.

He looked to Cara to make sure she was all right. Her eyes were bright with excitement. Her face was tilted upward as she listened to what was going on. Did she anticipate another kind of arrival? Something he hadn't yet perceived? He had felt another presence out there in the dark, but hell, had that presence announced itself in a way that others here had recognized?

The thunder of running feet was uncommonly loud in the silence that had fallen. His father would come armed with weapons and packmates, ready to rumble. And yet even as the pack entered the clearing to shift the odds of victory in Were favor, the monsters made no attempt to face them. The arrival of reinforcements didn't seem to matter to these monsters at the moment. In spite of that strange fact, Rafe breathed a sigh of relief when his father stood beside him.

"What is it?" his father asked as several Weres warily gathered around.

"I have no idea…and yet at the same time, I kind of do," Rafe replied abstractly, moving closer to Cara as he reloaded the gun. This had something to do with her. He was sure of it.

"Fill me in," he said to Cara. It was clear that she knew something no one else did. He saw this in the way her eyes pleaded with him to wait, and to stand down.

His nerves buzzed. His muscles twitched with the sudden inactivity. What was everybody waiting for, exactly? And was it a good thing, or bad?

When Cara stepped forward, he stopped her with a hand. She didn't look at him now. Her attention was riveted to the shadows across from them…and the slow approach of the creature that had caused such a ripple in the night.

Chapter 34

Cara's heart pounded frantically as the shadows parted. She took a shallow breath, then another in anticipation of an event she had thought she'd never see.

Her father was here.

A warm wash of familiarity hit her square in the chest as Colton Killion appeared. The ghost wolf had left his self-induced seclusion and had quite possibly saved the day.

It was he who had torn through the monsters like a lightning bolt of pure monster misery. No one could have equaled her father's exemplary fighting skills or brought such abject terror to his opponents. Without the ability to speak at the moment, her father allowed them all a good look at one of the fiercest werewolves on the planet, a Were who had died to his former Were self and returned as something else twice as formidable.

All white from head to toe and furred up like only

the rarest of pure-blooded Lycans, his height and the mounds of muscle clinging to his frame gave her father the appearance of an ancient wolf god. He stood in the blinking, fading headlights of Rafe's car like the legendary ghost everyone believed him to be.

And they all stared.

But he wasn't alone, and he hadn't been the lure for the creatures that had attacked Cara tonight. The ghost wolf, as stunning as his appearance here was, hadn't been good enough or strong enough to garner the kind of rapt attention the vampires and demons that had been left standing exhibited.

Her father, regal, terrible, in his colorless half-human, half-wolf form was merely the hors d'oeuvre before the main course. He was the guardian of a secret weapon that had once rendered monsters useless and had driven many of them so deep underground, it had taken almost twenty years for them to dare to emerge.

Her father had brought his mate. Cara should have known he would, because he never so much as left her side. Rosalind also had returned to Miami…and no one was ready for that.

The fear that drenched the clearing had its own smell and taste. One of the demons shrieked in anger. Two vampires hissed.

"Colton," the Landau alpha muttered with awe as Cara's father stepped aside to make way for his bride.

Cara felt the heat of Rafe's attention on her. "Christ," he said. "This is your dad?"

Rafe's remark faded as the headlights finally winked out, but no light was necessary for Rosalind's entrance onto the battlefield. She came as a large wolf on all fours with her black coat glistening and her ears pricked forward. Her delicate muzzle had drawn back in a snarl until her eyes, more human than wolf, found Cara. Then she reared up on her hind legs, shook her head hard and began her next shape-shift.

The black fur disappeared in the time it took for Cara to blink her eyes. Her mother's skin lightened to a smooth shade of ivory. Her limbs, slender and muscularly defined, took on a human shape. All that was left of the wolf Rosalind had been seconds before was her face until that melted into human cheeks, chin and long black lashes that rimmed a pair of light, serious eyes.

Rosalind Kirk stood before this gathering, tall and naked. Waist-length black hair infused with streaks of white partially curtained her torso as she raised a hand in greeting to Cara, then moved her arm to point at a pool of darkness beyond the trees nearest to the car. She spoke to those shadows in a deep, raspy voice. "You tried this one before, vampire. What made you imagine you would fare any better with my daughter?"

Rafe's hand slid to Cara's wrist, but she couldn't look at him yet. She didn't dare. The dark spirit inside her was twisting its way to the surface, drawn like everyone else to the sound of Rosalind's voice.

Rafe wanted to rub his eyes to make sure he was seeing correctly, but doing so would have meant letting go of his hold on Cara. *Legend* didn't begin to cover the pair of Lycans that had entered the clearing. He could not possibly have conceived of anything like this in his wildest imagination.

Still, Cara was his only concern. Cara's welfare. Her thoughts. What she might be feeling now when everyone here had gotten their first look at her parents.

At first, Cara seemed to be okay with the surprise appearance and the possibility of being reunited with her family. However, tiny quakes shook her arms as her gaze rested on the vampire that floated out of the darkness. Rosalind had called this old bloodsucker from its hiding place, and it was a bastard he and Cara had met before.

Still, Rafe kept his attention on Cara, whose shaking was getting worse with each passing second. He dropped her wrist and put his arm around her, able to feel how cold she was, thinking that odd when they had just exerted themselves and the night's temperature was soaring.

When her skin below the sleeves of her shirt began to darken, Rafe experienced a bobble in his stance. As the features of Cara's face began to rearrange, he fought the urge to shout for everyone to give them some space.

Rosalind was the most formidable presence he had ever experienced. The air in the clearing seemed to caress her, as if she had the power to call the smallest breeze. Colton, looking like a wolfish phantom, was a close second. And yet neither of Cara's parents could hold a candle to the daughter they had sent to Miami to find a mate. Because Cara had slipped away while he held on to her, and in her place was the dark thing that had glared at him from the tree in the park.

Exhaling a slow breath, Rafe looked this entity in the eyes, tightened his arm around her and said, "We meet again, Banshee."

Several things happened at once. The old vampire that had heeded Rosalind's call flew at Cara and the spirit that had taken hold of her. Rafe moved in front of her to ward off the first blow the vampire issued. He supposed a Banshee didn't require any assistance, and that as the right hand of death, she was the scariest, most dangerous creature here. But that assumption didn't take Rosalind and her many talents into account.

Cara's mother slid between Rafe and her daughter. Her pale lips parted for a whisper of sounds, the meaning of which Rafe couldn't comprehend. With a free hand, Colton caught hold of the bloodsucker's coat and spun it around. The old vampire was slower than its younger companions and in need of a meal that its age prevented it from getting.

This vampire wanted the dark spirit for itself. Rafe understood quite clearly that if that were to happen, vampires would no longer need to hide. With a vamp leader in solidarity with a Banshee, all bets for human survival would be off.

He fought with all his strength to prevent that from happening, even though he wasn't sure if such a union was possible. Vampires were undead creatures, and the Banshee called the living to their deaths. Besides, Cara would die before letting the spirit go.

Colton was there with him, beside him, tall, huge, all wolfed up and mean as sin. Colton had the thing by its scrawny neck and, with a growling heave, simply tossed the bloodsucker away. When it came flying back, along with a few undead friends, Rafe felt Colton's hand on his shoulder. He was torn away from Cara before he realized the predicament that left her in.

He couldn't get back to Cara fast enough. He saw Colton step away from her, leaving way for three vampires to flood in. Rafe's heart stopped. Although he couldn't catch his breath, Rafe hurled himself toward his lover, determined to end this once and for all.

He should have realized that Colton had backed off because he knew Cara wasn't in danger, and that he needn't have worried. All four vampires stopped before reaching her. In confusion, they stared at two exact replicas of the dark spirit in corporeal form. There were two Banshees, each as darkly threatening as the other. It was like seeing double. So which one was the real death caller?

This might have confused the bloodsuckers, but Rafe suddenly got it. Rosalind, with her talent for shapeshifting and adopting the form of whatever creature she got close to, had become a Banshee. *The* Banshee? Maybe it was a glamour that Rosalind had used to fool them. Perhaps her abilities were advanced enough to actually become a copy of the dark spirit that she had once hosted. No one could tell which of the dark duo standing there was the real thing. The tables had turned. Instead of Cara having that thing inside her, she was now inside it.

That confusion was all it took for Rafe, Colton, Rafe's father and his packmates to spring into action. Working together in a coordinated series of lunges and growls, they sent all of the vampires and demons in the clearing to their final spiraling oblivion.

When the fighting was over and the air was thick with ash and smoke from the leftover flames of demon fire, Rafe looked to the Banshees with his senses wide-open and his heart drumming. Cara was in there somewhere, and his ravenous hunger for her hadn't weakened one bit. If this night had taught him one thing, it was that one sorrow didn't have to piggyback on another. He would work hard to make Cara happy if she'd stay. Hell, she had to stay, because of those chains that bound them to each other.

Didn't she?

He could feel the love Colton and Rosalind shared. That love beamed from them. Following the awareness of that was the key to Rosalind's disguise. Turning to face one of the dark spirits, sure he had to be right, Rafe said, "You must see now that our lives depend on trust, honor and the need for friends. Please come back to me, Cara."

Rafe's second request was to the dark-eyed thing that had taken hold of his lover. Searching for Cara in the intense and wavering gaze of that entity was like looking into the realm of death. Gathering his courage, he said, "You must allow this. If you do, it will ensure your protection and our fealty for the next several years. This, I swear to you."

Cool fingers feathered over hers. Cara shuddered again. Rafe's voice reached her in spite of the dark spirit's rise. Its familiar soothing quality made her heart skip. She wanted to return to Rafe. She had to. If she did, she would never leave him again. *"A vow. My promise to you, Rafe."*

Cara tried to send that message to him.

"Dark spirit. Help me."

The icy chill remained. It was possible she had gone too far and had been too lenient in allowing the dark spirit her freedom so many times in a row. She felt the spirit expanding. Freedom was what every species craved. *"I understand that. I do."*

Did she hear Rafe speaking to her? Her heart raced faster.

"Please come back to me, Cara."

"I will. I want to. Rafe, can you hear me?"

There was something more in the distance, a faint whisper that had to do with fealty and protection. That whisper wasn't directed to her.

She spoke internally to the Banshee. *"I have done*

my part. My family has done theirs. Now you must listen to me and return my freedom."

Did the dark spirit listen? Had she understood? Like a running tap that was suddenly turned off, the burst of power she had felt began to recede. The flow became a trickle. Then a drip.

And when the final vestiges of the Banshee retreated, at least for the time being, and she could again breathe without pain, Cara opened her eyes.

Chapter 35

Rafe's breath hitched as Cara flung herself into his arms. Or maybe it was the other way around and he was the one who had rushed to gather her close. Either way, they were holding each other, their bodies pressed tight. His prayers had been answered by whoever had been watching this night play out, and for that he would be grateful for the rest of his days.

His lips hovered above hers. He was so very hungry for Cara and for the future he could perceive. He didn't give a damn about the others who were present—his packmates, his family and hers. This was what both families had hoped for. This pairing had been their plan all along, and rather than feeling used or manipulated, he was elated that it was going to work out. Cara had promised him that. He had heard every word.

As his mouth closed over hers, he heard his father say, "Thank you, Colton. It was you who placed the body near our wall, wasn't it, to alert us to demon presence? You've been here, watching over Cara from the start?"

Cara's lips parted. No sound came out.

In the hazy distance, his mother said, "A demon made the kill. If so, that poor human, good or bad, stood no chance."

Rosalind was there, too. Her presence was a powerful one unlike any other, living up to the legends surrounding her. She was so like Cara, only more so.

That thought also faded as Rafe deepened the kiss, needing to devour and reclaim what he had very nearly lost. His hands explored Cara's body, sliding over her back, her hips, her thighs. She growled softly to encourage him, and for a hungry wolf like Rafe, that was the ultimate seduction.

Could a death caller sense the pleasure moving through him, or classify it? Maybe he'd let her know.

Get used to it, Banshee...

He kissed Cara without letting her up for air, because every damn fiber of his being demanded it. And she kissed him back with a fervor that rivaled his. There was nothing tame about two werewolves mating. They would make love in human form tonight, and in a few days' time when the moon was full, they'd mate as wolves.

He was never going to take this for granted. It was enough, for now, to savor her taste...or so Rafe told himself.

Cara's body trembled as she leaned into him. An internal beat of pressure in his chest spurred him on. There was more about Cara to discover. There would always be more.

The sun was rising at last. Pink light edged the tree-tops, and there was new warmth in the air. In the back of Rafe's mind was a reminder that there would have been another death yesterday. The Banshee had predicted this, and Cara had let him know. Thank God his family was all here, and most of his friends were accounted for. So who was it going to turn out to be?

"A Were," Cara said when he gave her breathing room. "I don't recognize this one, and I'm sorry, Rafe. He fell near the edge of the trees before we arrived. Maybe he was watching the area? Someone from the hospital?"

He was sorry, too. Damn sorry that there had been a casualty here when the results of this fight had seemed so promising, and that it could have been someone he knew. He messaged that information to his father, who nodded with sadness.

There was nothing he could do about that death now. He would have to help his family tend to it later. He was finished with fighting for the time being, and with death and foreordained plans. Life lay ahead. He reached out to grasp it with both hands.

It was impolite to leave the others who had come to help in this fight, and to ignore both the latest victim of this battle and the keen observation of both sets of parents…but Rafe's emotional state demanded it.

Cara was hurting. She was alive and she was everything to him. Before he did anything else, he was going to prove that to her.

So he reluctantly took her hand. Then he turned, nodded an apology to everyone there, and ran.

Rafe had no idea how much time had passed as he rose from the comfort of Cara's naked body, panting from exertion and covered in sweat. Sometime during their wild, prolonged lovemaking session, daylight must have come and gone again. The night was quiet and almost eerily calm. Not even a breeze stirred the silence. Above them, the moon shone with a silver gleam, but it wasn't full, and nowhere near as powerful as what he held in his arms…

"No," Cara said, putting a finger to his lips to interrupt the sensations he was experiencing. "It's their
memories you've tapped into. You're seeing the end of
this through Colton and Rosalind's eyes. The spirit is
showing you that picture, and it's nothing but a view of
old memories, Rafe. We have to make our own."

Rafe blinked back his surprise. Hell, it had seemed
so real. But he and Cara were backed into a corner of
Fairview's chain-link fence, and not on the ground. The
sky was still pink with a new dawn, and they were still
hungry for each other and half-dressed. It turned out
they hadn't even gotten to the best part yet.

Another thing to be grateful for.

"Keep your damn images to yourself," he muttered
to a distant Colton Killion. "It's our turn."

A slow smile lifted the corners of his mouth. As
Cara's eyes met his, her face lit up with a beautiful smile
that showed no gleam of fangs. And it was one of the
best things he had ever seen.

He laughed out of pure joy. As she laughed with him,
Cara's green eyes danced with a mixture of longing and
mischief. Yes, he loved her. Rafe loved everything about
her. And with that acknowledgment, the next phase of
their life began in earnest, punctuated by the sound of
Cara's zipper on a slow, downward slide.

This mating was going to be no simple thing. Their
love would have meaning for their pack's future, and
also for the future of the werewolf species. If Cara bore
a child, the dark spirit would again be passed on and a
new breed of werewolf would continue to be loosed on
the world. And the world would change.

Cara knew the ramifications and responsibilities of
housing the Banshee, and like Rosalind, would be able

to help her daughter to prepare if he and Cara were to be blessed with female offspring.

Maybe this Banshee had a say in determining the sex of a child in order to preserve herself and her hiding place. If she had a say, did that make the Banshee a selfish entity, or merely a survivor?

Those were serious questions, but nothing he could come right out and ask. Not yet, anyway.

And hell…it was possible that dark spirits appreciated changing their hiding places now and then.

All that somehow seemed okay to Rafe as he left a trail of kisses across Cara's feverish neck, her chest, and in the valley of her breasts. She had thrown her head back, caught up in the throes of ecstasy. And her all-seeing eyes were closed.

For now, Cara was the only thing that mattered to him.

As for that future…

Late at night when the moon called and death was imminent in the city, the Banshee would howl, the black wolf would prowl, and he and Cara would fight for the right to keep their secrets and be who they were, together, in a world that was only beginning to comprehend the extent of the populations of other creatures that lived among them.

The thing was…neither he nor Cara—the love of his life, and the lover in his arms—would have wanted it any other way. So Rafe lifted her up, listened to the soft patter of her pants hitting the ground, and despite any lingering activity in the distance, wrapped her long, bare legs around him.

"Future memory number one," he whispered to Cara, meaning every word of that vow.

* * * * *

Jane Godman writes in a variety of romance genres, including paranormal, gothic and romantic suspense. Jane lives in England and loves to travel to European cities that are steeped in history and romance—Venice, Dubrovnik and Vienna are among her favorites. Jane is married to a lovely man and is mom to two grown-up children.

Books by Jane Godman

Harlequin Nocturne

Otherworld Protector
Otherworld Renegade
Otherworld Challenger
Immortal Billionaire
The Unforgettable Wolf
One Night with the Valkyrie
Awakening the Shifter
Enticing the Dragon
Captivating the Bear

Harlequin Romantic Suspense

The Coltons of Red Ridge

Colton and the Single Mom

Sons of Stillwater

Covert Kisses
The Soldier's Seduction
Secret Baby, Second Chance

Visit the Author Profile page
at Harlequin.com for more titles.

ENTICING THE DRAGON

Jane Godman

This book is dedicated to my new grandson, Harry.
Welcome to the world, little one.

Chapter 1

It didn't matter how many ways Hollie Brennan looked at the information on her laptop screen—the same pattern emerged every time. Only too aware of the problems the evidence posed, she had reviewed it over and over. Her faith in the computer program should have been absolute. She had been the person to devise it, and she had done it with just this sort of scenario in mind. It was used by fire investigators all over the country. Now she was doubting the information it was giving her. Instead of trusting it, she had gone back to basics. As she drank her early-morning coffee, the table in her small apartment was littered with maps, scribbled notes and scrawled diagrams.

She had even woken with a start at three in the morning, tearing herself away from her dreams of enchantment and mystery, before jumping out of bed to double-check one of the locations. But no. She had been right all along...which meant, no matter how crazy it sounded, she had to take this to her boss.

You have to listen to what the data is telling you, even if it appears bizarre. It was part of her introductory talk to trainee fire investigators. On this occasion, she was finding it increasingly difficult to take her own advice.

The streets were clear as she drove toward the office. This was one advantage of being up and about so early. She was half listening to the radio, her mind tuning in and out of the news stories, when the first bars of a rock ballad caught her full attention. It was the latest release from Beast, one of the biggest bands in the world. It was also, on this particular morning, the ultimate irony. After listening for a few moments, Hollie switched the radio off.

On arriving at the office, she was pleased to see her boss's car was already in its designated parking space. There was a joke among the agents at the Newark Division of the FBI that, since no one ever saw her come or go, Assistant Special Agent-in-Charge Melissa McLain might actually spend the night there.

Hollie didn't subscribe to the same view as her colleagues. ASAC McLain was a professional, but she wasn't an automaton. Maybe it was because of Hollie's unique role within the Bureau, but she had been granted occasional glances beneath the steely mask. They had even, now and then, gone out and gotten mildly tipsy together. No, McLain was human, and she was mightily pissed about their inability to catch one of the most prolific and deadly arsonists to come the Bureau's way.

On reaching the third floor, Hollie knocked on McLain's office door and waited for the abrupt instruction to enter.

"I come bearing caffeine." She held up the carton

from her boss's favorite coffee shop. She knew from experience that stopping on the way into work to purchase the strongest, largest espresso worked well in two ways. It softened McLain's mood slightly, and it meant she was forced to look up from her desk and focus on Hollie while they talked.

"It's never good if you have to bribe me." McLain removed the lid from the carton and closed her eyes as she inhaled.

"Not only is it not good—" Hollie sighed as she sipped her peppermint tea; the coffee had been tempting, but she needed a clear head for this conversation "—it's so weird I don't know where to start."

"How about the beginning?" McLain's direct gaze didn't allow for hesitation.

Okay. Deep breath. "You know I like rock music?"

A corner of McLain's mouth lifted. "I'm more of a classical fan myself, but I won't hold your musical preferences against you. Is this going anywhere?"

"Bear with me. About a week ago, I was looking at dates, hoping to get a ticket for Beast's next tour. They're like gold dust." *The facts. Stick with the facts.* "Anyway, there was a sidebar on the webpage, showing all the places they'd toured in the last few years. And it got my attention."

"Because?"

Hollie reached for her file of paperwork. "Because, in the last four years, the places Beast has toured are the towns the Incinerator has targeted. Our random arsonist is not so random, after all."

McLain's brows snapped together. "Let me see if I've got this straight. You're saying our arsonist set his fires in the same towns that this rock band tours? Does he do it at the same time?"

"Typically, the fires take place the day after a Beast concert. Sometimes two days," Hollie said. "But there's more. Once I found the link, I did some checking into Beast's international tours. Guess what?"

McLain took a gulp of her coffee, some of her customary poise deserting her. "Our guy has a passport?"

"It looks that way. In the four years we have been hunting the Incinerator, Beast has traveled to Europe, Australia and Asia. I checked with the police in each of those countries, and during each Beast tour, there were classic Incinerator fires in every location. Generally, the intervals between the international concerts and the fires were longer. Often they were weeks apart. But they always happened."

"Damn."

Hollie took her maps out of her file and placed them on the desk. "There's a problem."

"No, don't give me problems." McLain groaned. "Not when you've just given me the closest thing we've ever had to a breakthrough in this damn case."

Hollie pointed to the two maps. "This is a map showing the location of every Incinerator fire. This one shows every place Beast has toured. The two match up every time…except for recently." She pulled in a breath. Now for the hard part. "The last three Incinerator fires were set in towns that were *not* the location of a Beast tour."

McLain muttered a curse under her breath. "Why have you brought me this if you've already disproved your own theory?"

"Because there is another link." Hollie drew her electronic tablet from its case. "I reasoned that the Beast link was too strong to be overlooked." She brought an image of the band up on the screen. "This guy is the lead singer, Khan. He got married recently and the birth of his baby daughter twelve months ago coincided with the band's decision to take a break from touring. During that time, the other members of the group have done some solo projects."

Sensing McLain's impatience, she played a brief recording of the group. On the screen, dense smoke rolled like fog from the stage. Within it, colored strobe lights danced in time with the drumbeat. Giant LED screens at the rear of the stage projected alternating images of roaring fire, close-ups of snarling animals and Beast's logo, a stylized symbol resembling three entwined number sixes. At the side of the stage, explosions went off at random intervals, shooting orange flames high into the night sky.

Beast was a fire-storming force of nature, but McLain appeared unimpressed. "Why do I need to see this?"

"I want you to look at this guy." Hollie zoomed in on the front of the stage. Tall and muscular with his dark red hair drawn back into a ponytail, the man she indicated was all burning drama and flickering movement. Even on a screen, it was clear that the air around him sizzled into life as he timed the sweeping arc of his hand on the guitar to the explosions at the side of the stage. As they watched, he gestured in the manner of a conjurer, igniting a flickering blue blaze along the front of the stage.

"Looks like he enjoys playing with fire. Who is he?"

Hollie ended the recording. "Torque. Lead guitar."

The reason I wanted that Beast ticket. It was hard to explain her feelings about a man she had never met. Luckily, she didn't think McLain would require the additional information.

"You can match him to the other three Incinerator locations?"

Hollie nodded, withdrawing a third map from her file. "I tracked each individual member of Beast to find out what they have been doing during the past twelve months. Torque did a solo tour of small venues around the Midwest. We wondered why the Incinerator had changed his targets from big cities to small towns? It's because Torque did."

McLain leaned back in her chair, gazing at the ceiling for a moment or two. "You know what this means?"

Hollie nodded miserably. She was one step ahead of McLain. She'd already made the connection her boss was about to voice.

"We either have a crazed fan who is setting these fires as a tribute to his favorite, fiery rock star..."

"Or Torque is the Incinerator."

There were things Torque missed about touring with Beast. He enjoyed traveling. Since distance was meaningless to him, he particularly relished journeying across continents and oceans, although he found conventional means of reaching his destination restrictive. After twelve months of seeing his bandmates only occasionally, he could honestly say he was missing them. Even though they could collectively, and individually, bring him to a point where it felt like his head was about to explode, they were his friends. Too much alpha-maleness in one place was usually the problem. On their tour bus Beast was a cocktail of testosterone and shifter genes that meant one wrong look, or a word out of place, and the vehicle was in a constant state of near combustion.

Strangely, it was Torque, the fieriest member of the

group when performing, who often acted as the peacemaker offstage. Alongside Ged Taverner, their manager, Torque could defuse a situation with his calm manner and quiet good humor. When Khan, the lead singer, and Diablo, the drummer, were engaged in one of their snarling exchanges, most people stood back. Torque was the one who got between them and made them back down. That was probably something to do with shifter hierarchy.

There were plenty of things he didn't miss about being on the road. Torque hated being at the mercy of someone else's schedule, and touring felt like the ultimate restriction on his freedom. Food was always a problem when the band was on tour, both in terms of quality and quantity. Torque ate meat, and plenty of it. Well-done red meat. Everywhere he went, it was the same story. It didn't matter what country he was in, or what the establishment was. There was always an assumption that he would want salad, or bread, or some other trimming. The only accompaniment he wanted with his meat was more meat. Flame-grilled until it was black. No one ever understood that.

The other disadvantage to touring was the lack of privacy. There had been a time in the past when confidentiality wasn't an issue, when finding wide-open spaces away from prying eyes was easier. Now, of course, technology presented its own set of problems, taking surveillance to a whole new level. It meant he had to constantly stay one step ahead. But Torque was an expert at keeping secrets. He had been doing it for a very long time.

Unlike some of his bandmates, Torque had no problem with the rock-star lifestyle. Late nights? Parties? Groupies? He could handle anything fame threw his way. Yes, there were aspects of his life he didn't care to share with his fans, but he had learned how to strike a balance. And having billions of dollars at his disposal… well, that helped him maintain the life he wanted. It helped a lot.

He thought about that as he stood at the edge of his private beach, looking out across Pleasant Bay. When they weren't touring, the other members of Beast were based in New York, close to their recording studio. Torque owned an apartment in Manhattan, but this was his home. It had nothing to do with the celebrity life-style and everything to do with his personal needs. He didn't want glamour. This tucked-away, luxury Maine property had a perfect addition for anyone seeking the sort of isolation Torque needed. From where he was standing now, he could just about see the outline of his own secluded island.

Maybe it was thinking about his bandmates that had done it, but he was feeling restless. Having his own re-treat was all very well. It was here when he needed it, but on this particular evening, his need for company was stronger than the desire for solitude. It was a short walk into the town of Addison, and the regulars in the Pleasant Bay Bar didn't get starstruck by the presence of one of the world's most famous men. A few were fans and asked about tours and forthcoming albums. Others clearly had no idea who he was…and didn't care. Torque found this as refreshing as the beer.

The route from his house into town was one of his favorite walks. The dramatic coastline, with its craggy rocks and wild waves, was on one side and soaring pine forests on the other. It was a landscape from another time, making Torque think of days gone by. Of knights and maidens and heroic deeds. When humans looked beyond the veil of possibility and believed in magic.

It was still early and the Pleasant Bay Bar was quiet. The contrast as he walked from sunlight into shade made him blink. His eyes were extraordinarily sensitive, but they took a moment to adjust. The background music was a country ballad—*definitely not one of ours*—that suited his mood. Yes, this had been a good idea.

A couple of regulars were engrossed in a card game and didn't look up as Torque approached the bar. Another guy, whose name he couldn't remember, nodded a greeting. A few others didn't even turn their heads. Since there was no sign of Doug, the bartender, Torque leaned on the bar, content to enjoy the atmosphere. It was the complete opposite of many of the places he visited with Beast, lacking the crowds, the noise level, the darkened corners and gimmicks. Torque's moods were mercurial, but right now laid-back and quaint was what suited him.

Doug appeared from the storeroom at the back. "That's about it." The words were addressed over his shoulder to the woman who followed him.

As she emerged fully from the room and Torque got a good look at her, he had the feeling of time standing still. Dressed casually in jeans and a white linen blouse, she was of average height and slender build...and everything about her took his breath away. She had thick golden hair that bounced on her shoulders, an impudent, button nose and full ruby-red lips. Aware that he was staring, and that his interest was being returned by a pair of huge emerald-green eyes, he roused himself from his trance.

"Hi, Doug." He winced at a greeting that felt lame,

mainly because he hadn't withdrawn his gaze from the bartender's companion.

Doug didn't seem to notice. "The usual?" He held up a tankard and Torque nodded. "Did I tell you I'm finally taking that leave of absence so I can go traveling? This is my replacement..."

The woman at Doug's side gave Torque a shy smile. It made him want to leap across the bar to get closer to her.

"Hi, I'm Hollie Br..." She caught her breath, bringing a hand up to her throat with a nervous laugh. "I'm sorry. I've been a fan of yours forever. That's why I can't even remember my own name. I'm Hollie Brown."

That's why I can't even remember my own name? Ten minutes later and Hollie could still feel the blush burning her cheeks. How to blow her cover before she even got started. One look from Torque's unusual eyes and she had almost blurted out her real name. Not that he appeared to have noticed. He was still glancing her way every now and then, but the looks he was giving her didn't seem suspicious.

He seemed... Now that she gave it some thought, she wasn't sure how he seemed. Bemused? That might explain the tiny crease at the corner of his mouth when he stared at her. Nervous? How was that even possible? This was a man used to performing before thousands, even tens of thousands, of adoring fans. What was there about this situation that could possibly make him experience the same fumbling awkwardness she was feeling? Even so, his hand shook ever so slightly as he raised his glass to his lips. Most of all, Torque's expression was that of a man about to step over a boundary into the unknown. It was fear and excitement in equal measures.

Was it possible she was projecting her own emotions at this first meeting on to him? When she told him she had been a fan forever, it was the truth. Her love of Beast had always centered on Torque. For someone as grounded as Hollie, her adoration of a rock star had always been a slight annoyance to her. It almost felt out of character, like something she should have been above. And that starstruck sensation when she had gone to their concerts and seen him onstage? *So not me.* Even though he had been a speck in the distance, the pull of attraction had been so strong it had brought tears to her eyes.

To come face-to-face with her idol in these circumstances was the ultimate irony. To feel that same attraction up close, while under pressure to do her job…no wonder she was having trouble thinking straight. As she performed the routine tasks behind the bar under Doug's supervision, her stomach was churning and her hands were clammy.

Hollie had never worked undercover, and once McLain had decided to place Torque under surveillance, things had moved fast. Checking out the area around his home, local agents had come back with information that the owner of Torque's favorite bar was a former cop. If they could get someone in there, right up close to their target, just for a few days… Someone who could observe a celebrity rock star without arousing his suspicion…

"Have you ever worked in a bar?" McLain's sharp eyes had narrowed as she studied Hollie's face.

"I had a summer job when I was studying…" She had caught the trend of her chief's thoughts and trailed off. "No way." Blatant insubordination was not her style, but this was out-and-out crazy. "You need an experienced undercover agent."

"I need someone who knows the Incinerator. You've worked this case from the start, Hollie." Things were serious when McLain used her first name. "You understand everything about our fire starter." McLain had flipped over a sheet of paper. "This John 'Torque' Jones. You also know about him. This is highly sensitive. If we screw this up, the press will be screaming harassment of a superstar and the Incinerator case will become public property. No one else can replicate your intuition about this. I want you to get up close to Torque and find out if there's a chance he's our guy."

Get up close to Torque? Hollie was twenty-eight years old, but that instruction still made her heart rate soar as if she were nineteen and attending her first Beast concert. She told herself those words had nothing to do with why she was here. She was a professional. Catching the deadly arsonist whose trail of destruction had led to billions of dollars' worth of damage and more than twenty deaths was all that mattered. That was why she had agreed to McLain's request. For the next few weeks, she wasn't Agent Hollie Brennan, Chief Fire Investigator. Instead, she was Hollie Brown, bartender.

As she felt Torque's eyes following her, she thought back to her eighteen-year-old self. How often had she gazed at the image on the cover of *Fire and Fury*, Beast's most successful album? It depicted the band in evening dress, all of them looking glamorous as hell and slightly debauched, as though the shot had been taken the morning after a heavy night. While the others were pictured leaning against a whitewashed wall, bow ties hanging loose and hands thrust into dinner jacket pockets, it was always Torque who drew her gaze.

In the picture, he was apart from his bandmates, half sitting, half lying on a set of stone steps. With his flame-red hair tossed over one shoulder, bronzed skin tones and long legs encased in daringly tight black pants, he could have been a fashion model. The black top hat he wore was tilted low, its shadow concealing the upper part of his face, but his beautiful mouth and chiseled jaw were visible. His hands were raised as though his long fingers were strumming an invisible guitar. It was a stunning, iconic image.

The man who tilted his empty glass toward her now with a raised brow wore torn, faded jeans and work boots. His black T-shirt clung lovingly to his biceps and emphasized his dramatic coloring. Even in everyday clothing, Torque was breathtaking. Even with his features that looked like they had been lovingly carved by the hand of a master sculptor, it was still his eyes that drew her attention. Just when they appeared a nondescript gray, the light caught the multicolored moonstone flecks in their depths, making them shimmer like opals in sunlight.

Those eyes watched her again from beneath heavy lids as she refilled his glass. "What brings you to Addison?"

Keep it simple. That was what the veteran undercover agent who had given her an intense induction course had told her. Vince King had coached her in every aspect of the role, going over and over what she needed to know until she was word perfect. *Stick to a short, basic story and don't elaborate.*

"I like Maine. I thought it would be a nice place to spend the summer." She smiled. "Don't worry. Although I'm a fan, I'm not a stalker."

She'd seen his smile on her TV and laptop, on the pages of magazines, on the huge LED screens at the back of the stage at concerts. Now she was experiencing its full force across a distance of a few feet. As her knees turned to Jell-O, she gripped the edge of the bar to keep herself upright.

"Good. I don't want any more of those."

So Torque had a stalker. His words implied there was more than one. Could the Incinerator be an obsessive fan? Torque was well-known for his fiery onstage antics. Were the arson attacks a sick tribute?

Or was Hollie, already a Torque fan herself, now feeling the hit of his attractiveness close up, reluctant to accept that he could be the man they were looking for? Whatever the truth turned out to be, she needed to take care. She had come here to unmask a fire-wielding killer. After only minutes in Torque's company, she was already in danger of getting burned.

Chapter 2

Days of yore. Torque liked that phrase. It was all-encompassing, conjuring up images of chivalrous knights in armor on white chargers, maidens in distress and, of course, the obligatory dragon who terrorized the neighborhood by demanding a regular blood or virgin sacrifice.

Except legend didn't always get its facts straight. Sometimes the maidens did the rescuing, the knights were the ones who terrorized and the dragons were in charge of chivalry. To Torque, *yore* was more than just a nostalgic word for describing a bygone era. It summed up a time when the veil between worlds had been thinner. When the line between magic and mundane was blurred. When mortals had accepted the evidence of their hearts and their souls. Science had brought humankind a long way. Its benefits were far-reaching, but it had closed down many of those instincts. People looked with suspicion upon the very things that had once sustained them. Witches were cast out, charms and spells were frowned upon, alchemy faded into insignificance.

And dragons? What of those unique creatures who, most people would say, had only ever existed in legend? Even the believers, the humans who truly wanted dragons to have been real, would shake their heads sadly and mourn their loss, holding on to them through their games, paintings and stories.

It was better this way, of course. The last of the true dragons had died out five hundred years ago, spending his last days on a remote island in the South China Sea. Now only the dragon-shifters—a unique breed of half human, half dragon beings—remained. If the world ever discovered their existence? Torque clenched his jaw hard. *Not on my watch.* He had no desire to end his days in a cage, poked and prodded in the name of research. Even worse would be to become an exhibit in the name of entertainment, paraded and ogled like an elephant in a circus.

Torque was a dragon-shifter, but he no longer bore any responsibility to the others of his kind. His leadership had been brought to an abrupt end and the world had moved on from the days of dragon clans and oaths of fealty. He was the last of his kin. The mighty Cumhachdach had been wiped out by powerful magic, his own life saved only because the sorceress who killed his clan had chosen to torture him by keeping him alive. There had been a time, once… He shook his head, clearing it of any lingering thoughts as he unfurled his huge wings and took to the skies. Once might as well be never. These days, his only loyalty was to himself.

He swooped over his private island, blending easily with the night sky. As he flew lower over the dense forest, his scales changed color to match the tones of the trees. Camouflage was the dragon version of invisibility. Had he ventured into a city skyline, he would have become concrete gray. When he passed over an ocean in daylight, he was the exact blue of the waves below him and the sky above.

Torque's eyes scanned the landscape, homing in on a tiny creature moving in grass and the tilt of a bird's wing many miles away. His ears isolated individual sounds, locating rustling leaves and human voices along the coast. Dragon senses were the keenest of all, but on this night he was distracted by his human emotions. Feelings he barely understood were pulling at the edges of his consciousness, forcing his attention away from the beauty of the landscape.

After centuries of being alone—and liking it that way—he had felt something deep inside him stirring. And he knew why. All it had taken was a pair of green eyes, a shy smile and an enticing figure. It wasn't as if he lived a hermit's life as a human. He was a rock star. Temptation came his way and he didn't turn it down. Beast worked hard and played harder. Although the dynamics had changed now that Khan, lead singer and former party-animal-in-chief, had become a happily married man.

Torque knew why his emotions were in turmoil. The Pleasant Bay Bar's new employee had shaken him so much he couldn't think of anything but her. Hollie Brown was undeniably good to look at, and she had admitted that she was a fan. A plume of white smoke rose from his nostrils into the night sky as he snorted. He encountered fans all the time. His head wouldn't be turned by nothing more than a pretty face.

No, this was about something deeper and far more dangerous. Throughout the many centuries of his existence, Torque had never considered the possibility of taking a mate. Dragons mated for life and so did shifters. Fortunately, his mortal persona wasn't bound by the same constraints. When it came to his sex life, Torque preferred to be guided by his human genetics. They had served him well…up to now.

Now, suddenly, his instincts were telling him things were changing. It was crazy on so many levels. He knew nothing about Hollie. But he knew everything he needed. As soon as he had looked into her eyes, he had recognized two things. The first was that she was his. As if that wasn't earth-shattering enough, the second was that she wasn't who she claimed to be.

So, let's take a second to analyze this... My mate just strolled into town. And she's lying to me.

It wasn't the best start to a long-term relationship. And he had to accept that his instincts must be wrong. Because Hollie couldn't possibly be his mate. She was *human*. Dragons and humans? How could that ever be a thing? Other shifters could take humans as mates. It was rare, but when it happened, the humans could choose to become converts. That meant they could take the bite of their mates and be transformed into shifters themselves. Although it was a huge commitment, Torque had known of a few occasions when it had happened.

Not for dragons. To maintain the purity of the dragon bloodline, the option to convert a human mate didn't exist for them. A dragon could have a relationship with a mortal, but it could only ever last as long as the human's lifetime. They could never truly be fated mates.

Even supposing he decided to initiate the whole "mates for your lifetime" conversation, he couldn't picture it going well. *I'm a dragon...* He just couldn't see it working as a first-date conversation starter.

Normally, Torque looked forward to these nighttime flights. Maine wasn't Scotland, the dramatic land of his birth, but the scenery wasn't entirely dissimilar. Tonight, his heart wasn't in his exercise routine. He had a feeling those green eyes and that shy smile might be responsible for his apathy. Something about Hollie had reminded him of the past. Yore. In those days there had been a creed, a code of honor, and she had reawakened it within his breast. Although nothing about their encounter had led him to believe Hollie needed his protection, Torque's senses were on high alert. *If* she had been his mate—and that was one hell of a big if—and *if* there had been a looming danger, back in the day he would have been beneath her window, watching over his lady while she slept. Simpler times, easier solutions.

Circling the bay one last time, he landed on a slope close to the trees. His huge claws gripped the soft ground, gouging deep into the grass. Folding his wings close to his body, he shifted quickly back to his human form. Naked, he stretched his limbs, enjoying the sensation of the cool air soothing his heated flesh.

He had left his clothes in the boat and he shrugged them on, weighing up whether to spend the night on the island. The little cabin in the trees was basic, but comfortable, and he kept the refrigerator stocked in case he decided to stay over. But he needed Wi-Fi if he was going to check his emails for details of Beast's forthcoming tour. And he wasn't sure the isolation of the island suited his current restlessness.

Torque could have easily rowed the distance across the bay, but he liked the soft chug of the motorboat. Although he enjoyed the peace of the bay from the skies, now he was seeing a different view. This time—the hours between midnight and dawn—the old witching time, was when that veil between worlds was thinnest. When it almost seemed there was still a hint of the old magic in the air.

His inner dragon was a creature of contrasts, craving wide-open spaces when in flight but seeking solitude when grounded. The cinematic depictions of dragons living underground, guarding their hoards of treasure, were an exaggeration, but he liked enclosed spaces. Out here, on the water, he felt small and alone. Un-dragon-like. It wasn't unpleasant, but it challenged his shifter senses. And speaking of senses…

He tilted his head, trying to figure out what was different. As he neared the wooden jetty in front of his mainland home, he caught the first whiff of smoke. It was delicious and woody. The scent of burning called to his dragon the way catnip affected a kitten. Except something was wrong. The scent was out of place and the night sky over the town shouldn't be lit by a golden glow.

Leaping out of the boat, Torque broke into a run as he realized what was happening. The Pleasant Bay Bar was on fire.

Hollie's room was tucked away at the top of the old building. Doug had been apologetic about it. "I don't know why the boss suddenly changed his mind about letting me go traveling. Don't get me wrong—I'm glad he managed to find a replacement—but the short notice meant I didn't have much time to get this room ready."

She had assured him that the room was fine. And it was. A little on the small side, but it was clean and comfortable. Since she wasn't going to be in Addison for long, it hardly mattered. There was no point finding an alternative. Once Torque left Maine to go on tour, she would be returning to Newark. This was somewhere to sleep, to use her laptop to record her notes, to call in to McLain and to gather her thoughts.

Ah, her thoughts. They should be all about the job she had come here to do, shouldn't they? But they weren't. She was totally shaken by how much the encounter with Torque had affected her.

You are a twenty-eight-year-old FBI agent, for heaven's sake. You cannot still have a crush on a rock star.

It didn't matter how much she reproached herself, how hard she tried to concentrate on typing up her notes, half her mind remained firmly fixed on a pair of shimmering eyes and a very disturbing smile. Torque's mouth had lingered in her imagination as she drifted off to sleep. The disturbing, but pleasant, fantasy of feeling that full lower lip against her own had been achingly real...

The dream came quickly and she tumbled into it, welcoming it like a familiar friend. She couldn't remember a time when she hadn't experienced this slumbering adventure. It was warm, comforting and thrilling all at the same time.

Her sleeping self approached the giant creature. The beautiful red-gold dragon lay still, his breathing deep and rhythmic. A faint thrumming issued from his chest, and wisps of smoke curled from his nostrils, but she knew his inner fire would be subdued in slumber. His powerful hind limbs and huge coiled tail were tucked beneath him, and he slept on top of his hoard. His precious gems and jewels were scattered all around him, their brilliance dulled by the light of the cave.

When dream-Hollie approached, the dragon's eyes opened as if a switch had been flicked. Smoke poured from his nostrils, and there was a sound of scales sliding over coins as he shifted position. Keeping his wings tucked in tight, he lifted his head to gaze at her. Hollie raised a hand to touch his face...

She came awake abruptly, angry that her dream had been interrupted. Her annoyance dissipated fast as she realized what was happening. Hollie had been in too many fire simulations not to recognize the real thing when she was thrust into the middle of it.

Subconsciously, when she arrived at the Pleasant Bay Bar, she had done what she always did and checked out the fire safety systems. The bar itself had been fine. As a business, it needed to comply with industry standards. When it came to an escape route, her bedroom was not ideal. It had only one door and a small window high above the street. She hadn't realized, when she checked those things out on her arrival, that she would be putting them to the test quite so soon.

Smoke was already filling the room. Sliding from the bed, she found the T-shirt she had taken off when she undressed and tied it around the lower part of her face. Crawling commando-style in order to stay low, she made her way across to the door. Just as she had feared, one touch told her everything she needed to know. The wooden panels were hot beneath her fingertips. It meant the fire was raging on the other side of the door.

Although the window was her only escape route, she already knew it wasn't going to be easy. She was two floors up and there was no fire escape. A thirty-foot drop onto concrete faced her. *Break the glass and make some noise.* That was about the best plan she had as she crawled her way back across the room.

This was no coincidence. That thought hammered through her mind as the toxic smoke stung her eyes. The stench of synthetic carpet burning and electrical wiring melting made her gag. Above the roar of the fire, she could hear the whine of a smoke alarm. But it hadn't done its job. It hadn't warned her in time. It was a discordant thought, one for which she didn't have time. She spent her life fighting fire, but this one was personal. This one was meant for her.

As she reached the window, the noise level changed. There was sound that could have been a roar of fury and the door came crashing in. *That shouldn't happen.* Hollie knew how fire behaved. Although it could be unpredictable, it didn't kick down doors. Through the choking haze, she saw a tall figure, framed by shimmering tongues of fire.

It's too late. I've inhaled too much smoke...now I'm seeing things.

She sank helplessly to the rug, her eyelids drifting closed as the flame-haired figure strode toward her. She was swept up into strong arms...or maybe swept away on a tide of unconsciousness. It was impossible to tell which as she felt the searing heat on her exposed skin and through her lightweight pajamas.

Opening her eyes, she gave a horrified gasp. She was in Torque's arms, and he was advancing toward the door. He was purposefully carrying her into the source of the fire. Desperately, she squirmed against him.

"Keep still." His voice was different. Authoritative, slightly rasping. "If you move as we go down the stairs, I can't protect you from the flames."

This couldn't be happening. This man—one of the most famous rock stars in the world—couldn't seriously think he could get them down that blazing staircase. *I am about to be killed by my celebrity crush. Either that or I really am hallucinating.*

Unable to fight, she was helpless to do anything except press her cheek into the hard muscle of Torque's chest as he stepped into the flames. Her job made what was happening so much worse. Hollie had seen too many burned bodies, had attended too many coroners' inquests on people who had died in agony. This was a first. She had never come across a case in which someone had willingly walked through a blaze.

Yet, as Torque slowly made his way down the stairs, the strangest thing was happening. She could feel the heat of the flames, but it was like getting too close to a roaring coal fire. She was uncomfortable, but she wasn't being incinerated. Wrapped tight in Torque's arms, she had the strangest feeling that *he* was the source of her protection. But how could that be? It was like he was fireproof. She caught glimpses of what was going on around them. Flames were licking at his arms and shoulders, catching the long length of his hair and dancing gleefully like a halo around his head. Torque was on fire...but he didn't flinch.

As they neared the final step, one of the ceiling beams gave way with a weary groan. Orange cinders rained down on Torque's head as he reached up a hand and caught the blazing bar. Still holding Hollie tight against him with his other hand, he gave a grunt that sounded like it was half pain, half annoyance as he thrust the beam aside without breaking his stride. Two more steps and he was kicking open the door that led them into the street.

Her last memory before she passed out was of those moonstone eyes glowing bright with concern as he placed her gently on the grass.

Hollie slowly opened her eyes, hoping she'd been dreaming, fairly certain she hadn't. Her throat felt like she'd drunk a glass of chopped razor blades and her nose itched unbearably. Her eyes streamed with the effects of the smoke and she smelled disgusting. Lifting a hand, she could see thick black grime coating her skin. When she tried to sit up, everything ached.

A strong arm slid around her waist, and although she wanted to question its source, she was too grateful for the support. Leaning against a broad shoulder, she eased into a sitting position.

"What…?" The word came out as a feeble croak, followed by a coughing fit.

"I got you out before the blaze took hold of the staircase."

They were far enough away from the burning building to be safe from any explosions or debris, but she could still feel the searing heat of the blaze. When she tilted her head to look at Torque, he took away what was left of her breath. With his hair streaming in the breeze and his eyes glittering with that strange intense light, he appeared otherworldly.

Around them, a fire team bustled into action and paramedics approached. Hollie might be feeling the effects of the smoke, but her memory was clear. Torque was lying about what had just happened. He hadn't rescued her *before* the fire took hold. Like a comic book hero, he had carried her right through the heart of the inferno. And he was untouched, completely uninjured by the fire he had just walked through.

They should both have been incinerated. Instead, apart from the effects she was feeling from the smoke inhalation, they were unscathed. And Torque appeared… She searched for the right word. *Invigorated.* Perhaps it was the adrenaline rush of the rescue, but he appeared energized, his former laid-back manner replaced by restless, flickering presence he presented on-stage. Almost as if the fire had entered his bloodstream.

I am hallucinating.

As a paramedic knelt at her other side and placed an oxygen mask over her nose and mouth, Hollie tried to get to grips with her new, alternate reality. An existence that included a superhero rock star. A man who could walk through fire. How the hell was she going to explain *this* to McLain?

"My laptop." Her attempt at an exclamation was muffled by the mask.

"Pardon?" Torque leaned closer as he tried to hear what she was saying.

"All my clothes, my purse, my cell phone, my laptop… they were all in that room." Her voice was still a painful rasp, but she managed to get the words out.

There was nothing left of the top floor of the Pleasant Bay Bar. The roof had fallen in and bright orange flames were shooting into the night sky. It was a pyrotechnic performance of epic proportions, almost as if the fire itself was celebrating.

Hollie's professional senses got to work, weighing up what had happened. The fire must have started in the upper part of the building. Was it an arson attack? It was too soon to say. But it was an awfully big coincidence that Hollie, the person who was here to investigate the Incinerator, had almost died in a fire. The second thing Hollie noticed was that Torque had gotten here before the emergency services.

He had saved her life, and from that, she might assume he wasn't the Incinerator. Unless the rescue was a huge double bluff, designed to throw her off the scent? As she turned her head back to look at him again, she had the oddest sensation of her world tilting off balance. Was Torque the Incinerator, and was he capable of such cunning? If he knew she was here to investigate him, had he planned to set a fire and save her from it, thereby lulling her into a false sense of security? Her heart wanted to rebel against such an idea, to tell her he wasn't behind such deviousness, but her training and her experience warned her to be wary.

Hollie had been part of the team hunting the Incinerator for four years, wondering how the daring arsonist had set increasingly elaborate fires and escaped without injury. She didn't know how Torque had walked through those flames and emerged unscathed. If she hadn't seen it for herself, she wouldn't have believed it was possible. All she knew for sure was, she had to find out more about this phenomenon and whether it was linked to their inquiry.

The paramedic removed the oxygen mask. "How does that feel?" The woman had checked her over and found no injuries. The only concern was the effects of the smoke.

"I'm fine." Hollie knew better than anyone what the health risks were, but she could feel her lungs returning to normal. "I don't need any further treatment." She bit her lip. "I just don't have anywhere to go."

"You can stay at my place." Torque's breath was warm on her cheek.

His words triggered a world of conflict inside Hollie. She was here to investigate him. Staying in his house was certainly one way to keep a closer watch on him. It was also a good way to put herself in danger. She could almost hear McLain's response. Outraged caution followed by an insistence that she get her ass back into the office immediately would probably be the mild version.

Hollie's own internal warning system appeared to

be broken. In spite of everything, her heart's initial reaction to his offer was a leap of joy. Common sense refused to prevail, but maybe that was because her choices
were seriously limited. It was the middle of the night,
she was coated from head to foot in foul-smelling ash,
she could barely open her eyes and she sounded like a
donkey with asthma. The only clothes she possessed
were these once-pink, now-black pajamas. Even if she'd
had the strength to get to her feet, she didn't have her
ATM card to draw the cash to get herself home…

With a sound that could have been a laugh, but was
closer to a sob, she rested her head back against Torque's
chest. It was a very comforting place to be. "Thank
you."

Chapter 3

Torque showed Hollie to one of the luxurious guest bedrooms. He explained that there were toiletries and towels in the bathroom, and brought her a pair of his sweatpants and a T-shirt.

"They'll both be too big, but until I can get to a store in the morning, it's the best I can do."

She plucked at the front of her grimy pajama top with a grimace. "Anything will be better than this."

"You're sure you'll be okay on your own?" He realized how that sounded and held up his hands in a backing-off gesture. "Not that I'm offering to help you shower."

She attempted a laugh, but it ended on a cough. "I'll be fine."

Her bravery and resilience astounded him. She should have died in that fire. Did she know that? Even if she hadn't figured it out, she must be experiencing a profound sense of shock, yet her courage shone through.

When he first saw her, Torque had been drawn to her because of her looks. Seconds later, he had taken the whole never-meant-to-be, fated-mates hit. Now her spirit and strength attracted him just as powerfully as her physical characteristics.

Overcoming a fierce desire to pull her into his arms, he left her alone. But the urge to protect her remained strong. Torque never slept well. The same sorceress who had stolen his liberty and wiped out his clan had once cursed him with her trademark insomnia spell.

Yeah, Teine, the fire sorceress...what a charmer she had turned out to be.

Taking up a position just outside Hollie's bedroom window, he sat on the grass with his back against the wall and his long legs drawn up so he could rest his forearms on his bent knees. From this angle, he could make sure she was safe and watch the sun rise over the bay. Not that he was in any mood to admire the beauty of his surroundings. His mind was wholly occupied with Hollie and what had just happened.

Being a rock star brought many privileges Torque's way. This beautiful house with its sweeping grounds and its dramatic views, his island, his fast cars and faster motorbikes...any material thing he wanted was his for the asking. But there was a dark undercurrent to his fame, one at which he had already hinted to Hollie. There were always a few fans whose admiration spilled over into obsession. Enthusiasts who thought they owned him because they knew his face and read every article and interview about him.

Even among a band of big characters, Torque attracted more than his fair share of obsessive fans. Ged, his manager, put it down to Torque's fiery onstage personality. "They see you as Beast's torchbearer. Even though Khan is the ultimate showman and Diablo has the dark, brooding looks of a Hollywood leading man, you stand out because the photographers love to catch you surrounded by fire."

Ged knew who Torque was, of course. The man who had rescued him from the centuries-deep spell cast by Teine was also the man who had given him a new lease on life as a musician. It was a strange life choice, but one that worked. Torque was the only dragon-shifter in the band, but he was among equals. Tiger, jaguar, snow leopard, wolf...his bandmates were all shifters who had been rescued by Ged. Their manager was a businessman by day, a were-bear who saved damaged or endangered shifters by night.

No matter how knowledgeable Ged was, Torque wasn't sure he bought into the torchbearer theory. It wasn't just that he got *more* contact from obsessed fans than his bandmates. The contact he did get was on a crazier level. Ged called it stalking, but Torque wasn't sure letters and emails fitted that definition. No physical contact was made—he had never even gotten a disturbing phone call—no harm had ever been done to him or his property. And being a shifter in a human world, he found it difficult to know what to do about that. Determined to maintain their anonymity, shifters steered clear of the mortal forces of law and order. Since Torque's obsessive fans had, so far, limited their activities to strange confessions and occasional threats, he had done his best to ignore them.

Until now. He had a feeling tonight represented a crossed line. Because some of the confessions were very specific. Torque was the person who played a burning guitar. He walked through a wall of flame. He raised a hand and, like the conductor of an orchestra, coordinated a series of perfectly timed explosions along the edge of the stage. And he attracted a small group of people who were unashamed and fanatical about their love of fire. People who looked up to Torque because they sensed something in him that appealed to their fixation. For those very few, it was an infatuation that bordered on worship. They believed he was a fire-god and they offered him their devotion…whether he wanted it or not.

Not. His expression twisted into a grimace of distaste as he tossed a pebble toward the shimmering water.

Being a shifter meant that two parts of him lived in harmony inside one body. His inner dragon didn't just need fire, it defined him. Sizzling through his bloodstream alongside his mortal DNA. But he was also part human, and that side of him reined in his fiery self. He knew what flames could do. He didn't worship fire, he respected it. While it excited him, it didn't arouse him. He could play with its force without pressing the destruct button.

Some of the messages he got suggested his followers—he used the word even though he disliked it—were unable to display the same restraint.

"If anyone gets hurt, I won't be able to stay quiet." That had been his ultimatum to Ged when the tributes first started coming. "That's my deal breaker."

"You think it isn't mine?" Ged's reply had reassured him. "If we find out any of these crazies has actually gone beyond the letter-writing stage, we'll do something about it."

As far as they could see, the madness had stayed on paper. It was wild and disturbing, but harmless. Tonight had been far from benign. Tonight, Hollie had almost died. And no matter how hard he tried, Torque couldn't separate that event from his obsessive fan mail.

His intuition about the fire at the Pleasant Bay Bar scared him. For several reasons, it filled him with more fear than anything he had ever known. First, it meant he was being watched. It was a possibility he had never considered. He wanted to be more intuitive, to be able to say with absolute certainty that he would know if a malignant presence was tracking him. But he didn't. He was a creature of legend and mysticism, but hunches and premonitions evaded him. His dragon instincts were all sizzling energy and action. He left the finer detail to others.

All he had was an uncomfortable feeling in the pit of his stomach that Hollie had been targeted. She was the change, the common denominator. From the moment he first set eyes on her, Torque had been in free fall, as if he had given up control of his emotions. They no longer belonged to him; they were the property of a woman he barely knew.

If he was right, someone else knew what had happened to him in that instant. Someone else was aware of the profound effect Hollie had on him. That person had witnessed their meeting in the Pleasant Bay Bar…and he, or she, clearly didn't like it. It shook him to consider that an observer could have known the impact Hollie had on him. It had been devastating to Torque himself, but he had fooled himself he had hidden it well. It seemed his acting abilities weren't as good as he believed.

Even so, no matter how many times he reviewed that scene, Torque couldn't find anything out of the ordinary about it. Apart from Doug, there had been only a few regulars in the bar. While he didn't know any of them well, he couldn't picture any of them as a demented pyromaniac or a jealous stalker.

His thoughts turned to Teine, the sorceress who had

fallen in love with him. When Torque didn't return her feelings—*because, let's face it, she was evil as well as crazy*—she had destroyed his clan and imprisoned Torque in an enchanted cave. He would be there now if it wasn't for Ged. But Teine couldn't be the person responsible for the fire. She was dead.

Dawn had sneaked up on him and the rising sun was a huge golden disk in the cloudless sky hovering over the silhouette of the trees. Torque knew from centuries of experience that darkness wasn't the enemy. Nightfall merely provided a cloak for evil deeds. Even so, daylight offered a return to normality. Stretching, he got to his feet.

Within his nighttime reflections, he had been skirting around the central issue. When Hollie awoke, she would want to discuss the fire and Torque would need to make a decision. How much was he prepared to share with her? About his suspicions…but also about his feelings?

Hollie opened her eyes slowly, leaving her dreaming world behind. The images had been even more vivid than usual. She had clambered onto the dragon's back, clinging to his muscular neck and pressing her cheek to his scales as he soared over a landscape that was wild, restless and angry. High, towering hills were slashed through with steep valleys and dark, eerie lochs. As they flew, the weather ranged in untamed moods from soaring discontent to blazing sunshine with no thought of moderation between. Although there was no exchange between them, she knew this was *his* land and she loved it for that reason.

As wakefulness dragged her from her slumber, she knew she was in a strange place. Even so, she felt a curious sense of comfort, as though she was wrapped in a protective cloak through which no harm could penetrate. As memories of the previous night came flooding back, her feeling of well-being dispersed. By the time she was fully awake, she wondered how she could possibly have felt even a trace of security.

Not only did her intuition tell her she had been the intended victim of a targeted arson attack, she needed to call it in. McLain's reaction was going to make the flash point of that fire look like a failed firework.

Oh, and I have no belongings. No clothes, no money, nothing...

That wasn't strictly true, of course. When Hollie called McLain, her boss would be able to get her out of Addison within the hour. She could walk away from this undercover job and be back in her own apartment later that day. It would be the safe, sensible thing to do. With every fiber of her being, she did *not* want to take the safe, sensible option.

Ever since the Incinerator first came to her attention, Hollie had felt a personal connection to him. She always thought of the arsonist as male, but she couldn't pinpoint why. Until now, her role had never been hands-on. She was a scientist. Her colleagues called her a geek and she accepted the name with an element of professional pride. It had taken a lot of hard work to reach this level of geekery, one where she was called upon to give talks to experienced fire investigators on the science behind the blazes they studied.

Hollie's inclusion in the Incinerator task force was an indication of the seriousness with which the FBI took the case. She was one of six senior agents assigned to the investigation into possibly the most prolific and dangerous arsonist the agency had ever come across.

Her expertise included fire behavior, analytical chemistry and the use of technology to enhance fire scene investigation. She used those skills to enhance and support the team.

The Incinerator's legacy was the stuff of nightmares. He was a daring exhibitionist who didn't care about the loss of life as well as the damage to property. The current death toll was twenty-one, but that didn't include the information Hollie had gleaned from the other countries. Her colleagues had still been processing the details of the new cases when she left the field office to come to Maine. There had been a sense of urgency about starting the undercover operation because Torque would soon set off on tour.

Her thoughts were interrupted by a soft knock on the door. She scrambled into a sitting position.

"Come in." Her voice had benefited from the few hours of rest. Although it was still croaky, it sounded almost normal and at least she could speak without coughing. She wished she could blame smoke inhalation for the way her chest constricted and the breath left her lungs in a sudden rush as the door opened. But no. That was the Torque-effect.

He remained close to the door, studying her face. "I want to say you look better, but you're way too pale."

"Shock." Hollie made a movement to brush the hair back from her forehead and was surprised to find her hand shaking. Her lip trembled. "I'm sorry…"

He was at her side in a single movement. Although Hollie's current role kept her away from the action, her early training had brought her in contact with the survivors of fire. She knew she was suffering the classic aftereffects. The extreme physical impact of the shock was receding, but the emotional trauma still had her in its grip.

For an instant, Torque hesitated as though he had encountered an invisible barrier. His expression was guarded, and even in her distress, Hollie took a moment to wonder what was going through his mind. Then he appeared to shrug aside whatever doubts were assailing him. Sitting on the edge of the bed, he drew her gently into his arms.

As she leaned her cheek against the warm, solid muscle of his chest, Hollie spared a fleeting thought for the rules of undercover work. She guessed this probably broke several of them. Possibly it smashed them all into tiny pieces. As Torque's arms tightened around her, the trembling that had gripped her began to subside. Rules were fine if things were going according to plan. Any plan of Hollie's was ash blowing across Pleasant Bay in the early-morning breeze.

After a few minutes, she lifted her head and attempted a smile. The expression in Torque's eyes was even more disturbing than the aftereffects of the fire. It was probably best to avoid any close contact in the future. Professional distance. That should be the new plan. Reluctantly, she drew away from him. Some new intuition told her he was equally unwilling to let her go.

"It was just…you know…"

"I know." His lips hardened into a thin line, indicating he was well aware that the fire was no accident. Suggesting that he wasn't responsible? *Don't make assumptions.* "You don't need to explain. It was a horrible experience, and recovering from it will take time."

Her brow furrowed, the unspoken questions hanging in the air between them. Torque must know what she wanted to say. He had walked through a blaze as though his flesh was fireproof. More than that. He had some-how used his body to form a protective barrier between Hollie and the flames. She didn't need her years of study and hard-earned qualifications to tell her he had defied the laws of science. He could pretend it hadn't happened, make up a story that he had arrived before the blaze took hold. They both knew it wasn't true.

"You saved my life." The huskiness in her voice wasn't entirely due to the smoke damage. "I don't know how you did it. I know you didn't get there before the fire took hold—"

"Some things can't be explained. Your perception and mine are different." He got to his feet, bringing any further discussion of the subject to an abrupt end. "I need to go out and stock up on some provisions. I'm not used to having a houseguest." His smile dawned, swift and dazzling. "I'll get you some clothes, as well, although I don't claim to be an expert in women's fash-ion."

Hollie laughed. "I'll be glad of anything I can wear with dignity. Your sweatpants fall down when I walk."

"There is one important thing we need to talk about."

"There is?"

"Underwear." Torque rummaged in the drawer of the bedside locker and produced a piece of paper and a pen.

Hollie placed her head in her hands. "I can't believe I'm sharing my bra size with the man I've worshiped from afar for most of my adult life."

Torque's face changed from laughter to seriousness, his eyes darkening to a slate-gray color.

"What is it?"

He shook his head. "Just that expression. *Worshiped from afar.* It makes me uncomfortable."

She waited for him to elaborate, but he switched the

conversation to practicalities. Pointing her in the direction of the kitchen, he explained that there was fresh coffee already made and the toaster could be temperamental.

"I won't be long." She sensed he wanted to say more, almost as if something was troubling him. Whatever it was, he shrugged it off and headed toward the door.

"Can I make a call?"

"Of course." The moonstone glitter was back in his eyes. "My God, I never gave it a thought. Your family..."

"I don't have any family. I'm an only child and my parents are both dead. But I have a friend who looks out for me." Although it was stretching a point to call McLain a friend, it was the best explanation she could come up with. "She can be a bit of a dragon, but she worries."

Torque's rich, warm laughter poured over her. When she raised questioning brows, he shook his head. "There are worse things than having a dragon to watch over you."

When the call went straight to voice mail, Hollie's stomach did a bungee jump. This was the secure line Vince King had set up when she went undercover. McLain was her designated handler. The agreement was that she would be available on this number 24/7. Hollie had memorized the number so carefully she was actually able to recite it in her dreams. Her nondragon dreams. Voice mail was not an option.

Maybe she had gotten one of the digits wrong. Taking a steadying breath, she ended the call without leaving a message. Slowly, deliberately, she tried McLain's number again. And got the same bland voice mail message once more. Panic gripped the back of her neck like a mugger's hand.

Breathe. Think. After a moment or two, the mists cleared from her mind and some of her usual calm returned. She was letting the Incinerator get to her. Somehow she was making this about him, turning it into something personal. There could be a dozen reasons why her call wasn't connecting. There could be a fault with McLain's cell phone. A signal problem here in Torque's house.

She ignored the little voice that tried to tell her those arguments weren't plausible. Even so, she wasn't in any danger. If she wanted to, she could walk out of Torque's home right now. Okay, she was barefoot and she would have to hold up his sweatpants with both hands, but the point was, she wasn't a prisoner. She could go to Addison, get in a cab and get the hell out of here. Getting back to Newark wouldn't be easy, but she could do it. No one was after her. There was no reason to look fearfully over her shoulder…

The thought immediately made her cast a fearful glance behind her. *No.* She wasn't going to do this. She had no proof that the Incinerator had set fire to the Pleasant Bay Bar, no proof that anything had happened to McLain. Her imagination was working overtime as a result of shock. Pure and simple.

Her cell phone had died in the fire, taking all her contacts with it, but there was someone else she could call. It wasn't part of the undercover protocols they'd agreed, but things had already veered so far off script she'd lost sight of the original plan. One colleague calling another wasn't against the rules. There were other problems attached to calling Dalton Hilger, but they were personal. And they were in the past, she reminded

herself. Her history with Dalton was something she preferred to forget. Unlike his cell phone number, which,
for some strange reason, was imprinted on her brain.

She knew he hadn't changed it. Dalton was one of
the agents on the Incinerator task force and she'd called
him just last week to check some minor details. Her
businesslike approach always jarred with his wounded
pride. Five years ago, ending their brief relationship
had been difficult. Even now Hollie always finished
a conversation with Dalton feeling like she'd kicked a
puppy…which was why her finger hesitated for a moment over the call button. But she trusted him, and that
was what she needed right now.

"Hilger." The word was a hoarse mumble. A glance
at the clock confirmed it was still early. Dalton wasn't
a morning person and Hollie guessed she'd just woken
him on an off-duty day.

"Dalton, it's Hollie." Sliding open full-length glass
doors, she carried the phone and her coffee out onto a
terrace that ran the length of the house. Torque had a
rock-star view over the bay and she sank into a cush-
ioned chair, drinking in the stunning vista.

"Hey, Hols." He yawned loudly down the phone.
"McLain briefed the team that you were away on some
Incinerator-related business."

"I am, but I need to get in touch with McLain and
she's not answering her cell phone."

He yawned again and Hollie could picture him. Tall
and handsome, with brown hair that never quite did
what he wanted it to, endearing in so many ways…*just
not right for me.* Unfortunately, only one of them had
been able to see that.

"McLain's away."

"What do you mean '*away*'?" The word came out

as an undignified squeak and prompted another coughing fit.

"Damn it, Hols. Could you warn me next time you
plan on squealing like that? I have very sensitive ears."

"Where has McLain gone?" She regained enough
control over her voice to infuse a warning note into it.

"How would I know? She's the boss. She doesn't
share her itinerary with me."

Hollie's mind was racing. This was all wrong. No
matter how urgent McLain's business might be, there
was no way she would have left Hollie without a contact.
So what should she do now? Share her suspicions that
McLain's absence was linked to the Incinerator and the
fire at the Pleasant Bay Bar? She knew how preposter-
ous it sounded inside her own head. Trying to explain it
to someone else, even someone she trusted as much as
Dalton? *Not happening.*

Unprompted, her thoughts turned to Torque. Maybe
her perspective had become skewed when he walked
through fire for her. It had certainly added another layer
to the whole mystery. She faced a stark choice. Do the
sensible thing. Tell Dalton about the blaze at the bar and
end her undercover status here and now. Or play with
fire—the analogy brought a grim smile to her lips—
for a little longer.

There was more. It was something she couldn't define. Hollie was gripped by a powerful conviction that
she *needed* to be with Torque. It wasn't to do with him;
it was about her. She had no idea where it was coming
from, or why it had taken such a powerful hold. Maybe
it was that old crush, or the shock of the fire. All she
knew was she had never felt anything so strongly.

Torque was the link to the Incinerator. She was sure

of that. Did Torque know it? If she walked away from him now, she might never find out.

"Are you still there?"

"Yes." She drew a breath, ignoring the pain in her lungs as well as the misgivings. "When McLain gets back I need you to give her a message. Tell her my cell phone has been damaged, but I'm fine and I'll keep trying to call her."

"Okay, but I don't know when I'll see her." To her relief, Dalton didn't appear to have picked up on anything unusual.

"Can you get me a number for Senior Special Agent Vince King in the New Haven field office?" If she couldn't speak to McLain, she needed guidance from the agent who had prepared her for this undercover assignment. McLain had brought King in from the other field office, citing his years of experience. He was also skilled in offering support to rookies like Hollie. She had a feeling she wouldn't like his advice, but she should at least hear it.

"Sure." Dalton was silent for a few minutes. When he spoke again, Hollie could hear a note of bemusement in his voice. "No one of that name in New Haven."

"Are you certain?"

"Hundred percent."

She wanted to insist he go back and check again, but she knew Dalton wouldn't make a mistake over something like that. His attitude could be casual, but that was deceptive. He was razor-sharp at all times, one of the best agents she knew. Could she have got it wrong? She was sure those were the details McLain had given her... The feeling of discomfort intensified.

"Hey—" the casual way Dalton said the word alerted Hollie to the fact that there was nothing casual about what was coming next "—I may be able to get us tickets to see Beast. Some guy I know has contacts. Not quite front row, but not bad."

Not quite front row. It summed up her feelings about Dalton. She hadn't realized it until now, but she wanted front row. Actually, she wanted center stage. The thought coincided with the sound of a car pulling into the drive. "I'm not sure when I'll be back, but thanks for the thought."

She ended the call with that familiar feeling of guilt tugging at the center of her chest. It didn't matter how often she told herself Dalton was a grown man—*he's five years older than me*—with a successful career, and a wide circle of friends. He always managed to make her feel as if she had blighted his life.

Six months. That's how long we were together. It was fun, but it didn't set my world on fire. Speaking of which...

She turned her head as Torque walked into the kitchen carrying a variety of bags. He wore a sweatshirt she had seen him wearing in dozens of photographs. It was copied by fans around the world. Black and red, with an oversize hood, it had an image of a burning guitar on the back.

"I have food and clothes." He nodded at the phone in her hand. "Was your overprotective friend reassured?"

"I couldn't get in touch with her."

He stepped onto the terrace. "What will you do now?"

"I don't know." Her voice sounded hollow as she tilted her head to look up at him. She had come here to investigate him, had known him barely a day, so why did keeping secrets from him suddenly feel all wrong? And why did the thought of leaving him feel worse?

"In a few days, I need to join the rest of the band for the start of our tour."

Hollie bit her lip. "I understand—"

"I don't think you do." His lips curved into a smile, the one that warmed her insides and left her feeling slightly breathless. "How would you like to come with me?"

Chapter 4

Hollie looked tired and confused as she sat at the kitchen counter sipping coffee and nibbling at a pastry. She had showered and her blond hair was still slightly damp. Torque had done a good job of estimating her size, so at least she now wore sweatpants that stayed up and a pale gray sweater that suited her coloring and clung deliciously to her curves. Despite her pallor and the dark circles under her eyes, he couldn't drag his gaze away from her face.

"I can't just tag along on your tour." Ever since he had made the offer, there had been an underlying emotion about her that he didn't understand. It was like she was being torn in two different directions. He wished she'd just tell him the truth about who she was.

"Why not?" He leaned against the counter, just close enough to breathe in her warm, soapy scent.

"Because…" She flapped a helpless hand. "What

would people think? They would assume I was a groupie, or something."

"But you're not. Anyway, why does it matter what other people think?"

She laughed. "That's so *you*."

He shrugged. "Can't help being me."

"Torque, I don't want to seem ungrateful—"

He cut abruptly across her protests. "Where else will you go?"

Hollie hesitated and he got the feeling there was a lot she wasn't telling him. He wanted to explain to her that he didn't care. No matter what secrets she was keeping from him, he would fulfill his duty. She was his mate and that meant he had an obligation to keep her safe. But if he told her that, he would have to reveal a whole lot more. Like how he knew she wasn't safe. And how he had the ability to protect her. From *anything*.

"I don't know." The words were barely a whisper… and clearly a lie.

"Would you feel better if you had a job to do?"

"What do you mean?" Her brow furrowed, but he could see a glimmer of interest in the green depths of her eyes.

"My manager is forever telling me to get myself a personal assistant. I'm offering you the position."

"But you don't know if I'm qualified." Hollie appeared torn between laughter and incredulity. "And do all your bandmates take their PAs on tour? Because that sounds to me like one crowded tour bus…if that's still how you get around."

"My job offer, my rules. And yes. We use a bus. It gets a bit crazy, but I'll be there to look after you. Do you want the position or not?" He leaned over and took one of the pastries, biting into it as he watched her face.

Laughter shook her slender body as she gazed up at him. "I'll take the job. Although I can't help thinking you made it up just to give me something to do."

"You won't say that when you see my emails and letters."

Hollie shook her head. "Touring with Beast? This was my wildest fantasy when I was in college."

Before Torque could answer, the intercom for the electronic gates buzzed and he went to answer it. He pressed a button and an image of a man in uniform filled the screen. "Yes?"

"Jackson Kirk, Fire Investigation. I was told by the paramedics who treated Ms. Brown that she was here. I'd like to speak with her."

"She is here. But the decision about whether she's ready to speak with you is hers." He looked over his shoulder at Hollie, who sat up straighter, nodding her agreement.

Torque pressed the release button on the gates. When he opened the front door, Kirk was striding up the path. Torque got the impression the guy's shrewd, dark eyes were assessing him, the house and the grounds as he approached. Kirk held out an ID badge and Torque stepped aside to let him pass. He led Kirk through to the kitchen and introduced him to Hollie.

"The fire was started deliberately." It wasn't a question. She calmly stated it as a fact.

"How did you reach that conclusion?" Kirk asked.

"Because you're here."

Torque watched Hollie carefully as he made more coffee. Where she was concerned, his senses were finely tuned and his protective instincts were razor-sharp. He didn't need intuition to tell him her behavior was...unexpected. Until now, he'd had no dealings with victims of fire, but he didn't imagine they were the ones who usually led the conversation with a fire investigator.

"Was the point of ignition at the turn on the staircase?"

Kirk blinked. "Uh…yeah. Looks that way." He reached into his top pocket, drawing out a small notebook. "Although there were two other ignition points. One inside the bar and one in the storeroom. That's not always an indication of arson, but there were signs of a break-in."

Hollie appeared to be storing that information away. "How did he get in?"

That was it? That was her calm, collected question when faced with the information that a guy had broken in and set light to the staircase that led to her room? *Who are you, Hollie Brown?*

"Pried open a window at the back." Kirk nodded his thanks as Torque placed a coffee cup in front of him, indicating the cream and sugar. "The guy must have checked the place out in daylight, or risked using a powerful flashlight. That window was the only one large enough for him to climb through."

"You won't know what accelerant he used until you've run tests, but he would only have had what he could carry. I don't imagine there was anything in the bar he could use?"

Kirk flipped through his notes. He looked like a man who had come unprepared to an interview. "No. The staircase burned ferociously and it's been difficult to establish what happened there. My initial investigation suggests he stacked an absorbent, flammable substance—probably something he found in the bar, such as newspaper—at each ignition point before pouring his accelerant over it. He doesn't seem to have made any attempt to make it look like an accident."

Hollie nodded. "A professional torch."

Torque's lips twitched. *A professional torch? Oh, Hollie. Are you seriously proposing we keep up the pretense that you arrived in my local bar by chance?*

Kirk appeared not to notice the slip. "Looks that way. Which means we have to consider whether you were the target."

"Is there any question about that?" Torque asked. "If that fire was deliberately started on the staircase when Hollie was upstairs, it seems obvious that she was the intended target."

"We're right at the start of the investigation. It looks likely a crime was committed. We don't yet know whether that crime was arson or attempted murder. Which is why I'm here." Kirk turned back to Hollie. "Can you think of any reason why someone might do this?"

The hesitation was infinitesimal. If Torque hadn't been observing her so closely, he would have missed it. Or maybe it was because he was already so disconcertingly in tune with her emotions. "No."

"No recent breakup?" She shook her head. "Stalker? You haven't noticed anyone following you? No one who calls and then hangs up?" A shake of the head followed each question. "Nothing at all you can think of that has been out of the ordinary?"

"None of those things." It was just the wrong side of evasive. "Will you report this fire to anyone?"

Kirk frowned. "I'm the investigator. Who would I report it to?"

Hollie reached for another pastry, but seemed more intent on crumbling it into pieces on her plate than eating it. "I wondered if there was a database—" she waved a vague hand "—or something."

"Don't worry. I know how to do my job." Kirk finished his coffee. "Will you be staying here? With Mr.—?" He raised an inquiring brow.

"It's just Torque."

Kirk's glance managed to convey his disapproval of rock stars with long hair, big houses and unconventional names.

Hollie drew his attention back to her. "I'll be traveling and I lost my cell phone in the fire."

"You can reach us both on this number." Torque might not be the most organized person in the world, but he had succumbed to Ged's insistence and always carried a supply of his manager's business cards. He handed one of these to Kirk.

Kirk made a note of his own number on a page of his notebook and tore it out. He handed it to Hollie. "If you think of anything—"

"I'll be sure to get in touch."

Torque escorted Kirk to the door. "She seems to be taking it well." The investigator jerked his head back in the direction of the kitchen. "Most people would be shaken up after an experience like that."

"Shock affects people in different ways." Privately, he agreed with Kirk. Hollie seemed more intent on conducting her own investigation than on providing Kirk with answers.

He watched Kirk walk away, making sure the electric gates were closed behind him. His steps were uncharacteristically slow and deliberate as he returned to the kitchen. Hollie turned her head to look at him, smiling as he approached, and his heart lurched.

Everything about her enthralled him. The tendrils

of gold hair blowing about her face in the breeze from the open window. The faint blush on her cheeks as his gaze lingered on her face. Her scent, the aroma of *her* that he could smell beneath the vanilla and pine tones of the soap, made his inner dragon growl with lust. She was his mate. He wanted to sweep her up into his arms, take her off to a cave somewhere and show her what that meant.

The big green eyes scanning his face brought him crashing back down to earth. They were big green *human* eyes. Nothing about wanting Hollie made sense. Yet, from the moment he first saw her, she had become the most important thing in his life. Wanting her was something he would just have to fight. Not easy when all he wanted to do was grab her and growl out the truth. *Mine.*

Even so, it was torture. Exquisite but agonizing. How was he going to cope in even closer proximity to his mate?

"You look fierce." Hollie's smile wavered.

He laughed. "You have no idea."

Hollie was annoyed that she'd allowed her professional instincts to show through in the meeting with Jackson Kirk. She wasn't very good at this undercover thing. Her real self kept fighting to be let out.

She decided to tackle the subject head-on with Torque. "I suppose you're wondering what that was all about."

After Kirk left, they were seated on a bench in the garden, overlooking the wide sweep of the bay.

"I guess you'll tell me when you want me to know."

His gaze was steady on hers and she suddenly felt guilty. This man had saved her life, taken her into his home, bought her new clothes, offered her a job…and she was deceiving him. She was as convinced as she could be that he wasn't the Incinerator, that she could trust him, but her training told her instinct wasn't enough. Proof. That was what she needed. Until she had it, she should probably be wary of him. Instead of constantly wanting to get nearer to him.

"Torque…"

"Hollie." That glittering gaze held hers. "It doesn't matter."

The words jolted her, the sincerity in his tone almost knocking her off her seat. The message was clear. He understood that she was keeping secrets from him… but he didn't care. What *was* this? Everything about the situation she was in felt bizarre, yet she wasn't unnerved. It was somehow right. More right than anything she had ever known.

Needing to lighten the mood, she turned her attention to the job she would be doing. "Tell me about the tour."

"We're touring east to west, starting in New York, which is our base."

When Torque started to explain who the individual members of the group were, Hollie laughed. "You are talking to the girl who bought your first album and was hooked from day one."

"So you know all about us?"

Although Hollie still felt tired, the events of the previous day had receded. It was almost like a bad dream that had happened to someone else. There were things about the fire that nagged at the edge of her consciousness. Jackson Kirk had appeared unaware of the FBI database, but maybe he didn't feel it was necessary to discuss it with her. As far as he was concerned, she was a member of the public, not an expert. He didn't know she was the person who had devised the complex information system. It was the means by which the Bureau collated information about all fires and cross-referenced it with their existing records.

It frustrated her that she knew so much more than Kirk did. Although it appeared Hollie herself was the target of the fire at the Pleasant Bay Bar, she was even more convinced that Torque was the key. If she could discover why that was, she would be able to find her way to the Incinerator.

Then, of course, there was the issue of McLain's absence. That worried her most of all. But she had to have faith that her boss knew what he was doing. In the meantime, Hollie would continue to do her own job. She had decided to do that, even though every professional instinct told her she was wrong to remain undercover. Although the Incinerator had turned his attention to her, she felt safe with Torque. Safer than she'd ever felt in her life.

She was aware of him watching her, and pulled her attention back to his question. "Does anyone know all about you? For one of the most famous bands in the world, you guys have been incredibly successful at keeping yourselves private."

He was partly turned away from her and she studied his profile as he looked across the bay toward a small island. His gaze lingered there for long, silent moments before he turned back to her. Those unusual eyes glowed as he smiled. "I guess we just enjoy being enigmatic."

"How did you meet?" It was one of the things that had always interested her. The band kept their biographical details to a minimum. "I know Diablo is Native

American, Khan is from India, Dev comes from Nepal, Finglas is Irish and you…you like to be mysterious."

Torque held a hand over his heart in mock hurt. "I'm a child of the world. Wherever I lay my well-worn beanie, that's my home. As for how we met… Ged brought us together."

Ged Taverner was the mystery man of rock. Beast's hugely successful manager, he was the puppet master, the Svengali, behind the legend. The thought that she would soon be meeting him, and the members of the band, seemed unreal. Everything since she had arrived in Addison seemed unreal.

Except Torque. He was her new reality. Since they weren't touching, it must be her imagination that made her think she could feel the heat of his body warming her through her clothing. His eyes had a hypnotic effect on her. Once she stared at them, she couldn't turn away. And his lips… *Oh, dear Lord. Don't get me started on those lips.*

"Don't look at me that way." His voice was low. Not quite a whisper, almost a growl.

"What way?" She could no longer blame the smoke for the huskiness in her own tone.

"Probably the same way I look at you."

She edged closer. "Like you want me? Because that's how I feel about you."

"Hollie…" Although he said her name like it was made for his lips, he remained still, his hands splayed on his thighs.

"Oh." She let out a shaky sigh, slumping down in her seat. How could she have got this so *wrong*? "I see."

"No." He rubbed a hand over his face. "No, you don't see. Hollie, this can't happen."

"Torque, the only reason I can see why nothing can

happen between us is that you *don't* want me." When he turned to look at her, the raw agony on his face told her everything she needed to know. Her desire for him—her *craving* for him—wasn't one-sided. "Or if there's someone else in your life?"

He leaned forward, placing his head in his hands. When he started to laugh, there was no humor in the sound.

"What did I say that was so funny? *Is* there someone else in your life?"

Torque straightened, and the desolation in his eyes tugged at her heart. "I suppose there is, but not in the way you think." He caught hold of her hand and raised it to his lips. "Trust me. This way is better."

He got to his feet and Hollie watched him as he walked away. *Better for whom?*

Two days later, Hollie opened her eyes wide as she reached the rooftop terrace of Torque's New York apartment. Turning in a full circle, she took in the iconic views, the private pool, the sauna and the hot tub.

"I'm starting to think I died in that fire and this might be heaven." She turned to look at Torque. "You do know I may never leave?"

"You haven't started on that paperwork yet." Although he kept his voice light, the thought of Hollie staying in his life sounded just fine to Torque. If they could close the door on the rest of the world for eternity, that would be okay with him. He had grown used to her company with frightening speed. And if he could shut out everything else, he would be able to keep her safe from the person who had started that fire, from anything that might harm her. It was so damn hard. He would go to the ends of the earth for this woman…but he couldn't tell her that.

Ever since the conversation in his garden when Hollie had confessed to wanting him and he had turned her down—*like an idiot*—they had been tiptoeing around the subject. The attraction between them burned brighter with every passing minute. They were just doing their best to ignore it. Which was somehow making the whole situation even more tense.

Torque felt like he was living in a constant state of arousal. He was intoxicated by Hollie, drinking her in until his senses were filled with her. Unable to concentrate on anything else, he was barely aware of the practicalities of the forthcoming tour. Much to the annoyance of his manager.

"I have to go out in about an hour to a rehearsal." He grimaced. "Ged isn't happy. He thinks we haven't spent enough time together before we hit the road."

They headed back down the stairs into the open-plan living space. Although this place was incredible, it never quite felt like home to Torque. He had given a designer free rein with the decor, and the end result was stunning. The white and chrome furnishings were comfortable as well as classy, with everything chosen to make the most of the views. Even so, it had always been just a place to stay. He had only ever had one home. The mountains of Scotland had been forged in fire around the same time that the Cumhachdach dragon clan was born. Now the closest thing he had to a home was the house in Maine.

"How important is it to rehearse? Don't you already know your songs and each other really well?" Hollie asked.

"We do, but we have other people onstage with us.

Backing musicians and singers, some dancers. And our special effects are always evolving."

"Nothing will ever beat the display you put on a few years ago in Marseilles." Her eyes shone with excitement. "The one where it looked like wolves stormed the stage."

"You liked that?" Although Torque smiled at her enthusiasm, he remained wary. The band had done its best to cover up what had happened in Marseilles. In reality, there had been a genuine werewolf strike during one of their concerts. The band had all shifted in response and fought off the attackers. Caught on film, they had been forced to pass the whole thing off as one of the greatest special effects displays ever. They had succeeded, but they were constantly trying to cover up the reality.

"Liked it? It was incredible. I only wish I'd been there to see it in person. The atmosphere must have been amazing."

"You could say that." He decided a quick change of subject was in order. "Anyway, this week will be intense. It's always hard work just prior to the start of a tour, but Ged is right. He always is. The rehearsals are necessary."

Her gaze scanned his face. She was getting good at reading him. Just not too good, he hoped. There were many hundreds of years of secrets he didn't want to reveal. "I'd always wondered what made Ged so important, but when you speak about him, I can see it. It goes deeper than affection, doesn't it?"

It was a scarily perceptive comment. Ged was the glue that held Beast together, but he was so much more. He was the reason they existed. Each member of the band owed his life to the giant bear-shifter. "Yeah. Ged is a good guy." Such an understatement.

Hollie shook her head. "Do you ever *stop* being enigmatic?"

He laughed. "Only long enough to get coffee. But first, let me show you to your room."

There were four bedrooms, each with its own dressing room and bathroom. Hollie held up a small gym bag. "How will I ever fit all my stuff in?"

"We have to get you some new clothes."

"Torque…" She groaned. "That was *not* my way of trying to get you to purchase me some expensive new things. You've given me a job. I can buy my own clothes."

"That reminds me, we didn't discuss your salary. And I should probably see about giving you an advance—"

She dropped her bag and marched toward him. Reaching up, she placed a hand over his mouth. The action started out as a joke, but it violated their unspoken "no contact" rule. As soon as her fingers touched his lips, heat blazed from the point of contact through every part of his body. He saw Hollie's eyes widen and knew she was feeling it, too. So much more than attraction. It was their own firestorm and they were helpless against its power.

And…he wasn't quite sure how it happened, but his hands appeared to have developed a life of their own. His intention had been to move her gently but firmly away. Instead, his unruly body disobeyed him as he gripped her waist and pulled her closer. Now what was he supposed to do? With her parted lips so achingly close, there seemed to be only one solution to his dilemma.

As Hollie swayed closer, the temptation to kiss her grew into a necessity. Every reason why this was a bad idea had just flown out of his head when they were interrupted by a buzzing noise.

Hollie blinked as though she had been roused from a trance. "What was that?"

"It's the concierge. I'm expecting a delivery."

She sighed, resting her forehead briefly against his chest. "Then I guess you have to go." The disappointment in her voice almost undid his resolve.

"Come with me." He took her hand. "This is for you."

Hollie quirked an inquiring brow in his direction, but followed him without comment. When he opened the door, the uniformed concierge handed Torque a small package. Once he had tipped the doorman and closed the door again, he gave the box to Hollie.

"It's a cell phone."

She turned the carton over in her hands. Her expression was hard to read, but Torque was caught up in that swirl of conflicting emotions coming from her once again. She was feeling regret and sorrow. *Why, Hollie? What's bothering you?*

"You are such a good man." When she raised her eyes to his, he caught a glimpse of tears before she blinked them away.

"Tell me." The words were out before he knew he was going to say them.

"Pardon?" He knew she'd heard him.

He shrugged the question aside. Now was not the best time. "Nothing. You need a way to keep in touch with your overprotective friend."

"If she's taking calls." She placed a hand on his shoulder and pressed her lips to his cheek. "Thank you, Torque."

To hell with restraint. Her warm, soft mouth felt perfect on his skin, and just for a moment, he let it happen. Allowed himself that one, tiny indulgence.

"While I'm out you can try and contact her." He grabbed his jacket, turning back as he reached the door. "Be careful."

Her brow wrinkled. "About calling my friend?"

"Until Kirk gets in touch to say the guy who set fire to the bar has been caught, you need to be careful about everything."

She looked sweet and vulnerable—and so incredibly beautiful—that it took every ounce of self-control he possessed to walk out the door.

Chapter 5

Hollie took the new cell phone through to her bedroom. Her feet felt heavy, the sensation slowing her down, and she kicked off her shoes in an attempt to make herself comfortable. It didn't work. Her discomfort wasn't physical. Torque had been so generous, and asked nothing in return, not even an explanation. She hated taking advantage of his kindness. Sometimes she wondered if she should just tell him everything, but even though they had grown closer, there were still those nagging doubts attached to him. She was as sure as she could be that he wasn't the person who had tried to kill her, but there was still a mystery surrounding the night of the Pleasant Bay Bar fire. No matter how many different ways she looked at it, no matter how many explanations he gave about timing, Torque should not have been able to walk through those flames.

If she was honest, she'd admit there was another reason for her reluctance to tell him the truth. Once

Torque knew she had deceived him, things wouldn't be the same between them. It was unlikely they could continue the way they were. When she examined her motives, this was the strongest. She didn't want to leave Torque and this enjoyable bubble in which they were living. It was that simple.

She wondered if he was aware of the Incinerator's activities. The arsonist had received some press attention, but because the attacks were geographically so far apart, there hadn't been the same sensationalism as if he was operating within a smaller area. And McLain had done a good job of keeping the details out of the public eye.

The thought of the chief made Hollie eager to call her. Surely by now McLain would be back in her office and everything would be right with the world? They would clear up the issue about Vince King and Hollie would persuade her boss that sticking with Torque was a good idea. If that didn't happen? She frowned. It had to happen. She wasn't giving up on this now. As she set up the new cell phone, she tried to analyze what *this* was. Was it still the Incinerator investigation? Or was it something new, something to do with the unbreakable ties that bound her to Torque? By the time she had completed the setup process, she still hadn't decided.

When she tried McLain's number, her hands were shaking. Because she already knew what the outcome would be. Sure enough, she got the same voice mail message as last time. Bowing her head, she took a few deep breaths.

Okay. There were other ways to contact McLain. Trying the field office, she got through to the main telephone operator. "I'd like to speak to Assistant Special Agent-in-Charge McLain, please."

"I'm sorry, the ASAC isn't here right now. We're not sure when she'll be back…"

Something was very wrong. Hollie had already known that, but now she was unable to push aside the feeling of doom. Calling the service provider for the new cell, she explained that she wanted ID blocking enabled on her account. When that was in place, she called Dalton.

"Hollie, where the hell are you? And why are you withholding your number?"

"I don't have much time." She used the excuse as a way of not answering his questions. "What's going on with McLain?"

"No one knows. She seems to have vanished. It's crazy here right now. But, Hols, there's something else… I don't know how to tell you this…"

She could hear the distress in his voice and it triggered answering prickles of dread along her spine. "Just say it, Dalton."

"Your apartment building burned down yesterday."

She sat down abruptly on the bed, closing her eyes as the room began to spin. "Was it the Incinerator?"

"It's too soon to say, but it's looking that way."

A wave of nausea washed over her. She wanted to run to Torque, to cling to him and be comforted. But she couldn't. Partly because he wasn't there, but also because to him she was Hollie Brown…and Hollie Brown didn't have an apartment. All those precious things the Incinerator had destroyed? The books, photographs and mementos? They belonged to Hollie Brennan, FBI agent, and Torque had never met *her*.

Her thoughts skittered around wildly. The attack on the Pleasant Bay Bar had been personal. That was bad enough. But this latest fire meant the Incinerator knew her real identity…

"Are you still there?" The sympathy in Dalton's voice made the lump in her throat swell until it felt like she was choking. "I'm sorry, Hols. Some things shouldn't be done over the phone."

"Can't be helped when I'm on the road." Her voice was gruff as she fought back the tears. *On the road. Careful, Hollie.* She didn't think Dalton could pick up on where she was and what she was doing from those words, but it showed how easy it was to slip up.

"I don't know what's going on with you, but you need to come in. Let us keep you safe."

She could hear the concern in his voice. It wasn't just because he was a colleague. He still cared and this had shaken him up.

He was talking sense. Dalton was what she *knew.* Okay, so she didn't love him, but he represented the real world. *Her* world. For some reason, the Incinerator had switched his attention to Hollie and she needed protection. She shouldn't hesitate on this. There was no way she should be considering staying with Torque. Ever since she had started this job, her head and her heart had been at war. Her head was trying to convince her to give it up, while her heart prompted her to stay with Torque. Now things had gotten a whole lot scarier.

She should do what Dalton was suggesting. Let the might and resources of the FBI protect her. She should go home…except the place she had called home no longer existed. And the nearest thing she had to it now was the man who had walked through flames for her.

She guessed her choices were that stark. Dalton and the FBI represented her head. They were security and reason. Torque? He was fire and magic. He was her heart.

Hollie had never believed in gut reactions. Her response to those who did was always with facts. Data, figures, science, proof…they were the things that mattered to her. Now her world had been tipped on its head. Her instincts were telling her, loud and clear, that she needed to stay with Torque. It was a primal warning, coming from somewhere deep within her. If she left his side, she was doomed.

"Got to go, Dalton. I'll call you soon." She heard his blustering protest as she ended the call.

Flopping back on the bed, she held the phone to her chest for a moment or two. The tears were fading. In their place, her determination to catch the Incinerator was growing stronger. So he had chosen to switch his attention to her? Well, he had been her enemy for the last four years. Now they would find out who was stronger.

If the arsonist was trying to scare her, he was succeeding. But, for some reason, alongside the fear there was a feeling of empowerment. The woman who had walked into that bar in Addison was not the same one who was here in New York. Fundamentally, she was still Hollie, but something inside her had shifted. It sounded foolish, but she had been living a half-life until now. Having experienced the difference, she wasn't going back and settling for less.

A knock on the door shook her out of her musing. "Hollie?" Torque's voice was muffled by the thick wood. "Rehearsal finished early. How do you feel about pizza?"

"Um, hold on a second." She padded barefoot across the thick rug. When she opened the door, he scanned her face. His gaze was like a caress. How did he do *that*? It was almost as though he knew how she was feeling and he was using his presence to comfort her. "How do

I feel about pizza? Pretty much the same way a drowning woman feels about a lifeboat."

He grinned. "After we've eaten, we'll get you some new clothes."

Hollie had been subdued since they arrived in New York. No, Torque could pinpoint exactly when her mood had changed. She'd been fine at first. Then, after he'd left her alone and gone to his first rehearsal, he'd returned and they'd gone for pizza. Although Hollie had done her best to maintain the pretense that nothing had changed, Torque could tell she was upset. Every now and then, she'd lapse into silence and he would catch a glimpse of real anguish in her expression.

It caused an answering tug of pain in his own chest. Something had happened while he was at his rehearsal. The most likely possibility was that she had called someone during that time and what she'd heard had caused this distress. More than ever, Torque wanted to put an end to this charade. To tell her once and for all that there was nothing she could do or say that would turn him against her. If he could find a way to do it that didn't involve explaining about shifters, fated mates and the reasons why he wasn't able to offer her a normal life, he would do so in a heartbeat. Instead, he tried to offer her a reassuring presence.

Torque sensed Hollie was grateful for his understanding, and the knowledge made him angry. Even though he could never have it, he wanted more than her gratitude. He didn't want to be viewed as the kindly friend with the broad shoulder on which she could lean. When he looked into her eyes, he saw everything he wanted. Love. Passion. Laughter. Warmth. All of those things and more. Forever.

"I'm still not sure this is a good idea."

Hollie's words drew Torque's attention back to another, more mundane problem.

Persuading her that meeting Beast prior to the tour would be fun had been hard work. They had been in New York for five days and the first concert was taking place in two days' time. Despite Torque's reassurances, she clearly viewed the approaching evening with dread. They were in a cab now on their way to meet the others, and her expression had been growing more apprehensive with each passing block.

Finding a place to eat that catered for the different tastes within the band was always difficult. Torque supposed that was true of any diverse group, but Beast was unique. Not that Ged was likely to share the precise details of their differences with a New York restaurateur. A booking for a dragon, two werewolves, three big cats and a bear? Oh, and Hollie would be joining them…so, yeah, they'd need the mortal menu, as well. Celebrities got away with a lot of weird stuff, but that wouldn't slip by unnoticed.

Being part of Beast was a curious balancing act. Living in the human world was all about one simple rule. Mortals must never know shifters walked among them. Anonymity was key, and all shape-shifters, no matter what animal form they took, went to great lengths to maintain it. Yet the members of the band were rock stars, constantly in the limelight.

Being a celebrity was high-energy, high-profile and high-stress. Torque had known how it would be when Ged rescued him from a life of servitude. This was the new beginning Ged had offered him, and Torque had embraced it with gratitude. He was good at what he did. He was an outstanding musician and a brilliant performer. But his inner dragon didn't want to be on display. Along with his bandmates, his life was a constant battle to meet the needs of both sides of his persona.

Things had improved over time. Fame had brought great wealth, which meant they could buy themselves some privacy. Since Khan's marriage and the birth of his daughter, Karina, everyone had reevaluated the pace and decided to slow down. But walking down the street without being recognized? That still wasn't an option. Going out in a group? They'd had to resort to some creative measures to make sure they didn't disrupt the entire restaurant.

The solution was Daria's, a small, family-run restaurant located in a Brooklyn side street. Since Ged knew the owner—Ged knew *everyone*—and Daria was prepared to close to other customers, privacy wasn't a problem.

"What will they think when you tell them I'm coming on the tour?" As they vacated the cab, Hollie tugged nervously at the new top she was wearing.

"They already know." Torque removed the shades he always wore when he went out. Along with the beanie he used to cover his hair, they constituted his standard disguise. "I told them."

"Oh." She chewed her lower lip for a moment. "What did they say?"

He draped an arm around her shoulders, propelling her toward the restaurant door. "Hollie, this is no big deal. Sometimes other people join us on tour."

He felt her indrawn breath. "But they must usually be…you know…"

"People we're having sex with?"

She turned her head to look at him and he enjoyed the sensation of her hair tickling his cheek. "Isn't that what they'll think? That this job you've given me is just an excuse?"

"Probably. Does it matter?"

She regarded him thoughtfully for a moment or two. "No. Because if it was up to me, we *would* be having sex."

Heat streaked through him, pooling deep in his abdomen, hardening his whole body. "Hollie." Her name was a groan on his lips, a brand on his heart.

"I'm being honest, Torque." She touched one finger to the corner of his mouth, a simple caress that almost brought him to his knees. "I wish you would."

"You want to talk about honesty?" He drew her closer, even though the action inflamed him further, spiking his arousal almost to the point of no return. "You want to go there?"

Fear flared in her eyes, but she tilted her chin defiantly. "If that's what it takes."

"Hey, guys, making out in the street? Way to get papped." It was Khan, the biggest, baddest tiger of them all.

"Later." Torque kept his eyes on Hollie for a moment longer and she nodded before they turned to greet the new arrivals.

Khan and Sarange were the ultimate celebrity couple. He was Beast's lead singer; she was a singer songwriter. He was a tiger; she was a wolf. At first glance, it wasn't a match made in shifter heaven, but it worked for them.

"This is Hollie," Torque said as he kissed Sarange and was lifted off the ground in one of Khan's over-exuberant hugs.

He was aware of his friends regarding Hollie closely and he could guess what they were thinking. Their dragon friend was with a mortal woman. A woman who didn't know who he was…didn't know any of them were shifters. It was going to be an interesting evening.

Torque had asked Ged to organize this meal so Hollie could get to know everyone before they embarked on the tour. He'd already explained to his bandmates that she was unaware of his true identity. He'd also told them the story of the fire and his obligation to protect her. Although he had been able to feel caution coming off them in waves, their loyalty to each other was absolute. For Torque's sake, they would accept Hollie and keep his secrets.

It wasn't the first time they had been in this position. A few years ago, their former bass guitarist, Nate Zilar, had helped a mystery woman called Violet when she lost her memory. Violet had joined Beast on tour and they had protected her from a pack of vicious werewolves. Nate left the band when he and Violet got married. Of course, Violet had turned out to be a werewolf herself, so the circumstances weren't quite the same. Hollie was human, which meant she needed special treatment.

Special treatment that does not include dragon sex. Given the steamy exchange between them and her enticing behavior just now, it was probably a good time for Torque to remind himself of that.

When they entered the restaurant, Diablo was already there. Beast's drummer exuded raw, brooding vitality, and suppressed menace. With his blue-black hair flopping forward to cover his face and bulging, tattooed biceps, he was even more stunning up close than onstage.

There was barely time for introductions before Dev and Finglas arrived. Hollie could already identify them, of course. Dev, with his white-blond hair and pale skin, was the ice-man. Finglas, the replacement for Nate Zilar, was the youngest and newest member of the group.

Hollie picked up on the bond between Torque and his friends instantly. Sarange was part of it, but it was strongest between the men. They didn't need to speak. Although they went through the ritual of back-slapping and a few joking insults, there was an unusual warmth linking them together. Perhaps it had been forged during all those years of working in such close harmony. She wondered if they were even aware of it.

Then another man entered, and the feeling intensified. There was no mistaking him. Just from his size, this had to be Ged Taverner. It was incredible the way she could sense the affection the others felt for him. Having been a Beast fan for a long time, she knew the band members held him in high regard, but he must be special to generate this sort of devotion.

"Hollie." He came straight to her. "Hi."

Her hand was wrapped in a warm clasp and she found a pair of golden eyes assessing her. She understood what that gaze meant. He wanted to be sure she wasn't going to hurt Torque. Clearly, this group of alpha males looked out for each other.

What if I don't pass the test? Ged's gaze was scarily perceptive. What if he could somehow see through her? If he could tell she wasn't who she pretended to be?

She risked a glance in Torque's direction and he quirked a brow at her. The message was clear. *Stop worrying.*

When they sat down to eat, she found she was at a disadvantage. Daria already knew what everyone else would be having. And the food choices were seriously weird. Ged was having fish. Dev, Diablo and Khan wanted lamb, cooked so it was still pink. Sarange and

Finglas both had a liking for steak so rare it almost jumped up off the plate and ran away. Torque, on the other hand, wanted his own giant piece of beef well-cooked. Actually, when it arrived at the table, it was charred. She had shared many meals in his company recently, but she hadn't seen him eat anything like this.

Hollie, having ordered a pizza, was astonished at the sheer amount of meat her companions ate. "Are you guys on some sort of low-carb diet?" she asked Finglas as the Irishman started on his second steak. She couldn't help noticing that no one ordered sides. No fries, bread or vegetables. The only person who even touched his salad garnish was Ged.

"You could say that." Finglas choked back a laugh. "Touring uses up a lot of energy."

It had to be one of the unhealthiest diets she'd ever seen, yet they all appeared to be glowing with vitality. Maybe it was a celebrity thing. Possibly they had the same personal trainer who advocated this regime. Whatever it was, she wasn't going to be tempted to join them.

"Torque tells me you're going to help him make sense of his paperwork." Ged's deep voice suited his large frame.

"That's the plan. He has warned me it may not be an easy job."

"That's an understatement. Fan mail is only one part of it, of course, but it illustrates his disorganized approach. I'd be surprised if Torque has ever done anything other than look at it and put it to one side, both email and paper." Ged turned his head to look at Torque. "Has he mentioned he has some unusual followers?"

"Followers? That's a strange choice of word."

"Some of them are strange." Ged took a slug of his

beer. "One of the downsides of fame is that some people feel they know you. They read about you in the press, or online, and they have no cut-off mechanism. They feel you owe them a part of yourself. It can be a fine line between fanatic and lunatic."

His words made Hollie shiver. "Is that what Torque has to deal with? People who are crazy?"

"Not face-to-face. That has never happened. But sadly, he does seem to attract more than any of the others. I've spent a lot of time trying to analyze why."

"Have you reached a conclusion?" Hollie looked at Torque, who was talking to Khan. It scared her that he might be in danger. It frightened her even more to acknowledge how much she cared.

"Fire," Ged said.

"Pardon?" That single word, so much a part of her life, rocked her back in her seat.

"I don't know how to explain it, but having read some of the letters and emails, I think that's the link. They see him playing around with it onstage. He gives off these fiery vibes. And these people see him as some sort of fire god who has a message for them. Someone they can worship."

Hollie regarded the rest of her pizza with a rising feeling of nausea. Ged's words were confirmation of one of her wildest suspicions. Was the Incinerator one of the people who viewed Torque as a deity? Had the fires she had spent so long investigating been started as a tribute? It made a horrible sort of sense. If the arsonist believed that Torque craved, or even controlled, fire, then his avid follower would be eager to give him what he wanted. Until she delved into Torque's chaotic paperwork, she wouldn't know if the fire starter had ever contacted Torque to tell him what he'd done in his honor. If he had, the reference must be obscure. She knew Torque well enough by now to be convinced he wouldn't ignore it.

There was a flaw in that line of thinking, and it related to Hollie herself. If the Incinerator was an avid fan who believed Torque was something more than a rock star, maybe something more than mortal, how had he, or she, switched his attention to her so fast?

There was an answer, and it was an obvious one, but she didn't like it.

"What has Ged been saying to make you look so worried?"

She hadn't noticed Torque swapping places with Finglas. "He confirmed that your filing system can only be described as chaotic." She did her best to keep her voice light. As always, she got the sense that he knew what she was feeling.

"Now the truth." Color shimmered in the depths of his eyes.

"This is too one-sided. I should be able to know what you're thinking and feeling." Although they were surrounded by other people, it felt like they were cocooned in their own little world. It had been that way since the first moment she met him.

"That's not how enigmatic works. Tell me what's troubling you, Hollie."

"It was something Ged said about your fans. About how some of them believe you have a connection to fire?" He nodded, and she sensed a new alertness in him. "I wondered if the person who set fire to the Pleasant Bay Bar might be one of them."

"It had crossed my mind."

"But if that's the case, that person had to know about me—about our first meeting—really fast." She bit her lip, not wanting to voice the next uncomfortable thought. Saying it out loud would make it real. "Don't you see what that means? One of your crazy fans must be watching you."

"I'd realized that, as well."

He clasped her hand, holding it between both of his, and she experienced that curious sense of her troubles slipping away.

"I can take care of myself, Hollie. I can take care of both of us."

"I hate to interrupt—" Daria came out of the kitchen in her chef's whites. "But there's news coming in of a fire in a luxury apartment building in Tribeca." She handed Torque her cell phone to show him the images. "Isn't that where you live?"

Chapter 6

Although the blaze hadn't reached Torque's apartment, the fire department was still at work when Torque and Hollie arrived at the building.

"Do you know what started it?" Even though Hollie asked the question, she was aware that she was wasting her time. She already knew the answer. It wasn't a "what" it was a "who." She looked around the darkened street. People had gathered to watch what was going on. She had profiled enough arsonists to know that the Incinerator was probably here somewhere, watching from the shadows. That would be even more likely if he believed he had a link to Torque.

Show me your face. After four years, she had built up an image of her opponent. In her mind he was half laughing, half snarling, barely human.

"It's too early to say." The chief fire officer at the scene spared a few minutes to talk to them, but he was busy directing operations. "Luckily, the concierge acted fast and the system is excellent. No one was injured, but there is some structural damage in the lobby. I'll have it made safe by morning."

"You can stay with us tonight." Sarange, who had driven them, linked her arm through Hollie's.

Khan and Sarange lived a short distance away in another luxury building. When they arrived at their home, the obvious difference between this apartment and Torque's was that it had been adapted to make it child-friendly. There was less glass and chrome, more rounded edges and a distinct lack of white.

Hollie was surprised when Sarange paid off the sitter. "I thought you'd have an army of nannies." She bit her lip. "I'm sorry. That sounded judgmental."

Sarange waved aside the apology. "We like our privacy. Let me show you to your room." She grinned. "And you have to admire our little tiger as we pass the nursery."

"Tiger?" Hollie followed her up the stairs.

She detected a hint of annoyance in Sarange's expression, as though she'd said too much. She shook the thought aside. *I must be tired.* Or the Incinerator was getting to her again, playing havoc with her imagination.

"Khan reminds me of a tiger, and Karina takes after him," Sarange explained.

The baby was sprawled on her back like a starfish in her crib, and Sarange rearranged the blankets over her.

"She's beautiful." Even in sleep, Hollie could see the little girl had inherited the good looks of both her parents.

Sarange smiled. "I already liked you. Now it's official." She checked the baby monitor was on before closing the door.

She led Hollie down the hall to a beautiful guest suite. The soothing creamy tones of the furnishings made Hollie feel instantly relaxed and she regarded the vast bed with pleasure. Although whether she would sleep with the Incinerator's latest attack on her mind was doubtful.

"Will this be okay for you and Torque?"

Ah. Now would be a good time to explain Sarange's mistake. Just a few simple words to clear up the confusion. *Torque and I are not in a relationship.* That should do it.

"This will be fine."

Because wasn't this what she wanted? And no matter how hard he tried to resist, it was also what Torque wanted. *So, let's see where sharing takes us.*

Aware that her thoughts of Torque had kept her silent for a long time, she shook her preoccupation aside. "Are you touring with the band?"

"I'm not performing with them, but I'll join them when I can. Although it's not easy with a baby, Khan and I made a decision when Karina was born that we would try not to spend more than two nights apart." Sarange glanced at her watch. "Do you mind if I leave you to settle in? Karina will wake up soon for her supper and I want to change out of these clothes before she does."

When she was alone, Hollie went to the window and stared out at the dramatic views. Three Incinerator fires were now linked directly to her. She couldn't ignore that. She also couldn't escape the reality that she was responsible for bringing the arsonist closer to other people and specifically to Torque. Prior to her arrival in his life, the Incinerator had been content to worship him from afar. Now he was pushing for a more meaningful relationship. And it looked like Hollie had been the catalyst.

With no way of contacting McLain or Vince King, she was running out of choices. Going back to Newark and letting the Incinerator team know what was going on seemed like the only option available to her. It felt like stepping back in time. Going back to the same routine. Picking up the pieces of a four-year investigation that hadn't caught the Incinerator yet. And it wasn't what she wanted. If only there was another way.

"So we're sharing a room?" She hadn't heard Torque approach until he was standing right behind her. Close enough to touch, but not touching. It didn't matter. His gaze was like a caress.

"Unless you don't want to?"

"You know I want to." His voice was gruff. "Like I said, we need to talk before we even consider anything else."

She nodded. Maybe there were other options after all. "I'm ready."

"So am I. But I came to tell you that the other band members have just arrived." His smile was rueful. "I decided Khan and Sarange needed some extra protection if you and I were going to be here tonight."

Hollie covered her mouth with her hand. "I should have thought of that."

His gaze remained fixed on hers. "We've both just given something away without even trying. You didn't ask how my bandmates can provide the protection we need… And I didn't ask why you should be the one who knows about the arsonist's next steps."

"I guess neither of us is very good at keeping secrets."

He ran a finger down her cheek, sending delicious

heat shimmering along her nerve endings. "I wouldn't say that."

They had done this many times. When it mattered most, Beast was a formidable team. Onstage, they all came together as a unique entity, but their main strength was as a fighting force. This was what they did best. When one of their group was threatened, they closed ranks and worked together to protect that person.

They were shifters who lived in the human realm, and their responsibilities straddled two worlds. When they dealt with a problem that could draw the attention of mortals, particularly of law enforcement, they had to tread carefully, not only for their own sake. If their cover was blown, if the world became aware that the stories, movies and legends were more than hype, and that shifters lived among them, nothing would ever be the same again.

It was a fine line they always walked. On the whole, the supernatural world was a quiet one, but that could change in an instant. Passions ran deep and centuries-old conflicts could be reignited with a look or a word. Battle lines would be redrawn and shifters who believed they were living out their lives in peace might suddenly find themselves renewing ancient loyalties. With no immortal peacekeeping force, shifters had to find their own protection. For Beast, that meant relying on each other. And that suited Torque just fine.

Diablo, Dev and Finglas stayed at street level, taking turns to patrol the lobby and the sidewalk outside the building. Although their opponent was unknown to them, with their quick, shifter reflexes and heightened perceptiveness, they would notice anything unusual before the building's security guards did. Torque, Khan and Ged stayed in the apartment. Sarange was there, as well, but her focus was on the baby.

"What if this arsonist doesn't approach the building?" Ged asked. "What if he tries a different method this time? Some sort of remote control device, even a bomb?"

"He won't." Hollie's voice was calm, her expression resolute. "That's not his style. He gets up close."

Torque, who was seated next to her on the sofa, spoke quietly so only she could hear. "And the reason you can say that with such confidence is one of those things we need to talk about."

She turned her head, and he drank in the purity of her features. "No more secrets."

Could he do that? Tell a mortal woman everything? Would those clear green eyes still look at him with such trust once she knew it all? He would soon know.

A muffled cry over the baby monitor brought Sarange to her feet. "She's usually hungry at this time of night."

"Can I come with you?" Hollie asked. "I'd love to meet her."

"Of course, but be prepared to duck." When Hollie looked confused, Sarange explained. "Karina's eating habits are still hit and miss."

When the two women had left the room, Khan took Hollie's place. His expression was serious. "Do I want to hear this?" Torque asked.

"I'm your friend…"

Torque leaned back, looking up at the ceiling. "Whenever a conversation starts with those words it means I *don't* want to hear it."

"I just want to know you've thought this through. I mean, the whole dragon-mortal thing."

Torque knew Khan only had his interests at heart. He was saying exactly what Torque had just been thinking. But Torque didn't want to hear the words spoken out loud any more than he wanted them inside his head. He didn't want anything to come between him and Hollie, even if it made sense.

"You thought Sarange was mortal when you first met her," Torque said.

"That's not true. I always knew Sarange was a were-wolf. *She* was the one who didn't know it." Khan placed a hand on his shoulder. "Take my advice. Stay away from mortals." As Torque got to his feet, he raised his brows. "Where are you going?"

"See that?" Torque pointed to the glass door that led to the roof terrace. "I'm going to put myself on the other side. That way I don't have to hear your advice." He knew he was being unfair. He also knew it didn't matter how far away from Khan he got. He would still have to listen to the same doubts playing inside his own head.

Once he was outside, he sat on a bench that gave the sensation of soaring out over the rooftops. The height and the fresh air soothed him, but he craved a wilder setting. City living didn't appease his inner dragon. He ached for soaring mountains, swooping valleys, wild rivers and tumbling waterfalls.

"Care for some company?"

He looked up to see Sarange standing in the open doorway. One of the most famous and beautiful women in the world was dressed in baggy sweatpants and a faded, off-the-shoulder top. Torque decided against telling her that she had something that looked like oatmeal in her long, dark hair.

He scooted along the bench to make room for her. "Where's the baby?"

"With Ged." It afforded everyone in the band endless fascination that the giant were-bear and the tiny half wolf, half tiger got along so well.

"Did your husband send you to talk sense to me?"

"I thought we were friends. Does it matter why I'm here?"

He huffed out a breath. "I guess not."

They sat in silence for a few minutes. "Khan thinks I should forget her because she's mortal." Torque wanted to be strong and silent, but the temptation to talk about Hollie was overwhelming.

"Khan's a cat. They're not known for giving good advice. Too self-absorbed." They shared a smile. "But if you want her in your life, you have to tell her."

"How can I do that?" The anguish in his voice matched the misery that tore at his heart every time he contemplated telling Hollie the truth. Because he knew that, once he did, he faced the prospect of watching her walk away.

"It won't be easy, but you'll find the words. And maybe simple is best."

"You mean I should say 'I'm a dragon' rather than 'I'm a winged, fire-breathing, mythical beast of legend'?"

"You'll find a way. And if she loves you, she'll love all of you." She grinned. "Even the scales."

"My scales are my best feature, furry girl. And, by the way, you have baby food in your hair."

She patted his cheek. "Talk to her."

"That's the plan."

Hollie was drawn back again to the bedroom window with its view over the city. *He* was out there somewhere. She knew it. The Incinerator would not have left town. Even if he wasn't planning an attack on this building, he would be drawn close by Torque's presence. Probably hers, too. She had been involved in the profile they had produced on him. Profiling wasn't her area of expertise, but she knew the classic traits of an arsonist by heart. Usually white male, unstable childhood, above average intelligence but poor academic performance, inability to form stable relationships, possible mental illness. And the biggest one of all…fascination with fire.

The profiler had been cautious about the Incinerator. "The information available suggests the arsonist is a man, but the deciding factor about gender will be motive." *Unhelpful.* "If the perpetrator is driven by excitement, vandalism or money, then it's a man. If the motive is revenge or extremism, the chances that you are looking for a woman will increase considerably."

In other words, until they could figure out the motive, the shadowy figure would remain unclear.

This time, when Torque opened the door, she heard him and turned her head. He remained where he was for a moment or two, just watching her face. Then he crossed the room until he was standing beside her. They looked out at the view together.

Although it was long past midnight, the tiredness that had gripped her when they first arrived here was gone. In its place was a tingling excitement.

"It's time to tell me your secret, Hollie Brown."

She took a deep breath. "My real name is Hollie Brennan. I'm an FBI fire investigator."

His lips quirked into a grin. "That's it?"

"I thought it was pretty explosive." The irony of the word wasn't lost on her and she returned the smile. "I'm guessing you have something better?"

His expression immediately became serious. "I'm not sure you're ready for this."

Hollie shook her head. "That's not how it works. We had an agreement. You don't get to back down just because you think your secret is too big for me to handle."

He was silent for a moment or two, staring down at her with a look she couldn't fathom. The opal depths of his eyes glowed brighter than she'd ever seen them before. When his lips parted, she was no longer sure she really did want to hear what he had to say. Wasn't sure she wanted to know the truth about the man the world called Torque.

"Very well. You want to know how I can walk through fire without getting burned?" His eyes darkened, their depths becoming haunted. "The answer is easy, but it's one you'll have to open your mind to understand."

Torque was an entertainer, but Hollie had the strangest feeling none of this was for show. It wasn't a big buildup. He was steadying his nerves as much as he was preparing her.

She placed her hand on his arm, feeling the heat of his flesh warming her fingertips. "Tell me, Torque."

"I'm a dragon."

That was unexpected. She frowned, trying to assess his meaning. "Is it a club? A society? I'm not sure I'm following you…"

He gripped her forearms, holding her steady and drawing her closer. "Hollie, I'm a shape-shifter. I'm part human, part dragon."

That was the moment her dream ended. It had been too good to be true. She had always feared that the man she had fallen in love with from afar couldn't really be everything she had believed him to be, and now she was finding out he wasn't.

Torque was crazy.

As she made a move to pull away from him, Torque

slid his hands up her arms to her shoulders, and she shuddered. How could her body betray her this way? Thinking he was deranged as she did now, how could his touch still send that thrill through her?

"I can't do this." She said it with genuine regret. No matter what his problems were, she cared about him. And he had saved her life. Was that all part of this delusion? Had he been wearing some sort of protection so he could pretend he was a fireproof beast? She followed that thought a step further.

Oh, Torque. Are you the Incinerator, after all? Her heart was starting to race with fear now as she gazed up at him. Why had she never noticed the way his eyes could glow with inner fire?

"I can prove it."

"Torque, don't put yourself through this. Don't put *us* through it." All she wanted to do now was walk away, leave this situation while there was some dignity left. For both of them.

"You talked about the concert in Marseilles. The one where the wolves stormed the stage?"

She nodded, fascinated at the way he was staying so calm about this. As if he truly believed it.

"It wasn't special effects, Hollie. They weren't wolves. They were werewolves."

She broke free of his grasp and headed for the door.

"Watch that concert again with me now."

She paused with her fingertips touching the door handle. *It wasn't special effects.* She had never tired of watching the film footage of that concert. Like everyone else, she had pored over those incredible scenes, had devoured the comments from technology geeks about how it had been achieved. Just how had Khan changed into a tiger right in front of an audience of thousands?

How had Diablo been playing his drums one second and become a prowling black panther the next? And Torque…what the hell kind of digital genius had come up with an effect that had him casting aside his guitar, pounding across the stage and taking flight, unfurling giant wings as he ran. Because…

She turned to face him, her back pressed against the door as the blood drained from her face. "You turned into a dragon."

"I *am* a dragon." This time, when he said those words, everything about him was different. His stance was proud, his voice was a low rumble originating deep in his powerful chest and the fire in his eyes became a blaze.

Despite every instinct screaming out to the contrary, she believed him. More than that, she wanted to bow before him, to honor him. It was clear that Torque wasn't just any dragon.

"I can't…" As her knees started to give way, he was at her side, scooping her up with one arm beneath her thighs and the other around her waist. Hollie raised a hand to touch his cheek. "It's true."

Torque placed her on the bed. "Let's watch that film."

"I don't need proof." Even though everything she knew about her world had just been thrown off course, his word was enough.

Torque's lips quirked upward into a smile and he lifted her hand to his lips. "Thank you. But I want you to see me."

His gaze ignited tiny fires along her flesh.

"To know me. I can't shift here in the city. Not without triggering a major incident. That film will show you the other half of who I am."

Even though he came and sat next to her, there was at least two feet of mattress between them. Torque reached into a drawer of the bedside table and withdrew an electronic tablet. When he'd connected to the internet and found the clip he wanted, he held the device out to Hollie.

She didn't take it. Instead, she closed the distance between them, colliding with his hard, warm body. "You said we'd do this together."

His indrawn breath reverberated through her. "Okay."

Hollie could feel his determination and something more. Tilting her head, she viewed his profile. The hard planes of his features were more obvious from this angle and she could see the tension in his jaw, the tightness around his eyes. Was he *scared*? Afraid of what she would think when she watched this film? Hollie had seen it before, of course, but she would be seeing now with a new awareness.

She couldn't make him any promises about her reaction. Sitting on a bed with a dragon…she hoped she would continue to see the man she knew. But this was so far outside anything she had ever experienced, her thoughts were in a whirl. All she knew was that no matter what happened next, her life had just changed completely. "Let's do this."

He nodded, swiping the screen to start playing the film. The concert had been filmed as part of a documentary about Beast, but the incident had also been captured on dozens of cell phones. It began with five figures plowing their way through the audience to the front of the arena and leaping onto the stage. The men landed in a crouch and simultaneously shifted into wolf form. Crouching low at the far edge of the stage, they bared their teeth at the band members.

Beast was playing up a storm. Behind the members, the LED screens were like a giant art installation showing their signature three-sixes logo, roaring flames and the snarling jaws of various wild beasts. Believing the invasion to be part of the show, the already excited crowd went into a renewed frenzy. The band's symbolic sign of the beast was being made throughout the stadium as howls of appreciation rent the air.

Onstage, everything went from stillness to action. Adding to the sense of theater, Beast turned as a group to face the werewolves who had invaded their performance space. Khan, leading the advance, had a bring-it-on snarl on his face as he moved forward with muscle-bound stealth.

In the blink of an eye the stage erupted. The werewolves sprang from their crouching position as a series of incredible transformations took place. Khan's clothing burst apart. Beneath it rippled brilliant orange fur slashed across with diagonal stripes, each as thick, black and straight as a hand-drawn charcoal line. In Khan's place a giant tiger covered the distance across the stage in one bound, his lips drawn back in a snarl that revealed huge white fangs.

At the same time, Diablo disappeared and, in his place, a muscular black panther was prowling the space before joining the tiger as an unlikely ally. Finally, Dev cast aside his guitar, shifting stealthily as a ghost into a huge snow leopard, sharp and white in contrast to the blur of color around him, before throwing himself into the fray. Landing on the back of one of the startled wolves, the mighty creature lowered his head and used its lethal fangs to tear a chunk of flesh from its victim's neck.

The crowd, still convinced they were watching a series of awesome special effects, continued to cheer and howl. At the side of the stage, Ged could be seen gesturing wildly to the security team at the side of the stage. He wasn't fast enough...

Striding across the stage, Torque raised his hands and unleashed a series of explosions in his path. As he walked, he grew in stature until he towered over everything around him. Even on the screen, Hollie could see his eyes were bright red, the color filling the entire surface. The pupils had become vertical black slits. As he blinked, both top and bottom lids moved in time to meet each other.

As Torque broke into a run, his clothes tore from his body. His arm and leg muscles thickened, and he dropped onto all fours, giant claws the size of a mechanical digger churning up the surface of the stage. His skin was replaced by shimmering scales that reflected the neon colors of the strobe lighting. Giant wings unfurled, and a spiked tail flicked out before he opened his mouth to shoot a stream of blue-white flame in the direction of the wolves. Transfixed, Hollie watched as Torque became a stunning, fearsome dragon. He rose and hovered, his wingspan covering the entire stage.

Then the stage lights went out, black screens came down and a film of Beast playing one of its biggest hits was projected onto it.

Hollie sat very still, unsure what to do with all the emotion coursing through her. Dragons were creatures of magic and mystery. They had captivated her when she was a child, but she had put aside that fascination as she grew older. Except in her dreams. Now she knew dragons were real…and there was one sitting right next to her.

She pressed her hand to Torque's chest, feeling his heart beating beneath her palm. "You're beautiful."

He pulled her close, pressing his face to her hair as though he was inhaling her. Placing a hand on each side of her face, he dropped a single kiss on her parted lips. At his touch, white-hot fire scorched through her. The need for more became a burning ache and she moved closer.

She was in control of what she was doing, but at the same time, she was lost in sensation. Her body had shifted to autopilot. Every muscle was tense, every nerve on high alert. Torque's eyes locked on to hers with an intensity that took her breath away. His mouth on hers was harder this time, demanding everything she needed to give. A soft sound escaped him as he parted her lips with his tongue. A groan that came from somewhere deep in his chest. It sounded like he'd found forever.

That noise was everything Hollie had ever wanted. Her whole body vibrated with pleasure as she slid a hand behind his head. Heat built in the pit of her stomach, radiating outward until the pressure became a sweet, unbearable pain. The air around them crackled with electricity as Torque's tongue caressed hers.

Hollie came alive in the storm that broke over her. Torque's touch sent a lightning bolt straight to her heart. She gave herself up to the tempest, allowing it to consume her, emerging on the other side of a moment that changed her life.

When she raised her head and looked into Torque's eyes, she saw confirmation of her own thoughts. "I haven't changed my mind, Torque. I still want you."

Chapter 7

Even though Hollie had accepted his true identity, there were still reasons why Torque needed to keep his distance. No matter how strong this attraction was, Khan was right. There were too many barriers between them. Hollie had a regular job, Torque was a celebrity. She was mortal, he was immortal. She was human, he was a dragon. So many lifestyle differences to overcome.

That was before he even started on the sorceress and seer who had sworn to destroy Torque and everything he touched. Happiness would never be for him, that was what Teine had told him all those centuries ago. If she couldn't have him, she would make sure no one else did.

Even as his head was reminding him of all the reasons why he should gently remove Hollie's hands from around his neck and leave the room to spend a sleepless night on a sofa, Torque's lips were returning to hers. Over and over.

It didn't matter what his rational self tried to tell him, she was in his blood. His mate was in his arms, and everything else faded away.

"Hollie…" He made one last attempt at doing the right thing.

"No more talking." She pressed a finger to his lips. "Unless it's to tell me what you like."

The sound that began deep in his chest was a groan of surrender. "You, Hollie. I like you."

Sliding a hand behind her, he eased them both down the bed until she was lying on her back and he was on top of her. Using his knee, he pushed her legs apart and settled between them as he returned to the heaven of kissing her. Tugging her lower lip between his teeth, he suckled the plump flesh before thrusting his tongue deep into her mouth. Hollie murmured with pleasure and arched up to him.

She took one of his hands in hers, sliding it under the crisp cotton of her blouse and sucking in a breath as his calloused fingers moved over the soft flesh of her stomach. When he reached the swell of her breast, Torque covered the plump mound and pushed aside the lace of her bra. Finding her nipple, he rolled it between his thumb and forefinger.

Her breathing was becoming erratic and Torque lifted his head to watch her face. A faint flush tinted her cheeks, and her eyelids were heavy. Pleasure jolted him. *Mine.*

Lifting her blouse higher, he bent his head and lightly flicked his tongue over the exposed rosy tip. Hollie shuddered with pleasure and Torque's erection jerked in response. She brought her legs up to cradle him, holding him pelvis to pelvis. When she rocked against him, Torque hissed out a warning.

"If you do that again, this won't last long."

Her laugh was shaky. "Good, because I don't think I can wait."

"Clothes." He seemed to have lost the ability to speak in sentences. "Off."

In a flurry of activity, their clothing was flung aside. When they were both naked, Torque ran his hands up from her hips to her breasts. She looked so pale and dainty in contrast to his muscular hands and arms. So why was he the one who felt helpless every time he looked at her?

He drew in a rasping breath as Hollie mirrored his movements, spreading her hands over his torso, raking her nails over his flesh. It was too much. Too much raw heat and sensation powering through his veins, flooding his whole system. He grabbed her hands, bearing her onto her back again as he moved over her. Skin on skin. Heat on heat. Pleasure spiked and demanded release.

Not yet.

He moved slowly down her body, kissing along her neck, down her collarbone, until he reached the soft flesh of her breasts. He sucked at her rock-hard nipples, biting them and flicking them with his tongue, first one, then the other. Hollie dug her nails into his shoulders, crying out in delight.

Torque slid lower, licking and nipping the curve of her waist, her jutting hip bones, and the flat plain of her belly. Gripping the inside of her knees, he tugged her legs apart, holding her open to his gaze as he kissed his way along her inner thighs. Hollie writhed wildly in his hold, lifting her hips and offering herself to him.

Torque paused, his heart expanding as he gazed at her. She was perfection. Long-limbed, slender, pretty as a portrait. Elegance and light. Her emerald eyes glimmered at him from between half-closed lids, her lips were the color of rubies, her hair had the sheen of spun gold. The thought snagged a memory, then drifted away. There was no room for anything except his craving for her.

He wanted her so much it was an ache, but he was determined to make this moment last.

"So beautiful." Using his fingers to part her outer lips, he gazed down at her. "Pink and sweet…" He ran a finger through her center. "And so very wet."

Hollie's toes curled and her head thrashed from side to side. "Please, Torque." She buried her fingers in his hair. "No more teasing."

Obediently, he lowered his head and drew her clit into his mouth. As she began to tremble wildly, he sucked hard on the little nub. Panting, Hollie raised herself up on her elbows so she could watch what he was doing. Almost immediately, he felt her thigh muscles begin to tremble.

She threw her head back, her whole body bucking uncontrollably under the force of an instant climax. Torque didn't stop. He kept his mouth on her, circling her clit with his tongue, absorbing the ripples that crashed through her. He kept the waves coming and still continued to suck her.

"It's too much." Her voice was almost a sob. "No more, Torque, I can't…"

He eased up, slowing his movements and withdrawing gradually. His own breathing was coming harsh and fast as he moved back up the bed. Hollie gazed up at him with a dazed expression before wrapping her arms around him. Reaching a hand between them, she curved her fingers around his rock-hard shaft and stroked.

Luckily, a tiny part of Torque's brain was still clinging to a slither of reason. Leaning over the side of the bed, he snagged his discarded jeans with one hand. Hollie murmured a protest at the interruption.

"Condom."

"Are dragons always this well prepared?" Her voice was husky with a combination of laughter and residual breathlessness.

"This is my human side." He tore open the foil packet. "My dragon would choose to live dangerously."

Her hands traced molten lines of fire along the muscles of his back as he reached between them to get the protection in place. His erection felt like a steel girder, lying hot, hard and sheathed, pressing against her. Torque could feel Hollie's heart hammering a wild beat into his chest.

He couldn't wait any longer and Hollie's hands on his shoulders indicated she didn't want him to. Sliding his hands under her buttocks, he lifted her to him. She used a hand to guide him and he slammed all the way into her waiting warmth.

Hollie gave a little cry and he paused, looking down at her in concern.

She shook her head, her eyes tightly closed. "Don't stop."

He smoothed a finger over her furrowed brow. "I need to know you're okay."

"I'm okay." She opened her eyes. "It's perfect. New. Different, but perfect."

Different, but perfect. The ultimate high. If he hadn't known before that she was his mate, he knew it now. Adrenaline flooded his body, powering him into action. He surged into her in heavy, powerful strokes. Hollie slammed up from the mattress in time with his movements. Every thrust increased the pressure, built the intensity, destroyed a little bit more of the control. Hollie went wild, writhing beneath him, clawing at his shoulders and upper arms. She called out his name, tensing as she came again.

Torque felt the tendons in his neck straining, his facial muscles pulling tight. Thrusting powerfully one last time, his body convulsed in time with Hollie's as his own climax hit. He pulsed deep inside her, and Hollie clenched around him, holding on tight. It was like lightning striking his spine and sending aftershocks along his nerve endings. The room started to spin as he rocked into her, gasping out her name. Everything faded except this. His heart was ready to burst. He couldn't believe he'd wasted so much of his life not experiencing this delicious joy.

Gradually, he came back down to earth. He could draw a breath, his heart was starting to beat normally. But he would never be the same again.

Returning from the bathroom, Torque lay on his side facing Hollie. Gently, he brushed long strands of hair back from her face. A glimmer of a smile touched her lips when he leaned over, kissing her lightly.

She turned into his embrace, her eyes widening as her gaze traveled down his body. "Um, is this a dragon thing?"

He was harder than ever. Huge and throbbing. "I'm a dragon, but this has never happened to me before."

She ran her tongue along her lower lip. "I'm human... but I feel the same. I still want more."

As Torque reached for another condom, her blood felt like honey, running thick, slow and sweet through her veins. What she was feeling went beyond arousal. A thousand wonderful sensations blossomed from

Torque's touch, warming from her toes to her fingertips. Her naked skin was fever-hot, and the cooler air
in the room felt like ice in contrast.

Patience wasn't an option. They both needed fast and
hard. Hollie didn't stop to question why. This was her
new reality. Her new perfection.

She pulled Torque toward her and he pressed deep
inside, muffling a groan as he began to pump his hips.

"Too good." His lips crushed hers as they rocked
together.

Her own breath caught at the back of her throat. How
could it be even better? She ground her pelvis against
his, lifting to meet him, matching his demands.

When he pulled out, she called his name, trying to
draw him back to her. Flipping her over onto her front,
he drew her hips up so she was on her hands and knees.
"Oh, yes."

She spread her knees wider, arching her back as he
moved into position and drove into her from behind.
He felt even bigger and thicker from this angle and she
pushed herself up as he buried himself to the hilt. He
held her steady as he pistoned into her in a series of
frenzied thrusts. The pressure built, instantly taking her
to the breaking point. Hollie clutched at the bedcovers,
helpless to do anything other than hang on.

Barely recognizing the animal sounds that issued
from her lips, she jerked, letting out a strangled gasp
as every part of her body constricted and then slowly
released in shuddering, luscious waves. Her eyelids
fluttered shut as she shattered into a million pieces,
writhing in place for a few seconds before going limp.
Torque gave a low growl of appreciation, his grip tightening just enough that his nails bit into her skin.

"Feels like heaven when you come around me," Torque murmured, grinding his pelvis against her.

Hollie gasped and shuddered through her climax as he thrust harder and faster. He drove in hard one last time and held himself taut. Then his whole body started to shake and he buried his head in her neck, nipping the skin lightly with his sharp teeth before collapsing on top of her.

As his hands slid away from her hips, Hollie sank forward. Torque slipped to one side of her, draping an arm over her back.

"I don't know what just happened." His fingertips were warm and slightly rough along her spine.

She turned her head to look at him. "Nor do I, but it was wonderful."

His expression lightened and he reached out a finger to touch her cheek. "It was, wasn't it?"

Her body was reeling and her head was spinning. This was Torque, the man she had worshiped from afar for years. He had also just confessed to being a dragon. She really needed to take some time to process what had become of the life she thought she knew. But she couldn't. Not while Torque was looking at her with a touch of anxiety in his expression. As if he was afraid he hadn't met her expectations.

She traced the perfect lines of his lips with her finger. "I want more of that."

He looked startled. "Now?"

She laughed. "Maybe not immediately, but sometime soon."

"I promise you there will be more and it will be soon." He drew her close and she wrapped her arms around his neck. "And dragons always keep their promises."

Lying in the semidarkness with him felt comfortable and right. And un-dragon-like. "Where are you from?"

"It's a long story."

She tilted her head to look at him. At the bladelike planes of his face and the grim set of his lips. "I'm not going anywhere."

A corner of his mouth lifted. "I'll tell you the abridged version. It began when the world was young and time was new, when elves and faeries walked the earth without hindrance. When humans understood the need for magic and sorcerers were all-powerful. In the land now known as Scotland, a sorceress reigned over the Highlands. One day, she entered a cave and spoke the words of a spell. The ground shook and split and flames roared up from the cracks. When the blaze died down, there were two huge eggs in its place, one white and one black. The following day, the eggs hatched into two dragons. The white one was the Cumhachdach, or the mighty, and the black was the Moiteil, or the proud. They were the founders of the first of the Scots dragon-shifter clans."

"Clans?" She tilted her head to look at him. "Like a family?"

"Exactly." He traced circles on her shoulder with the palm of his hand. "I am the only remaining member of the Cumhachdach."

Although his voice was neutral, she knew, from the tension in his body, that this was not a subject he wanted to discuss. Leaning on one elbow, she pressed her lips to his and felt him relax slightly.

"Maybe we should get some sleep? I have some plans for later that may need you to conserve your strength."

He smiled, drawing her back down to him. "I'm not good at sleeping, but I'll gladly watch while you get some rest."

* * *

When they were able to get back into Torque's apartment building, Hollie took time out to view the damage. It was minor and the concierge explained his theory that a bogus delivery driver had started the blaze.

"The guy gave me a stack of paperwork to fill out. When I'd finished it, he was gone. Soon after that, the fire alarm went off." The concierge showed them the point where the fire had started. "He didn't think it through. This lobby is mostly marble—it's not going to burn easily. And a building like this is going to have a sophisticated fire prevention system."

"It doesn't sound like the Incinerator," Torque said when they were alone again. "He's good at this. Surely, if he wanted to burn this place down, he wouldn't make any mistakes."

"It was him." Hollie sounded certain. "This was just to let us know he's in town."

When they reached the apartment, she took his hands in hers. Standing on the tips of her toes, she reached up and drew his head down until their lips were almost touching. Torque was enchanted by her, bound to her body and soul. He'd even managed to get a few hours of sleep with her in his arms. It seemed Hollie's presence was the antidote to Teine's centuries-old insomnia spell.

"I want you to do something for me." Her voice was a whisper.

"Anything."

"Show me this legendary paperwork of yours."

"I can think of other things we could be doing." He slid his hands down to her waist.

"I'm guessing that's the laid-back attitude that got you in this administrative mess." She took his hand and led him toward the room he used as a study. "I'll strike a deal with you. Let me see what I'm up against, and then I'm all yours."

He gave an exaggerated sigh. "You're strict."

She grinned mischievously. "Well, if *that's* what you want…"

This was what his life had been missing. This easy, comfortable warmth. When they'd woken up that morning, he wondered if things would be awkward. It wasn't exactly an everyday situation. How would they deal with the whole human-dragon thing? But they'd slipped into their own natural rhythm. Maybe it was pretense. They were living in the moment and ignoring the big stuff—the crazy guy lurking in the shadows, the imbalance in their DNA, the ridiculous age difference, that whole mortal-immortal, dragon-human thing—but they were having fun. And Torque had forgotten about fun. He was one of the most famous men in the world, and he was enjoying himself for the first time in… He tried to remember.

A thousand years? Two? It didn't matter. He was going to relish these precious moments, even though he knew they couldn't last.

Half an hour later, Hollie was seated on the rug with paper piled all around her and a look of intense concentration on her face. Torque, who had wandered away to the kitchen, returned with sandwiches and soda.

"Am I beyond salvation?" he asked as he joined her on the floor.

"Pardon?" Hollie looked up with a frown. "Oh, no. I didn't realize the sheer quantity of mail you get. No wonder you don't reply. Why haven't you employed someone to deal with it before now?" She took a bite of her sandwich before answering her own question. "Ah, I see. Privacy. I'll send a standard letter to most of these."

"It's more than I was going to do." Torque nodded at his laptop. "And there are the emails."

"As I go through it all, I'll search for anything that could be from the Incinerator." She stretched her arms above her head. "I may see clues you didn't. Did you never see the connection? That there had been fires in the towns you'd visited?"

"When we're on tour, it's a whirlwind. We visit a town, do a performance and move on. Never look back." He grimaced. "I hate to say it, but I'm not great at keeping up with the latest news. If it's not front and center in the headlines, I don't read it. If these fires really were a tribute to me, I haven't been very appreciative. I honestly didn't notice."

Hollie tapped a finger on one of the stacks of paper. "If I'm right and you are the connection, I think the Incinerator will have told you. Somehow he, or she, will have sent you a message. But it's unlikely to be straightforward. He's not going to confess up front. For one thing, he wouldn't be that stupid. And for another, it's more fun to keep us guessing."

Torque regarded her in fascination. "You talk as though you know him."

"In a way, I do. I've never seen his face, but I've been inside his head." The corners of her mouth pulled down. "It's not a nice place to be."

"You said you have no family. Is that true, or was it part of your undercover role?" Torque asked.

"No, it was true. Other than my last name and why I was in Addison, I didn't tell you any lies. My parents were killed in a car crash when I was a baby and I was raised by my grandmother. She died five years ago. I never knew any other members of my family."

"So neither of us has any clan?" Torque linked his

fingers through hers, enjoying that immediate connection of her hand in his. "But you have your friend? The one you needed to check in with?"

"Ah." A faint blush stained her cheeks pink. "That's another thing I was less than truthful about. McLain is my boss. I was calling to let her know what was going on with my investigation." A frown pulled her brows together. "But she's disappeared."

"You mean you can't get in touch with her?"

"No, she's actually gone missing. I spoke to one of my colleagues and he told me McLain hasn't been seen since I went undercover." She lifted worried eyes to his face. "And my apartment building burned down at the same time."

Torque sat up straighter. "What? Why the hell didn't you tell me?"

"Um… I was undercover, remember?"

"But—" He ran a hand through his hair. "You lost your *home* and I didn't know about it? My God, Hollie."

His every instinct was on high alert, his emotions strained to the point of breaking. This was his mate, and she was being threatened. Her home had been destroyed and *he should have known.* Even if his human had no clue, he was half dragon and he should be doing more to take care of her.

"I can't help thinking the Incinerator is behind both those things," Hollie said.

"It certainly seems suspicious." Torque forced himself to remain calm, to keep the conversation going, even though he wanted to let his inner dragon loose, to snort smoke and belch fire and find the person who was responsible for the scared look in Hollie's eyes. "But it could be a coincidence. What does your colleague think?"

"Dalton? He wants me to go back, so the team can take care of me." A faint smile lit the depths of her eyes. "I didn't mention that I have you to do that for me."

"I can't imagine the FBI would approve of one of their agents consorting with a dragon-shifter."

"And Dalton definitely wouldn't." Torque raised inquiring brows, and she went on to explain further. "We dated a few years ago and although it was well and truly over at the time, I sometimes wonder if Dalton got that message." She shifted into professional mode. "Other than a crazed fan, can you think of anyone who could be the Incinerator?"

Torque hesitated. He'd come this far. Hollie knew who he was and she had accepted him. More than that, she still desired him. The thought made his whole body thrum. She had received the information that she would be traveling around the country with a group of shape-shifters with raised brows, but she had taken it well. Could he take that next step? Tell her all of it?

Aware Hollie was watching him in concern, he drew a breath, unsure of what he was about to say until the words came out. "No, can't think of a single one."

Was it his imagination, or did he see disappointment in those emerald eyes? He consoled himself that he was telling the truth. Teine was dead. He had seen her die. The sorceress who killed his family had felt the full force of Torque's own dragon fire before she plunged into a ravine.

"Torque?" Hollie's voice pulled him back from his recollections.

"Yes?"

"I said that once I'd seen what I was up against, I'd be all yours." She placed her sandwich down and crawled across the floor toward him.

With his lap full of Hollie, there was no room in his head for bad memories. His fingers moved to the top button of her blouse. "All mine." Right there, right then, it was the only thing that mattered.

Chapter 8

The stage was set on a huge island in the center of the stadium, bathed in brilliant white light. Hollie thought it had the appearance of something that had dropped there from outer space. She had been to many concerts, but this time it felt like there were too many people crammed into the vast arena. The crowd surged in a relentless wave like the ocean during a high tide. The band's iconic, sign-of-the-beast logo was everywhere.

The sound level was off the scale. Her eardrums were coping at a point just short of pain. She had arrived at the venue in the car Torque sent for her and she had been able to hear the pulse of the music through the surrounding streets as she approached. Now she could feel it in her blood. The ground beneath her feet moved in time with Diablo's drumbeats, each vibration passing up through her body. Even her teeth were chattering along with Beast's music.

Onstage, the band members were a constant burst of

passion and energy, their gymnastics and pyrotechnics growing wilder with each number. Khan was as outrageous as ever, but it was Torque who drew Hollie's attention. His hyperactivity was more evident than ever. Never still, he wore a path across the stage as he ran back and forth, leaping, gyrating, scissor-kicking and diving. As he moved, explosions and fireballs followed him. He was electrifying, and Hollie, standing to one side of the stage with Ged and the security team, knew she wasn't the only one who thought so. The crowd was going wild throughout the whole performance, but it was Torque who drew the most applause.

The atmosphere was euphoric. Hollie looked out across the sea of bodies. The familiar fingers at the side of the head, the devil-horn gesture, were everywhere. She had no real expectation of noticing one person, or singling out anyone acting suspiciously in such a mass of people. There was no way of knowing if the Incinerator even attended Beast's concerts before moving on to set his fires.

The security team and police had been alerted about the danger. She wondered whether there were FBI agents here. How much had McLain shared before she went missing? Did the Incinerator team in Newark even know about the Torque connection? Maybe that was something she should ask Dalton. Except that would bring the whole investigation crashing down on them. She didn't want to do that to Torque and his friends. Putting them under that sort of scrutiny would be the worst kind of torture. She wasn't ready to do it. Not yet.

She was the person who knew the most about the Incinerator. For the last four years they'd been trying to catch him using conventional methods. Now that she knew there was a paranormal element to the case, perhaps that explained why they'd been unsuccessful. With Torque at her side, she might have a better chance of catching him by unconventional means. She at least wanted the chance to try.

Hollie knew Torque was holding out on her. When she asked him if he knew of anyone who could be the Incinerator, she had seen his hesitation. She had seen his pain, as well. He had lived for centuries and experienced many things about which she could only speculate. Maybe she shouldn't be shocked that his life story included deep troughs, but the depths of agony in his eyes had shocked her. It had also hurt her. She wanted to take it away, to soothe him. The only way she knew how to do that was with her presence.

She hid a smile. It seemed to work. Torque was *very* appreciative when she distracted him with her body. And who knew sex with a dragon could be so incredible? If it wasn't for the Incinerator lurking in the background, she'd be having the time of her life.

This concert was the start of the tour. Right after this, they'd be getting on the bus, the one the band called the Monster, and driving to a hotel in Philadelphia, ready for their performance there on the following night.

The Incinerator would follow them. She knew that with absolute certainty. And he would target her again. Ged had tightened security around all of them, and Hollie could barely move without a muscle-bound security guard at her side. The arsonist had been part of her life for a long time. Now it felt like she could almost reach out a hand and touch him. She was getting close, but he was still in the shadows.

Ged touched her arm and gestured to the exit, indicating that the band was about to start its final number. The crowd reached frenzy level as Hollie, flanked by two huge guards, followed Ged out of the stadium.

The Monster was unlike any bus Hollie had ever seen. More a traveling hotel than a vehicle, it had every luxury the band could cram into it. In addition to a comfortable living area and a smaller room that Ged used as an office, it had a well-stocked kitchen, a shower room, two restrooms and a long narrow hall lined with bunks. Torque had explained that they used hotels when they could, but the bus was their home away from home when they were on the road.

"Just be glad we're not on the Monster overnight." Ged held up the coffeepot, but Hollie shook her head. "The postconcert high is usually a killer. It can take hours for the band to come down."

"I'm not surprised." Hollie took a seat on one of the surprisingly comfortable sofas. "That sort of performance must use up some energy."

She was conscious of his penetrating gaze as he sat opposite her. "Torque told you who we are."

"Yes." There didn't seem to be much else to say.

"And you're okay with that? With us?"

She smiled. "I'd have been running in the opposite direction if I wasn't."

He laughed. "I guess you would. I'm glad you're here. For Torque. What happened to him was…" He seemed to be searching for the right word. "Devastating."

Hollie didn't know what to say. Should she explain that she didn't know what he meant? If she asked him for details, it would feel like a betrayal of Torque, who clearly didn't feel ready to tell her more. She was saved from any further embarrassment when the five band members burst onto the vehicle.

Ged was right about their postperformance energy

levels. Although Torque came straight to Hollie, the other four were almost ricocheting off the sides of the bus with elation as they relived the atmosphere of the concert.

Dev pulled bottles of beer from the cooler and tossed them around. "Let's party."

"Let's not." Ged's voice was stern. "You have another concert tomorrow night, remember?"

"Ah." Dev sank back onto the sofa, chugging his beer. He quirked a brow at Hollie. "It's like high school around here, but without the long holidays."

"I think of it more as kindergarten," Ged said. "Tantrums, throwing up, eating and drinking the wrong things, taking each other's toys…"

Hollie laughed, snuggling closer to Torque as he placed an arm around her shoulders. "Is it always like this?"

"This is mild. Wait until Khan and Diablo try to kill each other."

"That's a joke, right?" She looked at the lead singer, who was almost horizontal on one of the sofas, and the drummer, who appeared lost in his own world.

Finglas, who had overheard, shook his head. "Happens at least once a day. It used to be more often before Khan got married and calmed down."

"Pass me one of those beers." Hollie gestured to Dev. "I don't usually drink much, but it looks like I might need to start."

As she spoke, the engines roared into life and the gigantic bus rolled out into the traffic. She was touring with Beast, a rock band of shape-shifters, and she had no idea where this adventure would take her.

Hollie couldn't sleep. The touring lifestyle didn't agree with her. After Philadelphia, Beast had performed in Pittsburgh, Cincinnati and Chicago. Now they were spending three nights in—her mind went blank. *Where am I?* Nashville. That was it. The home of country music was hosting a huge music festival, and Beast was one of the headline acts.

Leaving Torque, the self-styled insomniac, sprawled across the bed, she went into the sitting room of their suite and powered up the laptop. Torque had two email addresses. One was personal, the other belonged to his public persona. Hollie was simultaneously working her way through the stack of paper and his emails.

"I'm surprised Ged doesn't employ someone to take care of all this," she had said, referring to the fan mail. "You know, just have everything go through a management company."

"He does. Somehow people still manage to find me."

That had worried her. All these people had been able to contact him with ease. Once she had dealt with this backlog, she was going to tighten up his online security.

She started reading. Most of the emails were easy to answer. She was able to send the standard reply she'd composed—including an apology for the delay—before archiving the conversations. It had been the same with the letters. Most of the communications were genuine expressions of admiration.

Ged had been right about the extreme messages. Hollie thought she had seen everything when it came to fire, but some of these letters and emails opened her eyes to new extremes. From confessions of sexual arousal and sadism linked to fire, to occult and devil worship, they explored the darkest aspects of the human psyche. Some of them came close to threatening Torque, demanding he should share their fantasies.

She had started a database labeled *Possibilities*, listing the important information from each message and cross-referencing it to what she knew about the Incinerator. There was nothing that made her suspect the arsonist was among them. Maybe she was missing something.

She'd been working steadily for about an hour when she came across a message that made her pause.

Dark mists roll down the valley, blackened snow cloaks the peaks. Will ye no return again? The score remains unsettled, *mo dragon*, the fire unquenched.

Hollie frowned as she reread the words. There was no greeting and no signature. It was the date that made her pulse quicken. This email had been sent just over a year ago, but it was a forwarded message. The original had been sent three years earlier. Just before the first Incinerator attack.

The sender was Losgadh@ykl.com. A quick search revealed that ykl was an obscure internet provider with physical offices located in the United Kingdom. *Losgadh* was the Scots Gaelic word for "burning."

A prickle of awareness started at the base of her spine, working its way up until it lifted the hairs on her neck. For the first time ever, she felt like she had an insight into who the Incinerator might be. There was a motive here. The profiler had said the chances that the arsonist was a woman increased if revenge was the reason for the attacks. Did unrequited love count? Because that was what this message sounded like. She tapped a fingernail on the screen, following that thought. There was no clue that the writer was a woman; it could just as easily have been sent by a man.

She was still frowning over the message when Torque

appeared in the doorway. He wore sweatpants and was bare-chested and bleary-eyed, his long red hair rumpled.

"Missed you." The words were uttered on a yawn and a stretch.

Hollie patted the seat next to her. "I need you to look at this. It may be nothing, but it intrigued me."

Torque flopped down next to her. She moved the laptop so it rested across both their knees and she pointed to the three-line message. The words had a remarkable effect on him. All trace of lethargy vanished and he sat upright as though electrified.

"No. That can't be. She's dead."

Hollie was alarmed at the look on his face. It was as if the hounds of hell had been unleashed and were pursuing him. "Who is dead, Torque?"

He raised a hand, raking his hair back from his face. "Teine, the fire sorceress. The woman who was present at my birth. The same one who imprisoned me for centuries in a cave beneath the Scottish mountains. She was also a seer and she told me I would one day find great riches. Gold, emeralds and rubies would be mine."

A dozen questions swirled around in her head at those words, but she started with the most obvious one. "What makes you think it's her?"

"*Mo dragon*. It's Gaelic for 'my dragon.' That's what she used to call me." He appeared calmer now as he re-read the message. "And the tone of that message makes it sound like it's come from her."

Hollie remained silent, waiting for him to explain. After a few minutes of silence, Torque got to his feet. "I need to go for a walk. Some fresh air will help me clear my head."

"Can I come with you?"

He leaned down and kissed her. "I want you to."

They dressed quickly and slipped out of the hotel without being noticed. "Ged would go crazy if he knew we were out alone without protection," Hollie said as they wandered through the downtown streets.

"Hollie…" There was a distinct note of arrogance in Torque's voice. "You are with a dragon."

Even though the dawn light was just streaking the sky, there were still plenty of drinkers spilling out of bars and clubs. They walked in silence for a few blocks before Hollie spoke. "When you told me about the two dragon eggs that came out of the flames in the rock… one of them was you, wasn't it?"

"Yes. I was born from the fire that burned beneath the Highlands. I was the leader of the Cumhachdach." His lips twisted into a bitter smile. "I still am, for what it's worth."

"What do you mean?"

"Like I told you, I am the only one of my clan left alive." They had reached a low wall and Torque leaned against it. "Because Teine killed the rest of my family."

His voice was matter-of-fact, but Hollie could see the flash of pain in his eyes. Reaching out, she placed a hand on his arm. "I'm sorry."

He placed his hand over hers. "I've never been able to talk about it. Even to Ged, who was the person who rescued me from captivity. All he knew was that I was imprisoned by a sorceress. I never told him the story behind it."

"Can you tell me?" Hollie asked.

"I can try. We were the Highland dragon-shifters, born in the fire that raged when the mighty mountains were forged. I was the first, along with Alban, the leader of the Moiteil. Our followers came later. Teine saw us as her playthings. At first there was peace between the clans. The Highlands are vast enough for two dragon clans to exist in harmony, but that didn't suit Teine. Calm and coexistence are not in her nature. Over time, she turned us against each other and we became bitter enemies, stealing each other's treasure and fighting over territory."

As he spoke, there was a faraway look in his eyes as though he was looking back into the past. "Teine would favor one of us, then the other. First Alban, then me. But over time, it became clear that I was her favorite." Torque's lips twisted into a bitter smile. "More than that, I became an obsession with her."

Hollie shivered slightly. *Obsession.* It was a word that summed up the Incinerator, and possibly the writer of that email.

"When she realized I was never going to return her love, she cast a spell on me. I was imprisoned in the very cave where I was born, destined to be Teine's pet dragon for all eternity. Once I was helpless, she wiped out the entire Cumhachdach. It gave her great pleasure to come to me each day and describe the killings. She tortured me with the details."

Hollie moved closer to him, wrapping her arms around his waist, and Torque rested his cheek against her hair. They remained that way for several silent minutes. "You said she was dead." She lifted her head to look at him.

"I saw it for myself. When Ged came to free me, I thought I was imagining things. Another person entering the cave seemed to be an impossibility, but it's what he does. Don't ask me how, but he discovers the whereabouts of shifters who are in danger, or distress, and he rescues them. I was one of the lucky ones. He got me out of the cave, but Teine appeared as we were leaving.

There was no way I was going back into that prison. I breathed a stream of fire over her. She was engulfed in flames and staggered back, falling into a ravine." He pressed a fist into his open palm. "She couldn't have survived."

"But she was a sorceress. Didn't she have magic powers?"

He hunched a shoulder. "The sort that made her resistant to dragon fire and a fall from a mountain? She was good, Hollie, but she wasn't invincible."

Hollie tried out another theory. "Could the Incinerator be someone close to her? Someone who wants revenge for her death? If a family member, or someone close to her, knows you killed her, they could have sent that message."

Torque snorted. "I don't think Teine was the type to inspire loyalty. She has a twin sister, but they hated each other. Teine was fire and Deigh was ice—that's what their names mean in Gaelic—and they were opposites in every way. They stayed on their separate mountains and never met. It was a joke among the Highland paranormal community that no one had ever seen them together. I can imagine Deigh's main emotion at hearing about her sister's death would have been deep joy."

"But Deigh is still alive?"

Torque shrugged. "I assume so. The level of sorcery they had achieved made them immortal, but not invincible. Teine should have—must have—died when she was burned and fell from the mountain. As long as Deigh has avoided similar hazards, I guess, she still resides in her lonely ice palace on the mountain known as Càrn Eighe."

"What are we left with? A message that coincidentally sounds like it could be from Teine?" Hollie asked.

"That's how it looks." Torque didn't sound convinced, and his eyes, which were fixed on a point beyond her shoulder, had a hunted expression that made her uncomfortable.

"At least there haven't been any Incinerator attacks since we left New York," Hollie said.

Grasping her by the shoulders, Torque slowly turned her around. "I wouldn't be so sure about that."

Chapter 9

Torque gripped Hollie's hand tight as they walked toward the glow in the sky. He had known what it was as soon as he saw it. He was a dragon. Fire was in his blood; it pulled him the way a drug tempted an addict.

"It could be part of an organized display." Hollie shook her head. "I can't believe I just said that. We both know it's not."

She was right. There was already a large crowd gathered close to the burning building. It was an office block near the hotel where Beast was staying and just a few blocks from the concert hall where they had played on the previous night. Hollie pointed that information out to Torque as they stood behind the makeshift barrier the firefighters had erected. He nodded, pulling his beanie hat down as the group of people around them grew. The last thing he wanted was to be recognized.

The fire had taken hold fast, and every part of the structure was blazing, with flames creeping along the roof and bursting out of the doors and windows. Even though he was watching a destructive force at work, Torque still felt the inevitable pull of attraction as he stared into the blaze. Swirling orange, red and amber, even purple. It drew him in. Called to him.

Beckoning fingers of fire licked up into the air and reached out toward the surrounding buildings, trying to catch hold and make more. More heat, more smoke, more devastation. Finding nothing to cling to, they fluttered away, rising again minutes later in another direction.

Smoke, the headiest of all scents to a dragon, tugged at his nostrils. It was diluted by burning rubber and electrical cables. Nevertheless, he inhaled it greedily. Guiltily. Getting his dragon fix, secure in knowledge that the building had been empty. The firefighters had answered that question when someone from the crowd called out. Closed for the holiday weekend.

Is this for me, Teine? A little gift for the pet dragon?

The thought brought all the humiliation and pain of the past crashing back down on him. Torque was part mortal, part dragon. Both halves of his psyche were equal, but his dragon traits had a strong influence on his human personality. He was hotheaded, energetic, arrogant and loyal. He could tick all those boxes. But he was defined by his pride. Honor was the watchword throughout the Highland shifter clans. Torque's society had rules that were built on dignity, chivalry and dragon supremacy. Teine had known that and had used it to bring him low. She had stripped him of his power as a dragon-shifter leader. That feeling of helplessness came back to him now, rising like bile in his throat.

He scanned the faces of the other onlookers, unsure what he was looking for. If Teine had survived and she was doing this, she would be able to disguise herself in any way she chose. The sorceress he had once known could be anyone in this crowd. The middle-aged man standing slightly to one side? The youth taking tasteless selfies with the burning building behind him? The person who wasn't looking at the building at all, but who was staring at Torque and Hollie? He paused, looking again at the figure. He couldn't tell if it was a man or a woman. Most of the person's face was hidden by a hooded sweatshirt, but Torque caught a glimpse of the eyes. And a flash of venom in their depths.

As soon as Torque turned that way, the figure disappeared.

"What the...?"

Torque made a movement toward where he had seen the person. At that precise moment, there was a horrible groaning noise from the building as the roof started to collapse. The firefighters began moving everyone away from the scene. Torque, shoving his hands deep into his pockets and keeping his head down, went with the crowd, pulling Hollie along with him.

"What happened back there?" Hollie hauled on his arm. Becoming aware that she was having trouble keeping up, Torque slowed his strides to match her pace.

"I'm letting her get to me." He pressed the knuckles of one hand to his temple. "This is what Teine is good at. She gets inside your head and makes you doubt the evidence of your own eyes. Even after she's dead..." He took a breath. "It was nothing. I saw a person in the crowd. Whoever it was appeared to be watching us instead of the fire. When I looked their way, they disappeared."

"Disappeared, as in walked away? Or disappeared, as in vanished?"

"Back there, I'd have said vanished, but I'd been staring into a fire and inhaling smoke. Both of which used to be my favorite things." He was calming down now. Seeing a fire so soon after talking about Teine must have unnerved him. That was the explanation. Had to be. The person he'd seen had just blended into the crowd.

"Used to be?" Hollie hooked her arm through his. Looking at her upturned face helped him get some perspective. They were on a regular street; there was nothing sinister about the people walking past them. He could breathe normally again.

"Yeah. Then I met you and they dropped down to about a hundred on the list."

"Seriously, Torque." She looked back over her shoulder at the burning building. "Do you think it was Teine?"

"Seriously?" He didn't want to answer the question truthfully. He wanted to be able to brush it aside, to go back to their hotel room, close the door and pretend the rest of the world—including arsonists and sorceresses—didn't exist. "I think it could have been."

When they had returned to the hotel after the fire, it was almost dawn. Although they had attempted to snatch a few hours of sleep, it had proved impossible. The events of the previous day had chased away any possibility of slumber, and they had lain awake talking about Teine and the most recent fire. At least the day had been a busy one. Torque had spent most of it in rehearsals while Hollie had continued to plow through his old emails.

Now it was early evening, and to Hollie's intense relief, there was no performance that night. Some of the band were going out to a steak house, but others were catching up on sleep. Torque had gone with the early night option and they'd ordered room service. Having halfheartedly eaten some food, Hollie had decided she could no longer put off the task she'd been dreading. But she'd been standing in the bedroom, staring at her cell phone for at least ten minutes. Even though she'd rehearsed what she was going to say a dozen times, none of the words and phrases sounded reasonable. If she was truthful, all of them would sound crazy to her.

That's because all of this is *crazy.*

Blaming her reluctance on tiredness didn't work. She had been catapulted into a world that was wonderful, but that broke every rule of sanity.

Even without the inability to decide what to say, she was torn in two directions about calling Dalton. She desperately wanted to know if there was any news about McLain. And, of course, it would be good to find out how the Incinerator team was progressing with their inquiries. The ideal situation would be that they had arrested someone over this latest fire and the nightmare was over. She knew that wasn't going to happen, but it was nice to indulge in that brief moment of hope.

Hollie didn't want to call him because that other world was too far away. Her old life was another time and place. Since the last time she saw Dalton, she had fallen for a rock-star dragon-shifter. It was a pretty big lifestyle change and she felt like she no longer had anything to say to the people she'd once known. Although she still wanted to catch the Incinerator, she had no wish to go back to the things she'd once thought of as normality.

Anyone learning what had happened to her would have a reasonable cause to believe she'd undergone some sort of brainwashing. If Dalton got even a glimpse of her whereabouts and her companion, he was likely to suspect she'd parted company with her reason. But Hollie—sane, practical, *scientific* Hollie—had never been more sure of anything. She belonged with Torque.

Eventually, she decided the best way to do this was to just make the call and see where the conversation took them. Dalton was a friend as well as a colleague. They had once been close; he cared about her, and she knew he valued her professional opinion. He would listen to what she had to say. Probably.

"Hollie, my God. I've been out of my mind with worry."

He didn't have to say it, she could hear it in his voice. "Dalton, I'm fine."

"You need to tell me where you are right now, or go to the nearest field office." She could picture him pacing up and down as he was talking. "It doesn't matter where you are, I'll come and get you."

"Dalton, did you hear me? I said I'm fine." She didn't know whether to be touched, or irritated, at the depth of his concern.

"Hollie, we found a dead body in the burned-out ruin of your apartment."

It wasn't just the words that rocked her back on her heels; it was the change of pace from Dalton. Blunt, harsh, totally emotionless. If he was going for shock tactics, he was succeeding.

"Wh…what?"

"Specifically, she was in your bedroom." He waited a moment or two to let the information sink in. "And that's not all."

"No." Hollie didn't want to hear any more. Her mind

was already filled with awful images and she had a horrible premonition about what was coming next. "Please, no."

"It was McLain."

The phone clattered out of her hand as she dropped to her knees. The edges of her vision went dark and she was only vaguely aware of Torque, alerted by the noise, coming into the room.

"She'll call you back." Torque ended the call to Dalton before lifting Hollie off the floor and carrying her to the bed.

As soon as he placed her on the mattress, the whole room began to spin wildly and Hollie bolted upright, covering her mouth with one hand. She just made it to the bathroom in time. With her whole body shaking violently, she leaned over the lavatory as her stomach emptied its contents. After a few minutes, she felt able to stand up, rinse her mouth and wipe her face. On legs that still felt wobbly, she returned to the bedroom.

Torque was sitting on the bed, an expression of concern on his face. "What happened?"

"My boss..." Her throat felt raw and she was still shaking like a leaf in a high wind. Her mind was playing a series of images of McLain. First there were the good pictures. McLain in the office, sipping her megastrength coffee while she jabbed a finger to make a point. McLain when they'd gone on an occasional night out, drinking and letting her hair down. McLain when they got a result, buying donuts and high-fiving her team. But other images kept intruding. McLain lying dead on Hollie's bedroom floor, her body blackened by fire...

"Slowly." Torque took her hands, and his touch acted like a balm. Drawing her down next to him, he placed his arm around her shoulders and pressed his lips to her temple. "When you're ready."

"She's dead." The words came out on a gasp. "Burned. By the Incinerator. In my apartment."

His fingers tightened on her shoulder. The tears came then and she turned her face into his chest, unable to halt the storm of grief, shock and rage that took hold of her and flung her about like a rag doll. Vaguely conscious of Torque holding her and murmuring words of comfort, she clung to him. Guilt screamed inside her head.

Eventually, she straightened and took the wad of Kleenex Torque held out to her. Blowing her nose and wiping her streaming eyes, she tried to confront what she knew.

"This is because of me." She fought down a fresh wave of tears as she said the words. "I took the investigation in this direction. If I hadn't uncovered the link to you—if we hadn't met—McLain would still be alive."

"Hollie." Torque took both her hands in his. "You told your boss your findings because you are good at your job. And you were right. No matter how horrible this is, it proves that I *am* the link to these fires."

She nodded miserably. "By coming into your life, I've made things worse. The Incinerator doesn't like it."

"We can't live by the Incinerator's rules. This is probably not something you want to talk about right now, but I wonder why your boss had to die."

Hollie frowned, trying to follow what he was saying. "What do you mean?"

"From what you've told me of this case so far, the other deaths have been incidental to the fires. The people who died were tragically trapped in the place the Incinerator chose. But this couldn't be more personal. You have no family, so he, or she, targeted someone who was close to you. It's a powerful message."

"I don't know." Hollie was having trouble following that train of thought. "I have a few friends, people I socialize with. McLain and I occasionally went out for a drink together, but our working relationship was clearly defined. She was in charge and we never became good friends because we didn't cross those boundaries. If the Incinerator wanted to send me a message, why would he pick her? Why not Dalton, the guy I called earlier? Of my work colleagues, I'm closer to him than to anyone, I guess."

"Who knows how it happened? I'm speculating now, but maybe he saw an opportunity and grabbed it?" Torque said. "I'm assuming she didn't die in the fire?"

"I don't know." Hollie cast a look of distaste in the direction of her cell. "I need to call Dalton back to find out the details. I grayed out right after he told me McLain was dead."

"Do you want me to stay with you?"

She nodded gratefully, wondering how she had ever gotten by without his strength. But she had never dealt with anything like this. Although her grandmother's death had been a sad time in her life, it had come at the end of a long illness. Sorrow had been combined with relief, and Hollie had dealt with the trauma in her usual, practical way. Nothing had ever derailed her like this. The sensation that someone else was in control and that person's venom was directed at her was terrifying.

Torque's presence sustained her as she called Dalton back.

"Who was that guy?" Dalton's voice was harsh, giving her no time to speak. "What's going on, Hollie?"

"I'm safe and I'm with friends. That's all you need to know."

"Are you kidding me?" He shouted the words so

loudly she shifted the phone away from her ear. The action brought a frown to Torque's face and Hollie shook her head slightly to indicate everything was fine. She guessed she'd react the same way if she was in Dalton's place and he was the one who'd gone missing.

"Dalton, listen to me. I promise I will keep in touch so you know I'm not in any danger. Right now you can help me by telling me how McLain died."

"She was too badly burned."

Hollie could hear him battling to get his emotions under control.

"There was no way of knowing…" He took an audible breath. "The medical examiner identified her from dental records."

Hollie closed her eyes, letting the horror of that information sink in. "Have you any more information about the fire in which she was found?"

"Apart from McLain's body, it had all the signs of being a classic Incinerator attack." Thankfully, Dalton had calmed down and slipped into professional mode. "We need you here, Hollie. No one can analyze this the way you can."

"There are three other fires you may want to look at, if you aren't already considering them as part of the Incinerator investigation. Do you have a pen and paper?" She knew Dalton. He wouldn't have a pen and paper.

"Um…hold on."

Hollie rested her head on Torque's shoulder as she listened to the sound of long-distance rummaging.

"Go ahead."

"The first fire was at the Pleasant Bay Bar in Addison, Maine. A week later there was a small blaze in the lobby of the Tribeca Trinity apartment building. It only made the local news, but it was almost certainly set by the Incinerator. Then tonight, the head office of the Go Faster Cargo Company in Nashville was the target."

"You want to tell me how you know this? Or if there's a link between these three fires that I should be aware of?"

Hollie paused. The question instantly pulled her in two. She had told McLain about the Incinerator's link to Torque. Instead of sharing that suspicion with the rest of the team, her boss had come up with the plan to send Hollie undercover. It had been McLain's way of keeping the possibility that one of the most well-known men on the planet could be their suspect. Her decision on how to proceed would have depended on what Hollie discovered.

Right now it appeared that the only people who knew about the potential connection were Hollie and the members of Beast. Dalton was asking her to make a choice between her two worlds. If she told him the truth and admitted what she knew, she would be choosing her professional world. Keeping quiet would be about her own private motives, reasons that were entirely to do with the man at her side.

There was that feeling again. That deep-seated unease. It was the same additional sense that told her she could trust Torque. She had no idea where it was from. All she knew was she couldn't ignore it. She consoled herself that she wouldn't be lying to Dalton if she ignored his question. After all, nothing had been *proved*.

"I have to go now. Just one final thing…don't ignore the possibility that the Incinerator may be a woman."

Aware that she had left out the key piece of information, she ended the call. *The woman you are looking for may have magical powers*. She could predict Dalton's reaction. It would be exactly the same as her own would have been before she'd met Torque. To be fair, Dalton was likely to be more measured in his response. She'd have advised the person offering that information to seek medical help.

Sighing, she nestled closer in the circle of Torque's arms. "This is hard."

"Why don't we get out of here?" He gripped her chin lightly with his fingers, tilting her face up to his. "Your choice. What do you want to do, right here, right now?"

"Anything?" Would he go with it? She wouldn't know if she didn't ask him.

The iridescent lights in his eyes shone brighter. "Tell me your wildest fantasy."

"I want to see you as a dragon."

Chapter 10

Shifting in a built-up area was risky, but Torque had checked a map of the local area. There were a few islands on Percy Priest Lake, which was just outside the city. He made some calls, organizing a cab to take them there and a fishing boat so they could get out to one of the islands.

Hollie watched him with an expression that was somewhere between laughter and astonishment. "I wondered if you might be reluctant to do this."

"Hollie, I told you I need you to see the real me." He took her face between his hands. "If you're sure that's what you want?"

"I want all of you. The human you. The dragon you." She grinned mischievously as she led him to the door. "Let's go. I can't wait for you to breathe a little fire on me."

He groaned. "That's the sort of talk that would have

had a white knight on a charger seeking me out and trying to slay me back in medieval times."

They traveled down in the elevator to the hotel lobby. Torque donned his hat and shades, tucking his trademark fiery hair inside his denim jacket.

"Nobody would dare slay you these days. Dragons are cool," Hollie said. "They feature in books, movies, games, comics…" She ticked them off on her fingertips.

"There are worse things than being slain." Torque's face was serious. "Imagine what it would be like if my identity became known. You think I'd be left in peace? I'd end up in a research facility. Or a zoo."

The corners of Hollie's mouth turned down. "I never thought of that. No wonder you work so hard to protect your anonymity."

The traffic was light and the cab journey took less than half an hour. When they reached the lake, Torque told the driver he would call him when they wanted to be collected. He led Hollie to the water's edge, where a motorboat was waiting for them.

"There are advantages to the celebrity lifestyle," he said as he helped Hollie into the little craft. "One of them is that you can call up a local fishing charter company and hire a boat at short notice. Of course, I paid twice what the damn boat would cost to buy, just for a few hours' use."

He started the engine and the boat was soon skimming over the moonlit waters. Behind them the edge of the lake, with its rocky shoreline, began to fade. They passed a few small islands before they reached a larger one. It was roughly horseshoe in shape, covered in spiky pine trees, and with a jagged cove into which Torque steered the vessel.

When they stepped onto the land, it was fully dark

and a breeze was blowing off the lake. Torque pulled the boat up onto the pebbly shore. Before they set off, he had made sure that this was one of the islands that wasn't used by campers. He really didn't want to spark a major news story about a dragon sighting over the local tourist area.

There was a clearing in the center of the small land mass that was surrounded by trees, and Torque paused there. Casting a measuring eye over the ground, he nodded. There would be just about enough distance for him to spread his wings and take flight.

"Do you need to do anything?" Hollie asked. "Any rituals? Incantations to help you get in the zone?"

"I'm a human *and* a dragon," Torque explained. "Both beings are inside me all the time. I don't need to make an effort to find either of them. The word *shifting* perfectly describes what happens. It's a simple change from one to the other."

"And you don't mind that I'm here…watching you?" She gripped her lower lip between her teeth.

He took her hand and placed it on his chest, letting her feel his heart. The organ that powered his human and dragon selves. "I want you to see me. All of me." He grinned. "And now I have to remove my clothes."

The air chilled his skin as he stripped the layers of garments away. What he'd told Hollie was true. Shifting was in his DNA. Although it was magical, there was no skill or mystery to it. As he closed his eyes, Torque tried to remember the first time he had shifted. It was lost in the mists of dragon time, one of those memories of his Highland home he had put aside because it pained him to think of it.

You close your human eyes, now look inside your dragon. Shrug off your human instincts. Feel the for-

*est around you. Mold your body. You no longer have
a foot, instead you have dragon claws. Flesh becomes
scales. Breath turns to fire.*

His mind ran through the swift, subtle changes as his
muscles relaxed into the familiar shape of his dragon
self. He was ready. With a swish of his giant tail, he
crouched low on all fours and opened his eyes.

With her back pressed tight against the trunk of a
tree, Hollie was gazing up at him with an expression
he couldn't define. It could have been fear. He believed
it was wonder.

It was probably a good time to remind herself that
she had asked Torque to do this. And Hollie wanted to
see him shift, but that didn't mean she wasn't nervous
as hell about it. Once it started, it all happened so fast.

One minute Torque was standing naked in the moonlight. Then he shimmered before her briefly. Next thing
he was gone. In his place was the dragon from the Beast
concert in Marseilles. He was the most magnificent
creature she had ever seen, with wings that spanned
the clearing. When he lifted them, they billowed and
created an updraft that blew Hollie's hair back from her
face. His claws were like giant scimitars, driving into
the ground as he moved. Sleek, iridescent scales covered his muscular body, each one catching the glinting
light and pulsing in time with his dragon breath. Wisps
of smoke issued from his elegantly carved nostrils.

Moving slowly away from the tree trunk, Hollie approached him. Even though the dragon towered over
her, as she looked up at his proud features, she could
see a trace of Torque still remained. A slight smile softened her face and she relaxed. This was *her* dragon. The
thought made her shiver.

Reaching out a hand, she placed it on his leg. Instead of the roughness she had expected, his flesh was soft, smooth and very warm. Torque lowered his head and Hollie leaned closer, resting her cheek against his face. She stayed that way for several minutes, listening to the sound of his slow, rhythmic breathing.

"My dragon." She ran her hand along his neck and felt a tremor run through his giant body in response. "I want to see you fly."

She stepped back as, rising upon all fours, he spread his wings. Breaking into a run, Torque lifted his head toward the sky and, with a flick of his tail, was airborne. Hollie watched in wonder as he gracefully soared above her, into the darkened clouds. Circling the bay several times, he swooped low as if checking on her before climbing higher, then disappearing from view.

Hollie sank down onto the grass, tucking her knees up and resting her chin on them. She tried to analyze what she was feeling, but her emotions were like splinters of glass. Too tiny, too painful, too delicate. She reached a hand up to her cheek and found it wet with tears.

Torque was the last of his clan, the only remaining member of a noble breed of dragon-shifters. And he had trusted her with his incredible secret. It was like tasting honey and acid at the same time. He was everything she had ever wanted, and she would never be able to hold on to him.

Too much emotion had been poured into her heart, filling it to a point where it was ready to burst. The wonder of watching him shift, the joy of knowing he belonged to her, however briefly, the recognition that this was *real*…each of those was counterbalanced by a matching darkness.

Their worlds had met right here, right now, but they

were dancing to the tune of the deranged fire starter who had brought them together. And when this madness ended, they would have to face reality. Just as Torque's night flight must soon come to an end, so would the dream in which they were living. They had some serious talking to do about what the future could hold for a dragon and a mortal.

The sound of beating wings alerted her to Torque's return and she tilted her face back toward the heavens. It was hard to see him until he was immediately overhead. His body blended with the velvety darkness. Then he was there. So much power in one body. The man and the dragon were both perfection. Torque circled one last time before landing. His claws churned up the grass and he used the momentum to come to a halt. As he stopped, he shifted back. When he turned to face Hollie, there was a trace of uncertainty in his eyes.

She got to her feet, going to him and wrapping her arms around his waist. "You are beautiful."

She could feel the tension leave his body. "I should get dressed."

"Not yet." Hollie rose on the tips of her toes, fitting her body more intimately to his.

"Here?" Torque's lips quirked into a smile.

"Maybe somewhere less open?"

He picked Hollie up and carried her, and his clothes, toward the shelter of the trees. She twined her legs around his waist and hooked her arms about his neck, clinging to him and kissing along his jaw as he walked. Although her body pressed tight against him was the most delicious distraction, Torque clung to the remnants of his sanity long enough to find a secluded place among the trees. No one knew better than he did what

the view was like from above. While he didn't anticipate any helicopters or drones would be flying over this
area, he wasn't taking any chances.

"One of us is wearing way too many clothes." He
placed Hollie on the grass.

"You should probably do something about that."

The moon filtered through the trees, giving just
enough light for him to see her. It reminded Torque of
bygone days. Of gloomy forests and beautiful maidens
and treasure untold.

He kept his gaze on hers as he undid the buttons
on her blouse and pushed it down her shoulders. Hollie helped him remove it by wriggling her arms free of
the garment. Torque laid her back against the ground
and trailed kisses down her neck to the point where her
breasts swelled above the lace of her bra.

Behind her back, his hands worked on the fasten-
ing on her bra until he was able to toss it aside with her
blouse. Leaning over, he brushed featherlight kisses
across one nipple, then licked the delicate pink flesh.
Taking the tender bud between his lips, he sucked it gently. Hollie's back arched, her breaths coming in bursts
of sharp gasps. Pausing to smile down at her, Torque
moved on to the other nipple.

While he pleasured her breasts, Torque undid her
jeans. Hollie lifted her hips to help him as he sat back
and removed her boots, jeans and underwear. Pressing
her legs apart, he knelt between them. "Your scent—"
he lapped once before circling her clit with his tongue
"—your taste, everything about you, is perfect."

Moving over her, he reached between their bodies
and slipped two fingers inside her, caressing her as he
used his other hand to circle her nub before pausing to
reach for a condom in the pocket of his jeans. Once the

protection was in place, he positioned himself at her entrance. Gazing down at Hollie's features in the moonlight, he felt the greatest peace and passion of his life surge through him. A treasure more than emeralds, rubies and gold. That was what she was to him. She was what Teine had foreseen he would one day find. Hollie was his dragon hoard.

As he entered her, he pressed a kiss onto her mouth. His tongue swirled around hers and Hollie caressed him back. His beautiful mortal was showing him how much she loved all of him.

Hollie raised her hips to meet him, and Torque groaned at the near unbearable pleasure. He was fighting not to rush this, but his feelings threatened to overwhelm him. He lifted her so she was fully opened to him, and she bucked her hips, matching each long, powerful thrust. Reaching around his back, she dragged her nails along his muscles.

Torque's breath came faster and harder as his thrusts grew wilder. Primal instincts overtook them both. Her cries urged him on as her ankles locked around his hips. He pulled them up higher so he could drive even deeper.

"The feeling of you wrapped around me is the most perfect dream. I want it to last forever."

Pounding faster, he felt the first spasms hit her. Hollie threw back her head, crying his name to the treetops as her body shuddered in a series of unrelenting waves.

Feeling her explode around him, Torque held her closer, thrusting once more as deep as he could. Her inner muscles clenched hard around him, triggering his own release. Torque gasped, his cock spasming wildly. Hollie's hands locked on to his shoulders, pulling him tight to her as she jammed herself against him, every part of them in contact from groin to neck. He kissed her, and she cried out into his mouth.

Hollie's eyes were closed, her cheeks flushed and her lips slightly parted. *Forever.* If there was one moment Torque could choose to last that long, it would be this one. He gazed down at her, continuing to thrust slowly, even as the storm subsided and his body softened. Never wanting to break this connection.

Finally, his movements stilled as the shuddering stopped, his breathing slowed and his racing pulse ebbed. With their lips locked in a kiss, he withdrew and rolled onto his back.

Hollie rested her head on his chest. "Is it strange, when we have a luxury suite back at the hotel, to think this is the perfect way to spend a night?"

"Every night with you is perfect."

Torque gazed up at the stars, enjoying her warm, sweet weight against him. He had no need of anything except this. Even if he searched for another immortal lifetime, he wouldn't find the same joy he felt when he looked into her eyes.

Hollie was his treasure, his dragon hoard, and he would guard the enchantment she brought him the same way he had once guarded a looted treasure from a rival clan.

After the band left Nashville, the next few days seemed to be a blur of big arenas. Hollie felt like she spent the whole time getting on and off the tour bus with barely time to eat, sleep and shower in between.

"When we get to Dallas, you can take a break," Ged said, regarding her with sympathy. "We have two performances there, but we have three nights before the first one."

Hollie stretched her arms above her head in anticipation. "You mean I get to sleep in a real bed instead of a bunk?"

Khan flung himself down on the sofa next to her. "And you won't have to listen to Diablo snoring."

The drummer threw a plastic water bottle at him, narrowly missing his head. "Can it, tiger boy."

"Is Sarange bringing Karina when she meets us in Dallas?" Hollie asked. She had seen enough of the legendary clashes between Diablo and Khan to know it was best to deflect their attention from each other.

Khan's expression changed, becoming one of delight. "Yeah. Can't wait to see my girls."

Torque was asleep on one of the bunks and Hollie had the laptop open. The marathon task of making her way through Torque's emails still occupied much of her time and she hadn't found any more messages from Losgadh@ykl.com. Although she had come across a few more items for her *Possibilities* file, nothing else shouted out to her and made her think it could be from the Incinerator.

She was so deep in her task she barely noticed the downshifting of the Monster's engine and only looked up from the screen when the vehicle came to a complete standstill.

"Where are we?" She looked out the window, but could see only an empty parking lot, surrounded by trees.

"I asked Rick to find a quiet place to stop." Ged leaned forward to look out the window. "Somewhere we have a half-decent chance of not being recognized. I want to stretch my legs and grab a burger. There's a restroom here and a small convenience store."

He called out to Rick, the head of the band's security team who was driving the bus, to give them half an hour. As the others bounded from the bus, Hollie considered joining them and decided against it. She was wearing sweatpants and a Sign of the Beast extralarge tour sweatshirt. Her hair was half in and half out of a braid and she couldn't find one of her sneakers. Life on tour with a rock band wasn't as glamorous as she'd once imagined it might be.

Torque emerged from the bedroom area looking rumpled and confused. And adorable.

"What's going on?" Since he placed a hand over his mouth to muffle a yawn, she only just managed to decipher what he was saying.

"Your friends have made a bid for freedom." She jerked a thumb over her shoulder. "The last I saw of them, they were running for the hills."

He grinned. "Burgers and coffee, huh? You want anything?"

Hollie considered the question. "Cookies. And soda." He turned to go. "And ice cream." He looked slightly alarmed and she laughed. "Don't worry, I'm stir-crazy, not pregnant."

The words hung between them for a moment, filling the atmosphere with a new sentiment. Hollie couldn't identify it. Was it a simple acknowledgment that a family would never happen for them? It felt like more. For the first time, she experienced a tug of longing for children of her own. Children she would never have. Loving Torque meant she would never be with someone else in the future. Hard on the heels of longing came regret. A deep, profound sorrow that she would never have normality with the man she loved.

"So, sugar and plenty of it?" Torque broke the loaded silence. She could see her own pain reflected in his eyes.

How many ways could she fall in love with him, only

to be reminded that it couldn't last? Seeking to lighten her thoughts, she indicated her bare feet. "If I could find my other sneaker, I'd come with you."

Torque knelt to retrieve something from under the sofa. "Is this yours?" He held up the shoe she had spent hours searching for.

Hollie slipped it on. "Lead me to my sugar rush." Reaching up a hand, she felt her braid and grimaced. "On second thought, let me find something to cover this."

Torque slipped his iconic guitar-in-flames hooded sweatshirt over his head. "Will this do?"

She pulled it on and placed a hand over her heart, batting her eyelashes at him. "Torque, you don't know what this means to me."

He flapped a hand at her. "Let's go before Ged eats everything in the store." Snagging another sweatshirt from his bunk as he passed, he tugged it over his head. "Can't be too careful. You never know who's watching."

They both drew their hoods up as they exited the bus. They had almost reached the store when Torque muttered an exclamation. "Left my cash on the bus. There's a handful of notes and coins on the table."

"I'll go back for it while you order what we want." Hollie was already running back toward the bus as she spoke.

She clambered quickly up the steps, dashing into the living area. As she snatched up the money Torque had mentioned, the laptop pinged with an incoming email. Her attention was instantly caught by the address... Losgadh@ykl.com.

Holding her breath, she read the message.

Look close into the shadows, *mo dragon*. Your maiden of gold and emeralds will be the sacrifice.

She was moving fast, on her way back to Torque, when the vehicle was rocked from side to side by an explosion. Staggering from the impact, Hollie emerged from the central living area to see flames engulfing the driver's cab and licking their way along toward the kitchen.

Her fire investigator instincts kicked in. It looked like a firebomb had been thrown in through the driver's window. Turning back, she headed along the bunk-lined corridor toward the emergency exit in the rear of the bus. Before she reached it, there was a sound of glass smashing. An orange ball of flame filled the area that Ged used as his office.

Hollie was trapped in the middle of the bus and all the exits were blocked.

Chapter 11

Torque was at the counter of the convenience store when he heard the noise. He knew all the sounds fire could make, and this was the unmistakable *whumphing* of a firebomb being thrown. Instantly, the hair on the back of his neck prickled and he ran outside.

Rick had been Beast's head of security since the band became famous. Torque often wondered if he knew they were shifters. He figured the big, long-suffering guy at least knew there was something very unusual about the rock stars he guarded. Since Ged paid Rick well for his discretion, there were no questions asked on either side.

Rick's specialty was protecting the band's privacy. Instinctively, he had parked the bus under a clump of trees, as far as possible from any prying eyes inside the store. Now Torque watched in horror as flames began to pour from both the front and rear windows.

"Hollie!" He raised a hand, signaling to the others to follow him.

Breaking into a run, Torque shifted, his feet pounding the tarmac. He could hear his friends behind him. As his dragon muscles burst through, his clothing tore from his body. By the time he reached the bus, he was already in dragon form, his giant wings unfurling.

Hovering a few feet above the burning vehicle, he hooked his claws into one end of the metal roof, rolling it back like the lid of a tin can. Throwing the torn metal aside, he lowered his head to get a better view of the interior of the bus. The driver's cab was fully alight and the rear appeared to have recently started to burn.

Hollie was in the living area, in the center section. Crouching low to avoid the smoke, she appeared unharmed and was crawling toward the fire extinguisher. Conscious of the need to move fast before the fire reached the bus's gas tanks, Torque landed beside the vehicle. Raising one mighty claw, he ripped a hole in the side of the bus. Shifting back, he stepped through the jagged gap.

"Torque." Hollie leaped up and closed the space between them. "We don't have long."

He could tell his beloved scientist had already analyzed the situation. "Let's get out of here." He lifted her through the opening, handing her to Ged, who was waiting on the asphalt.

Getting away from the bus fast was Torque's first priority. He would worry about his nakedness and any possible witnesses later. They headed for the cover of the trees with the rest of the band following, making it just as the bus blew up. Flames spiked and black smoke billowed. Glass and metal rained down onto the parking lot.

"I didn't get your ice cream," Torque said as he pulled Hollie down onto the grass with him.

She stared at him for a moment, her eyes huge and round; then she started to laugh. At first he thought she must be in shock, but her amusement was genuine. He raised questioning brows at her. Shaking her head, she pointed at the bus. "It's just as well it blew up. I can't imagine what my fire investigation colleagues would make of the way you casually ripped that bus apart to get me out." She became serious. "But I'm very glad you did."

"Did you see who did it?"

"No, I didn't see anything."

Torque turned to look at his friends. "You guys?"

"Nothing." Khan looked disgusted. "Whoever did it got away fast."

That was one of the many things racing around in Torque's head, but he decided to deal with the practicalities first. "This is one of those times when it will be impossible to avoid the human forces of law and order. I'm guessing the cashier has already called them. First, we need to discover if there is security camera footage of the parking lot." He grimaced. "It would be useful to see who did this, but I don't want anyone to get hold of film of me shifting."

"I'll go check that out before the cops get here." Khan left the trees and headed toward the store.

"Meanwhile, maybe Rick could find me something to wear?" Torque asked Ged. "It isn't the first time one of us has unexpectedly lost all our clothing, but the circumstances have often been different."

Ged laughed. Beast's hell-raising exploits were legendary and Rick had often been called upon to extricate one, or more, of them from a difficult situation. "Rick can do that while he arranges alternative transport for the rest of the tour. Dev, Finglas, come with me. You can keep a lookout for the cops."

When they'd gone, Hollie turned to Torque. "This is not quite the same atmosphere as last time you were naked in the woods."

Although she made an attempt at humor, he could see the panic in her eyes. It mirrored his own alarm. Twice the Incinerator had come close to killing her. If Torque hadn't been a dragon-shifter, Hollie would have died in that blazing bus.

"There was another message. It came through just before the bus caught fire. It said you should look into the shadows and your maiden of gold and emerald would be the sacrifice." Hollie shivered as she spoke. "He, or *she*, must have been following us. That blaze wasn't started remotely."

Torque forced himself to concentrate. He had been so focused on his concern at what had just happened to Hollie, so wrapped up in the terror of losing her, that he was barely able to think straight. He had convinced himself that this attack was about her, but what if it wasn't?

"What if he thought it was me on the bus?" He was thinking out loud, the words racing ahead of his thoughts.

"What do you mean?" Hollie asked.

"You were wearing my sweatshirt with the hood pulled up. Okay, you are a lot shorter than me. But if he wasn't close, he'd have seen a figure who looked like me getting back on the bus. Alone."

Comprehension dawned on Hollie's face. "So we don't know if the target of the attack was me or you."

It didn't matter to Torque. An attack on Hollie was an attack on him. She meant more to him than his own life. He had to stop this monster from taking control and paralyzing him with terror. Torque knew what fear could do. It could be a knife in his gut slowly twisting deeper, or a hammer pounding inside his head. Fear could shackle him…or it could drive him forward.

He drew Hollie into his arms, feeling her begin to relax as she rested her head on his shoulder. Drawing strength from her at the same time as he comforted her, he knew what he had to do. If Teine was out there, he had to find her. And he knew where to start his search.

Hollie was growing accustomed to her own capacity for dealing with the highs and lows of this new life. Her body amazed her with its capacity for absorbing shock and moving on. She suspected Torque's presence had something to do with that. He was her comfort blanket. After he had rescued her from the bus, her insides felt icy, her stomach muscles tightly contracted. Inside her chest, her heart had been an explosion waiting to happen, while her skin had been clammy, her breathing fast and hard.

Torque only had to place an arm around her and those physical symptoms receded. Within minutes, the horror had receded. It wasn't gone, but she was able to dig into her own reserves of strength and deal with it.

The practical aftermath of the bus fire was surprisingly calm. Hollie quickly learned that the members of Beast had the experience and the resources to deal with anything that came their way. Khan had discovered that there were no security cameras on the secluded area of the parking lot where Torque had shifted. That was fortunate because it meant they weren't facing a situation where the police might stumble across the biggest scandal of the century. Scrap that. A man shifting to become a dragon in rural Texas would be the biggest story *of all time*. Add in the fact that the man concerned was John "Torque" Jones, legendary guitarist with mega rock band Beast, and the world would go wild. Luckily, the cashier hadn't witnessed the incident because he had been calling 911 at the time Torque shifted.

At the same time, it was unfortunate that there was no CCTV. If they had been able to get their hands on any film before the police arrived, they might have been able to see who was responsible for the attack. The cashier confirmed that no one had been into the rest stop convenience store in the half hour prior to Beast's arrival. Rick was adamant that, even though he had chosen a secluded location, there were no other vehicles in the parking lot when he arrived.

"If someone was following us, how did they approach the bus within minutes of us stopping if they didn't pull into the parking lot?" Torque asked. That was the puzzle to which they needed to find a solution.

Rick explained to the cashier that one of the band had been sleeping naked when the bus caught fire. The guy was a Beast fan and he had been overawed by the whole situation. The sweatpants and T-shirt he had donated were stretched taut over Torque's muscles, but at least he was covered up. As he and Hollie explored the trees behind where the bus had been parked, there was no longer a risk of him stumbling naked upon a hiker or dog-walker.

It didn't take them long to find a dirt track that ran parallel to the road leading into the parking lot.

"There." Hollie pointed to evidence of recent tire tracks. "If the Incinerator was following the bus and saw us pull off the highway into the rest stop, he could have driven down here."

There was a line of trees and shrubs between the track and the parking lot. As they pushed through knee-high, scrubby grass, Torque gestured to a flattened section. "Looks like he stopped right over there."

From the place he indicated, the whole rest stop area, including the location where the bus had been parked, could be observed.

They stood in silence for a few minutes, surveying the wreckage of the Monster. It was no longer recognizable as a vehicle. Chunks of smoldering metal lay strewn across the asphalt, and the air was thick with the smell of burning gas, oil and plastic. Some of the debris was still on fire, while acrid smoke rose in black plumes from other parts.

"He was just waiting for a chance, wasn't he?" Hollie said.

"Looks that way."

She looked back at the fresh tire tracks in the dirt. "If Teine did this, would she need to follow us in a car?"

Torque's expression was grim. "She has magic powers, but they are limited. Teine can't transport herself from one place to another. In that sense, she is as restricted in her means of travel as a human. But this?" He indicated the destruction on the parking lot. "This is the action of a human. I don't know what to think anymore, but maybe that's what she wants. Teine is good at screwing with people's minds."

Two police cruisers pulled into the parking lot, ending the opportunity for further conversation. Torque turned to look at Hollie. "This is your call. If you talk to the police about what just happened, your colleagues in the FBI will find out where you are. I can make sure the police get all the information they need without telling them you were involved. No one needs to know you were on that bus."

How far had she come? Mere weeks ago law-abiding Hollie Brennan would have been shocked at the suggestion that she would conceal information that could help with any inquiry, let alone the Incinerator case. Now she clutched at Torque's suggestion like she was drowning and he had thrown her a life preserver.

She couldn't analyze why it was so important for her to remain hidden. It wasn't as if she was doing a good job of hiding from the Incinerator. He had found her at the Pleasant Bay Bar and now, if she was the intended target, it looked like he had found her here. All she knew for sure—and it was not a sixth sense or a hunch—was that she needed to be with Torque. Whether that was for her security or her well-being, she didn't know. There was a strong possibility it could be both.

"I want to stay out of it," she said.

"Leave it to me."

Those words summed up everything about what had happened to her since she'd met Torque. No matter what else life was throwing her way, no matter how bizarre the situation, she knew she could place her life in his hands.

Hollie thought she'd coped well with everything life had thrown at her over the last few weeks. Rock stars who were really shifters, a dragon lover, attempts on her life…she'd taken them all in her stride, emerging, if not unscathed, at least quietly restrained.

But *this*? This was taking irrational to a whole new level.

"Let me get this straight. You are going to fly from here to Scotland—*crossing the Atlantic Ocean*—and you want me to ride on your back?" Her voice was getting higher and higher as she spoke, ending in something that was close to a screech.

"It's perfect timing." Torque appeared not to notice her near stratospheric levels of incredulity. "We have a few rest days in Dallas, so we can be there and back before the next performance."

When she tried to discuss the logistics, including important things like her survival at altitude, he waved them aside. "Och, you'll be with a dragon. Trust me."

"Did you just say 'och'?" She regarded him in bemusement.

"It must be the prospect of a return to Scotland." Although he smiled, she heard a touch of apprehension in the words. Going home after all this time would be hard on him. Going home in search of answers about the woman who had destroyed his family? That had to hurt his soul. And Torque was doing this because Hollie was in danger.

She placed a hand on his arm. "I do trust you, but I can't help thinking of all the things that could go wrong. What if I fall off?"

A smile glinted in the opal depths of his eyes. "Then I'll catch you."

She believed him. He had saved her from death twice, and both times he had done it in a way that no human could have achieved. "Okay. Let's do it." She gave a squeal as Torque seized her and spun her around.

Having made this decision, Torque seemed invigorated by it. His energy levels, always high, were off the scale as he paced the hotel room, throwing items into a backpack that Hollie would carry. When they were ready to leave, they stopped by Ged's hotel room.

When Torque explained his plans, Ged regarded

him with a thoughtful expression. "And you finally feel ready for this?"

"At long last, I believe so."

"Then be careful." Ged turned to Hollie. "Since Torque has no sense of time, I'm relying on you to get him back here for the next performance."

She smiled. "I'll do my best, but he's in charge of the travel arrangements."

Torque had checked a map of the area and chosen the nearby Cedar Ridge Nature Preserve as the best place to shift. They took a cab to the scenic area. As they left the vehicle and followed an isolated trail, the moon was full and round.

"Perfect for a dragon ride." Hollie's voice quivered with nerves. She still couldn't quite believe she'd agreed to this. "Sorry, bad joke."

Torque grinned. "Every night is perfect for a dragon ride."

When they found a sheltered clearing that suited his needs, Torque slipped off his clothes and handed them to her. Hollie placed them in the backpack, ready for when they reached their destination. Even though she was prepared for him to shift, Hollie still found she was holding her breath. If she lived to be a hundred, she would never tire of this moment. If only she could live to be *more* than a hundred...

Torque shifted quickly, almost impatiently. Neck stretched out and wings held high, he crouched low, waiting for Hollie.

So, we're really doing this. I'm really going to fly halfway across the world on the back of a dragon. Or die trying...

Hoisting the backpack in place on her shoulders, she caught hold of one of Torque's wings and levered herself up onto his back. Settling into position, she straddled the base of his powerful neck, just in front of his wings.

Once she was in position, Torque spread those incredible wings to their full extent. Hollie could feel his muscles tensing in preparation. His mighty feet pounded across the ground as he broke into a run, gaining speed before launching into flight. Flattening herself tight to him, Hollie felt her face stinging as the air rushed past. When she risked a look down, her stomach swooped alarmingly. The ground dropped away as they soared above the trees, quickly reaching altitude.

It was like riding a horse bareback, with the same rocking and bucking motion, but on a larger scale. They flew up into cloud and down into clear skies. Time became meaningless, and in the darkness below her, Hollie caught glimpses of oceans and land masses, of vast cities and of mountains and rivers. Although the air around her was cool, she could stand its bite. Pressing close against Torque's scales, she let the heat of his body warm her. No, she shouldn't have been able to survive at this height. But she was riding on the back of a dragon. Nothing about this made sense. It was magic. Reason didn't come into it.

When Torque swooped and soared, it was as exhilarating as the most white-knuckle fairground ride. The wind brought tears to Hollie's eyes and the wind whipped her hair straight out behind her like a flag on a pole. The best part of the flight was when Torque stilled his wings to glide, letting the air currents carry him for long distances. Without the heaving *whumphing* sound of his beating wings, there was only silence. Except when she pressed her cheek to his scales, then she could hear the strong, rhythmic beat of his dragon heart. Impossible as it seemed, she might have slept.

Or maybe it was an illusion, the sense of time passing too quickly. Because long before it should have been, the night was over. Daylight was streaking the sky, and Torque was dipping low over snow-covered summits.

When they landed, Hollie looked around in amazement. The low ground was dark, with patches of purple heather and green gorse. The mountain peaks glowed white against a sky that was endlessly gray. It was beautiful, majestic and forbidding. She knew this place. She had been here many times in her dreams.

Torque shifted back and slipped on the clothing she handed him.

"Welcome to Scotland." There was a fierce pride in Torque's voice. "The weather is unpredictable. It could hail, snow, rain or shine. And it could do all of those things within the next hour. These Highlands will show you their moods with no room for misunderstanding."

"You love this place." It was evident in everything about him. Even the way he held himself had changed. There was a new pride in his bearing.

"Aye."

She'd never heard him use that word before.

"It's my home."

"But this is the first time you've been back here since Ged rescued you from Teine?"

He tilted his head up toward the mountains as though drawing strength from their beauty. "There was too much pain for me here. And too many memories. But now we've an arsonist to hunt down." He took her hand. "And I have you. The memories are still here, but they don't hurt as much with you by my side."

She leaned in close, nestling her cheek into the curve of his neck. "I'll be by your side as long as you want me."

"How about forever?"

Neither of them took the thought further, even though the reality was always with them. There was no happily-ever-after for them. A human and a dragon? That whole mortal-immortal thing was a real barrier. They could do long-term, but it would last for Hollie's lifetime. Which meant Torque was left staring down the barrel of a long, lonely forever. The Fates had gotten it wrong this time. When they decided to interfere and make them mates, it was like a magic trick that had gone wrong.

"Let's get going." Torque pulled on his beanie and shades, apparently feeling the need for his disguise even in this remote location. "If we walk to the nearest road, we can catch a bus into Inverness."

Hollie started to laugh. "Maybe you can make the switch that quickly, but I'm having trouble adjusting. One minute I'm flying on a dragon's back, the next I'm a regular tourist taking the bus into town?"

"Welcome to my world. Straddling the human and the paranormal is all in a day's work."

Chapter 12

Hollie soon learned that Torque hadn't been joking about the weather. They waited at the roadside for the regular bus from Fort William in drizzling rain, but by the time they arrived in the city of Inverness, the sun was shining.

"Who are we here to see?" she asked as Torque led her down a narrow street. "Tell me it's not a sorceress."

"No." He grinned as they halted outside a quaint bookstore. "It's a dragon."

He pointed to the sign above the door. *The Book Hoard*. It was accompanied by an image of a dragon guarding a pile of leather-bound books.

Before she could respond, he was ushering her inside. The interior was gloomy and it had that old-book smell that was instantly recognizable but couldn't be categorized. Hollie thought of it as aging paper, with a dollop of dust, and a hint of incense. It always made her feel slightly giddy, as though she was in a place of magic and mystery. The difference was that, on this occasion, her instinct told her that was exactly where she was.

The store was long and narrow and the walls were covered from floor to ceiling with book-filled shelves. Oddly matched easy chairs were dotted about the place, and a large ginger cat dozed in the middle of a sagging red velvet sofa.

"It's like something out of a fantasy story," Hollie whispered.

"It may have featured in one or two," he whispered back.

The shop was quiet, with only a few people browsing the shelves. Torque walked confidently through to the rear, until they reached an office with glass windows that overlooked the whole shop. As they approached, a man who was seated at a desk inside the tiny room, looked up. He went very still, his hand hovering in the act of pushing his half-moon glasses up his nose.

Hollie had heard the expression "cut the atmosphere with a knife," but she'd never felt it until now. As Torque and the other man stared at each other, the air seemed to heat up and thicken. She could feel the relationship between these two. Although she couldn't understand how, the memories and emotions of centuries were right there in that curious old bookstore. It was as if she could reach out a hand and pluck them from the motes of dust that floated around them.

"Hollie, I'd like you to meet Alban."

The man who rose from the desk was stick-thin and very tall. He had the slightly stooped air of someone who has spent his life trying to compensate for his height. His shoulder-length hair, pointed beard and neatly trimmed mustache all shimmered silver. Everything about him, including his long, hooked nose and piercing blue eyes, seemed to enhance the impression of a wizard who had accidentally wandered out of his own time period.

"Alban?" Hollie muttered the word out of the corner of her mouth. "Isn't he…?"

"The enemy?" Alban came out of the office. Hollie's first impression had been that he was old. Now that he was up close, it was impossible to judge his age. "Have you been telling tales about me, Cumhachdach?"

"Only the truth, Moiteil."

As they gazed at each other for a moment, the outcome appeared in doubt. Hollie wondered if they were about to fight or embrace. Then Torque moved forward and grasped Alban's forearm. "Too long."

The other man clamped a hand on Torque's shoulder. "It was your choice to stay away."

"You know why." Torque's voice was rusty with pain.

"Aye." Alban shook his head. "She did for you. Just as she promised she would. What brings you back now?"

"Her. Always her." Torque's jaw muscles were tight. "Can we go somewhere to talk?"

Alban looked around the store. "Give me a few minutes."

He walked away and Hollie watched in amazement as he started hustling his few customers out the door. "Closing time, folks." He pointed to the scarred grandfather clock in the corner of the room. "Och, I know the sign on the door says we're open until five, but you cannae always trust those things."

"Isn't that bad for business?" Hollie asked when Alban had locked the door.

"Possibly." He beckoned for them to follow him up a flight of stairs that was tucked away behind the office. "But I do this more as a hobby than for profit. I've a pretty hoard tucked away." He lowered his voice and cast a look in Torque's direction. "But don't tell yon thieving Cumhachdach."

"I've a tidy sum of my own. I've no need to raid the Moiteil cave," Torque said. "Not this time."

"The stories about dragons and their hoards are all true, then?" Hollie asked. She was in Scotland, in the company of two dragons, sharing a joke with them. Life didn't get more surreal than this.

"Aye, we like our gelt. But you'll be pleased to know we know longer demand the sacrifice of a pretty maiden." Alban led them into an apartment above the store…and took them back in time.

Everything about the place, from the heavy wooden beams that meant Alban and Torque had to stoop low, to the wood-burning stove, seemed to be from another era. Hollie looked around her with surprise and pleasure. This was the home of a fearsome dragon leader? These cozy, floral cushions, woven rugs and fringed lamps were straight out of a 1950s English detective movie.

"I like my home comforts." Alban seemed to follow the direction of her thoughts. "If you've a long life ahead of you, why not enjoy it?"

As he spoke, another cat, this one a huge black-and-white ball of fluff, wandered into the room. Favoring them with a look of disgust, it jumped onto the window ledge and proceeded to ignore them.

"Tea? Or will you take a wee dram?"

Since Alban was already reaching for the whiskey bottle that sat on a table beside a winged chair, there seemed to be only one answer to that question. Alban's idea of a "wee dram" was a hefty slug of fifty-year-old Scotch, and Hollie sipped the heady liquid cautiously.

"She's dead, Torque." Alban didn't mince his words. "We both saw her die."

Hollie looked from one to the other in surprise. "Alban was with you when Ged freed you from captivity?"

Torque nodded. "I told you Teine delighted in playing us off one against the other. When she imprisoned me, she thought Alban would be pleased. His enemy was destroyed. The Moiteil would reign supreme."

"It doesn't work like that." Alban swirled the whiskey around in his glass. "We dragons are honorable. What Teine did to the Cumhachdach was murder most foul. My clan was not going to tolerate that."

"Alban and the Moiteil tried to rescue me," Torque said. "It didn't go well."

"No." The look in Alban's eyes reminded Hollie of Torque's expression when he talked of Teine. "It couldn't have gone any worse."

Torque raised his whiskey glass in a half-mocking salute. "You are looking at the last of the two Highland dragon-shifter clans."

"She killed the Moiteil, as well?" Although Hollie had already heard the horror story of what Teine had done to Torque and his family, it was hard to believe that she had repeated her atrocities.

"Like I said, she considered us her playthings. But Teine was like a child having a tantrum, and when things didn't go her way, she stomped on her toys. The dragon-shifters who lived in these Highlands were the casualties."

"She threw me into the cave with Torque. Told me if I had become so fond of him, we could spend eternity together." Alban's laughter had a hollow ring to it. "I thought we would. Which reminds me, how is Gerald?"

"Ged," Torque explained when Hollie raised questioning brows. "He's fine. Still saving the world, one endangered shifter at a time."

"We saw her die, Torque." Alban returned to the subject of Teine. "There is no more to be said."

"We saw her fall." There was a challenge in Torque's eyes. "Can we be sure she died?"

Alban sighed. "I suppose you have a reason for asking this?"

"Someone is lighting fires that appeared to be a tribute, but have now become a warning, to me."

Torque drew a piece of paper from his pocket. On it was the message from Losgadh@ykl.com. When Alban read it, his already pale complexion lightened by several shades. "It certainly appears to be from her."

"I came to find out if you'd seen, or heard, anything that might make you think she could still be alive," Torque said.

"Hell, no. If I thought that, I'd seek her out and kill her all over again myself," Alban said. "And enjoy every minute." He tapped the piece of paper. "But if Teine is behind this, she wouldn't have returned to her old, secluded life here in the Highlands, would she? She's a sorceress, but her powers are not unlimited. She would need to be able to travel around and start these fires."

"What can she do?" Hollie decided it was time to find out more about the enemy. "And why do you call her a sorceress and not a witch?"

"There is a hierarchy of magic, and at each stage the practitioners can be male or female," Torque explained. "Witches can learn their magic, or they can inherit it. The most powerful are those who use a combination of both. Their spells are low-level. Love potions, healing, finding lost pets…that sort of thing. Although they can also turn their hand to darker spells like relationship breakups and spoiling crops. The next step up is to wizardry. Wizards combine alchemy with witchcraft, exploiting science and mathematics to create magical potions. The final stage, having mastered wizardry, is sorcery."

"Let me guess." Figuring she wasn't going to like what she was about to hear, Hollie took a slug of her drink. "They are the rock stars of the magic world?"

"Oh, yes. They make Beast look like amateurs. Sorcerers must progress through the ranks, but they must also have magical parentage. Once they reach that level they are more or less all-powerful, within certain limits. They can act as a force for good or evil, but their magic must have a target."

"So, when Teine decided she wanted to kill your families, she had to come up with a spell that was aimed specifically at them?"

"Yes. She can't fly, or make herself invisible, and she doesn't have superhuman strength. So Alban is right. If Teine is the Incinerator, she would have to physically be in the place where the fires took place. She would have to get close to the building to focus her magic on it. If she traveled back and forth each time she started a fire, she would do it as a mortal, on an airplane, in a car or by whatever means necessary. Which means she must have a human identity."

Hollie's two worlds were colliding and nothing was making any sense. She could understand why Torque and Alban would believe Teine, if she was still alive, was behind the fires. They had been raised in a sphere where magic was the ruling force. The supernatural was normal to them and the evil sorceress had ruled over their whole existence. When anything bad happened, it must be natural for them to suspect she was behind it.

But Hollie came from a different place. Her world was one of logic. She had studied for years to gain an understanding of science and technology. She needed facts, data and hard, cold evidence. And after hunting the Incinerator for four years, she knew what she was looking for.

"What you are saying doesn't fit with the way the Incinerator operates. He—" Hollie still couldn't think of the arsonist as a woman "—sets the fires himself. He's what we call a professional. By that we mean he keeps it simple and he prefers to use fuels he finds at the scene. That way, he minimizes the risk of being caught. So, he takes trash he finds at the scene and piles it up. Then he uses copier toner to light it. If he can't find any toner, he raids the janitor's store and searches for another accelerant. He knows what will work. Paint, glue, mop cleaner, uncured polyester resin, brush cleaner... He's used all of those things." She frowned. "If Teine could stand within sight of a building and cast a spell on it to set it alight, why would she go to all that trouble?"

"Hollie has a point." Alban tilted his glass toward Torque.

"But that message is from Teine." Torque's tone was insistent. "Has to be."

They lapsed into silence as they finished their drinks. "You know what we need?" Alban asked.

"A crystal ball?" It was hard to tell if Torque was joking.

"The next best thing."

"Dinner at Kirsty McDougall's?"

"Och, that's mighty nice of you." Alban's eyes twinkled appreciatively. "I'll fetch my coat."

* * *

Kirsty McDougall's was an unashamedly traditional Scots restaurant located in the heart of Inverness. Serving dishes such as clootie dumplings, rumbledethumps, Arbroath smokies and cranachan, it was popular with locals and tourists alike. It was one of the places Torque had missed most while he was away. As soon as he walked through the door, the smell that met him made him feel at home.

Alban was greeted with a hug from a short, plump woman with a broad accent. "It's about time. I've no seen you for at least a month." She looked beyond him to Torque, and her hand went up to cover her mouth. "Is it yourself indeed?"

"It really is, Kirsty." As he stooped to kiss her cheek, she punched him so hard in the shoulder he went staggering back.

"Aye, you may well look shocked." She placed her hands on her hips. "Think you can forget me for all these years, then stroll back in and expect a warm welcome?" After glaring at him for a moment or two, she burst out laughing and embraced him. "Och, I cannae stay mad at you for long. It's a sight for sore eyes you are."

She ushered them to a table, talking constantly and eyeing Hollie with interest. When Kirsty bustled away to fetch drinks, Hollie leaned close to Torque. "Is she…?"

"Witch." He nodded. "Harmless." He rubbed his shoulder. "Mostly."

Kirsty returned with the inevitable bottle of whiskey and four glasses. She took a seat next to Alban. "I've told them in the kitchen you'll be having haggis, neeps and tatties."

Hollie looked slightly alarmed. "Haggis with turnips and potatoes," Torque said. She didn't appear even slightly reassured by his explanation. "It's a national dish."

"Tell me why you're here," Kirsty said. They were seated in a booth, slightly apart from the other diners, where they were able to talk without being overheard.

"We wondered if you'd heard anything about the fiery one," Torque said.

Kirsty's pleasant face instantly twisted into an expression of distaste. "We're about to eat."

"Is there any chance she's still alive?" Torque persisted.

"I'll tell you what this is." Kirsty spoke directly to Hollie. "This is a dragon plot to spoil my peaceful existence. You didn't know what it was like when *she* was alive. None of us knew what she'd be about next. It was all about Teine. All that mattered was what she wanted…and if she didn't get it? Hoo! Stand by for fireworks. I've a touch of the third eye myself. It's a mere fraction of Teine's skill for seeing the future. And I try to use it for good, whereas she used her mighty gift for personal gain." She pointed a finger at Torque. "Do I think she's still alive? No. And I'll tell you for why. Because my teeth dinnae ache when I say her name."

"Seems pretty conclusive to me. Kirsty knows everything that goes on in the Highlands." Alban raised his glass in a toast. "I suggest we eat."

Torque reluctantly agreed. He still wasn't convinced. Ever since he'd seen that email, he'd been sure Teine had somehow survived the fall and was determined to get back at him. It made a strange kind of sense. Although Teine had believed she loved him, Torque didn't think the sorceress was capable of love. What she felt for him was more like ownership. When her toy dragon hadn't done what she wanted and returned her feelings, she'd been incensed. Her revenge had been all-consuming.

Even so, watching him from afar, burning buildings in towns he'd visited…it wasn't quite Teine's style. If she was going to turn into an evil stalker, she would be more hands-on. But who knew what might be going on in her twisted mind? She could have decided on a change in approach just to be infuriating. She could take her time. Like him, Teine was immortal.

The dramatic change in pace and approach when Torque met Hollie definitely suggested Teine was the arsonist. Seeing him with another woman would have sent her into a frenzy. There was no way she'd tolerate that. He almost laughed out loud. *Tolerate?* He was surprised they weren't both a pile of ashes already, consumed in the fire of her jealous rage.

And maybe that was another reason to believe Teine *wasn't* the Incinerator. Could she have learned restraint since he'd watched her plummet off a mountain in a ball of flame? He didn't think Teine was capable of learning. She just *was*…or had once been. The frown between his eyes as he tried to think it all through was making his head ache.

Instead of trying to unravel the mystery that might not even exist, he turned his attention to the more enjoyable task of watching Hollie. He was instantly soothed. No matter what else was happening, he would always rather be watching Hollie. The food had arrived and she was viewing the haggis on her plate with suspicion. A corner of his mouth quirked up.

"It's a traditional sausage made from lamb's liver, lungs and heart mixed with oatmeal, onion, suet and seasoning." His grin widened. "All stuffed into a casing made from a sheep's stomach."

"Yum." She gave him a challenging look. "I flew here on the back of a dragon, Torque. You think you can scare me with a sausage?"

"Is that the whiskey talking?"

"Possibly." She started eating. "It's actually really good. Where are we sleeping tonight? Tell me it's not in a cave."

"Och, lassie. Dinnae fatch." Kirsty waved her fork at her. "You'll stay in my spare room, of course."

As they ate, Torque was content to listen while Alban and Kirsty talked of people and places he knew. It seemed the thriving paranormal community that lived alongside the humans was having some problems. He hadn't realized until now how much he'd missed his Highland home, hadn't understood what that ache in his heart was all about. He'd believed he had to stay away because the memories were too painful. After Ged had freed him from his captivity, he hadn't wanted to see the familiar faces and places. At that time, all he'd wanted to do was get as far away as he could and stay away forever.

Guilt and sorrow had been twin demons gnawing on his heart. He had blamed himself for the annihilation of his clan. If he'd handled Teine differently, been able to predict her reaction, even pretended to love her... No matter how hard he tried, he had never been able to shake off the feeling that he could have—*should* have— done more. Burying himself in his new life, reinventing himself as a rock star, had helped, but it had never driven away the anguish.

Now that he was here, he could acknowledge the truth. He had been desperately homesick all that time. Although he had tried to suppress the cravings, they had never gone away. This was his land. These Highlands owned him and they would never let him go. Torque didn't want them to. He was stronger when he was here.

His attention was drawn back to Kirsty, who was tapping on the table with her fingertip to make a point. "It's become an epidemic."

"What has?" Clearly, whatever they were discussing was serious.

"Och, it's the strangest thing," Kirsty said. "When it first started, it was barely noticeable, so no one talked about it to their friends because they thought it was just *them*. Then, gradually, it got worse. People started sharing their stories and we realized it was affecting more and more people. Now it seems the whole paranormal community is afflicted by insomnia."

Torque sat up straighter. "What?"

"Aye." Alban nodded. "Every single one of us. No matter what we try, we cannae sleep. What do you think it is?"

"I think it's the final proof we need that Teine *is* alive." Torque dashed off the last of his whiskey. "She's cast her trademark insomnia spell on all of you."

Chapter 13

Kirsty's spare room was small and cozy, but the only things that interested Hollie were the wood-burning stove and the double bed.

"So tired," she said as she kicked off her boots and held out her hands toward the warmth.

"Really?" Torque came close, running his hands through her hair. "How tired?"

When he kissed her, the world fell away. It was soft and slow, soothing her in a way she hadn't known she needed. More than words could ever have done, the touch of his lips drove away the strangeness of everything that had happened. His hand rested below her ear, his thumb tracing her jawline as their breaths mingled. She slid her hands beneath his sweater and around his back, pulling him closer, wanting no space between them, needing to feel his heart beating against hers.

"Maybe not *that* tired."

His mouth moved to her neck, his stubble rasping deliciously over her skin. Soft kisses, sighing breaths, tiny nibbles…each one had her squirming with delight. Then he kissed her lips again, demanding more this time. Like he couldn't get enough. *She* couldn't get enough.

"Clothes off," she murmured. "At least it's warmer in here than the rest of your homeland."

When they were naked, Torque's mouth was on her flesh again, tracing a line from her collarbone to her breasts. His hands slid down her spine as he pulled her close, letting her feel his erection. Lost in sensation, she writhed against him. Swinging her into his arms, he carried her the short distance to the bed.

"It's been a long day, we'll go slow."

"Slow sounds like heaven."

Placing her down gently, he turned her onto her side, spooning his body tight against hers. His chest hair was warm and rough on her bare back, his lips igniting fires over her neck and shoulders. Hollie held his arm and tucked it across her waist, twisting her head to reach his lips.

He stroked his hand down her side, idly circling his fingers on the sensitive skin of her hip as he kissed her bare shoulder. Soft sighs left her lips as his touch soothed away thoughts of everything except here and now. Torque kissed along her back, his hand cupping her right breast and circling the nipple with his finger, making the flesh harden into a peak. "Lift your leg."

As she raised her thigh to her chest, opening herself to his touch, Torque cupped her buttock, kneading the firm flesh. Lowering his hand, he ran a finger down her cleft, and her muscles twitched in anticipation. Circling her wetness with his finger, he applied more pressure each time he pushed against her entrance. Not entering, just teasing.

"Please…" Her breath hitched as she writhed against him, impatiently pressing into his hand.

Torque obliged by slipping a finger inside her, stroking softly. He pulled out slowly, then pushed forward again. Taking his time, he caressed her tenderly and her body welcomed him with a rush of overwhelming pleasure.

As he added another finger, she felt his erection pressing hard into her spine. Gripping the edge of the mattress, she surrendered to sensation, loving how her walls stretched to accommodate the width of his fingers and her muscles clenched.

Finding her clit with his thumb, he gently flicked the swollen bundle of nerves as he hooked his fingers inside her. Hollie gasped as she spasmed around him and Torque muffled a groan into her shoulder as he continued to stroke and rub.

"Need you now." Hollie managed to gasp out the words on a wave of approaching orgasm.

The bed dipped as he moved away and her body adjusted to the sudden cold. She heard him rummage in his clothing and the sound of foil ripping. Then he returned and his warmth was tight up against her again.

Tilting her hips to meet him, he slid into her from behind. Hollie bit her lip at the feeling of raw power filling her slowly, inch by inch. Torque's teeth were sharp on her shoulder; then they both remained still for a few moments, relishing the perfect connection. His hands reached down, stroking her thighs, making her skin tingle in the wake of his touch.

"You're so…" She gasped as he pulled out and slid in again. "Torque!"

"Ah, Hollie. Nothing sounds as good as hearing you say my name when I'm inside you."

She felt his teeth against her earlobe. Then he groaned as he started to pump.

Each time, when he slid in, it felt like he was impossibly deep. Hollie thrust back against him, and he groaned with every thrust.

Torque kept his movements slow and luxurious, his hands kneading her breasts and teasing her nipples. Even though she begged him to hurry, he continued to move with deep, lazy strokes. Every now and then, he pressed his lips to her ear and whispered dark, carnal words that stoked her passion to a fever pitch. Hollie's whole body was quivering as he kept her poised on the edge of climax, her senses filled with Torque and this magical, erotic moment.

She reached a hand behind her, raking her fingernails over his sensitive flesh and cupping him in the palm of her hand.

"Oh." His head dropped onto her shoulder. "Oh, Hollie. Just like that…"

He held her hips harder, pulling her tighter to him and thrusting faster now. Hollie arched into him, crying out and squeezing her eyes shut. He was so big, strong and virile. Every stroke pushed her to limits she'd never known existed. She felt her release building like a gathering storm. Her cries were coming in time with his groans, the slick sounds of their bodies moving together filling the room. She clung to the mattress, matching his movements.

"So close." He hissed out the words. His hips jerked wildly as his whole body shuddered and one hand tightened in her hair.

Her breathing hitched as she felt it begin. A moan

started somewhere in the region of her curling toes and then she was crying out, her whole body juddering. Torque was still thrusting, but she could tell from the tensing of his muscles that he was close, too. She bit her knuckles, riding the waves of pleasure washing over her as she felt Torque stiffen and heard him groan. His fingers dug into her hip while he rode it out, his grunts matching her panting breaths. He wrapped his arms around her, pulling her up to his body as she trembled in his embrace.

After several long minutes, when the room was quiet except for the sounds of their sighs, Torque rolled over, taking Hollie with him.

"At first I thought the Fates were mad to throw us together. I thought they must have got it wrong, that nothing good could ever come of this. How could a dragon and a human be together?" His voice was quiet and reflective as he ran a hand down the length of her hair. "Now I'm starting to wonder if the Fates knew what they were doing, after all."

"What do you mean?"

"There's a fight ahead, and before I met you, I didn't have the strength or the heart for it. We don't know who the enemy is yet. But whether it's Teine, or some other faceless evildoer, there's one thing I do know..." He smiled down at her, the glow in his eyes warmer than the heat from the stove. "With you at my side, they don't stand a chance against the last of the Cumhachdach."

Torque woke early. Easing carefully away from Hollie's sleeping form, he pulled on his clothes and slipped quietly from the room. When he stepped outside the building into the chilly morning air, he wasn't surprised to see Alban waiting for him. They walked in silence along a road that led them out of the town.

Alban spoke first. "There is no getting away from it."

"No." Torque gazed up at the mountain peaks.

"She is the only one who will know for sure if Teine is alive."

"Yes." The snow-covered mountains stood out against the gray skies. Càrn Eighe couldn't be seen from where they were, but he could feel its presence. "She doesn't welcome visitors."

Alban snorted. "That's an understatement."

Torque sighed, digging his hands deep into the pockets of his jeans. "I suppose there's no other way?" Even as he asked the question, he knew the answer.

For thousands of years, Teine and her twin sister, Deigh, had ruled over the Highlands. Teine was the Scots Gaelic word for *fire* and Deigh meant *ice*. The two sisters lived up to their names. Teine ruled over a kingdom of heat and fury. Deigh was icy and unmoving. Unlike most twins, they had no love for each other. Even so, Alban was right. Deigh might be able to tell them what was going on with Teine. Most important of all, she would be able to discover where her sister was. If she chose to cooperate. Where Deigh was concerned, *if* was a very big word.

"You made this journey," Alban said. "Do you want to leave wondering, or knowing?"

Torque nodded. Alban was right. He and Hollie had to leave that night. He wouldn't get another chance like this until after the tour was over. If they didn't approach Deigh now, he would be left in a constant state of speculation about what she knew. Even worse than that, if there were more fires—and more deaths—he would question whether he could have prevented them by speaking to her.

"Okay. Food first, crazy ice woman later. There's only so much insanity a man can take before breakfast."

They retraced their steps, pausing on an incline to watch the city as it came to life.

"So… Hollie?" Alban's face was turned away, his voice expressing mild interest. Torque wasn't fooled. They had been born from the same fire. Teine might have turned them against each other once, but the bonds that existed between them had been reestablished when she imprisoned them both and destroyed their families. Even though they were from different clans, they were as close as brothers.

Alban didn't have to tell Torque what it would mean if he fell in love with a human. A human life span was the blink of an eye to an immortal dragon-shifter. If he was foolish enough to fall for a mortal…well, he would be storing up a pain-filled future for himself.

"Yes?" There was no fire in the word. Alban could see through him. He would have been aware of Torque's feelings as soon as he first saw him with Hollie.

"We are the last of our kind. I wish with all my heart that wasn't so." When Alban turned to look at him, his expression was anguished. "We will never find one of our own kind, you and I. Teine saw to that. I can see you love Hollie, and I wish I could shake your hand and wish you well. But I have to say this."

"No." Torque's throat tightened painfully, so the word came out as a croak. "No, you don't. I already know."

Alban's hand on his shoulder felt like the heaviest weight in the world. "The Fates are supposed to guard against a dragon and a mortal falling in love. When it happens for other shifters, they can choose the difficult step of converting their mate with a bite. We don't even have that."

"Yeah. The Fates don't let that sort of screwed-up madness happen. Do they?" Torque asked. "Except it has happened. And I can't undo it. I can't make these feelings go away." They had reached Kirsty's place and he looked up at the window of the room where he had left Hollie sleeping. "I don't want to."

"Then, when this madness is over, you, my friend, must find another way," Alban said.

"You think there is one?" Torque was aware that he was clutching at possibilities…or maybe impossibilities.

"I don't know." Keeping his hand on Torque's shoulder, Alban guided him inside the restaurant, where the aroma of bacon and coffee greeted them. "But there is someone who will have the answers you seek."

Torque frowned, trying to follow what he meant. After a few moments, realization hit him. Of course. There was one person who was a walking reference book about shifters.

"Ged." Torque said his friend's name like it was a revelation. "What he doesn't know about our history and legends isn't worth knowing."

"Will you tell Hollie about you and Deigh?" Alban's voice acted like a bucket of cold water extinguishing the tiny flicker of hope he had just glimpsed.

Torque thought about it. Would he explain to Hollie that he had once been stupid enough to get involved with the frosty sorceress? It had lasted about as long as it took him to realize that, although she wasn't as demented as her fiery sister, Deigh had a block of ice in place of a heart. He had no reason not to tell Hollie;

it was just where to start. *Of all the stupid things I've done in my life...*

With perfect, or perhaps imperfect, timing, Hollie appeared in the doorway, cutting short any further conversation on the subject. Torque's heart flipped over at the sight of her. There had to be a way for them to make this work. He couldn't feel this way only to let her go. As she took a seat next to him, he turned that thought into a vow. He would find a way.

Càrn Eighe wasn't a difficult climb, but Torque and Hollie didn't have much time. They had to get back to Dallas in time to rejoin Beast for the next concert.

"One last flight?" he asked Alban.

"No." Alban shook his head. "One *more* flight."

"You're right." Torque nodded. "I haven't come back only to stay away for good. We will fly together again. Many times."

He and Alban had engaged in a lengthy discussion about whether Hollie should go with them. Torque explained to her that the mountain was popular with walkers and climbers, but they weren't taking any of the traditional routes. Once they reached the summit, they would be stepping into a mystical realm, one known only to those who were not mortal. Beyond the physical peak, the temperatures plummeted and the world became a hostile, icy kingdom ruled over by a ruthless sorceress. Torque hadn't been sure he wanted to expose Hollie to either the weather conditions...or to Deigh.

Hollie was not about to be sidelined by a pair of alpha-male dragons who thought they knew best. She had listened to their arguments, then faced Torque with a stubborn expression. "I'm coming with you."

"Deigh isn't Teine, but she can be vicious."

"You've seen me before I've had my morning coffee. I can match any evil sorceress." Hollie slid her arms around his waist. "This is my investigation, Torque. Okay, it's taking some unexpected turns, but you can't shut me out of it."

"Okay. But you do as I say."

She opened her mouth to protest and he silenced her with a finger on her lips. "This is not about me being an arrogant dragon-shifter, Hollie. This is about facing a devious magician who will target you because you don't have the same powers she does. Together, Alban and I can protect you from Deigh. We were defeated by Teine because she caught us unawares. I will never let that happen again. But you have to trust me to know how to handle this."

"I do. I trust you completely." She grinned at him. "I was going to ask if we have time to buy some warmer clothes before we set off."

He laughed. "We're in Scotland. The stores are full of warmer clothes."

They went to one of the larger chains that catered to hikers and walkers. When they set off toward Càrn Eighe, Hollie wore thermal undergarments beneath her jeans and a sweater with waterproof outerwear over the top. Sturdy boots and thick gloves completed the look. Her movements felt slightly clumsy, but at least she was warm.

Once they reached the lower slopes of the mountain, the two men found an isolated place and prepared to shift.

"Shifting and flying in daylight is always risky, but at least we are in a remote part of the world and our camouflage hides us once we take to the skies," Torque explained.

When they had removed their clothing, Hollie placed it in her backpack, since they would need it again once they shifted back on the mountaintop. She took a moment to consider how her day was going. She was halfway across the world from her home. No one from her former life knew where she was. The two naked men standing before her were about to transform themselves into dragons. She had been in some unusual situations as a fire investigator, but no one could call this an average working day.

When Torque and Alban had shifted, they unfurled their giant wings. Both dragons were a similar size, but Torque was more muscular. Alban's scales were darker and more silvery than Torque's and his eyes retained some of their blue sheen.

Torque crouched low so Hollie could climb onto his back, and once she was in place, he broke into a run and immediately took flight. Alban was right behind him. It was easier for Hollie to see how the dragons blended into their environment now that she could watch Alban. As he soared high, his scales changed to match the murky gray of the low cloud, but when he swooped lower, he became part of the brown and black of the mountainside.

The mountaintop was a horseshoe ridge, and the dragons followed its edge, dipping low into a snowy basin. Hollie gasped in surprise as they almost immediately left the bleak Highland scene behind and entered a whole new world. This was a land blanketed in ice and snow, a wonderland of white where even the air glistened and the icy gale cut through Hollie's warm clothing as if it wasn't there.

Torque and Alban landed on a snowy plateau and

Hollie was shivering by the time they had shifted and quickly dressed.

"There." Torque placed an arm around her shoulders and indicated a point just above them. Although it was difficult to see through the swirling snow, she could just make out the outline of a building.

As they moved forward, ice cracked beneath her feet and her breath frosted the air. The snow began falling more heavily and the wind howled out in fury.

"Is the weather getting worse because of *us*?" Hollie had to shout to be heard.

"Yes," Torque yelled back at her.

It was almost impossible to keep going. The world had become a swirling mass of screaming white. Hollie raised a gloved hand to shield her eyes, but it had no effect against the onslaught. The wind was razor-sharp on her face, and the snow blinded her. All she could do was to bow her head until her chin was touching her chest and try to stay upright. Her feet were starting to freeze as they sank into the drifts with each stride, slowing her almost to a standstill.

Torque placed an arm around her waist, keeping her tight against his side and using his own strength to propel her forward with him. It helped, but it still felt like the weather was going to win the fight.

A high-pitched screech, like ice scraping over rock, claimed her attention. Without warning, the gusts died away and every snowflake hung in the air in perfect, frozen stillness. As her vision cleared, Hollie saw they were only a few feet from the building. With gleaming towers and turrets, it looked like a palace carved from ice.

The sound she had heard was a giant door opening. Pressing closer to Torque, she watched as it was pushed wider, shards of ice cracking and shattering all around it as it moved. When the opening was wide enough, a woman stepped into view.

"I do not wish for visitors." Everything about her was white. From her ivory skin, to her silver hair, and her flowing, misty robes. The only hint of color was in her light blue eyes.

"We dinnae come expecting a dram and a tattie scone," Alban said. "Although, if you're offering..."

Ignoring him, the woman turned her attention to Torque. Her expression didn't change, but the ice in the air glimmered brighter. "Cumhachdach."

"Deigh." He bowed his head. "We come in peace."

"Mine is a land of ice." She swept a hand around her, and fresh snow fell in a shimmering arc. "There is no place here for fire-breathers. You mistake me for my sister." She turned to go back inside.

"Wait." Torque spoke urgently and Deigh paused. "How can we mistake you for Teine? She is dead."

A slight smile touched her colorless lips. "Of course. How foolish of me to forget."

Torque took a step forward. "Deigh, you have no more love for Teine than we do. If she is alive, you can help us by sharing what you know."

Hollie watched the sorceress in fascination. She was like a china doll, beautiful, but unblinking. It was almost as if her thought processes had been slowed down by the cold.

After a few minutes, Deigh sighed. "You should come inside." For the first time, her eyes flitted over to Hollie. "Humans don't last long in the cold."

"It doesn't look much warmer inside," Hollie whispered as they approached the building.

"Stay close to me. I'll give off enough heat for both of us." Torque kept his own voice low.

The interior of the palace was jaw-dropping. Everything about it was elegant and fit for a fairy princess... except it was all carved from ice. Hollie was reminded of movies she had watched and fairy tales she had read as a child. This was the enchanted castle that existed in the frozen wastelands. This was the place the characters sang about.

Except the reality was she couldn't feel her feet and she didn't like the way Deigh was looking at Torque. It was like she had been waiting her whole life for a dragon-shifter to adorn her home. Hollie cast a sidelong glance in Torque's direction. Could he feel it? Did he know Teine wasn't the only sorceress who had a massive crush on him? It was a reminder of the chasm that existed between them. All those centuries of his life about which Hollie knew nothing.

"Is that why you came here after all this time? To ask me if Teine is still alive?" There was no escaping the look in Deigh's eyes as she fixed her gaze on Torque's face. It was raw longing. "No other reason?"

Hollie felt almost embarrassed for her. For an instant, she was gripped by an insane desire to tell Deigh to have a little dignity. *Don't make it so obvious. Try for a little subtlety.* It was probably a bad idea to offer relationship advice to a magical being on account of that whole possibility of violent death thing. *Plus, he's my dragon-shifter.*

"Deigh, I have to leave Scotland soon. People are dying. I need to know if there is a chance Teine survived." Torque's manner reminded Hollie of an adult talking to a child. Patient, but firm.

Deigh laughed and the sound made Hollie think of ice tinkling in a glass. "Anything is possible."

"There is a problem within the Highland paranormal community," Alban said. "We seem to be under a spell that leaves us unable to sleep. Do you know anything about that?"

With an obvious effort, Deigh dragged her gaze away from Torque and turned to Alban. "The spell is Teine's."

"That was what I thought," Torque said. "But if she cast it, where is she? Teine enjoys watching her victims suffer."

For the first time, Deigh really smiled and Hollie glimpsed how stunning she could be if she let the icy persona drop. "Don't we all?"

"Is she alive, Deigh?" Torque seemed to be losing patience.

Her eyes rested on Hollie's face. For an instant, something flickered in their depths, rocking Hollie backward. Despite the subzero temperatures, the ice sorceress had scorched her. Before they settled back into a neutral expression, pure venom was overlaid on the porcelain features.

"She may be."

"How do you know?" Torque asked.

"You came onto my mountain uninvited. You asked me a question. I answered it. You don't get to demand proof."

Hollie could sense Torque battling to maintain control of his temper. "It would help us if we knew how she survived and where she is now," she explained.

There it was again. That flash of otherness as Deigh looked her way. But she was at the top of the sorcery hierarchy. It was hardly surprising that she gave off unexpected vibes. "I don't deal with mortals."

"Just tell us, Deigh." Torque spoke through gritted teeth.

"It's a twin thing." The sorceress lifted one slender shoulder. "As for where she is…" The pause went on a little too long. There was the hint of a sly smile. *You know, but you're not telling.* "We were never that close."

"Well, that was helpful," Alban said. "I don't suppose you know a way to counteract the insomnia spell?"

She cast a look of dislike in his direction. "Tell your witch friend to make an infusion from the leaves of lavender and chamomile. It must be used when the moon is full and the songbirds are silent. Do not drink the liquid. Inhale the steam through the fronds of a fresh young fern. Once you remember how to sleep, the spell will be broken." The air around Deigh glittered brighter as her mood changed and she took a half step toward Torque. "Are you back for good? As you know, there are circumstances that can tempt me down from my mountain."

There are? Hollie cast a sidelong glance in Torque's direction, but his expression was closed.

"No." He took Hollie's hand. "We have to leave." If looks could kill, Hollie would be dead on the spot with a shard of ice through her heart. "Thank you for your help."

Hollie was inclined to agree with Alban. Apart from a grudging suggestion of how to break the insomnia spell, she couldn't see that Deigh had been of any use. A vague hint that Teine might be alive? It didn't move their investigation on a single step.

When they stepped outside, the storm had died down. The air was still and crisp, and thick snow lay like cake frosting over the ground. Instead of the disappointment Hollie had expected, Torque and Alban exchanged a smile.

"She's alive." They spoke the words together.

Chapter 14

"I don't understand." Hollie looked from Torque to Alban in bewilderment. "Deigh didn't tell you anything. How can you possibly walk away from that conversation and say with certainty that Teine is alive?"

"Because Deigh told Alban how to undo the insomnia charm. It's not her spell. Only the person who cast it knows how to reverse it. Teine must have told Deigh what to do."

"Why would she do that?" Hollie asked. "I thought you said they had nothing to do with each other."

"Think about it." Torque took her arm, propelling her through the deep drifts. "Imagine you are an evil sorceress, you've just been burned by dragon fire and fallen into a ravine. Against all the odds, you survived. Everyone in these Highlands hates you and is celebrating the news of your demise. You need help and a place to recover. Where do you go?"

"To the only other evil sorceress in the vicinity," Alban said. "Your icy twin."

"But why didn't Deigh turn her away? They didn't love each other, but they were both in love with you." So Hollie had noticed that. To be fair, it was hard to miss. Deigh wasn't exactly subtle. "If Teine was her rival for your affections, why not let her die?"

"They don't understand love. Either of them. Who knows why she chose to help her? Maybe it was, as she said, a twin thing."

Alban snorted. "You mean foul blood is thicker than water? It's a pity you don't have time to take her up on her offer."

"What do you mean?" Torque asked.

"You know. Tempt her down from her mountaintop. Sweeten her up with that Cumhachdach charm of yours. Find out what really happened." Alban appeared oblivious of the glare Torque was giving him.

"Alban has a point," Hollie said.

"Is this a conspiracy?" Torque growled. Why would Hollie want him to spend time with his crazy ex? Not that she knew the details about the depths of how unhinged Deigh could be.

"It's obvious she'll talk to you." She stopped and looked back at the ice palace. "You should set something up."

He tapped his watch. "We don't have time. I have to get back for this little matter of a concert in front of thousands of people."

"Invite her." He blinked at her. "Not to the one we are rushing back for, but to the next one in Denver. Ask her to be your guest at that."

"Hollie, we probably need to have a serious talk

about some things. Set a few relationship boundaries, but not right now—"

She caught hold of his arm. "Torque, listen to me. I don't want you to spend time with a mad ice witch who looks at you like she wants to lick every inch of you. But I do want to catch the Incinerator. And if you giving Deigh a VIP pass to a Beast concert and taking her out to dinner is what it takes, I can live with that." She paused. "I'll hate every second, but I can do it. I think."

"I could offer to be Deigh's traveling companion," Alban said. "It won't be much fun of a trip, but at least we'll know what she is doing."

"Do you have a passport?" Torque asked. "I doubt Deigh does."

"I'm sure she can conjure one up for herself, but I actually keep mine up to date." Alban grinned at Hollie. "While yon Cumhachdach deals with the icy one, you could take me out for a decent, well-done steak."

"So you two get to go out and have fun, and I get to go on a date with Deigh? Build her hopes up and spend the night fighting her off?" Torque groaned in frustration. "Thanks, guys."

"Isn't it worth it to find out, once and for all, if Teine is the Incinerator?" Hollie asked.

"If there was any other way…" He gave a sigh of surrender. "Wait here."

As he walked back toward the ice palace, Alban's sympathetic tones followed him. "Och, you cannae blame him. Deigh is as mad as a box of frogs in a thunderstorm."

Torque knew a moment of longing for the days when Alban was the enemy. A good dragon fight, with claws and fire-breathing…that was just what he needed right now to release his tension. He was supposed to be in charge around here, so how the hell had he ended up in this position? More time than was necessary with the very woman he had spent the best part of several centuries avoiding was not an option he liked. And tricking a sorceress? Never a good move.

At least Deigh didn't have Teine's legendary fortune-telling talents. If she had been able to see into the future and know what was coming, they'd be storing up a world of trouble. He frowned. He didn't *think* Deigh had the same skill. She'd never mentioned them, whereas Teine boasted of her ability to predict the future.

But Hollie was right. This was about finding the Incinerator. Nothing they'd tried so far had brought them any answers. Maybe it was time for an unconventional approach. He just hoped he could keep it low-key. He bit back a laugh. This was *Deigh*. Back when the first King Kenneth had been on the throne, Torque had glanced her way once and she'd been ordering her bride clothes. Unfortunately, he hadn't known about that and had worked on the assumption that she was sane when he got involved with her. It hadn't taken long for him to discover his mistake. "You came back." Deigh turned to him with shining eyes as he walked back through the frozen portal.

Even though he knew iced water ran in her veins and she had a cruel streak a mile wide, he pitied her in that instant. If there had been another way to get this information, he'd have taken it. Recalling some of her deeds helped stiffen his spine. This was the woman who had caused a landslide and buried a whole village. The reason? She overheard someone say that one of the maidens was prettier than her. And that time when the crops failed for three consecutive summers? Deigh had been harboring a grudge because a visiting sorceress had been welcomed into the home of a Highland witch. Both the witch and her guest had been found incarcerated in a block of ice—even though it was high summer—and hundreds of people in the surrounding area had starved.

Yeah, he could harden his heart against Deigh's hopeful smile. Particularly if she was covering for her even more sinister sister.

"I wondered if you might like to take a trip."

Hollie hadn't timed Torque's last trans-Atlantic dragon flight, but she knew they were cutting it dangerously fine if they were going to make it back to Dallas for the concert. Even factoring in magic, dragon speed and time differences, Ged would be tearing his hair out and cursing Torque's legendary unpunctuality. Leaving a dozen questions unspoken, they said goodbye to Alban on the summit of Càrn Eighe.

"Och, won't I be seeing you again in just a few days?" Alban winked at Hollie. "Remember what I said. Steak. Well done. No sides."

She stood on the tips of her toes to kiss his cheek. "I'll take you to the best steak house in Denver."

Alban grinned at Torque over her head. "I think I did better than you out of this deal. At least my date is sane."

"I knew there was a reason why we fought the Moiteil for all those years." Torque scowled. "Just get Deigh to America in three days' time. I'll have someone contact you when the travel and accommodation arrangements are made."

"Separate rooms, right?" Alban's flippant air was replaced by a hint of nervousness.

Torque's smile was pure mischief. "I'll have to see what I can do. Hotels get so busy at this time of year."

"Stop tormenting Alban." Hollie lightly punched his upper arm. "We have to get going. *Right now.*"

Flying back felt different. Perhaps it was because the exhilaration was there but the fear was gone. And a whole new side of Torque's life had been opened up to her. He was a dragon, but he had spent most of his life living among humans. Those humans were also shifters, or, like Kirsty, they had additional powers. But they lived otherwise normal lives. Their hopes, fears and dreams looked a lot like Hollie's own. Except for the wicked sorceress who had lurked in the background, of course. Even so, Hollie's own world wasn't very different. Instead of enchanted spells, the villains carried guns and knives.

It was still right against wrong, still ordinary people trying to get on with their lives, sometimes in the face of monumental evil. That brought her thoughts back to the Incinerator. Her world and Torque's had collided because of the arsonist. But which of those worlds did the fire-starter come from? Had he stepped from her world of science and logic into Torque's magical sphere? Or was it the other way around? Would they catch him with conventional weapons, or could he only be defeated with supernatural powers?

Tired of thinking, she rested her head against Torque's neck, letting his warmth and strength soothe her. It seemed like only minutes later that he was swooping low over the dark outline of the Cedar Ridge Nature Preserve.

"How much time do we have?" he asked as soon as he had shifted back.

"The concert starts in an hour." Hollie drew his clothes from the backpack and handed them to him.

"Plenty of time."

She managed to stop her mouth from dropping open. "Dear Lord. You're serious."

He pulled her close, kissing her quickly on the lips. "Let's go."

Taking his cell phone from the back pocket of his jeans, he called a cab as they walked along the moonlit trail. They reached the highway and waited only a few minutes before the driver drew up at the edge of the sidewalk. When Torque gave him directions to the stadium where the concert was being held, he shook his head.

"I dropped two guys off there an hour ago and the streets were already blocked. No way we'll get near that place now."

"Get us as close as you can." When the driver started to protest, Torque withdrew a wad of cash from the back pocket of his jeans. "And fast."

"I'll see what I can do." He turned the cab around.

Hollie could see the arena as they approached. The huge building was located on a hill just outside the city, and searchlights positioned on the edge of the open roof lit up the night sky. As they got closer, the traffic slowed to a crawl and then came to a standstill. Police cruisers blocked the exit roads. Although there were people on the sidewalk, the lack of crowds was an indication that the concert was about to start.

"We'll walk from here." Torque shoved another handful of money into the driver's hand and gestured for Hollie to follow him out of the cab.

"Torque." She was torn between laughter and dismay. "We are still at least ten minutes from the venue."

"Then we need to move faster." Grabbing her hand, he broke into a run. Powering past people who were walking toward the stadium, he kept going, only pausing occasionally to check that she was okay.

Laughing, Hollie nodded. "Just get there. I promised Ged," she panted.

By the time they reached the entrance, her lungs were about to collapse and her leg muscles had given everything they had. Luckily, the security guard on the door recognized Torque and waved him through.

"Ged?" Torque asked.

"He's backstage. Along this corridor and turn right."

The opening bars of the first number were playing as they dashed toward the stage. Hollie could see a stand-in guitarist in Torque's usual position. At the same time that Khan erupted onto the stage from the rear, Torque vaulted on from the front. Grabbing his guitar from the stand-in, he high-fived the startled guy, grinned at Dev and gave one of his trademark leaps into the air. The audience, clearly believing it to be part of the performance, went wild.

Hollie sidled around to the rear of the stage to where Ged was standing with his arms folded across his huge chest. His expression was unreadable as he glanced down at her.

"Thanks for getting him back on time." Even though he had to yell to be heard, she picked up on the sarcasm in his voice.

After a minute or two, Ged nodded toward the stage, where Torque was on his knees. He was bent backward so his head touched the floor and his flame-colored hair fanned out around him. As they watched, he jumped to his feet and powered across to the other side of the stage. Explosions followed in his wake. Even from a distance, Hollie could feel raw power coming off him in waves.

"I didn't think it was possible for Torque to have even more energy," Ged said. "But something has invigorated him."

Hollie nodded. She had seen the love he had for his Highland home. Now that he had been back there and accepted that it was part of him, could he continue to stay away?

The following morning, over breakfast, Ged brought them up to speed with the police inquiry into the bus fire.

"There is very little to tell. What was left of the vehicle was in such a poor state the fire investigation team didn't have much to work on." Ged turned to Hollie. "You'll probably already know what I'm about to say next. There was no trace of an additional accelerant, so it was likely he used gasoline. Since there was gas in the tanks, however, that can't be taken as conclusive. They are working on the theory that a container, probably a bottle, of some sort was thrown through the front window and then the same thing through the rear window."

"A Molotov cocktail," Hollie said. "The simplest and most effective way of making a firebomb. You fill a bottle with gasoline, or another accelerant, stuff a rag in the neck, light the rag and throw the bottle through the window of the building or vehicle you want to set fire to. As the bottle breaks, the accelerant spills out and catches alight."

"There was a lot of glass and fabric remnants at the scene, as you'd expect from a bus that was a home on the road, but it hasn't been possible for the investigators to get anything useful from them."

"What about the person who did this?" Torque asked. "Have the police come up with any ideas, even any suspects?"

He had told Ged about Teine and the plan to bring Deigh to Denver in an attempt to get more information from her. It was always helpful to have Ged on his side and Beast as backup, particularly now that Hollie's safety was at risk.

"Nothing so far. Obviously, they don't think it was a random attack. Their advice was to increase security, which I've already done. From now on, Rick's security team will be following the new bus. When we stop, they'll patrol the exterior."

Hollie slumped back in her seat. "So we are no closer to knowing who is responsible?"

Torque leaned across the table and took her hand. "All we know for sure is that this is escalating."

Although he couldn't say why, he felt like the end was approaching. A final confrontation was looming and he had to put himself and Hollie on the right side of it. It was just so hard to achieve that goal when their opponent remained faceless.

The encounter with Deigh had brought him an answer…of sorts. It seemed his conviction that Teine was alive had been proved correct. There was still a long way to go before he could confirm the connection between Teine and these fires. And then he had to do the hardest thing of all. He had to stop her…

Even if Teine wasn't the Incinerator, if she was alive, she was trouble. One day, Torque would have to face her again. Since he was never going back into captivity, that meant he had to defeat her. Or die trying.

When Ged left, Hollie regarded him over the top of her coffee cup. "We never did talk about you and Deigh."

"Does that bother you? It shouldn't."

She tilted her head to one side as she considered the question. "No, it doesn't bother me in *that* way. How could I be jealous of something that happened in your past? I suppose I'm curious. You and her?" She shook her head. "I can't see that."

"I'm not going to pretend to be a victim, but the Deigh I became involved with wasn't the woman you saw on that mountaintop. We met in the valley—yes, she left her ice palace—and she appeared normal. Did I think she was the love of my life? No. Was I attracted to her? Yes. I was stupid, or horny. I guess the two things can often be the same. I got into a relationship with her without knowing anything about her. It didn't take me long to realize she was insane. And, of course, I discovered she was a sorceress, who just happened to be Teine's sister. While I was backing off, Deigh thought she was in the middle of the greatest love affair of all time. Our breakup wasn't pretty."

"Did she leave her ice palace specifically to seek you out?" Hollie asked.

"I never thought of it that way." Torque considered the question. It was so long ago, and some memories were better left in the past. "Why do you ask?"

"I'm not sure. It just seems strange that both sisters had this intense thing for you." She gave him a teasing smile. "Not that I don't get it, of course. But I wondered if Deigh came looking for you as a way of getting at Teine. You said they hated each other, and it would be the ultimate way to hurt her sister. Steal the guy she's crazy about. How did Teine react when she knew you and Deigh were together?"

"I don't know. I can't imagine she took it well, but I never saw the two of them interact. Like I said, it was well known in the Highlands that they kept well away from each other." He scrubbed a hand over his face. "God, this is hard."

Hollie returned the clasp of his hand, anxiety in the depths of her eyes. "What is?"

"All of it." He raised her hand to his lips. "I'm a dragon. I should be able to control this. Whatever the hell *this* is."

"If we hadn't met, none of this would have come your way…"

He was out of his seat and at her side in one explosive movement. "Don't ever say that." Dropping to his knees, he wrapped his arms around her waist. "Don't even think it. When you came into my life, you changed everything. You made the world right. If only there was a way—"

She rested her cheek against the top of his head. "A way we could have forever?"

"If there was, would you take it?"

When she lifted her head to look at him, her eyes had filled with tears. "I would do anything."

At that moment, there was a knock on the door. Muttering a curse about bad timing, Torque went to answer it. Since the security team wouldn't allow just anyone to approach his room, he knew it had to be one of his friends. Sure enough, it was Sarange and Karina.

"Khan asked me to remind you about the sound check," Sarange said as she kissed Torque on the cheek.

"Was he as polite as that?" Torque asked.

She laughed. "He may have used the words 'sorry,

unpunctual, dragon ass' somewhere in the original message."

She placed Karina on the floor. The baby had just learned to walk, but faced with a new environment, she reverted to a devastatingly fast crawl. As Sarange darted after her, removing objects from her grasp, Torque turned to Hollie.

"Let's continue our conversation at another time."

She nodded. "I meant it. Anything."

What he saw in her eyes was the future he wanted. There was no more pain and darkness, only love and light. He wanted to see that every day, to have the assurance that it would never go away. He wanted Hollie in his heart and in his arms. He didn't want to watch her grow old while he stayed young, or to wake one day and find that she was a dear, sweet memory. *Forever.* It had to be within their grasp.

"I'll find a way."

Chapter 15

One of the consequences of the bus fire had been that
everything the band had with them was lost. Clothing,
cell phones, electronic devices, bank cards…everything
had to be replaced. Rick had gotten organized and most
things had been speedily replaced, but it meant Hollie
only had a few outfits. And she didn't like any of them.

"I'm really not a combat gear sort of girl," she explained to Sarange as they drank mint tea in her hotel
suite and took turns to extricate Karina from trouble.
Although the baby had a pile of toys, she was ignoring
them. The silken fastenings from the drapes had been
chewed and cast aside, elegant cushions had been flung
to the four corners of the room and a glossy magazine
had been carefully shredded.

"Ew." Sarange wrinkled her dainty nose. "Rick is
great, but would I trust him to buy my clothes? I'd rather
send Khan, and that's saying something. Why don't we
go shopping now?"

Hollie was torn. The prospect of buying some new clothes was appealing, but the shadowy image of the Incinerator rose before her eyes. "I don't know."

"I always have security with me when I go out," Sarange said. "And I wear a disguise. This won't be any different. It just means you need to do the same."

Hollie succumbed. "Let's do it."

Organizing security and getting Karina ready took some time. Just as they were about to leave, Sarange covered her mouth with one hand. "Give me a minute." She dashed toward the bathroom.

Hollie squatted next to Karina's stroller. "I guess Mommy isn't feeling too great."

Karina grinned and punched the toys that hung in front of her. Clearly, she hadn't noticed her mother's distress. When Sarange returned, she looked pale, but composed.

"Are you okay?" Hollie asked. "Could it have been something you ate?"

"Morning sickness." Sarange grinned. "I was the same with Karina."

"Oh, my goodness." Hollie jumped up and hugged her. "Congratulations."

"You are the only one who knows," Sarange warned. "Apart from Khan, of course. We're going to tell the other guys at a special meal after the final concert."

"I won't say a word," Hollie promised. "Do you want to stay here and rest instead of going shopping?"

"Are you kidding? I'll be fine now. Let's hit those stores."

Three hours later, Hollie was starting to wonder if pregnancy hormones had given Sarange a burst of energy. Her own head was spinning and her feet were aching after they had dashed in and out of a dozen stores in the high-class mall. The upside was that she had managed to purchase some new clothes during the whirlwind tour. Now, as they flopped into a booth in a coffee shop, she let out a long sigh of relief. "Do you always shop like it's a competition to reach the finish line?"

Sarange, who had her long, dark hair tucked up inside a hat, lifted her shades to give Hollie a pitying look and kept her voice low. "I'm a werewolf. Everything I do is a competition to reach the finish line." She grinned. "Plus, I don't get out much."

After they ordered drinks, Sarange took Karina, who had just woken up, to the restroom for a diaper change. While she was gone, Hollie glanced around, her eyes seeking out the security guards who had remained at a discreet distance from them during the retail expedition. She was reassured to see the two burly figures standing close to the door.

Her attention was caught by another man. He was close to the serving counter, talking on his cell, with his back to Hollie. Dressed in a dark suit, he was tall and slim with light brown hair. There was nothing unusual about his appearance. Except she knew him. She'd have recognized him anywhere. As he turned and she got a clearer view of his profile, her heart gave a curious, uncomfortable thud. What was Dalton Hilger doing in this coffee shop?

Abandoning her packages, Hollie was on her feet and moving toward him without thinking. This couldn't be a coincidence. The only reason for Dalton to be in Dallas was as part of the Incinerator inquiry. The coffee shop was crowded and her progress was hindered as she made her way around busy tables. By the time she got close, Dalton had slipped his cell into the inside pocket of his jacket and was on the move.

She called out his name, but he was out the door and mingling with the crowds in the mall before she could reach him.

"You want me to go after him?" One of Rick's security guys was at her side in an instant.

Hollie shook her head. Feeling dejected and confused, she returned to the table, where Sarange was waiting with a look of surprise. She could call Dalton, but if she told him she'd seen him, she'd be giving away her location. If she questioned him about the Incinerator case and any connection to Dallas, would he even talk to her about what was going on? She no longer knew what her status was regarding the investigation. The truth was that she had cut all ties to Dalton and the FBI. They were no longer a part of her life, but she hadn't told anyone about it yet. On balance, it was probably just as well he'd gone before she could speak to him. Having a big, life-changing conversation thrust upon her unexpectedly wasn't the way to go.

"Someone you know?" Sarange asked as Hollie slid back into her seat.

"Just a mistake." She smiled. "Now, where are those drinks we ordered?"

When Torque returned to the hotel and found Hollie was still out with Sarange, he decided now was as good a time as any to talk to Ged. They headed for the bar.

"Is this a conversation that requires the good cognac?" It was a tradition within the band. The more serious the subject, the better the brandy needed to be.

"Yeah. Go for it."

The room was almost empty, but they took their drinks to a quiet corner where there was no chance of being overheard.

"This is about Hollie." Ged opened the brandy bottle and sloshed the aromatic liquid into their glasses.

"Of course it is." Torque sipped his drink. "How can this have happened to us? How could a dragon-shifter and a human have been fated to become mates?"

"It's an unusual, but not an unknown, situation in the shifter world. Over time werewolves, were-bears, were-tigers and others have all taken humans as their life partners. Of course, the mortal must become a convert. He, or she, must be willing to take the bite of their partner and transform into a shifter themselves." Ged studied Torque over the top of his glass. "It's never an easy decision."

"I can't imagine how anyone asks that question of their partner," Torque said. "Where do you start when it comes to giving up being human?"

"Once the step has been taken, there's no going back. But I guess it's a lot like proposing marriage. You both give up your old lives and begin a new one. In the case of a human taking the bite of a shifter, it's just more dramatic." Ged's gaze was searching. "Is this leading somewhere?"

Torque shrugged. "Can it? I suppose that's my question. You know what my problem is. Dragon blood must remain pure. I've never heard of a human taking a dragon bite."

Ged tented his fingers beneath his chin, his expression thoughtful. Torque wanted to hold his breath. What if the answer was a simple negative?

No, you can never claim Hollie as your permanent mate. Prepare to spend the rest of forever in hell.

His heart had soared when Hollie said she would do anything to be with him. But what if there wasn't anything she *could* do? Dragons were unique among shifters. He had been raised to believe in the proud purity of the dragon bloodline. The simplicity with which other shifters could convert a mortal was not for them. Now he longed for that ease. Asking Hollie to become a shifter wouldn't be something he took lightly, but he would love to have that choice.

Just when he thought Ged was never going to speak again, his friend nodded slowly. "Have you heard of the dragon mark?"

Torque was about to shake his head, when he paused. There *was* something, way down deep in the mists of his memory. "Forged in fire?" His hand shook as he dashed off the rest of his drink and reached for the bottle. "That's it? That's the best you can do?"

Ged held out his hands, palms upward. "That's all I've got."

"The dragon mark was a way of ensuring fealty to a clan leader." Torque frowned as he dredged up the ancient ritual from the recesses of his mind. "It was never about mating."

"That's true, but I heard a story, many centuries ago, in China. It was the tale of a dragon prince who fell in love with a human. His father, the king, refused to hear of his marriage to a mortal unless she *could* be converted. The only way was to use the ancient rite of fealty. She took the dragon mark and became his dragon bride."

Torque sat up a little straighter. "You saw it for yourself?"

Ged shook his head. "No. I only heard about the story."

"So if I want to be with Hollie forever, I have to ask her to step into a pit of fire with me while I sink my dragon fangs into her neck? All based on a story you heard a few hundred years ago?"

"That sounds like an accurate summary." Ged tilted his glass toward him.

"Damn it all to hell, Ged. How do I introduce *this* into a conversation?"

"That is a question that will require a second bottle."

Torque was in a mildly alcoholic haze when his cell buzzed with a message from Hollie letting him know she was back in their room. The brandy hadn't numbed the shock of what Ged had told him, but their conversation had given him some thinking time.

The dragon mark had always been more the stuff of legend than reality. He'd never known anyone who wore it, never heard of a human who had taken that step. To blindly walk into a fire for love? All based on a story that Ged had once been told? He couldn't ask that of Hollie. She had said she would do anything, but she hadn't known the reality of what "anything" might mean.

When he reached their suite, he found her unpacking a number of bags. Although she smiled when she saw him, he could tell there was something on her mind. As he drew her into his arms, she sniffed the air.

"My goodness. I'm surprised your dragon fire didn't set light to all that alcohol," she teased.

"Ms. Fire Safety." He kissed the tip of her nose. "What's troubling you?"

"I saw Dalton Hilger today."

"Your ex? The FBI guy?"

She nodded. "He was in the coffee shop Sarange and I went to. He didn't see me, but I know it was him." Her eyes grew more troubled. "He must be in town because of the Incinerator."

"That's not necessarily a bad thing. It could mean they're getting close."

"I tried telling myself that." Her expression became even more gloomy. "But what if it turns out Teine is the Incinerator? Human cops won't be able to arrest her. That means Dalton is in danger."

"But you can't call him and warn him because you'll give away your location," Torque said, following her thought processes.

"Exactly, although I could live with telling him everything if I thought it would end this nightmare. It's more about not wanting to draw the FBI's attention to you and your friends." She sighed, resting her cheek against his chest. "Anyway, Dalton would think I was crazy if I tried to tell him all of this mayhem was caused by a woman with supernatural powers."

Sensing her need for reassurance, Torque held her close. It was always this way when her two worlds were in conflict. He knew she had made a commitment to him and this new life, but sometimes she was torn. The scientist in her was strong. Hollie hadn't been raised in the ways of magic and legend. and even after a dragon flight, it was hard for her to accept them.

After a few minutes, she raised her head. Lifting a hand to stroke his cheek, she smiled. "You know how to make me feel better. I love you so much, Torque."

Emotions stormed through him, setting his blood alight. Even though he had always known Hollie loved him, it was the first time she'd said those words out loud. Hearing them from her lips made his world feel right. No matter what else happened, he would always treasure this moment. Before he could push past the lump in his throat to respond, Hollie was speaking again.

"When we talked earlier about finding a way to have forever...that would mean everything to me." Her eyes were shining with unshed tears.

He loved Hollie more than life. She was his mate. She loved him in return. Ged had told him of a way they could be together... Torque almost lost it and told her about the dragon mark. Almost.

"I love you, too. More than words can say." He kissed her forehead. "And I'll keep on searching for a way to find forever."

"I miss the Monster." Dev was lying stretched out on a sofa in the bus, eating potato chips and drinking soda.

Hollie looked up from her new laptop. "This bus is almost identical."

He gave a theatrical sigh. "It doesn't have the ambience."

"You mean it doesn't have the same memories and beer stains," Torque said.

They had left Dallas immediately after the performance, traveling overnight. The mood was curiously subdued, but Hollie wondered if that could have something to do with Khan's absence. The larger-than-life lead singer was driving Sarange and Karina in their own car.

"Rock 'n' roll and baby sick? I don't think so." That had been Sarange's official explanation. Privately, she'd told Hollie that her morning sickness was getting worse. "All-day sickness, more like."

The closer they got to Denver, the more restless Torque was becoming. Hollie knew the reason, of course. Beast had one sell-out performance on the following night, but that wasn't the explanation for his nerves. No, his roller-coaster mood was all about the approaching reunion with Alban and Deigh. Ged had arranged VIP passes for Torque's guests and they would be staying in the same luxury hotel as the band. Hollie had emailed Alban with the arrangements and they would be arriving in Denver on the following day. All Torque had to do was charm Deigh into revealing more about her sister without raising any false hopes that he was in love with her. No pressure.

Hollie was worried, as well. The high drama of the encounter on the snowy mountaintop was fresh in her mind. While she trusted Torque to protect her from Deigh, she didn't want to feel all that malevolence up close once again. She had enough to think about without Deigh's ice-dagger stares and swooning glances in Torque's direction.

She had left Dallas on a sigh of relief, feeling she could breathe again when she saw the city's bright lights receding in the distance. There had been no Incinerator attacks there. Could that be because the arsonist knew the FBI were on his tail? Or, if Teine was the arsonist, had Deigh told her sister about their visit to her chilly lair? Whatever the reason, Hollie was glad there had been no fire-related drama recently.

In addition to his unease about meeting Deigh again, Hollie sensed a deeper trouble going on inside Torque. She knew it was linked to her. It was evident in the way he watched her. As though she was a dear memory that would soon be gone. It scared her, but when she tried to talk to him about it, he became evasive. Now, unable to focus on the screen in front of her, she wandered into the kitchen in search of coffee.

Ged was there and he poured her a cup, pointing to

cream and sugar. Hollie shook her head. "Strong and black is what I need."

He was watching her face with something that looked a lot like sympathy. "He told you about the dragon mark, then?"

She paused in the act of blowing on her coffee. She had always known this man was not what he appeared to be. The hold he had over the members of the band was stronger than just that of their manager. Once she knew they were shifters, Torque had talked about the part Ged played in rescuing them. Now it seemed he might also have another role. That of confidant.

"Hmm." It was as noncommittal as she could get. She wanted to encourage Ged to keep speaking without admitting she had no idea what he was talking about.

"It's a huge step. Walking into a pit of fire and allowing your mate to sink his fangs into your neck? All so you can become a dragon convert? It's not quite the same as the whole dress, flowers and cake scenario most mortal women dream of. I expect you need some time to think about it."

"Yeah." Hollie cast a glance along the corridor toward the living area. She could just see Torque's profile as he leaned against the window, gazing moodily out at the view. "I guess I do."

When she returned to her seat next to Torque, she tucked her feet up under her and rested her chin on his shoulder. They watched the scenery flash past in silence for a minute or two. "What were you and Ged talking about in there?"

She turned her face into his neck, hiding a smile. "How to play with fire."

"I guess you're already an expert on that." There was a hint of surprise in his voice.

"It's a subject about which I aim to become even more knowledgeable."

Chapter 16

Alban called Torque to confirm that he and Deigh had arrived and they arranged to meet prior to the concert. Apart from the fact that his old friend was in town, Torque could find nothing positive in the situation. The truth was he hated subterfuge. He hated bringing Deigh into his new life. He hated that Hollie was being pushed to the sidelines while she was here. He hated every goddamn thing about it.

"If the Incinerator would step out of the shadows and face me, none of this would be necessary." He slouched moodily around the hotel suite as the time to leave drew closer.

"I don't like this any more than you do, but if Deigh gives you some more details about Teine, then it will be worth it." Hollie linked her fingers behind his neck, pulling him down for a kiss. "Just as long as she keeps her icy hands to herself."

"Hollie, I am going to take her to dinner, ask her

some questions and leave. You can't possibly be worried there will be anything more to it."

She laughed. "I'm not. And I'll be with Alban."

"You'll have more fun." He frowned. "And you should be with me now when I'm going to meet them."

Hollie shook her head. "The idea is to get on Deigh's good side. There's no point in antagonizing her by turning up with me holding your hand. If I stay in the background, it may keep her sweet."

Torque ran a hand through his hair. "Deigh is mad. Did I mention that? I can't believe we're having a conversation about keeping her sweet. It's like discussing the best way to feed a rabid dog."

Hollie stepped back, studying him with her head on one side. "If looks have anything to do with it, she won't be able to resist you."

He growled. "I am not a sacrifice to the ice sorceress. What will you do while I'm gone? The concert doesn't start for hours."

"I told Sarange I'd take Karina off her hands. I'll take her out for a walk."

"Won't Sarange go with you?" Torque asked.

"I don't think she's feeling too great."

Torque spared a moment to feel surprised. Sarange was a werewolf and a superfit human. He'd never known her have a minute's illness. "I hope she's okay."

"I'm sure she'll be fine." Hollie placed a hand in the small of his back, pointing him toward the door. "I don't want to send you off to meet another woman, but this has to be done."

"Kiss me again to make it bearable."

When her lips met his and her taste flowed through him, everything else faded away. His inner dragon surged, demanding release, urging him to possess her.

Forcing himself to retain control, Torque still couldn't keep his hands from her. Gripping her hips in a rough, possessive hold, he pulled her tight against him, letting her feel his arousal. Hollie gasped at the pressure and pushed back. Shaking at the effort to maintain control, Torque covered her mouth with his, dominating her, forcing her to open for his possession. Her enthusiastic response stoked the fire higher and higher until they broke apart trembling.

"Ah, Hollie." He rested his forehead against hers. "What you do to me."

"Maybe you could be a few minutes late…"

Torque sucked in a harsh breath, leaning back against the door as she sank to her knees. A tremor of pleasure ran through Hollie's body as she grasped his thighs and leaned into him. She paused for a moment, pressing her face to the bulge in his jeans as she inhaled his scent.

When she reached for his zipper and button and freed his straining erection from the confines of his jeans, Torque's heart rate skyrocketed. Tangling his hands in her hair, he gave himself up to a firestorm of emotion.

A soft whimper came from Hollie as she moistened her lips and pursed them to form a heart shape. When she leaned forward and softly kissed the head of his cock, Torque almost went into orbit. Hollie's eyelids fluttered closed as she sighed. Slowly, she kissed down his shaft and back up again.

Opening her eyes, she kept her gaze fixed on Torque's face as she licked all the way around his sensitive tip. Her pink tongue was warm and slightly rough and his flesh twitched at the delicious sensation.

His erection hardened and tightened as she moved her mouth along it, kissing and licking, judging to perfection where the most sensitive nerve endings were concentrated. Now and then, she applied a slight sucking pressure that spiked his pleasure even higher.

"Hollie…" He couldn't take much more of this.

Shifting position, she brought her open mouth to him and closed her lips over the crown. Bobbing her head in a slow up and down motion, she relaxed her mouth on the downstroke, sucking and tonguing him as she glided back up. Watching his throbbing flesh slide in and out of her mouth was the most erotic thing he had ever seen.

The pressure began to build deep inside him, the veins at his base pulsing and burning, aching for release. Holding the sides of her head, he moved his hips in time with her mouth, feeling her moans vibrate all the way along his length. "So close."

With Hollie's hot, sweet mouth surrounding him and her tongue lapping him, he was lost in her. Throwing his head back, he closed his eyes, and braced his leg muscles, letting it hit. An orgasm close to explosion pounded his hypersensitive nerve endings at full force. Rapture was like liquid fire being poured into him, triggering a series of stunning aftershocks. Slowly, he came down from the searing high.

Feeling Hollie gently withdrawing her lips, he opened his eyes and looked down at her upturned face. Her eyes were bright with tears. His hands were still on either side of her head, but his grip was light. Even during the storm of his emotions, he was sure he hadn't tightened it.

"Tell me I didn't hurt you." His voice was shaky.

"Of course you didn't hurt me." She smiled and he was reassured that her tears were an expression of how intensely she had felt their physical connection. "You're my dragon."

Leaning down, he placed his hands under her arms

and lifted her to him. Time. Since they'd met, it was the one thing they had never had enough of. Even if they managed forever, would he be able to find the words to tell her how she made him feel?

"And you're mine, Hollie. All mine."

Hollie had researched places to go with a one-year-old and decided on the aquarium. It proved to be a hit with Karina, who was fascinated by the sea creatures. Cooing and babbling, she waved her arms delightedly as Hollie, with two bodyguards following at a discreet distance, pushed the stroller around the exhibits.

Hollie herself was even more entertained by Karina's delight than she was by the creatures around her, but nothing could keep her thoughts from straying to Torque. She knew how emotionally draining the meeting with Deigh would be and wished she was there at his side to support him. Anything that took him back to his past was hard for him. Knowing the story of what Teine had done to him, she could understand why.

Alongside the grief he felt for his family and the life he had lost, his pride and self-esteem had been destroyed. Torque was an alpha-male, a leader among dragons. Teine had taken that from him, leaving him with no one to lead and shackling him to her. Hollie's heart cried out at the thought of her proud dragon-shifter chained and imprisoned, unable to soar.

As well as her concerns for Torque's well-being, she was still buzzing with erotic memories from the recent scene in their hotel room. Although her body had been overheated, it was the emotional connection that burned deepest. Torque was in her soul, and that was what made sex between them so good. She bit back a smile. *Good? I meant rapturous.*

Although Karina couldn't talk, she was good at making her needs known. When she lost interest in her surroundings and started lifting her arms up to come out of the stroller, Hollie figured it was time to stop for refreshments. Finding a seat in an area away from the crowds that thronged the main walkways, she took Karina's bottle out of its thermos and lifted the little girl onto her knee. The baby gave a sigh of contentment as she started to drink.

Sarange's instructions had been clear. Karina would have formula and then some solid food. Next would come a nap in the stroller, followed by a diaper change.

"You're going to be gentle with me on that one, aren't you, sweetheart? I'm new to all this." She murmured the words into Karina's hair, and the little girl gently patted Hollie's cheek as she drank.

Hollie became vaguely aware of someone approaching her, only looking up when that person paused right in front of her. Her gaze traveled upward from a pair of hand-stitched tan shoes—*I know those shoes!*—following the suit pants, white shirt and navy tie upward until she was looking into Dalton's frowning gray eyes.

Among the dozens of thoughts swirling through her mind in that instant, there was only one that mattered. Once again it fixed itself in her mind.

This is not a coincidence.

"Did you follow me here?" Of course he had followed her. The chances of seeing him in the coffee shop in Dallas were remote. Seeing him a second time in Denver? Hollie's mathematical brain tried and failed to calculate those odds.

"It's nice to see you, as well, Hols." He took a seat next to her, nodding at Karina. "Whose baby?"

"A friend's. Answer the question, Dalton. Did you follow me?"

Conscious of one of the bodyguards signaling to her, she caught his eye and shook her head, the gesture so slight that it went unseen by Dalton. Hollie and Karina were in no danger and she needed answers.

"Kind of." He grinned and she relaxed a little. This was *Dalton*. He was her friend and her colleague. Or ex-colleague. She still didn't know what was going on with her FBI status. Right now it was about the least important thing about this whole situation. "Would you believe me if I said I saw you coming out of your hotel? I mean, once that happened, I had to go after you, didn't I?"

"Why didn't you approach me as soon as you saw me? Why wait until now?"

"Jeez, Hollie. Why all these questions? This is *me*." He looked slightly bemused as he echoed her own thoughts. "If you must know, I was making sure you weren't being followed by anyone else."

"Oh." She subsided, chewing her lip. His reply sounded reasonable. Scary, but reasonable. "This is about the Incinerator."

"Of course it is. What the hell else did you think it was about?" He gave her a sidelong look. "So you finally did something about it."

Hollie could guess what was coming, but she was going to look him in the eye and force him to say it. "About what?"

"Come on, Hols. *Him*. Torque. You're obsessed with him. Always have been. It's what split us up. Now you're with him."

Dalton used to laugh about her "*Torque-thing*." It had been a joke between them. *It's what split us up?* It was like he was trying to rewrite history. It was also *not* like Dalton.

She drew in a breath. "I wouldn't have this sort of conversation back when we were dating, Dalton, so I'm sure as hell not doing it now. You know better than to think I would give you a say in how I live my life."

"The difference this time is it matters to an investigation." There was a hint of triumph in his voice.

"I know that," she snapped back at him. "*I* told McLain the Incinerator was targeting places Torque had been. Now instead of trying to score points because you don't like him, tell me if you are any closer to finding the person who killed her."

Hollie forced herself to get a grip on her anger, partly because it wasn't helpful, but mostly for Karina's sake. Cuddling the little girl's warm, plump body close, she reviewed the situation. Dalton had shown no sign of surprise when she let slip that she had told McLain about the connection to Torque. That must mean the FBI had been investigating the link all along. She wasn't sure whether that was good, or bad. On the one hand, no one had come pointing any fingers at Torque or interrogating him and his friends. On the other, they hadn't caught the Incinerator, either.

"I'll be honest with you, this case is as puzzling as ever." Dalton dug his hands into his jacket pocket and stretched his long legs in front of him.

"But you're here," Hollie persisted. "There must be a reason for that."

"You've been right so far. Wherever Torque goes, the Incinerator follows. It made sense for the investigation to be there, as well."

"But no one from the FBI has spoken to Torque." Hollie was confused. She had assumed that, when the investigators kept their distance, it must mean that McLain hadn't told the team of Hollie's suspicions. If they knew Torque was the link, keeping their distance made no sense.

"We haven't needed to do an interview, Hollie. Not when you've been right up close to him."

The note in Dalton's voice surprised her and she turned her head to look at him more closely. She could see hurt in his eyes, and it shocked her. After all this time, he still cared that much?

The pained look deepened. "Even sharing a room. When McLain sent you undercover, she couldn't have expected that sort of dedication from you."

"McLain told you I was working undercover?" Hollie frowned. "You never mentioned that when I called you."

His smile was lopsided. "I guess you're not the only one who's good at keeping secrets."

"This isn't about scoring points, Dalton." A little flare of anger made her speak more harshly than she'd intended. "We're on the same side here. We both want to catch a dangerous arsonist before he does any more harm."

As she finished talking, Karina drank the last of her milk and sat up straighter. The baby regarded Dalton with wide golden eyes for a moment or two. Apparently deciding she didn't like this stranger, she nestled closer to Hollie, burying her face in the front of her blouse and starting to cry.

"Look, you're busy and I have to go." Dalton got to his feet.

Hollie wanted to cry out in annoyance. All Dalton had given her was a series of nonanswers. "I'll call you."

Her priority was trying to soothe Karina, but the whole situation was intensely frustrating. If anything,

Dalton's presence in Denver had deepened the mystery. As she watched him walk away, the questions she wanted to ask rose to her lips. She couldn't pursue them now, but she was determined to get the answers from him. He had spoken as if her undercover role was still being treated as part of the investigation. Well, if that was the case, he could step up and brief her fully.

"Hey, sweetheart." She reached into Karina's bag and produced a tub of pasta. "Want some of this?"

Karina did a quick check to make sure Dalton had really gone before clapping her hands to express approval of the plan. As she fed the baby her lunch, Hollie's thoughts returned to Torque. She really wanted to see him, or call him, to tell him about the encounter with Dalton. Bumping into her former boyfriend at the same time Torque was meeting his evil ex was the worst kind of timing.

"These days, there doesn't seem to be any other kind," she said to Karina. In response, the baby cheerfully smeared pasta sauce onto the front of Hollie's blouse.

Torque met Alban and Deigh in the hotel lobby. Alban greeted him with a look of relief that told Torque everything he needed to know. Not that he had ever imagined a trans-Atlantic journey with Deigh would be easy.

He had seen Deigh away from her mountaintop often enough to know that the key to her behavior lay in the decisions she made. When she chose, she could be charming. It never lasted long, but she could sustain the appearance of normality for short periods. It was, after all, how she had tricked Torque into their brief relationship.

With relief, he observed that, on this occasion, she appeared inclined to be pleasant. The only oddity was her clothing. Although she had disposed of her ice princess robes, she hadn't taken account of the hot and humid weather. Deigh wore white jeans and a pale blue sweater with a long white coat over the top.

"Did you mention that, even at night, it's over seventy degrees?" Torque murmured to Alban as they headed out to a waiting cab.

"No, because I've given up on trying to make conversation of any kind," Alban said. "If it's not about you, my friend, she doesn't want to know."

Torque winced. Those words didn't inspire him with confidence that he was going to be able to keep this light and walk away. His mood lowered even further when, once they were in the cab, Deigh pressed up close to him, her eyes shining as she gazed at his face.

Ice sorceress unleashed. Was this really such a good plan?

That night's performance was at Denver's iconic Red Rocks Amphitheater. The naturally formed, outdoor venue was world-famous for its acoustics and ambience. Torque had been looking forward to this concert more than any other on the tour. Now he was wishing himself a thousand miles away. Just him and Hollie on a deserted island somewhere…maybe recreating the scene from the hotel room earlier.

Aware that Deigh was talking, he pulled himself back from the edge of a delicious fantasy.

"Where is your little pet?"

Torque's inner dragon fired up at those derogatory words used in connection with Hollie. With an effort, he forced himself to remain calm. This was what Deigh did best. By prodding and pushing, she would get him to reveal his feelings. If he let her. "I don't know what you mean."

Even away from her natural environment, her laugh sounded like breaking ice. "Come, now. Your golden girl with the emerald eyes."

He stared at her for a moment. The words were uncomfortably close to Teine's prediction about his future and to the words of the latest email. But he was on edge, unnerved by Deigh's presence, uncomfortable with this whole situation and missing Hollie. Jumping at shadows. Or seeing coincidences where they didn't exist.

"We're here." Relieved to have a distraction from Deigh's probing, Torque pointed out of the window at the majestic jutting rocks. The cab took them around to the rear of the stage, where they exited the vehicle.

The other band members were already there and Torque experienced a profound sense of relief when he saw them. As always, the team came together in times of difficulty and he could feel the hostility toward Deigh coming off his friends in waves. The problem was, he was fairly sure she could feel it, too. A slight smile tugged at the corners of her lips as she looked around her. Torque wanted to warn his bandmates. *She thrives on conflict. Hating her will only make her stronger.* He consoled himself that the members of Beast could look after themselves.

Alban provided a contrasting ray of light in the tense atmosphere. Abandoning his naturally serious demeanor, he appeared genuinely stagestruck and interested in the workings of the special effects. As Ged gave him a guided tour, Torque was left alone with Deigh. He sent a help-me glance in Khan's direction. To his relief, the tiger-shifter sauntered over. It was a classic case of antagonism at first sight.

"I don't wish for company." Deigh tried her usual icy tones.

"I have a daughter who has that same attitude." Khan's grin was more of a snarl. "She gets away with it because she's only twelve months old. And she's pretty."

The drop in temperature had nothing to do with Deigh's powers. She turned to Torque. "When do we leave here?"

He indicated the stage and, beyond that, the audience of thousands. "There's the little matter of a concert for all these people who have paid good money and traveled to see us."

She hunched a shoulder. "I hope you will make sure it is over fast."

It was with relief that Torque handed her and Alban over to Rick so he could escort them to the VIP area. Once they'd gone, he tried to focus on the performance. Those fans had come to see Beast, and he wasn't going to sell them short.

A tap on his shoulder made him turn abruptly and he encountered Hollie's mischievous smile. Instantly, his restless spirit was soothed. "I'll be with Ged." She jerked her thumb in his manager's direction. "When I saw Alban and Deigh leaving I wanted to say hi."

Casting a quick glance around, he backed her up against a bank of speakers, kissing her until she murmured a protest. "I think the others are ready to go onstage."

He groaned. "I hate it when real life gets in the way."

She patted his cheek. "We can finish this later."

"Oh, we will." He watched with pleasure as the blush stained her cheeks pink. "I owe you from earlier, remember?"

With one final kiss on her parted lips, he bounded

toward the stage. A heavy, thumping beat filled the air, and Torque caught a glimpse of the almost ten-thousand-strong audience. Excitement, anticipation and exultation showed on the waiting faces. Thick, theatrical smoke rolled like fog from the stage and out into the waiting crowd and, within it, colored strobe lights danced in time with the music.

Giant LED screens were positioned at the rear of the stage. On them, alternating images of fire, close-ups of snarling animals and a stylized symbol that looked like three entwined number sixes flashed up. At the side of the stage, random explosions went off, shooting orange flames into the air.

A glance at the VIP area showed him Alban was getting into the mood of the concert. Torque could see him joining in with people around him and putting his fingers on either side of his head to make devil horns as he moved in time with the beat. Next to him, Deigh stood as still as an ice statue.

The tension built further as the crowd sensed something changing. The lighting shifted, becoming focused on a podium at the rear of the stage that supported Diablo's vast, gleaming circular wall of drums. Even above the music, the roar of the crowd filled the air as the drummer ran on from the side of the stage and vaulted into his seat behind the drums. His chest was bare and his tattooed biceps bulged as he pounded out a furious beat, his blue-black hair flopping forward to cover his face.

Torque nodded to Dev on the opposite side of the stage and, synchronizing their movements to perfection, the two of them dived into place. For this time, while he had his guitar in his hands and those devoted fans in front of him, he could lose himself in the moment.

The band was more than the sum of its parts and the members reenergized each other through their music.

Torque let the power of Beast wash over him, secure that Hollie was close by. He needed this, needed the contrasting raw power of the performance and the healing balm of his mate. Both would help him conserve his strength for the coming battle of wits.

Chapter 17

After the concert, Hollie took Alban to the Mountainview Steak House. Having eyed the menu thoughtfully, he cast it aside.

"You know what I'd like?"

She regarded him with a smile. "A large steak, burned to a crisp, and no sides? Better yet, two large steaks."

"How did you guess?"

"I may have dined with a dragon once or twice before tonight."

She gave their order to the waiter, opting for a slightly more conservative choice of burger and fries for herself.

"Ah, yes." Alban gazed out the window at the nighttime view of the city with its mountain backdrop. "I wonder how Torque is getting along with his quest to learn more about Deigh's evil twin."

"Is there an evil twin in that partnership?" Hollie asked. "From what I've seen of Deigh, she's not exactly one of the good guys."

"But you have never encountered Teine," Alban pointed out. "She makes Deigh look like a Girl Scout."

"Were they born evil? Or did something happen to make them that way?" Hollie asked.

"Now, there you have me." Alban frowned over the question. "As you know, to become sorcerers, they had to rise through the witching ranks and must also have had magical parentage. Their father was one of the greats. Known throughout the Highlands and beyond, he was Draoidh. The name itself means 'magic.' His time was before my birth, you understand, but the legends have been passed down."

Alban was a natural storyteller and Hollie found that listening to him, sipping her beer and enjoying the mood all took her mind off her worries about what Torque must be enduring.

"Although Draoidh was powerful, he was benevolent. Until a rival came along. Her name was Eile. She was a sorceress who wanted to steal Draoidh's place as the dominant force in the Highlands. The only way she could do that was to take Draoidh's magic from him. The two fought constantly, with no true outcome. Gradually, Draoidh changed. He was no longer the benign presence the Highlands had come to trust. Driven by his desire to defeat Eile, he became bitter and vengeful. One day, the two met in a mighty confrontation. Storms raged over the mountains for days. The outcome was unexpected."

His story was interrupted by the arrival of their food. Once they were alone again, Hollie, who had become engrossed in the ancient tale, leaned forward. "What happened?"

"Somehow Eile had managed to overpower and kill her stronger rival. A glimpse into her method became clear when it was seen a few months later that she was pregnant. Once or twice, she boasted that she had seduced Draoidh and murdered him while he was...um, distracted."

"Nice lady. I'm guessing she didn't find herself another partner?"

Alban laughed. "I don't think she was looking. Eile also claimed that she had absorbed all of Draoidh's power. She was now twice as strong. When her child was born, it would have enough magic for two. It was later seen as a prophecy."

"Because she had twins?"

"Yes, although their separateness started right from birth. Eile kept them hidden up on her mountaintop and didn't show them off among the villages. All anyone ever knew was that they were fire and ice."

"What happened to Eile?" Hollie asked.

"The rumor is that Teine killed her. Some argument over her mother trying to stop her throwing rocks at the mountain goats. No one knows for sure, but Eile disappeared about six years after the twins were born."

"Whoa." Hollie spluttered on a mouthful of beer. "You're saying Teine could have killed her mother when she was *six*?"

Alban tilted his head to one side. "She may have been seven," he conceded.

Hollie held her hands up. "Maybe Deigh is the good twin, after all. Have you ever seen them together to make a comparison?"

Alban shook his head. "I don't know anyone who has."

"Weird."

"Look at the parents," Alban said.

Hollie started to giggle. When he raised his brows in a

question, she tried to explain. "I can't believe I'm sitting here with a dragon, talking about two evil sorceresses."

He wagged a finger at her. "That's because you are used to the company of a rough-and-ready sort of dragon. I'm an intellectual. I prefer the slow and steady approach. Some things cannot be rushed. Time finds a way to heal all wounds and settle all scores."

"What do you mean? Are you talking about Teine setting these fires as revenge?"

He took a sip of his drink. "Strangely enough, I'd forgotten about Teine."

Torque had no idea what sort of cuisine would impress Deigh, but he knew she liked snow and mountains. The Rooftop Restaurant had views across the whole city toward the distant peaks. The care he had taken in choosing somewhere that would appeal to her appeared to have been wasted, however. Deigh barely spared a glance at her surroundings, preferring to fix her gaze on Torque's face.

There was an awkward moment when they were shown to their table and the server approached her. If looks could kill—and Torque reminded himself that, in Deigh's case, looks actually *could* kill if she chose to let them—the poor guy would have dropped dead on the floor the instant he raised his hands in her direction.

"He's offering to take your coat."

"Oh." She appeared to weigh the situation. Surely she wasn't going to keep it on? After a moment or two, she shrugged the garment off and handed it to the server. Her thick high-necked, long-sleeved sweater still kept her well covered.

They took their seats and Torque ordered a beer. "What do you want to drink?" he asked Deigh.

"Iced water." She waved an impatient hand.

Figures. Her veins probably needed a top-up.

"Tell me why I'm here."

Torque was pinned in the light blue beam of her gaze. "Pardon?"

"I could continue to torture you while we pretend you brought me all this way because you want my company, but we both know that's not true." Deigh smiled and Torque's skin went cold all over. "I will regret bringing this little charade to an end. You know how much I enjoy causing pain."

Torque leaned back in his chair, relieved that the pretense was over. Of course, Deigh would not allow this deception to go unpunished. She would demand a retribution and he knew from experience she would do her best to make it hurt. His task now was to keep her focused on him. Deflect her attention from Alban. And, most of all, keep that icy glare away from Hollie.

"If you knew there was an ulterior motive, why come here?"

Her laugh would shatter an iceberg. "The temptation to torment you was irresistible." Her gaze softened. "*You* are irresistible."

Torque squirmed slightly. "This is about Teine."

Their drinks arrived and she sipped her iced water slowly. "It always is. Do you know how it feels to have spent my life fighting my way out from beneath her shadow?"

Of the two sisters, Teine, with her fiery personality, was the one who naturally drew the most attention. Had he given the question any thought, Torque would have said that was the way Deigh preferred it. Now it seemed he'd have been wrong.

"She's alive." He didn't need to phrase it as a question. He knew it was true.

Deigh sighed as she gazed out at the mountains. "I wish she wasn't."

"Where is she, Deigh?"

Something flickered in the depths of her eyes. Something dark and malignant. It rocked Torque back in his seat and planted a seed of doubt in his mind. Then it was gone and he was left questioning his own sanity.

"For once, look beyond your dragon arrogance." Deigh's voice was almost sad. "The answer is staring you in the face, but you refuse to accept it."

Torque wasn't in the mood for her games. "Is Teine the person who is setting fire to these buildings?"

"Can't you see it yet?" She got to her feet, leaning across the table until her face was inches from his. Gold sparks brightened the blue depths of her eyes. "Are you still so blind?"

Whirling away from him, she ran toward the exit. Muttering a curse, Torque threw some cash down on the table and followed her. Part of him wanted to let her go, but the consequence of leaving an angry sorceress loose in a built-up area wasn't one he wanted on his conscience. He found Deigh giving the elevator doors an icy glare. Clearly, she thought she could make them open by force of will.

He pressed the button. "Wait here while I get your coat."

Her eyes narrowed as she considered the situation, and then she nodded. Torque returned with her coat just as the elevator doors closed with her inside. Racing down the stairs, he reached street level in time to see Deigh exiting the building. Luckily, her silvery hair made her hard to miss even in the darkness. He chased after her, catching hold of her arm as she reached a quiet side street.

"Explain it to me, Deigh. Tell me what I'm missing."

She started to laugh, and the sound chilled him... because it didn't *chill* him. It wasn't Deigh's laugh. As he stared at her, she jerked her arm away from him. Because he still had a tight grip on her sweater, the fabric tore, revealing the skin of her arm. Torque started to apologize; then his attention was caught by the scars on her flesh. They were the marks of someone who had survived a terrible fire. The sort of blaze caused by the breath of a dragon...

He raised his eyes to her face. "Teine?"

She made a sound that was somewhere between a sob and a laugh. "You see it at last."

Torque watched in horrified fascination as a battle for control seemed to take place within her. One minute, Deigh's cool features were visible; the next they were replaced with Teine's stormy visage.

"I don't understand."

"Of course you don't. No one does." She dropped to her knees on the deserted sidewalk, wrapping her arms around her waist. "There never was a Teine *and* a Deigh. We are one, not two. Our mother told the story that she gave birth to twins because the enormous power we inherited was enough for two. We are fire and ice, but we both reside within one body and the fight for dominance is constant."

Torque ran a hand through his hair, trying to process what she was saying. Essentially, he was looking at a case of a magical split personality. Two people—two sorceresses—living in one body.

"What name do you prefer?" he asked.

Her lips drew back in a snarl. "I am Teine. Fire is always stronger than ice."

He stared down at her in fascination. Two beings who hated each other sharing a body? It must be the ultimate torture. No matter how much he hated Teine for what she had done to him, he pitied her for the torment he could see on her face. "Are you the Incinerator?"

Her laughter alternated between Deigh's icy tinkle and Teine's heated gales. "You are still not looking in the right direction. Open your eyes, *mo dragon*."

Then she was on her feet and sprinting away from him. Torque ran after her, closing the distance between them. Ahead of them, he could see bright lights, noise and people. If Teine headed that way, he would lose her. Worse, she could do untold damage in a group of mortals. He wasn't prepared to force her into a confrontation in a crowd and risk a demonstration of her powers.

As they drew closer, he saw it was a fairground. There were a few rides and stalls. To one side, an old-fashioned, steam-driven calliope wheezed out an annoyingly repetitive tune. As Teine darted into the throng of people, Torque lost sight of her.

Slumping against a wall, he pulled out his cell phone. His mind was reeling from what he'd just learned, but his first thought was for Hollie. Hopefully, she was still with Alban, and if Teine came for her, he would be able to protect her. If they were already back at the hotel, Torque could tell her to go to Ged or Khan and wait with them until he arrived.

He stared at his cell in fury as her number rang, then went straight to voice mail.

Although it was after eleven when Hollie and Alban got back to the hotel, once she reached her room there was only one thought on her mind. No matter how late it was, she was calling Dalton.

When she tried the number she had stored in her cell phone for him, she got a message that it wasn't recognized. Frowning, she tapped the digits in from memory. The message was the same. Of course, there was nothing to stop an FBI agent changing his number in the middle of an investigation. It was just…odd. And the prickling feeling of dread running down her spine intensified.

Calling the twenty-four-hour number for the Newark field office, she explained her problem to the operator. "I'm trying to get in touch with Agent Hilger."

Did she sense a slight hesitation? "Who's calling?"

"I'd prefer to speak direct to Agent Hilger. I just need his cell phone number."

"Agent Hilger is no longer on active duty—"

Hollie ended the call fast, her heart thumping out a mad, new rhythm. What the *hell* was going on? How could Dalton be in town as part of the Incinerator investigation if he was no longer on the team? And what had happened to get him taken off active duty? Her head was spinning out of control when her cell phone rang.

She experienced a wild moment of hope that it might be Dalton calling her to explain the misunderstanding. It was Khan.

"Hollie? I hate to ask you this so late at night, but Sarange is really ill. She's been throwing up nonstop for hours. I need to get her to a doctor friend of Ged's so he can get some fluids into her…"

"I'll stay with Karina." She was on her feet, placing her cell on the bedside table as she spoke.

"You're a lifesaver."

Khan and Sarange had a suite just along the corridor. When Hollie arrived, Khan was already waiting by the door. He drew her into one of his signature hugs. At his side, Sarange looked like a pale shadow of her usual self.

"Thank you." She kissed Hollie's cheek. "We can't go to the emergency room. Shifter DNA makes everything that bit more complicated. But we'll be back as soon as we can."

"Karina and I will be fine. You go and get well."

After they'd gone, Hollie checked on the baby. Karina was sound asleep in her crib. Going back into the sitting room, she paused, realizing she'd left her cell phone in her own suite. Wanting to let Torque know where she was, she called down to reception.

"When he returns, can you let him know I'm baby-sitting in the Colorado Suite, please?"

With a restlessness fueled by the information she'd been given about Dalton, she wandered the luxurious suite. It was almost identical to the one she and Torque were in, except this one had different views. Standing on the balcony overlooking the perfectly manicured hotel gardens, she drank in the mountain vista, trying to make some sense of her disordered thoughts.

When she had seen Dalton at the aquarium, there had been nothing in his demeanor to make her suspect a problem. He had been evasive, but otherwise he had appeared to be his usual self. *No longer on active duty.* That could mean so many things. Was he ill? Oh, dear Lord, was Dalton *dying*? She took a breath, getting her disordered thoughts under control. It was probably less dramatic. He could be on a misconduct charge. If that was the case, why would he be here, pretending to be part of the investigation? Could this all be a terrible mistake? Maybe the operator she spoke to had gotten the name wrong. Dalton was the most dedicated agent Hollie had ever known. The FBI was his life. She couldn't imagine he would allow anything to jeopardize that.

But those words had been so final. *No longer on active duty.* Not "unavailable" or "out of the office." Something drastic had happened, and it had happened fast.

Her musings were interrupted by a cry from the bedroom and she left the balcony with a feeling of relief. At least dealing with the baby would give her a break from her other problems for a while.

"It's okay, sweetheart, I'm here—" She walked into the bedroom and stopped in shock. Dalton was standing beside the crib holding Karina.

"She scratched me." Dalton cradled his hand against his chest, staring at the baby in horror. Blood was already running down his wrist and soaking into his white shirt.

"Good. I hope it hurt." Shock took second place to the need to care for the baby. Hollie strode forward, taking Karina from him and holding the sobbing child to her shoulder. Stroking her hair, she felt a fierce pride in the little shifter. "There, there. It's okay. I've got you now."

"What kind of baby leaves marks like that?" Dalton held up his hand, showing the deep cuts in his flesh.

One who has a tiger-shifter for a dad and a werewolf for a mom. Hollie decided not to mention Karina's parentage. "One that's scared out of her wits because you woke her up and she doesn't know you. What were you thinking? Why are you even here?" Trying to keep her anger and outrage under control so she didn't alarm Karina was proving difficult. "And how the hell did you get into this room?"

As she spoke, Dalton started to smile. Then she saw the gun in his other hand and everything fell into place. All at once. Horribly and easily. Hollie raised a shaking hand to her lips. "*You* are the Incinerator." Her voice refused to rise above a whisper. "Why, Dalton?"

His smile twisted, becoming something that made her glad Karina's face was still turned away from him.

"Why? Because, even when we were together, you wanted *him*. Do you know how it feels to be second best to an album cover? Well, now you've made your dream come true." He gave a mirthless laugh. "Only I'm going to turn it into a nightmare, Hollie. For both of you."

Torque had never wanted to shift so badly. His inner dragon was making a strong case for just forgetting convention and taking flight across the city. So what if he was seen? He'd cope with the wild speculation about dragons over Denver once he knew Hollie was safe. In the end, his human common sense prevailed and he ran faster than he had ever done. By the time he reached the hotel, his lungs were on fire. If Teine, or Deigh, or whatever the hell she was calling herself right now, had gotten there before him, it would only be because she'd found a way to teleport since the last time they met.

He was about to dash across the lobby to the elevators when the desk clerk called out to him. "I have a message for you from Ms. Brown. She asked me to let you know that she's babysitting in the Colorado Suite."

Calling out a quick word of thanks, Torque headed up to Khan's suite. As least he knew where Hollie was, although he didn't know why she was with Khan and Sarange. He also had no idea why she wasn't answering his calls.

Leaving the elevator at a run, he hammered on the door of the Colorado Suite…and was greeted by silence.

"Khan, open the damn door." Even as he shouted to his friend, he already knew the suite was empty.

The fury that surged through him was so powerful it took everything he had to contain his inner dragon. *Think. Focus.* He couldn't accept that there had been enough time for Teine to reach the hotel and snatch Hollie before he got here. And where the hell were Khan and Sarange? He was pulling his cell phone out of his pocket, ready to call everyone he knew, when the spots of blood on the carpet just outside the door caught his attention.

Squatting to get a closer look, he saw they were fresh and his heart ricocheted wildly against his rib cage. As he started to call Alban, his cell rang. He didn't recognize the number, but he answered it with a feeling of dread.

"Lost something?"

Torque was instantly disoriented. Having expected to hear Tiene's fiery voice, or Deigh's mocking tones, he was thrown off balance by the man's voice. "Who is this?"

"You don't get to ask the questions. I have Hollie and the baby. If you want to see them again, go alone to the Denver Image Company. It's a disused copy shop on Stockton Street."

"Let me speak to Hollie—" He was talking to dead air. The caller had ended the conversation.

Alone. For Hollie and Karina's safety, he would follow that instruction, but there was no harm in having backup waiting nearby. As he headed back toward the elevator, he was calling Ged.

"Get the guys together and head over to Stockton

Street, but stay out of sight until I give you a signal. You'll need to track Khan down. He's not in his room."

After he ended that call, the next person he spoke to was Alban. "This is a long story and I don't have time to give you all the details right now. Teine and Deigh are the same person and she's loose in the city. Find her."

His friend was still spluttering out a series of confused questions when Torque cut him off. Having reached street level, Torque was about to exit the building when he realized he was missing a vital piece of information. Turning back, he walked over to the reception desk. "Stockton Street. Walking distance, or a cab ride?"

The clerk looked startled. "It's probably a ten-minute walk, sir. But it's not a great area."

"That's okay." Torque's smile was grim. "I'm not in a great mood."

The ten-minute walk took him five, during which time he recalled Hollie's words about accelerants. *Copier toner.* That was one of the things she'd said the Incinerator looked for in the buildings he burned down. And now the arsonist was in a copy shop...

Bright needles of pain danced across his forehead and his skin felt too hot, too tight. He forced the surge of panic back down inside himself. He was no good to Hollie and Karina if he gave way to the tumult of emotion that was threatening to overwhelm him.

Stockton Street was a short street comprising a number of commercial units on one side and a weary looking high-rise block on the other. Several of the streetlights were out and Torque took a moment to catch his breath as he approached the boarded-up storefront of the Denver Image Company.

He paused before he drew level with the darkened

building, some instinct warning him to stay back. His intuition was telling him he would know if Hollie was inside that place. She was his mate. He would feel her. He didn't.

Now he had to weigh his options. Walk into what was probably a trap on the chance that Hollie and Karina were inside, or turn away, not knowing where they could be?

For a dragon, there was only ever going to be one answer to that question. Torque strode toward the door of the empty store.

Chapter 18

The streets were quiet as Dalton drove them away from the hotel. They had taken the back stairs down from the suite, leaving by a service exit to avoid crossing the lobby.

Hollie tried desperately to fix on something during the journey so she knew where they were going, but Karina was restless. Hollie had managed to snatch up a blanket from the crib and wrap Karina up in it as they left the suite, so at least the baby was warm.

"She needs something to eat and a diaper change."

"Too bad." Dalton kept his eyes fixed on the road.

He had ensured her cooperation as they left the hotel by keeping the gun pressed tight against her ribs. "I have enough bullets for the baby, as well."

Dalton, the scratches on his wrist still bleeding, ushered Hollie from the vehicle and into a run-down apartment building. All she noticed as she left the car was the fairground on the square opposite the building.

When they got inside, the elevator wasn't working and Dalton pushed her ahead of him up the stairs. She focused on counting. *Fifth floor. I don't know where I am, but I know how high. And that calliope music is already driving me crazy.*

She was still struggling to come to terms with what was happening. She had always believed the Incinerator fires were either a tribute to Torque or an act of vengeance against him. Now it turned out Hollie was the target. Yes, vengeance was the motive and Torque was the trigger. But this had been about *her* all along.

I was hunting a man who was pursuing me. And he was doing it in plain sight.

She remembered how Dalton had always joked about her fondness for Beast and her liking for Torque in particular. Back then, she hadn't seen it as a big deal. If anything, it had been a source of amusement between them. How had it come to this? A tear slipped down her cheek. How had it turned into this hateful obsession? And how had he committed these crimes while holding down his job as a federal agent? There were so many things that didn't add up.

Dalton kept the gun trained on her as he unlocked the door of one of the apartments. As he thrust her inside, the open-plan space was lit by a single overhead bulb. Hollie's gaze took in the piles of newspaper and cans of gasoline. Although she was confused about many aspects of what was going on, one thing was clear. She wasn't meant to leave this place alive.

Thankfully, Karina had fallen asleep again. Dalton gestured for Hollie to sit on an old sofa. As she did, he went over to the window, looking out at the street below. When he took out his cell phone, he turned to look at her.

"I'm going to call your boyfriend. If you make a sound while I'm talking to him, I'll shoot the baby. Understand?"

This couldn't be happening. It couldn't be *Dalton* saying those words. Dalton liked comics and computer games. He gave money to wildlife charities and would go to great lengths to avoid killing a spider...

"Understand?" He pointed the gun at Karina as he raised his voice.

"Yes. I understand."

"Give me his number."

With the gun still trained on the baby, Hollie stammered out Torque's cell phone number. Her whole body shook as she listened to Dalton speaking to Torque. There was a slight smile on his face as he ended the call.

"What happens now?" Hollie managed to get the words out despite the quivering of her lips.

"Now we wait." He threw himself down in a chair opposite her, his gaze fixed on her face.

"Why did you kill McLain?" She had so many questions, but that one bothered her most. Why did an innocent woman, one they had both known for years, have to die a horrible death?

He was silent for so long she thought he wasn't going to answer. Eventually he shrugged. "She wouldn't tell me where you'd gone."

"That was her job. I was working undercover and she was protecting me."

He didn't seem to be listening. "When you didn't come into the office and no one knew where you were, I tried asking McLain politely where you'd gone. She treated me like I was a kid in school. She actually had the nerve to tell me to back off and stay on my own side of the line. Guess she didn't realize who she was dealing with." His expression switched from a scowl to a smile. "She found out later that night when I followed her home. It took me a long time—she was one tough cookie—but I got the information I needed. Eventually. Of course, I couldn't let her live after that. So I took her to your apartment. Once she was dead, I made sure the place burned so good no one would ever know how she died."

The images of him torturing McLain to get the information about Hollie's whereabouts were sickening. *She died because she tried to protect me.*

"And Vince King? When I asked you to find his number, you said there was no one of that name in the New Haven office. Was that a lie?"

He laughed. "Yeah. I didn't even look for his number."

She swallowed hard. "Is Vince King dead, too?"

"Of course. They'll probably never find him. I tipped his body into a Dumpster and set fire to the whole thing. It was miles from his home and it burned for hours."

Hollie swallowed hard. "So when I spoke to you and you told me to come in so the Incinerator team could look after me, the truth was that you already knew where I was. And the only people who knew I had gone undercover were dead."

He grinned. "Clever, wasn't it? Of course, after I'd killed McLain and King, there was no need for me to keep turning up at the office each day. I knew where you were, so I followed you. The only times I needed to pretend that I was still on the team was when you called me and when I saw you at the aquarium."

Hollie shook her head in confusion. "But for the last four years you *did* turn up at the office each day. How could you be the Incinerator if you were also working for the FBI? You didn't have the time to travel across the country—across the *world*—to start those fires."

"It always amazed me that no one came up with the possibility of an accomplice. Even you, Hollie, with your databases and analytics, never once suggested that there could be more than one Incinerator." He shook a finger at her. "You're not as clever as you think you are."

Hollie's mind went into overdrive. An accomplice? It was an explanation that opened up a whole range of new possibilities. But who? And why? She supposed the obvious motive was money, but Dalton wasn't wealthy and paying someone to start those fires, as well as buying another person's silence...well, that wasn't going to come cheap.

Dalton laughed as he watched her face. "I can see you're trying to guess who it is and I'll bet you're thinking about it all wrong. I'd like to tell you the whole Incinerator thing was all my idea, but my partner came to me with the plan just after you and I split up."

Hollie was starting to feel that familiar trickle of dread down her spine. "But I don't understand. If this is about me and Torque, we didn't meet until I went undercover. No one could have known that was going to happen."

Dalton hunched a shoulder. "I don't know how it works. Something about a destiny foretold. Gold, emeralds, rubies and a dragon hoard. Anyway, my partner told me Torque would find you eventually. Looks like it was a pretty accurate prediction, doesn't it?"

As far as Hollie was concerned, that cleared up any doubt about who the accomplice was. It must be Teine. Who else could have engaged in such destructive forward planning? She could see into the future. Five years ago, she had set this trap. Preying on Dalton's weakness and his jealousy, she had begun this devastating series of arson attacks, escalating the stakes when Hollie and Torque met.

The odds were already stacked against us, but this? We never stood a chance.

"Dalton, she is dangerous..."

"She? I never said my partner was a woman."

The door to the copy shop was unlocked, a clear signal that it was a trap. *Too easy.* Nevertheless, Torque stepped inside. The place smelled of disuse. Of dust, old newspapers and something unpleasant. Like maybe an animal had crawled in there and died.

Torque stood still, his finely tuned senses seeking any sign of life. Any sound or scent that would tell him Hollie and Karina were in this building. There was nothing. His eyes adjusted swiftly to the gloom and searched every corner. He couldn't see anything out of the ordinary. There were abandoned copy machines and computer monitors, a stack of old chairs and a desk with three legs and a pile of bricks in place of the fourth. On top of the desk Torque's attention was caught by a cell phone.

It was out of place in this run-down environment and there was enough light for him to see that the area around it on the table was dust free. Which made it look like the cell had been left there recently. But that wasn't the most noticeable thing about it. The most important, glaringly obvious feature by far was that it was taped to a bottle of clear liquid...

As the cell phone rang, the explosion hit. Blinding white light was accompanied by a sound like the roar of an express train approaching at tremendous speed with a loud whistling, wailing noise. The blast hit him

at chest level, like an ocean wave, lifting him off his
feet and powering him backward. Helpless, Torque let
it take him, carry him back and slam him into the wall.
With the breath driven from his lungs at force, he slid
into a sitting position on the floor, feeling like a broken marionette.

But he wasn't broken. If that had been the intention,
it had failed. Although he was shaken, he was undam-
aged. Whoever had planted that bomb hadn't known
what they were up against. His inner dragon strength-
ened his mortal. He wasn't superhuman, but he was
close. Pushing himself away from the wall, Torque staggered to his feet. His ears were buzzing, his head was
pounding and his legs felt like they belonged to someone else. But his spirit was intact. And he was angry.
Tail-swishing, wing-beating, fire-breathing furious.

Come for the dragon, would you? Best not miss.

He looked around him. Part of the ceiling had fallen
in and the windows had blown outward. A pipe overhead had burst, allowing water to gush into the room.
Several small fires had broken out. Ignoring the devastation around him, Torque stalked through to the back
of the store. There was a locked door at the rear and he
dealt with it by giving it several swift kicks. The panels of wood soon gave way under his onslaught and he
barged through the ruined structure and out into the
night air, taking in great gulps as he walked.

What now? He had walked away from a pathetic attempt at a trap, but he had done it with no way of finding Hollie and Karina. Breathing hard, he was trying
to think what the hell to do next when his cell phone
buzzed.

"Did you enjoy my little warm-up activity?" It was

the voice of the man who had claimed to have Hollie and Karina.

"If that was the best you've got—"

"Best? I wasn't even trying."

Torque could hear a noise in the background. He forced himself to concentrate on that, trying to identify it. He had heard it before, very recently.

"Let's see how you like what comes next."

If this guy thought he was sending him on some sort of hunt… Torque had lived through a time of quests. In his opinion, they were mostly a waste of time and energy. Going straight to the main prize was so much easier.

"Head to the storage depot next to the railway station."

As he listened to the instructions, Torque focused on that noise. Jangling, discordant music. The wheezing of ancient pipes. It made him think of cotton candy and children's laughter. And he knew exactly where he had heard it.

"There is a container with a green door."

"Are Hollie and Karina there?" He knew damn well they weren't. They were near the calliope machine he'd heard earlier when he was chasing Teine.

"You'll find out when you get there."

"I hope you're prepared to die a horrible death when I find you."

The response was an amused chuckle before the Incinerator ended the call. Torque resisted the impulse to crush his cell phone underfoot. Instead, he considered the situation. All he had was an idea of the area where Hollie and Karina were being held. He didn't know the precise location. But he knew someone who might be able to help.

Ged answered his call on the first ring. "Are you okay? We saw an explosion."

"I'm fine. Any news on Khan and Sarange?"

"No. They're still not answering my calls."

That news was both good and bad. Sarange would have been the best person to track Karina, but she might have been distracted by concern for her daughter's welfare. But there was another werewolf on the team, and Karina was half wolf. Torque was hopeful Finglas would be able to pick up the baby's scent. And the Incinerator had left another trail for him to follow.

"Send Fin back to the hotel. Tell him to start at Khan's suite. I don't care how he gets in there. I want him to track Karina, so he needs to find something of hers to get her scent. The guy who is holding Hollie and the baby is likely to have taken them in a car, so he won't be able to follow the smell through the streets, but I know the area where they're being held."

I hope I do. He was pinning everything he had on that damn calliope. Torque paused to draw breath, aware that the words were spilling out too hard and fast. "They are near the fairground close to the Rooftop Restaurant."

"We'll meet you there." Ged's calm tone was as reassuring as ever.

"One more thing…there was blood on the carpet outside Khan's suite." Torque clenched a fist against his thigh, fighting the wave of emotion that hit him. *Let it not be Hollie's or Karina's.* "Fin may be able to use that as an additional way of tracking them."

He ended the call to Ged, aware he had one more thing to take care of before he headed over to the fairground. There was a booby-trapped container near the railway station. It was intended for Torque, but an innocent person could stumble across it at any time. He had to find a way to make it safe. Luckily, he wasn't the only fireproof person in Denver that night.

He made another call. "Where are you?"

Alban sounded mildly annoyed at the question. "Chasing around the streets of the city trying to find Teine, just as you asked me to. It's a big place and she's a small woman. If you could narrow the search area, I'd appreciate it."

"Forget that. Go to the storage depot next to the railway station and find a container with a green door."

"Any particular reason?" Alban asked.

"Yes. It will probably blow up as you enter."

Even on the fifth floor of the apartment building, the bright lights of the fairground and the calliope music were jarring. Hollie could feel a headache forming behind her eyes, but maybe it was unfair to blame the entertainment on the street below when there was a man with a gun sitting opposite.

"Your pet dragon is running around town obeying my every command." Dalton's gloating tones made her feel slightly sick.

"What do you mean 'my dragon'?" She tried to console herself that Dalton couldn't know the truth about Torque. No one could.

"I was there, remember? When he rescued you from the burning bus, I saw it all. That explosion wasn't meant for you. It was supposed to be for him. But you were wearing his clothes and I was too far away to see. It was your fault you got caught up in it, Hollie. But what came next, that was a revelation. A rock star who is also a dragon? I was too shocked to film what I was seeing, but I won't be so slow next time."

His next words chilled her.

"Soon the whole world will know the truth about Torque."

"Please, Dalton. You are angry with me. I understand that. But Torque hasn't done anything to hurt you." She hugged Karina tighter. "And let the baby go. She needs her parents."

He barked out a laugh. "He's done nothing to hurt me? How can you say that when he took you from me?"

The words frightened her even more than the gun that was hanging loosely from his fingers. If Dalton believed Torque had stolen Hollie from him, then his mind had become unhinged.

They had split up four years ago. Yes, Hollie had been a Beast fan back then, but she hadn't met Torque and there had never been any hope or prospect that she would do so. She hadn't even been an overzealous follower of the group. She had always written that strong pull she felt toward Torque off as imagination. She had certainly never spoken of it to anyone. If Dalton had somehow become convinced Torque was the reason they broke up, it was a problem *he* had; it wasn't anything Hollie had done.

"Dalton, you know that isn't true. I only met Torque recently…"

"But it was meant to be. You would never have stayed with me. Not when he was waiting for you." His teeth clenched in a tight, unpleasant grin. "You had a dragon in your destiny, Hollie. I was never going to be able to compete with that."

This mysterious partner of his, the other half of the Incinerator team, must have gone to work on him. Preying on Dalton's minor insecurities and jealousies, magnifying them until they became this huge, festering resentment. *For five years.* They had worked together, laughed together, been friends. And the whole time he was harboring this terrible secret.

Yet, even though he talked about destiny, his insistence that his accomplice wasn't a woman perplexed her. Who, other than Teine, could have seen into the future?

"And the baby is my way of making sure you behave. I know how feisty you can be, Hols."

She gritted her teeth. *Hols.* The man who used to call her that had been her friend. Whoever this was, he wasn't the Dalton Hilger she had known. She had to face up to that. This was the Incinerator. The enemy. He looked and sounded like Dalton, but she had to be prepared to fight him if she was going to get herself and Karina out of this alive.

"If you know who Torque is, you must know you won't be able to kill him," she said.

"There are worse things than death for his kind."

The words triggered a memory. What had Torque said? *There are worse things than being slain.*

"Once I expose him, once the world knows what he really is, he'll lose everything. Money, fame, freedom... you." He grinned. "When he's a circus exhibit, he'll wish he *was* dead. Better still, there could be a fortune to be made. Can you imagine how much people would pay to hunt a living, breathing dragon? Big-game hunting would be nothing in comparison. I could set up a company. Of course, I'd have to make sure he wasn't killed outright first time. Maybe the hunters could take trophies. A few scales at a time. The longer I let him live, the more money I'd make."

Hollie felt sick at the images he was conjuring. "You used to care about every living creature. Who did this to you, Dalton?" Tears burned the back of her throat as she asked the question. "Who made you into this person?"

For a moment, Hollie thought she saw a flicker of regret in his eyes. Then the mask came down again. "You did," he snarled.

His cell phone buzzed before she could say anything more. Dalton's expression changed as he looked at the screen. Anger became fear and something more. She'd have said it was awe, but he moved too fast for her to be sure. Getting to his feet, he went over to the window to take the call.

He was talking in an urgent undertone. No matter how hard she strained to hear, Hollie couldn't catch what he was saying. Whatever it was, she got the feeling something had gone wrong with his plan. Hope flickered inside her like a tiny star in a midnight sky and she tried not to pin everything she had on it. That little light was too small and insignificant to guide her out of this dark place, but for a brief instant, it felt good. And wouldn't it be wonderful if it was Torque who had somehow messed up Dalton's cleverly laid schemes?

When he finished speaking, he was breathing hard and his skin had taken on a waxy hue. He tried out a snarl, but it didn't quite work.

"Change of plan. It looks like the dragon boyfriend will have to die, after all."

Chapter 19

Karina woke up again and was weepy, clinging to Hollie and crying louder every time she caught a glimpse of Dalton.

"Can't you keep her quiet?" Dalton was pacing the small room. Hollie could see he was struggling to keep it together, and his earlier threats toward the baby terrified her.

"She wants her mommy. Maybe if I take her to the window, the lights will distract her."

He regarded her suspiciously for a moment or two, then shrugged. "Just don't get any ideas."

Bouncing the little girl against her shoulder and murmuring words of comfort to her, Hollie went to stand at the window. She wasn't sure what sort of ideas Dalton thought she might have, but jumping from this height with a baby in her arms wasn't on her agenda. The only reason she had come to look out at the view was to genuinely try and divert Karina from her distress.

She supposed there was a vague hope at the back of her mind that she might catch a glimpse of something—anything—happening on the ground to reassure her. Maybe she would even see a muscular, flame-haired dragon-shifter striding to her rescue.

She didn't see Torque, or anyone she recognized, but the sight of life going on as normal had the effect of grounding her. Torque would be doing everything he could to find her and he wouldn't be using conventional means. He also had a formidable team around him.

Dalton had said Torque would have to die, but he also knew Torque was a dragon. Hollie couldn't make those two pieces of information add up. At first, she had believed that Teine was the person responsible for changing Dalton from her friend into a ruthless criminal. That would have made sense. Teine had the power to kill a dragon. She had already done so, murdering two whole dragon-shifter clans back in the Scottish Highlands.

But Dalton had insisted that Hollie was wrong. His partner was not a woman. That made her blood run cold. Because it meant the other half of the Incinerator team was a man with the same powers as Teine. And there couldn't be many of *them* around.

Her thoughts were interrupted by the buzzing of Dalton's cell phone. That half fearful, half worshipful look crossed his face again as he gazed at the screen. Grasping Hollie's arm, he dragged her toward the bedroom.

"In here." He pushed her across the threshold. "And stay there. No matter what you hear."

He slammed the door closed and she was left staring at it in shock and fear. What now? Was this part of the plan, or had something changed? She had thought she was operating at the highest level of anxiety, but this new development kicked her stress levels up a notch.

Panic was like a silent fist tightening on her throat. Her eyes widened, darting around the empty room. Racing heart, brain on fire, nerve endings misfiring like a faulty car engine, thoughts that were a cluster bomb inside her brain, each new idea triggering a series of explosions...any attempt to function normally failed.

Karina wriggled in her arms, reminding her that she had to get past this. She *had* to calm down and think rationally. Hugging the baby close, Hollie pressed her ear to the hardwood panel. The silence was broken by three heavy knocks, presumably on the front door.

There was a murmur of voices and she strained to hear. She couldn't make out the words, and it might have been her imagination, but she definitely heard a wheedling note in Dalton's speech. He sounded like a child trying to make excuses for his behavior to an angry parent. There was obviously a seniority within the Incinerator partnership, and if she was right and the person who had just arrived was the other half of the team, Dalton was scared of his ally.

Then they passed the bedroom door and what she heard next rocked her back on her heels. One tiny word. Not even a word, more a sound, an unmistakable colloquialism. It was meaningless and out of context, but it told her everything.

Dalton's companion said, *"Och."*

Opening the bedroom door, she was face-to-face with Alban before she had time to think about the danger. "So that's why you kept your passport up to date. You needed to follow Beast around the world, starting fires in their wake when Dalton couldn't get time off from his day job." She was pleased with the way her voice remained perfectly calm as she confronted him.

"And that's why you said time settles all scores. You've been waiting a long time for this."

Unfazed by her words, he smiled. "Hello, Hollie. I didn't expect to ever see you again." His piercing gaze shifted from her, and the smile faded. "But I suppose I should have anticipated Dalton would screw this up."

Dalton's face went an ugly shade of red. He turned on Hollie. "I told you to stay in the bedroom."

"You told me a lot of things." Her panic was fading now and anger was bubbling up in its place. Alongside her renewed courage, she felt Karina's tears subsiding. It was as though the little girl was sensing Hollie's mood and drawing on this new surge of bravery. "Like how you were still investigating this case and you weren't a criminal."

She turned to Alban. As she did, her attention was briefly caught by the fact that the front door hadn't fully closed. Thoughts of escape flashed through her mind and were quickly quashed. There was a dragon standing between her and freedom. "You pretended to be Torque's friend."

He shrugged. "All's fair in love and dragon warfare."

"No, it's not." She practically stamped her foot at him. "You are the person who told me dragons are honorable. You said the feud between the Cumhachdach and the Moiteil was over when Teine imprisoned you and Torque together. Now I find out it was all a pretense and you were working behind his back all this time. That doesn't sound like the dragon way."

"He stole from me." Alban's expression was sullen.

"This is about *money*?"

"No. It's about dragon hoard. That which we value most. What the Cumhachdach stole from the Moiteil in the height of battle *was* treasure. The gelt we had accumulated over many centuries," Alban said. "Now the time has come to take from Torque that which he esteems most. That is no longer a material possession… It's you."

"No." Dalton's voice shook. As Alban cast a furious glance his way, he backed down from his initial protest. "I mean…you said you would let her live."

"Oh, come on, Dalton." Hollie turned the full force of her scorn on him. She swept an arm around her, indicating the piles of newspaper and gasoline cans. "You didn't seriously expect me to believe that?"

"This was another trap for your dragon boyfriend. I was to let him believe you died in a fire here." He cast a nervous look at Alban. "But Torque knows where you are."

Her heart gave a wild bound of delight. "He does?" *Then why isn't he here?*

"I hate to wipe that look of joy from your face, but he only has a vague idea of your location. That's why we're leaving right now," Alban said.

"And I hate to be the one to disappoint you."

Hollie gave a little cry of delight as she heard the beloved voice she had been longing for. Swinging around, she saw Torque standing in the doorway with Finglas just behind him. Fury burned in the opal depths of Torque's eyes. "But you are not going anywhere."

Rick had managed to get Finglas into Khan's hotel suite with a story about lost keys. Once there, the werewolf picked up Karina's scent from a soft toy he had found on the pillow of her crib. He had also found a patch of fresh blood on the carpet nearby.

Powered by anger as well as his wolf instincts,

Finglas led Torque to an apartment block close to the fairground.

"You're sure they're in here?" Torque looked up at the building in dismay. It was ten floors high. If the Incinerator got a hint that they were after him and started a fire in there, the outcome would be catastrophic.

"Positive. Karina is only half werewolf, but her scent is strong. And my tracking instinct, even as a human, is powerful."

"Do you know whose blood it is?"

Finglas shook his head. "It's not Karina's. That's all I can tell you."

That meant there was a possibility it was Hollie's blood. The thought that she had been injured while he wasn't there to help her chilled Torque to his soul. This was the side of loving no one had warned him about. That giving his heart to another so completely meant she had possession of his soul, as well. That if anything should harm his mate, it would come back and hurt him double, leaving him unable to function, barely able to breathe.

He had to take those feelings of helplessness and loss and turn them around, force them to become actions, or he would be useless. He pictured Hollie's face, her sweet, warm smile. Keeping her image before him, drawing strength from it, he pulled himself back from the abyss.

They were standing to one side of the building, away from the fairground and out of sight of any of the apartments and the front entrance. The whole team, apart from Khan and Sarange, was together awaiting Torque's orders. He hadn't heard from Alban since he'd sent him to check out the storage depot. It was infuriating because he needed confirmation from his dragon friend that he had neutralized the trap.

There was no time to waste. The Incinerator would be expecting to find out that his rigged explosion in that container had been successful. If Alban hadn't triggered it, or if something had gone wrong, he would get suspicious and that would put Hollie and Karina at risk.

"Finglas and I will go into the building," Torque said to Ged. "Hopefully, Fin can follow Karina's scent and lead me to the right apartment. The rest of you wait out here until I send for you."

"Be careful," Ged warned. "It could be another trap."

Torque turned to Finglas. "What do you think? Are you ready to walk into a trap?"

The young werewolf tilted his face upward. "Khan's daughter is in that building. Hollie is probably at her side. I'm with you."

The words summed up the spirit of Beast and powered Torque forward. Although he allowed Finglas to go slightly ahead of him, he was ready to surge in front at the first sign of trouble. If there was any fighting, a werewolf would be useful, but a dragon would be better.

There was an out-of-order sign on the elevator, but Finglas bypassed it and went straight to the stairs. Confidently, he led Torque up to the fifth floor. When they got there, he paused outside one of the apartments.

He sniffed the air before giving a nod of satisfaction. "This is the one."

The door wasn't fully closed and Torque could hear voices from within. One of them was Hollie's, and his whole body flooded with relief at the realization that she was safe. After listening for a moment or two, he could hear that she was alive, well and angry enough to be arguing with her captor. He spared a second to admire his feisty scientist. Then he recognized the answering voice and his blood froze.

Alban? Reality hit him hard, leaving him momentarily questioning everything he had believed about himself and his life.

Then the fire and fury of a centuries-old dragon feud crashed over him. Every slash, bite and flame-filled breath of Cumhachdach against Moiteil flashed before him and he knew what had happened.

He pushed open the door in time to see Alban seal his own death warrant by taking hold of Hollie's arm.

"Torque!" She wrenched herself free of Alban's grip and ran to him. The feel of her warm, trembling body was like heaven. A sweet, brief reminder of what he thought he'd lost. He dropped a swift kiss on the top of her head. And another for Karina, who, recognizing him, managed a tearful smile.

"Go with Fin. Wait for me outside." He looked over the top of Hollie's head at Alban. Met a pair of unflinching blue eyes. "The Moiteil and I have unfinished business."

"But I need to…" Hollie raised fearful eyes to his face.

"Tell me later." He placed a gentle hand in the small of her back, signaling to Finglas to go with her. "We will have all the time in the world when I'm done here."

"What about the guy?" Finglas jerked a thumb in the direction of a man who looked like he was trying to blend into the peeling wallpaper.

"I'll deal with him later."

"That's Dalton Hilger. He was working with Alban all this time because he somehow knew, even five years ago, that you and I would get together." Hollie cast a glance over her shoulder toward Alban. "Please be careful, but also make him pay."

"I intend to." His jaw was aching with the effort of talking while his teeth were so tightly clenched.

Alban seemed unnaturally calm. He had felt the force of Torque's anger before, but this? The Moiteil was about to discover what it was like to be caught up in the eye of the most violent storm the Cumhachdach could unleash.

Hollie carried Karina out of the apartment and Finglas, grabbing Dalton by the arm as he took his gun from him, marched out after them. Torque took a step closer to Alban. He had never felt fury like this. It was like molten lava building up inside him, creating a pressure so intense that, when the time came for release, it would scorch everything in its path.

"We were forged from the same fire, you and I. Enemies and friends. We hate each other and love each other with equal passion. But when we do it, we do it face-to-face." Torque's jaw was so tense he was having trouble getting the words out. "This? Hiding in the shadows is not the way of the leader of the Moiteil."

He could see his words had stung. Throughout the centuries of dragon clan warfare, the two sides had clung to their identities. The Cumhachdach were the mighty, the Moiteil the proud.

"Och, would you lecture me about dragon ways?" Alban attempted to regain some of his swagger. "You, the great Cumhachdach, who has been hiding himself away behind the swaggering rock star instead of facing his fears—"

The punch Torque swung missed its mark. Instead of connecting with Alban's nose, it caught him on his cheek, but it still rocked his head back. It provoked Alban to come swinging back at him. A balled fist caught Torque in the stomach and he doubled over.

Alban used his advantage and kicked his legs out from under him, getting him down on the floor and straddling him.

Torque had lost count of the times he had fought this man. Of the beatings, the broken bones, the blood and the dust. Each time, they had fought with honor and shaken hands at the end. This time it was different. Alban had threatened Hollie. There was no going back from that.

As they traded blows and swapped places, they knew there could only be one outcome. They were both breathing hard when Alban asked the all-important question.

"To the death, Cumhachdach?"

Torque jerked his head toward the window. "To the skies, Moiteil."

Hollie sank onto the grass at the side of the building. It was a warm night and the shivering that gripped her had nothing to do with the temperature. Nearby, Finglas stood guard over Dalton.

Ged came to kneel beside her, draping his jacket around her shoulders. "Torque will be okay."

"They are both dragons." She wished she could make her teeth stop chattering. "Both Highland clan leaders. They are equally matched and they are both fighting for a cause."

"But Torque's motive is stronger. He is driven by love," Ged said.

Hollie brushed away a tear, resting her cheek on Karina's head. "Have you spoken to Khan or Sarange?"

Her words were accompanied by a cry of relief from the open window of a car that pulled up on the street nearby. Sarange leaped out and darted over to them.

Scooping Karina up from Hollie's arms, she smothered the baby's face with kisses before checking her over. Karina chuckled with pleasure and waved her plump arms. Khan wrapped his arms around them both, holding them as close as he could.

"Oh, Hollie. How can we ever thank you for keeping her safe?" Sarange turned to her with eyes that were bright with tears. "When we were finally able to check our messages and realized what was happening, we were frantic with worry."

Hollie made an attempt to answer her. It was a miserable failure. Her voice didn't work and all that came out was a gulp. It was followed by a sob and soon she was weeping uncontrollably on Ged's shoulder as the full horror of the past few hours hit her.

When she could finally talk, she gestured toward the apartment building. "Torque." It was the only word she could say, the only thought on her mind.

"Torque can take care of himself—"

Khan was interrupted by the sound of breaking glass from high above them. Hollie got to her feet, covering her mouth with a shaking hand as two figures tumbled from the window of the apartment she had recently left.

The scene was perfectly illuminated by the lights from the fairground. Torque and Alban were in free fall, heading for the ground, arms and legs windmilling wildly. Hollie's every sense seemed heightened. The screams of the people watching from the attractions were overloud and the breeze in her face became an icy wind. For an instant she could almost have sworn Torque looked directly into her eyes. His gaze pinned her in place, searing into her mind, blazing into her heart.

With only feet to go before they hit the ground, there

was a sudden upward rush of air. A ricochet of force that sent Hollie reeling back. In an almost choreographed move, both men stretched out their arms, shifting in the same instant. Two giant dragons snorted twin plumes of smoke, banking around hard as they rose above the apartment building.

"Son of a…" Khan threw back his head, watching the spectacle above him openmouthed.

The dragons circled the building in a tight arc before facing each other across the roof. The ground shook with the depth of a single dragon roar. Hollie knew for certain that Torque was the challenger. When Alban's answering bellow came, it was equally thunderous.

All around her, people were gathering to watch the spectacle. Cell phones were raised to capture the scene for all time.

"Do something," she begged Ged. "He will hate this." *If he lives.* She shook the thought aside. He *had* to live. She couldn't think about the alternative. It was hard to watch the scene above her, impossible not to.

"I can't stop other people from filming. I can only try to limit the damage." Ged didn't take his eyes off the two winged figures in the sky as he drew his own cell phone out of his pocket.

Above them, Torque, distinguishable to Hollie because of his red-gold scales, launched a stream of fiery breath toward his opponent. Alban jerked violently as he absorbed the impact of the flames. Tilting his nose to the heavens and streamlining his body into an arrow shape, he took off with Torque just behind him.

Twisting and weaving to make himself a difficult target for his pursuer, Alban kept going until he had gained sufficient altitude. Then he pulled up abruptly. Seeing his intention, Hollie cried out a warning even though there was no chance of Torque hearing her.

Alban seemed to hang in midair before starting a nose-down strike. Torque, coming up beneath him, was flying too fast to turn. One of Alban's long-clawed feet hooked into his lower left flank and he spun away with a roar of pain.

Sarange handed Karina to Khan and came to stand next to Hollie, placing an arm around her shoulders. "I don't know much about dragon fights, but I know about good guys. We always win and Torque is the best there is."

Whirling back on course, Torque dove after Alban. From the ground, the next few minutes were a blur of aerial wrestling as they engaged in a tooth and claw battle. Straining to see what was happening in the eye of the dragon storm, Hollie glimpsed Torque's lethal talons tearing into his opponent. The hit to his upper right shoulder sent Alban reeling from the blow, knocking him off course. He fell, hitting one wing on a corner of the apartment building.

Alban emitted a high-pitched screech of pure fury and veered away. Torque was too fast for him. Lashing out again, he inflicted a long gash on Alban's already injured wing, limiting his ability to maintain height.

Gripping his victim in his claws, Torque opened his powerful jaws wide. Clamping on to Alban's muscular neck, he used his huge fangs to tear through the thick dragon hide. Although Alban struggled, he was powerless to break free of the excruciating grip and Torque gave him a final shake before sending him plummeting to the ground.

Chapter 20

As he landed and shifted, Torque could see Ged doing what he did best. Crowd control and public relations.

"Nothing to see here, guys." Ged was signaling to the other members of the band to help him out. They were working as a team to keep people away from the point where Alban had crashed to the ground, shifting into human form as he fell. Forming a human barrier against prying eyes, everyone was giving the same message.

"That's right. It was a promotional display for Beast's new album. Glad you enjoyed it. Realistic? That's what we were aiming for. Spread the word to your friends..."

Incredibly, Alban was still alive. Just. Torque knelt beside him.

"It was a good fight, Cumhachdach." The words were barely a wheeze. "Best dragon won."

Torque took Alban's hand, and his clasp was returned. "You did the Moiteil proud."

"No." A shadow crossed the other man's face. "You

were right. What I did to you…to Hollie…that was not the dragon way. I guess it was jealousy. It affected my ability to think straight."

"Jealousy?" Torque frowned.

"Teine once told me your most precious treasure would not be gold coins and jewels, but a human woman you would love. I never gave it much thought until five years ago when I got a letter telling me you would soon find her and, unless I could stop you making her your mate, the Cumhachdach would rise again. I believed Teine was dead, so I did'nae know who sent that letter. I know now, of course." A spasm of pain crossed Alban's face. "Even though I didn't know it was Teine who sent the letter, it named Hollie…told me where to find her. I tracked her down, and once I knew what her job was, I came up with the Incinerator plan. Jealousy is the only word for my motivation. I couldn't stand the thought that you would have all the things that would never be mine. A mate. A clan. A new life."

"I can't have those things. I'm a dragon-shifter. We can't convert our mates."

"Och, you can do anything you choose. You are the last of the Cumhachdach…believe in yourself, man." As he spoke, Alban's voice faded, his clasp on Torque's hand loosened and his eyes drifted closed.

Torque remained on his knees with his head bowed, only vaguely conscious of someone placing a blanket around his naked body. This man—this dragon—had been part of his life since he was born. All his memorable moments, good and bad, had been shared with Alban. The Cumhachdach and the Moiteil. The names were ingrained in Highland legend. Now the Moiteil were no more. The last of their name was gone.

Dragon honor. It was the code by which Torque lived,

the one by which Alban had died. The leader of the Moiteil had brought dishonor on himself, but that didn't make it any less painful for the one who had been forced to strike the death blow. To a dragon-shifter the shedding of dragon blood was the greatest offense one of their kind could commit, permissible only in battle, or for the punishment of high crimes.

The stupidest part of all was no matter how much he hated what Alban had done, Torque would mourn him for the rest of his life. Not this man, the warped criminal whose mind had conceived the Incinerator plan. The other Alban, the brave warrior, loyal friend and sensitive intellectual. The man who could make him laugh until he had tears in his eyes had now made him cry for an entirely different reason.

He lifted his head as a hand slipped into his.

"I know you loved him." Hollie's face was wet as she raised his palm to her cheek.

"I love you more." He gained strength from the words.

She clung to him. "When I saw you fall from that window, I thought I'd lost you."

He wrapped the blanket around them both and held her until his heartbeat was restored to normality. "Are you okay?" He looked around him to where Dalton Hilger was sitting on the grass with his head in his hands. Renewed anger pounded through him. "Did he hurt you? There was blood in Khan's hotel suite…"

She gave a shaky laugh. "It was Dalton's blood. Karina scratched him."

"She did?" Khan, who was standing nearby, overheard. "That's my girl." His face hardened as he looked at Dalton. "What's happening with that guy? He kidnapped my daughter…and you, Hollie. But…*my daughter.*"

"Maybe we should hand him over to the FBI. Let the human forces of law and order deal with their own," Torque said. "He can try and explain his involvement in the fires by telling them his partner was a dragon. Who knows? They may even listen."

Dalton took his hands away from his face. Across the distance between them, Torque could see the fury in his eyes. "You did this." Dalton's voice shook. "If it wasn't for you…"

Reaching behind him into the waistband of his pants, he withdrew a hidden gun. He aimed it at Torque, but two shots rang out almost simultaneously. The one Dalton fired missed Torque by inches.

A look of surprise replaced the furious expression on Dalton's face and he toppled forward. Behind him, Finglas held the gun he had taken from Dalton in the apartment.

"I thought he might try something like that," Finglas said. "I decided not to wait around and see if he was bluffing."

Ged stepped forward to check Dalton. "Dead." He looked around. "Which leaves us with an issue. We have two bodies here and I'm guessing the authorities may want to know what the dragon story that will be hitting the media any time now is all about. If they don't, the press will. Even if my claim that it's promo for the new album holds, it will draw a lot of attention our way. We should probably get out of here and do something about these bodies."

Torque got to his feet, clutching his injured side. Alban's claws had cut deep and the gash was still bleeding. "Alban may not have earned an honorable departure from this world, but I choose to give him one. His ashes must be scattered on the soil of our homeland."

"For the time being, would you settle for going back to the hotel so Hollie can tend to your wounds? You can trust me to deal with Alban's body with sensitivity and also leave this scene free from any trace of our presence," Ged said.

Torque nodded. "Very well."

Khan drove Torque, Hollie, Sarange and Karina back to the hotel. Ged, Finglas, Dev and Diablo remained at the scene of the dragon fight. Torque didn't know the details of what they were doing, but he knew Ged would be true to his word. When he had finished, there would be no trace of the dragon fight or of Beast's presence. The following afternoon, they would leave Denver and set off on the final stage of the tour.

Hollie's head flopped wearily against Torque's shoulder as they completed the short drive in silence. When Khan pulled into the hotel's underground parking lot, she stretched and yawned.

"You haven't told me what happened when you took Deigh out to dinner."

"Ah, hell." Torque ran a hand through his hair. "I'd forgotten all about her."

Hollie bit her lip as she knelt on the floor and studied the wound in Torque's left side. "This needs stitches."

"I can't go to a hospital." He was seated on the bed and he flinched as he moved his arm. "But there is a medical kit in my suitcase."

She attempted a smile. Given everything that had happened, she thought it worked pretty well. "You bring along a suture kit just for this sort of eventuality?"

He grinned. "It happens more often than you'd imagine."

Her lip wobbled and she took a moment or two to

get it under control. "I've never stitched anyone's skin before, Torque. I don't want to hurt you."

He used his right hand to grip her chin, tilting her face up to him so he could drop a kiss onto the end of her nose. "I need you to help me heal. And once you stitch me up, I'll heal fast. Shifter DNA," he explained in response to her look of inquiry. "It works quicker than the human kind."

Torque explained where the medical kit was, and once she had it, Hollie took it through to the bathroom and arranged its contents on the counter beside the sink. Returning to the bedroom, she took Torque's hand and he leaned on her as she helped him through to the other room.

"This will sting." The gaping cut in his side looked even worse in the harsh fluorescent light.

Torque gripped the sink hard as she poured antiseptic onto a swab and cleaned the wound. Beads of sweat broke out on his brow and he trembled violently.

Hollie bit her lip as she cleared the blood away and viewed the damage. It was even worse than she'd thought. The razor-sharp talons had penetrated deep, tearing through flesh and muscle as Alban had sliced into Torque's side with full force. It was a devastating injury.

Having thoroughly cleaned the wound to prevent any infection, she turned to the suture kit, checking the instructions carefully. The pack included a syringe and a local anesthetic. Taking a deep breath, she injected this into the area around the wound in Torque's side.

Forcing herself to remain calm, she prepared the needle and suture material. "Okay. I'm going to stitch you up now."

Torque smiled. "You say the nicest things."

"You do not want to make me laugh while I'm approaching you with a needle in my hand," she warned. Bending over her task, she managed to complete it quickly and effectively. "There. It may not be the neatest, but you no longer have a hole in your side."

Torque studied his reflection in the mirror. "Looks fine to me."

Hollie placed a dressing over the stitches and secured it in place. Then she gave Torque two painkillers washed down with a glass of water, before helping him back to the bedroom.

"I'm not completely helpless." He was torn between laughter and frustration.

"So you can get your own underwear on, can you?" She faced him with her hands on her hips, a teasing smile on her lips as she studied his naked body.

He held up his right hand in a gesture of surrender. "Um…maybe not."

Having helped him into his boxer briefs, she led him to the bed, drawing back the bedclothes so he could ease himself down.

"Where are you going?" he asked as she walked away. "I need you next to me."

"Give me two minutes. I just have to dispose of the medical waste."

He nodded sleepily. Having tidied up in the bathroom, cleaned herself up and stripped down to her underwear, Hollie slid into bed. The sound of his rhythmic breathing told her Torque was already asleep. After the events of the day just gone, she didn't expect to join him, but as she turned out the bedside light, slumber was already tugging at the edges of her consciousness.

The beat was so loud Torque could hear it in his teeth. A slow, heavy pounding. Half-time, slower than a human heartbeat, maybe more like that of a whale. Every light went out, plunging the huge arena into darkness. Screams and cries from the audience filled the night. Slow, lazy guitar chords joined the drumbeats.

Above the stage, a single beam became a whirling series of colored lights. Flashing, red-green, yellow-blue. Within the indistinct patterns, a shape began to emerge. Pure, pulsing light became a creature of fire and scales. As the beat picked up and the guitar faded, the dragon in the sky roared once, shooting a stream of fire over the heads of the stunned crowd.

Blackness reigned once more, and then the lights focused on Khan as he screeched out the opening lines of the final number. Los Angeles. Seventeen thousand people. The last night of the tour. The dragon special effect was Ged's way of answering the media frenzy that had followed the Denver dragon fight.

We are Beast. We gave you werewolves, tigers and other shifters in Marseilles. Now it's time for dragons.

As they bounded off the stage, Torque didn't feel his usual sense of elation. This time there was only relief. He was thankful the performance was over and was experiencing a sense of freedom now that this nightmare tour was finally at an end.

The whole band was staying at Khan and Sarange's luxury Beverly Hills mansion. Hollie and Sarange had left the performance as soon as it finished so they could prepare a celebratory meal. There had been times during this tour when Torque wondered if they would ever make it to this point. Now his thoughts were on the future and what it might look like.

There hadn't been any police backlash from the events in Denver. Ged had ensured that the scene was scrupulously clean. The following day, he had drawn

Torque and Hollie's attention to an online news report about a body found in a fifth-floor Denver apartment. The man, identified as former FBI agent Dalton Hilger, had died from a single gunshot wound. The room in which he was killed had been prepared as though for an arson attack. Investigations were ongoing and included the possibilities that Hilger, already under investigation for the killing of a senior officer, was responsible for a series of fires over a number of years and that he had been shot by an accomplice.

There was, of course, the issue of the bizarre dragon fight that had gone viral on social media. In Marseilles, Ged had done everything he could to play down the incident, assuring fans that it was an experimental special effect and there would be no repeat performance. This time, so many people at the fairground had filmed the spectacular beasts in the sky above Denver that he had been forced to take a different approach.

Refusing to name the digital geniuses responsible for the aerial display, Ged had given several interviews, simply stating that it was a promotion for Beast's new album. Luckily, he already had a reputation for being enigmatic and Beast was known for its commitment to its privacy. Ged had then arranged several other dragon-themed displays, including the one at the performance they had just given. They were intended as a distraction, but he suspected the questions would remain about how the animation in Denver had been achieved.

When they arrived at the house, Sarange had already sent the caterers away. If the team she employed to provide food for the party found anything strange in the meal they were asked to provide, Torque guessed they had been too professional to comment. Or too well paid. Meat, fish and salad—and plenty of it—was arranged on tables at the side of the swimming pool. The elegant gardens were the perfect place to unwind.

He sought out Hollie, who looked delectable in a flowered sundress, and wrapped his arms around her, lifting her off her feet. Although the wound in his side twinged, it was already healing. "The tour from hell is over."

"It wasn't all bad." Her smile sent electrical currents zinging through his bloodstream. "I can think of a few memorable moments. Some of the hotel rooms we stayed in will always have a special place in my heart... and so will some of the forests."

"Let's take a vacation." He hadn't thought about the immediate future until now, and it was a spur of the moment suggestion. "Where do you want to go? Anywhere in the world."

"I may have some thoughts about that, but I'll tell you later."

When he pushed her to elaborate, she shook her head mysteriously and led him to the drinks table. At least Hollie hadn't said the words he was dreading. She hadn't told him that tonight would be their last night together. But at some point soon they would have to have that conversation about the future. About how they could be together as humans, but how they couldn't have forever. And they would have to talk about children. He had watched her with Karina and seen how much she loved the little girl. Hollie would be a wonderful mother, but dragon-shifters would never accept those who were not pure of blood. Unless their parents were both dragon-shifters, their children would be outcasts. Torque was not prepared to bring a child into the world knowing he, or she, would be a misfit. He didn't think Hollie would do that to a child, either. Would she be prepared to face a future without a family of her own? It was yet another shadow hanging over them.

Even as he took Hollie's hand and enjoyed the prospect of a vacation during which they didn't need to look over their shoulders, his heart was heavy at the thought that this happiness could be on borrowed time.

Khan and Sarange made their announcement about the new baby to laughter and jokes.

"Did you think we hadn't guessed?" Dev raised his glass, anyway. "All that running out of the room and the sound of throwing up was kind of a giveaway."

While everyone was crowded around their hosts, Hollie approached Ged, who was standing slightly apart from the group. "Can I ask you a question?"

He smiled down at her. "Always."

She took a deep breath. "In your alpha-male world, have you ever heard of a dragon-shifter being proposed to by a human?"

"Now, that's a question." His gaze went over her head to where Torque was standing with Khan. "And the answer is no. No, I have never heard of that."

"Oh." Hollie considered his response in silence. She wasn't entirely surprised, but she had hoped there might be a precedent.

"Why are you asking me this, Hollie? Torque already approached me about the dragon mark."

"You told him I would have to walk through fire to receive his bite, didn't you?" Ged nodded. "That's the problem. It's the whole alpha-male thing. No matter how much Torque wants us to be together, he won't do anything that puts me in danger."

"I see. So you are planning to take the initiative away from him."

"Yes. Of course, he may just refuse."

Ged regarded her in fascination. "What would you do then?"

She smiled. "Walk into a fire, of course. Then he'd have to rescue me and he could bite me while we were there. But it would be so much easier if he'd just accept my proposal. Don't you agree?" He started to laugh and she watched him with a bemused expression. "What did I say that was so funny?"

"Nothing. I was just thinking that the dragon has finally met his match."

Torque came over to them then. "Are you two hatching secrets?"

"You could say that." Ged kissed Hollie's cheek. "Good luck."

"Good luck?" Torque watched as Ged walked away. "Why do you need luck?"

She took his hand. "Let's go somewhere private so I can tell you."

His expression was somewhere between confusion and trepidation as she led him to their luxurious bedroom. When she closed the door and turned to face him, her heart was trying to hammer its way out of her chest. Telling herself she had to go for it, she launched into a speech without being entirely sure what she was going to say.

"When you said you'd find a way for us to have forever, why didn't you tell me about the dragon mark?"

He muttered an exclamation. "I suppose it was Ged who told you about that?"

She shook her head at him. "Don't try to change the subject. And don't do that dragon frown at me, Torque. I asked you a question first."

His sigh seemed to come from the depths of his soul.

"Did Ged explain what the dragon mark entails? That, unlike when another shifter species asks their mate to convert, it is much more than just a bite. Before you received my mark, you would have to walk into a pit of fire to demonstrate your allegiance." His voice was tortured. "I could never ask you to do that."

"When the Pleasant Bay Bar was on fire, you walked through the flames to rescue me. If I stepped into a fire pit, surely the effect would be the same? You would be there to protect me."

"That was different. Your life was in danger and I had no choice. This time I would be asking you to do it." Torque's expression was anguished. "I can't do it, Hollie. I can't send you into a blaze not knowing for certain I can get you out of it."

"Then I'll make it easier for you." Slowly, with her heart pounding out a wild tattoo, she went down on one knee.

"What are you doing?" The words were a growl, originating somewhere deep in his chest.

"Well, if we were both human, I'd be proposing marriage. But since you're a shifter, I'm asking you to give me your dragon mark." She swallowed the constriction in her throat. "Be my mate, Torque. Give us forever."

"Hollie, you don't know what you're asking." He stepped closer.

"I do. I'm clear on the details. Fire and fangs." She took his hand, holding the palm against her cheek. "If you don't say yes, I may as well walk into that fire pit, anyway. You don't want eternity without me, but I don't want a human future where I have to watch you hurting. I don't want half a life."

He gave a shaky laugh. "Are you trying to blackmail me?"

"I'll do whatever it takes, my dragon…" She gasped as he hauled her to her feet, crushing her tight to his chest.

"You win." Torque's lips were hot and hard on hers. "I'm going to throw you into a fire. Then I'm going to bite the hell out of you."

"That's what I love about dragons. You are so romantic." Hollie melted against him, returning his caresses with a fervor that matched his own. "That answers the question of where I want to go on vacation. Take me to Scotland. We can scatter Alban's ashes and then have ourselves a honeymoon."

"We'll leave in the morning."

Chapter 21

Deep in the heart of the mountain, the fire leaped and twirled in a fiery dance, its glowing embers twinkling like stars in the heated atmosphere. Each time Hollie tried drawing a breath, the air was hotter and her chest grew tighter. This was the place where it all began. The pit where the Cumhachdach and the Moiteil were born.

Flames licked close to her bare feet, crackling playfully at the edges of the rock. Flaring higher toward the center, they flared and spat, showering sparks like a fountain, hurling plumes of gray smoke high into the air. Ash flew up high before showering the ground like great dirty flakes of snow.

"It's like a living creature." Hollie wrapped her arms around her naked body, gazing into the inferno. "A great hungry serpent, ready to devour everything in its path." She turned her head to look at Torque. "Ready to consume me."

His hands gripped her shoulders even tighter. "I'm here."

She let herself feel the fire's force, using her fear to drive herself onward. The blaze was regal and proud. Well, Hollie could hold her head up and stare into its yellow heart. For the sake of her future, she could take its hissing, spitting challenge. "Will it hurt when you bite me?"

"Yes." Torque's lips brushed her ear. "But the pain won't last."

She nodded. There were natural steps carved into the rock, and Hollie moved onto the next one, sucking in a breath as the scorching heat kissed her flesh. How beautifully the flames swayed and danced, reaching for her, inviting her to join them. She was so close now that her pale flesh had taken on a bluish tinge.

"It will be like walking into a river." Her voice was dreamy. "Waters of fire."

Behind her, Torque wrapped his arms around her and they took the last few steps together.

The blaze welcomed her with a brilliant display of color. Reds, oranges and purples bloomed all around her, bursting into life and fading to golden embers. As it heated her blood to boiling point, Hollie had a moment of perfect clarity. This was a mirror on her new life. Glowing bright and fading, only to be renewed seconds later.

Behind her, she could feel Torque shifting. His body was growing, his hands leaving her shoulders as his wings wrapped around her, his skin on hers becoming scales. Instead of the fear she'd anticipated, the fire acted as a balm, calming her nerves, warming her body and emptying her mind of care.

This moment, this commitment, they were all that

mattered. Tilting her head back against Torque's shoulder, she exposed her throat to his mouth. His sharp fangs closed on her neck and shoulder and Hollie hissed out a breath.

The searing pain was like a knife blade being driven deep into her flesh, but the agony quickly dulled to a throb. Time ceased to exist and she had no idea how long they stayed that way, his wings enclosing her, his teeth marking her. Slowly, he pulled away and shifted back. His human body was hard and strong against her, his lips tender on the skin of her neck. Sensation rushed through her, and her body became boneless. Hollie sagged against him, feeling Torque lift her off her feet as her vision darkened.

When she regained consciousness, she was on a ridge, close to the summit of Càrn Eighe. A warm blanket covered her nakedness and she was wrapped in Torque's arms. Both of those things felt just fine. She raised one arm, studying her unblemished flesh with a sense of wonder.

"No burns."

"How do you feel?" Torque's expression was concerned.

She felt for the tender spot on her neck and shivered. It wasn't painful. It was…delicious. "Different. And very turned on. Is that normal?"

His laughter held a note of relief. And something more. Her gaze traveled down his body, her eyes widening as she identified what the something more might be. "This is all new to me, as well. But I'm willing to learn."

"We should probably go with our instincts, but maybe find some privacy." Getting to her feet, she led him back into the cave.

Whatever had happened to her in that fire, she was

now aching and raw with desire. As soon as Torque pushed her up against the rocky wall and kissed between her breasts, Hollie was squirming and panting.

"Please, Torque. I can't wait."

He swirled his tongue over her diamond-hard left nipple several times before taking it in his mouth and sucking. Pleasure shot through her and she moaned. He reached up and began caressing the other nipple between his thumb and forefinger. The restless longing spiraled out of control.

"Need your mouth on me now." It was hard to talk, but she managed to gasp out the words.

He obliged by kneeling in front of her, pressing his face to the apex of her thighs. Hollie couldn't believe how close she was to orgasm already. Using his thumbs to hold her outer lips apart, he ran his tongue along the length of her sex. Hollie's whole body jerked wildly.

"Keep still." Torque used one hand to hold her hip, keeping her pressed up against the cave wall.

With the other hand, he continued to keep her open while he covered her with his mouth. Finding her clit with his tongue, he flicked the tiny bud before sucking it hard. Hollie gasped. Throwing her head back against hard rock, she instantly succumbed to a thunderous orgasm.

"Want you in me. Right now."

Torque threw the blanket down on the cave floor. As soon as they were lying down, Hollie pulled him on top of her.

"No condoms." He ground the words out just as he was about to enter her.

"We don't need them anymore, my dragon."

He gazed into her eyes, and she felt the strength of the connection between them more powerfully than ever. This was what they craved. This was forever. Torque pressed forward, pushing into her, and the pleasure that streaked up her spine made her cry out.

"Mine." It was a growl.

Hollie wound her arms around his neck. "Always."

As she arched her back and lifted her knees around his hips, he sank fully inside her. They both moaned at the exquisite feeling. Torque held himself still and Hollie closed her eyes, reveling in the delicious sensation. Before long, it became too much and she gripped his arms.

"I need you to move now."

In response, he pulled right out and plowed straight back in. Hard and fast. Hilt-deep. Hollie cried out with pleasure. He filled her completely and she instinctively squeezed her muscles around him. Torque repeated the movement, drawing out and thrusting in, over and over. Each thrust tipped her closer to a second orgasm. She could feel the familiar tingle building even though it felt impossible after only a few minutes.

When Torque began to tease her with shallow movements, she arched her back, and dug her nails into his shoulders. This time, when her release hit, there was no warning. She was thrashing wildly, flung into the most intense climax of her life. The fire she had walked through had entered her body, filling her veins and rushing through her bloodstream. Dragon pleasure. It was almost too much. As her vision grayed and the pressure inside her skull triggered a series of sunbursts behind her eyes, she clung to Torque as he continued to drive into her sensitive flesh.

His thrusts triggered a series of exquisite aftershocks and her muscles clenched tight around him, pulling him deeper into her.

"Ah, Hollie." His head dropped onto her shoulder

as he gave one final thrust before holding himself still. She could feel his own release shuddering through him.

After a few minutes, the reality of lying on the rocky ground intruded and Hollie sat up. Something more began to tug at her consciousness. It started out as a need, a hunger that filled her whole body, and quickly became a craving so strong she couldn't ignore it. She hugged her arms around her upper body, unsure how to express this new sensation.

Torque, who was lying on his side watching her, started to smile. "You need to fly."

She regarded him warily. "I do?"

"Trust me, I know exactly what you're feeling. And remember—" He got to his feet, holding out his hand. "I'll catch you if you fall."

Torque watched Hollie closely as she stood on the ridge. She was trembling all over, her expression a combination of trepidation and exultation.

"I don't know what to do." It was a wail of frustration.

"You are trying too hard. Shifting is a natural process." He tried to find the words to explain it to someone who had never done it before. "You are part dragon now. A creature of legend, born to fly, to hunt, to mate, to breathe fire, to bring up your young as part of a clan. Reach deep inside yourself and feel your inner dragon rippling in the depths of your muscles, and simmering in your bloodstream. Hear the call of the Highland skies beating in time with your heart."

As he spoke, Hollie closed her eyes. Her breathing slowed as she lowered her head and stretched out her arms. And slowly—oh, so slowly—she shimmered. He caught a brief glimpse of her dragon. Then a gasp left her lips and Hollie came back into view.

"Let it happen, Hollie."

She gulped and nodded, her expression becoming determined. "I felt her."

A second or two later, she shifted. A beautiful, graceful dragon stood poised on the edge of the ridge. Her scales were the color of shimmering aquamarine and she shyly unfurled new wings. She blinked as if waking from a deep sleep, and her eyes were like emeralds catching the light of the morning sun. As she raised her head toward the sky, white smoke drifted from her elegant nostrils.

Torque shifted quickly, wanting to be at her side when she took her first step off the mountain. Nudging her lightly with his snout, he swooped from the ridge, watching in delight as Hollie followed him. They soared together over the slopes and valleys, camouflaged against prying eyes as Torque showed his mate her Highland home.

Swooping over one dark loch, he hovered above a gaunt gray house that nestled among the tall pines. The exterior was as dour and unprepossessing as all Scots mansions of the same age tended to be. They had been built, after all, with the intention of repelling invaders, rather than welcoming guests.

When they returned to the ridge some time later and shifted back, Hollie was laughing with delight.

"I did it." She threw her arms around Torque's neck. "I really did it."

"Yes, you did. Now get some clothes on, or I won't be answerable for the consequences."

They dressed quickly in the hiking gear they'd left inside the cave and started the long walk back down the mountainside. By the time they reached Inverness, it was evening.

"I'm so hungry I could eat two charred steaks," Hollie said. "Maybe three."

"There speaks a dragon after my own heart." Torque pushed open the door of Kirsty McDougall's and stepped aside to let her enter.

Kirsty bustled forward to greet them, her face breaking into a beaming smile. "Have you brought that reprobate Moiteil back to us?"

Torque took her hands. "I have some bad news for you, Kirsty." He led her to a quiet table and the three of them sat down. "Alban is dead. We scattered his ashes on the slopes of Càrn Eighe this morning."

"Och, no." She burst into noisy sobs. "I suppose it was all his own stupid fault?"

"I guess you could say that." Torque decided to keep it diplomatic and say as little as possible about the circumstances surrounding Alban's death. "How's the insomnia situation?"

Kirsty dabbed at her eyes with a corner of her apron. "All cured. The remedy Deigh recommended worked like a charm." She gave a watered-down version of her chuckle. "Which is good, since I suppose it *was* a charm."

"And has anything been seen of Teine or Deigh recently?"

Kirsty shuddered. "Not even a glimpse of the whites of either of their eyes. Tell me it will stay that way?"

"I hope so, but I can't make you any promises."

Kirsty sighed heavily. "We'll live in hope. Now, can I get you some food? Neeps and tatties?"

"We'll have steak. Well done," Hollie said firmly. "No sides."

Kirsty looked from her to Torque and back again with interest. "Like that, is it? Well, I hope you'll both be very happy." A dreamy look came into her eyes as though she was looking beyond them and into the future. "Aye, I can see it. You *will* be happy, although your hands will be full in about nine months' time with the twin dragon-shifters that are coming your way."

"Twins?" Hollie gave an exclamation of surprise.

"Och, did he no mention that twins are common in the Cumhachdach clan?" Kirsty chuckled to herself as she disappeared into the kitchen.

"Twins." Hollie pressed a hand to her flat stomach. "Do you think we just…?"

"It's possible." Torque smirked. "We Cumhachdach are very virile."

She started to laugh. "We haven't even talked about where we're going to live."

He took her hand. "I showed you my ancestral home."

Hollie's brow wrinkled.

"When we were flying."

"That house beside the loch was your home? Torque, that place was incredible."

He nodded. "Home to the Cumhachdachs since my birth. Of course, my commitments with Beast mean we'd have to spend time in America, but we have the house in Maine and the apartment in New York."

"I'd be quite happy with just one home."

Torque's cell phone buzzed as she spoke, and he experienced a fierce desire to throw the damn thing against the nearest wall. *Just leave us alone.* Surely nothing else could happen? When he checked, it was a message from Ged with a link to a news report.

Might want to check this out.

The article was short. Denver police were appealing for help in identifying a woman whose body had been recovered from the South Platte River. Although there were no signs of violence, the medical examiner had released the information that her body appeared to have been frozen for some time prior to entering the water. The unknown woman was described as petite with pale coloring and unusual, silver-white hair that was natural. At some point in the past, she had suffered severe burns to her upper body.

Torque held his cell phone out to Hollie so she could read what was on the screen.

"Deigh won," she said when she finished.

"It looks that way. She finally defeated Teine, even though it was at the expense of her own life." He placed a hand under her chin, tilting her head up so he could look at her face. "Are you crying?"

"Only because I'm so happy. I can't believe, after everything that's happened, it's all going to be okay." She smiled through her tears. "You will no longer be the last of the Cumhachdach."

"And you, my beautiful dragon mate, need to start planning our wedding."

"But we had our ceremony." She blushed. "Up on the mountain."

"That was for us." He raised her hand to his lips. "But I want the world to know the truth. Next time I say it, I want it to be in public. You are mine, Hollie. All mine."

* * * * *

We hope you enjoyed this story from

Unleash your otherworldly desires.

Discover more stories from
Harlequin® series and continue
to venture where the normal and
paranormal collide.

Visit **Harlequin.com** for more Harlequin® series reads
and **www.Harlequin.com/ParanormalRomance**
for more paranormal reads!

From passionate, suspenseful
and dramatic love stories
to inspirational or historical...

With different lines to choose from
and new books in each one every month,
Harlequin satisfies the most voracious
romance readers.

ROMANTIC suspense

"I think I might be pretty good at motivating myself,"
Lila confessed.

"Everybody should know how to motivate themselves,"
Travis agreed with a wicked smile. "Aren't you going to
ask about my stress levels?"

"Are you stressed?" she asked, taking one step
backward.

"That depends."

"Depends on what?"

"On if you're interested in doing something about
it." His smile sexy enough to make her light-headed, he
moved forward one step.

Since his legs were longer than hers, his step brought
him close enough to touch. To feel. To taste.

She held her breath when he reached out. He shifted
his gaze to his fingers as they combed through her hair,

swirling one long strand around and around. His gaze met hers again and he gave a tug.

"So?" he asked quietly. "Interested?"

"I shouldn't be. This would probably be a mistake," she murmured, her eyes locked on his mouth. His lips looked so soft, a contrast against those dark whiskers. Were they soft, too? How would they feel against her skin?

Desire wrapped around her like a silk ribbon, pretty and tight.

"Let's see what it feels like making a mistake together." With that, his mouth took hers.

The kiss was whisper soft. The lightest teasing touch of his lips to hers. Pressing, sliding, enticing. Then his tongue slid along her bottom lip in a way that made Lila want to purr. She straight up melted, the trembling in her knees spreading through her entire body.

Don't miss
Navy SEAL to the Rescue *by Tawny Weber,*
available February 2019 wherever
Harlequin® Romantic Suspense books
and ebooks are sold.

www.Harlequin.com

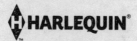

Want to give in to temptation with
steamy tales of irresistible desire?

Check out **Harlequin® Presents®**,
Harlequin® Desire and
Harlequin® Kimani™ Romance books!

New books available every month!

CONNECT WITH US AT:

Facebook.com/groups/HarlequinConnection

 Facebook.com/HarlequinBooks

 Twitter.com/HarlequinBooks

 Instagram.com/HarlequinBooks

 Pinterest.com/HarlequinBooks

ReaderService.com

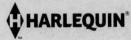

**ROMANCE WHEN
YOU NEED IT**

PGENRE2018

Love Harlequin romance?

DISCOVER.

Be the first to find out about promotions, news and exclusive content!

Facebook.com/HarlequinBooks

Twitter.com/HarlequinBooks

Instagram.com/HarlequinBooks

Pinterest.com/HarlequinBooks

ReaderService.com

EXPLORE.

Sign up for the Harlequin e-newsletter and download a free book from any series at **TryHarlequin.com.**

CONNECT.

Join our Harlequin community to share your thoughts and connect with other romance readers!
Facebook.com/groups/HarlequinConnection

HARLEQUIN®

**ROMANCE WHEN
YOU NEED IT**

Reward the book lover in you!

Earn points on your purchase of new Harlequin books from participating retailers.

Turn your points into **FREE BOOKS** of your choice!

Join for FREE today at
www.HarlequinMyRewards.com.

Harlequin My Rewards is a free program (no fees) without any commitments or obligations.

MYR18